BURNED

D0902626

A CADE RANCH NOVEL

GRETA ROSE WEST

Thanks for being a great Deathmate!

Love

Gia

PRESS

ALSO BY GRETA ROSE WEST

Wild Heart: Welcome to Wisper A Short Story

Join the newsletter for this short introduction into the Cade Ranch world and for extra goodies and scenes. Sign up on my website.

gretarosewest.com

BURNED: A Cade Ranch Novel

BROKEN: A Cade Ranch Novel

BUSTED: A Cade Ranch Novel

BRAVED: A Cade Ranch Novel

Coming December 2021

BLINDED: A Cade Ranch Novel

Coming Spring 2022

ACKNOWLEDGMENTS

This book would so not exist without many wonderful people.

To my boys: Thank you for supporting me in this. Wyatt, your courage showed me that it's okay to try. Our music is the foundation for everything I love, and even though I know you'll roll your eyes, you and Bok Bok led me to this whole freakin' thing. It's all your fault (though, I hope you never, ever, *ever* read this!)

To my Betas: Thank you. Christy: for pushing me and believing in me, and for reading every word I've ever written, even though cowboys are SO not your genre! You have no idea how much your faith in me helped me hit the "publish" button. To Tracy, Jackie, and Cece (!!! Dank je wel ;)) Thank you for looking inside my brain and for helping me to navigate through it. I'm so grateful none of you laughed when I said, "Um, so, I wrote a book. It's, like, a contemporary steamy romance novel with a little bit of suspense and some cowboy."

To Peter Senftleben, my editor (and BFF forever!): Thank you, thank you, thank you. I think you may have succeeded in rearranging my brain. Your wisdom and kindness guide me. I am so thankful to you for showing me how to mold that awful first draft into a book I love. I will NEVER forget your comments from Jack's book. They still make me blush. Thank you for seeing through my anxiety in the many, *many* convoluted and idiotic emails I send. Thanks for your sarcasm. It is now the reason I live.

To my very own Grammar Nerd, Joanne Machin. Thanks for being a steady voice in the thick of my punctuation freak-outs (and just regular ol' freak-outs).

M, for not comma shaming me, you are a Goddess. I'm so excited for us to figure all this shit out! And thanks for making sure I knew Christmas trees can't be replanted in the back yard.

Thank you to every single person who read this book, friends, family, ARC readers. I appreciate every single comment and piece of feedback.

I am greatly inspired by many authors. But there is one I need to mention: Aja James. Being a Muse opened up a new world to me, and by example, you have given me permission to do this thing I never knew I was being called to do. I've learned a lot from you. The beauty of, your efficiency with, and the words you choose are constant reminders to me that I use way too many. And just cuz I can, here's a vague winky face for you. ;) See how you like it.

And finally, GAI. You have inspired me beyond. It's immeasurable. Your words and the rhythm inside your mind have been a huge part of the soundtrack on the inside of mine forming the earth and the air of my imagination. I hope you won't deck me for mixing your metaphors but— You runnin' wave, you pull on this heart like you pull on the sea, and this is me in all my PJ glory. Dankie. Quick xo…

For Walter J. Finklefarkle
Wish you were here
313

Dear Reader,

I didn't know it at the time, but on the second anniversary of my dad's death, I began writing Jack's book. The whole month of September (and I'll be honest, October, November, and December...) can be difficult, and without realizing I did it, I threw myself into the Cade Ranch world to avoid my own and poured all I felt into this story.

This book, this series, is a labor of love. People always say that, but seriously, I have never *ever* loved working on anything more. It's not work; it's obsession. I don't know where he came from, but as soon as Jack introduced himself to me, I knew I needed to tell his story. I fell in love with him and Evvie and then the rest of the lovely, tortured—but satisfied—souls at Cade Ranch.

The characters came to life in my head, just like that. Music helped. It inspires me every day. If you're into it, check out my website and listen to each book's playlist as you read. gretarosewest.com

I live on the ranch in my mind, so much so, sometimes I forget to come back to reality.

Thanks for coming with me. There are many more stories to come, and I can't wait to share them with you!

Love always,
  greta
  greta@gretarosewest.com

CHAPTER ONE

JACK

I GUNNED the engine of my pop's old Ford pickup down Route 20 toward the hospital over in Jackson. The truck was old as hell, but Cade Ranch was too far out in the mountains for the ambulance to reach us in any measure of good time, so I drove as fast as I could. We were only a few more minutes away from pain medication and unconscious bliss for my brother Kevin, but I knew from experience minutes could feel like hours.

I was pretty certain I could see the pure-white bone of his fibula stickin' outta the skin of his right leg. No amount of bed rest would set him straight, not without some serious surgical intervention. He lay sprawled between Dean and me in the cab of the truck with his leg slung over Dean's and his head diggin' into my shoulder while I drove like a madman.

I'd never heard my pops or my father cry. I didn't remember ever cryin' myself, and I couldn't think of any time my brothers had cried, with the exception of when we were little kids, but boy, did Kevin cry now. He'd tried to be very manly at first, of course, but as soon as the truck hit the asphalt and we felt the bumps from the constant potholes along Route 20, he let out his first wail, and they only kept comin'.

"Fuckin' Christ! Drive faster!"

"I'm goin' as fast as I can, brother."

"Oh God, I think I'm gonna puke."

"Do whatcha gotta do," I said, and his head lolled when he passed out.

"Whatever you do, don't slow down," Dean said. "If the cops get after us, we can deal with it when we get there. I've never heard a man make that kinda noise before." The worried look on his face as he chewed his lip was enough to make me press a little harder on the gas pedal. I grunted my agreement and silently counted down the two minutes we had left to go.

We arrived at the hospital, and a couple orderlies lifted Kevin off Dean, layin' him on a gurney. They whisked him off and left us standin' in front of the ER entrance, speechless.

I parked the truck in the lot across the street, and we made our way inside so we could hurry up and wait. Dean sat, watchin' me worry, while I paced the little room.

"I dunno how we're gonna pay for this one. Emergency surgery, anesthesia, and he's gonna need a shit-ton of physical therapy down the line. You're leavin' for the auction in a few days. Goddammit. I warned him about that mare."

"We'll make it work. We always do. We got two horses ready to sell in what, two more weeks or so?"

"Yeah, that'll cover next month's operatin' costs, but not much more. You know what, never mind. I'll figure it out. Ain't your problem."

"It is my problem. The ranch belongs to all of us, Jack. It's up to all of us to keep it runnin'." Dean cleared his throat. We weren't much for talkin' about our feelin's. Offerin' support was about as far as any one of us would go in that department, but even that felt uncomfortable. Growin' up with two dicks for role models and no mama—well, you might say we were all a little emotionally incompetent, or maybe reluctant was a better word. "What about Jay's idea? You been considerin' that? It could work."

"I can't talk about this right now. I need to walk or somethin'. Text me if you hear anything."

He sighed. "Yeah, okay, brother."

Pushin' out the waitin' room door, I found my way to a nice long hallway I could pace in peace.

I appreciated his support. All of my brothers' support. They were always offerin' it. But the runnin' of the ranch had been left to me. Our dad had spent a lotta time teachin' me how to keep things goin'. He'd expected me to take the reins. He might be dead, but I had no intention of lettin' him down. My brothers had no idea what it took to run the ranch, apart from the actual trainin' of the horses. And maybe that was my own fault, but it had always been my job and my responsibility.

And with the way things had been goin', it would only get harder and more complicated.

The Cade Ranch had been in my family for five generations. A small operation, we owned the land for much more business but not the manpower or the money, though the business was pretty well-known throughout the western United States. People came to us from all over to buy the quarter horses we bred, raised, and trained for ridin', ropin', and a few for racin'. Just not enough people.

The easiest thing would be to sell off some of the land, but it was *home*, with all the memories, good and bad, to come with it.

When we were kids, we lived on the ranch with my pops

and granny, my mama and dad, and my uncle, Jon. My mama left us when I was nine, and Granny and Uncle Jon were killed in a car accident outside of Idaho Falls by a drunk driver a year later. Pops never really recovered from losin' 'em, so that was about the time I began workin' the land and the horses with my dad.

My brothers came on board as they got older, but the runnin' of things had fallen to me. I was the oldest. I'd been jugglin' everything on my own for the better part of two years, tryin' to find ways to stretch our money and expand the business, but things were changin' for farms and ranches, and times were tight. I'd been tryin' to figure out how to—

"Jackson Cade, is that you?" A familiar voice yanked me outta my annoyin' postulatin'.

I turned to see Mrs. Mitchum sittin' on a bench about twenty feet down the hall. *Ahh...* She was sick again. She wore a hospital johnny and some silly, pink, fuzzy slippers, and she looked so frail and tired. Dammit, I'd just seen her two days before, and she hadn't said a word. She was hidin' this from us, or she had been. *Cat's outta the bag now.*

"Yes, ma'am," I said, walkin' toward her. She pointed to the bench next to her, wantin' me to sit. I took off my hat and turned, and as I sat, she patted my knee softly, then hooked her arm through mine. I kept my eyes on the floor, not wantin' her to see the sadness I felt at findin' her there. She'd fought through two bouts of cancer already.

Seein' her there again, I knew by the dullness of her skin, the absence of strength in her muscles, and the look of defeat in her eyes, this would be the fight she lost.

"Whatever are you doin' here, Jack? I know you didn't come all this way just to see me," she said, and I heard the chagrin in her voice.

"No, ma'am. Kevin broke his leg. They took him back for surgery. I'm just passin' time while we wait."

"Well now, why'd he go and do a thing like that?"

"He was fu—messin' 'round with that ol' pregnant mare, ma'am, tryin' to put a halter on her. I told him just to leave her be, but you know him. He never listens." I caught myself before I cursed for fear of her conjurin' a bar of soap to shove in my mouth. She'd done it once when I was fifteen, and I never made the mistake again.

Tappin' her fingers on my forearm, she let me know she appreciated my discretion. She never judged us for bein' coarse; ranch life was hard, and we were five men livin' with little female influence for quite a few years now, but she wouldn't tolerate harsh language in her presence, even though I was sure she suspected we swore like sailors when she wasn't around.

"Well now, you know he'll be just fine. He's young and strong. Stop your worryin'."

"Yes, ma'am."

She squeezed my arm, scootin' closer to me. "I've been meanin' to come out to see you boys."

As if I might see through it to all the comin's and goin's below, I continued starin' at the floor. An uncomfortable silence stretched between us, and I knew she was workin' her way up to say somethin' important, so I didn't dare interrupt her.

She took a deep breath, and it whistled up through her old lungs before she said softly, "Jack, look at me."

I took a deep breath, too, held it, and did as she said. Her soft puff of short white hair lay flat against her head and looked lackluster at best. She had dark hollows under her eyes, her skin sallow and paper-thin. She must've started her medications already to look so weak and sickly.

"I'm dyin', Jack," she said, studyin' my face, lockin' onto my eyes with her own milky blue ones. I saw sadness in 'em, compassion, but mostly, a mother's love. "There's nothin' to be done about it. We're gonna try one more round of chemo, but the doctor doesn't hold much hope."

I released my breath slowly. "Yes, ma'am, I know."

It was more painful to admit than I'd imagined. This woman was the last tether to my grandparents, to my dad. I had my brothers, I knew, but when Mrs. Mitchum passed, it would be the end of an era. She and Granny had been thick as thieves when we were boys, and when Granny died, Mrs. Mitchum had taken to fillin' the role. She'd loved us boys as her family, helpin' out with the cookin' and cleanin', and she'd taken us shoppin' for new clothes and shoes when we'd needed 'em.

Oh, her strawberry rhubarb pie was so damn good. She made one for me still, and I waited for it every year at the beginnin' of summer. My brothers didn't even try to eat it anymore. They knew I'd beat their asses well and good if they did. I would miss that pie. I was an asshole for even thinkin' it at a time like this.

I would miss her.

Now the future was unknown, especially with the state of our finances, and for the first time since Granny died, I felt fear.

I'd borne the full weight and responsibility of the ranch for a long time, on top of responsibility for my brothers—my youngest brother's four years at school had been another large expense to worry over—and I'd been shoulderin' it all solely, learnin' how to control all the movin' parts. But with the unknown future loomin' out ahead of me, just outta my reach, I wasn't sure where we'd end up. I didn't know if I'd be able to keep hold of my precious control.

And that control was somethin' I was *not* prepared to lose.

Mrs. Mitchum pulled her arm from mine and stood. I jumped up to help her when a wisp of a girl appeared with a wheelchair, parkin' it in front of us.

"C'mon, Mrs. Mitchum," she scolded, "you know it's time for your medication."

Mrs. Mitchum sighed. "Yes, dear," she said, and I steadied her and led her to sit in the chair. Unlockin' the wheels, I felt the familiarity of the task and remembered the last time I'd been at the hospital with my dad, lockin' the wheels on his chair and helpin' him out of it and into a hospital bed. I stopped that train of thought right in its tracks. It wouldn't lead anywhere good.

I looked at Mrs. Mitchum and at the young girl whose face had turned beet red with the effort of tryin' to push the wheelchair into motion. "Here," I offered, "lemme help you."

"I got it."

Mrs. Mitchum chuckled. "Headstrong child. Don't worry 'bout her. She's stronger than she looks once she gets me goin'."

"Yes, ma'am." I took a step back. I'd learned a long time ago never to argue with my elders, so I didn't make a fuss. They took off a little too fast for my likin' and I winced, but they stopped again.

"Oh, and Jack?" Mrs. Mitchum called back to me, and I walked over, takin' her small outstretched hand in mine. She looked right in my eyes, smiled a mischievous grin, and said, "Don't you worry. I'll leave you the recipe for my rhubarb pie when I die. Maybe you'll find a nice woman to settle down with, one who can make it for you, hm? It won't ever be as good as *I* make it, but at least then you won't have to go without. Get to workin' on that, hear me, young man?"

"Yes, ma'am." I leaned down to kiss her paper-soft cheek.

"I'll get right on it." I tried not to sound too sarcastic, but she knew me too well.

"Don't you get smart with me, Jack Cade!" she called over her shoulder as the girl propelled the chair forward again.

"Yes, ma'am." I called out so she could hear me and chuckled to myself. I put my hat back on my head and stood for a minute, watchin' her go and wonderin' how long she had left. The world would be a lot less colorful without her in it. She'd been such a constant in our lives these last twenty years, and I felt sad at the eventual loss of her kindness.

Turnin' to resume my pacin', I saw a group of women standin' at the nurses' station, heads together while they whispered and smiled at me. I tipped my baseball cap to 'em and continued on my way.

A woman was the *last* thing I needed in my life. I didn't trust 'em and I had more than enough to worry about.

Kevin came home two days later. The nurses had a hard time gettin' his pain under control. Oh, he tried sweet talkin' 'em in his usual way, tellin' 'em he was just fine, but his elevated heart rate and the grimace on his face gave him away every time. As it was, though, he came home the proud new owner of three different nurses' phone numbers. He was the most determined flirt I'd ever met. He didn't care what a woman looked like, how old she was, or where she'd come from—if she talked sweet and smiled at him, he chased her.

He had the hardest time copin' when our mama left. She'd doted on him like he was some baby lamb, and for a time, I wondered if I wouldn't have to reteach him some basic manners—he'd been angry and confused. But after a while, he seemed to accept it like the rest of us. On a ranch there wasn't much time for feelin' sorry for yourself. There were always chores to be done, animals to be fed, and after a short while, life went on.

Like now. I'd been in the barn for an hour, waitin' on that mean old mare, and I needed to get back to work and set my contemplatin' aside. She'd finally gone into labor, and I needed to pay attention and try to keep her calm.

My brother Finn had installed a stereo system in the barn a few months back, somethin' my dad would never have allowed. At the time, I thought it just to be a waste of money, but the horses seemed soothed by the music so I turned it on. Some guy named Bon Iver sang about someone being drunk as hell and stacks. Stacks of what, I didn't know, but the guitar was nice. I let it play low and went back to talkin' about my day to the mare. It wasn't another twenty minutes till her foal dropped, a filly.

Watchin' her tryin' to stand and failin' miserably at it, I jumped when my phone rang. It still scared the shit outta me every time one rang in the barn. We'd just gotten halfway reliable service this far out in the foothills of the mountains not two months ago, but it could still be spotty sometimes.

It neared nine at night, so I knew the call would probably be important. When I pulled my phone from my pocket, I saw Mrs. Mitchum's name and answered quick as a fit.

"Ma'am, what's wrong? You okay?"

"Well, 'course I am, dear. Can't I just call to say hello?"

She never had before, and she never called this late unless she needed help with somethin'.

"Yes, ma'am, 'course you can." I waited for her to tell me what she would. I had a feelin' she was up to somethin' but didn't know what it could be.

"Well, fine then, I do need a favor from you, Jack. I need

a ride home from the hospital tomorrow. I already gave my grocery list to Dean, and he's gonna have everything set for me in the mornin' before he and the boys leave for Montana, but I'll need a ride. There's a volunteer who's gonna help to get me settled once I'm home, but she doesn't drive either, so we'll both need a ride. I'll expect you 'bout nine a.m."

"Yes, ma'am, I'll be there."

"That's real good, son. Thank you. See ya then," she said in a kinda sing-songy voice and hung up.

By then, the little filly was up and nursin' from her mama. I finished my chores and left a soft light on in the tack room, turned off the music, and headed back up to the house for a hot shower and my warm bed. A storm was headed our way, and I needed sleep to prepare for the next day. I wasn't lookin' forward to dealin' with *two* old ladies complainin' about my drivin'.

CHAPTER TWO

EVERLEA

THERE MUST HAVE BEEN a storm that I slept right through because when I woke to my kitty, Iggy, standing next to my head, patting my face with her paw, my alarm clock was flashing a big red 12:00. If I didn't hurry, I'd be late for my volunteer shift at the community hospital in Jackson, Wyoming. It was only about a twenty-minute drive from the little house I'd rented in Wisper, and if I'd left twenty minutes ago, everything would've been fine. But, of course, that wasn't how my morning went.

At this point, I was only ten minutes behind schedule, but when I went into the kitchen to snag my first of three cups of coffee for the day, I discovered my little coffee-pot-that-could had also succumbed to the storm and subsequent power outage. *Ughhh.* I had to have at least one cup in my system before my brain cells would fire at a rate acceptable enough to operate a motor vehicle. I didn't have a legal driver's license, so the least I could do for the safety of other drivers was caffeinate myself properly before getting behind the wheel. I reset the machine and went to get dressed while my blessed coffee brewed.

I then realized I'd fallen asleep the night before without switching my load of laundry from the washer to the dryer. The ancient set lived in the detached garage of the old house I'd been renting, so the last thing I remembered was being too warm and comfy in my full-size rental bed to trek all the way out there to deal with it. I'd already locked the house up tight, blocking all the windows and doors with furniture, like I did every night.

So, I woke up with nothing to wear. I didn't have a uniform per se, but I wanted to at least appear to be halfway put together. But I'd run out of time, so I just grabbed the first clean things I could find, which turned out to be a decent pair of jeans and a *Never Mind the Bollocks* Sex Pistols T-shirt.

After a quick dash to grab my coffee (which hadn't actually brewed because, apparently, my little coffee-pot-that-could, just couldn't), I realized my mistake on my way out the door and ran back to my room to change my shirt to something a little less... "in your face." I would be volunteering with the elderly, for crying out loud. I grabbed the first black shirt I could find and my thrift-store-style lilac cardigan. Lilac was an inoffensive color, right?

By the time I got out to my car, I realized I was still wearing my old scruffy tennis shoes, so I grabbed my extra pair of Chucks from the back seat, slid them on, threw the old shoes behind me, and hit the gas.

When I finally arrived in the hospital employee parking lot, I stepped out of the car and took a deep breath to reset myself. It was then I noticed the "less in your face" shirt I'd changed into was a Metallica tee that said, "Metal Up Your Ass." Could this day get any worse?

I would be meeting the new volunteer coordinator before helping Mrs. Mitchum get settled in at home. I would also be meeting Mrs. Mitchum's grandson of sorts. *Oh well, too late now*. And, of course, it could be worse. I was about to walk into a hospital, after all. My choice of apparel seemed a minor problem in the big scheme of things.

I was being silly. No one would even notice what I wore. I pulled my cardigan on over my horrible choice of a T-shirt, threw up a silent prayer to the universe to try to convince her to be just a tad bit kinder to me for the rest of the day, and walked in the direction of the hospital entrance.

"What the hell are you wearing? Does that shirt say *ass*? Change. Now," Linda Cummings, the volunteer coordinator, growled and pointed to her office door. "Do it quick, girl. You're late and Mrs. Mitchum and her family are waiting for you."

"I'm so sorry, Ms. Cummings, but I didn't bring a change of—"

"This is a hospital. I'm sure there are a pair of scrubs somewhere. Find them and get going."

"Yes, Ms. Cummings." I tucked my tail and turned to go.

"And Eve?" She looked me up and down. "You will report back to this office before your next shift to discuss what *appropriate* attire might consist of. That is all," she declared, and I hung my head and left her office.

Oh boy. Great first impression. Although, after meeting her, I had a feeling pleasing Nurse Ratched, I mean Ms. Cummings, might end up being an impossible feat.

I shortened my name when I signed up to be a volunteer. Usually, I used a fake name to keep my real name out of any databases or social media (there wasn't a situation I'd put myself in that would result in a selfie pic posted anywhere, for any reason), but I'd been in a hurry and had started to write my real name on the sign-up sheet, so I just stopped at Eve.

I wasn't a "real" volunteer. The hospital here in Jackson

had a buddy program for elderly people, but it wasn't official, so they didn't do a background check or anything too nosy. I had a fake driver's license and had never had insurance, so I pretended not to drive. I didn't want to put anyone else in danger because of my—unavoidable but necessary—negligence. But it usually worked for me, and volunteering gave me a little bit of purpose which, sometimes, I desperately needed to keep the silence in my head at bay.

I did locate a pair of scrubs from a harried young aide at the nurses' station right outside Mrs. Mitchum's room. They were at least two sizes too big, but I was in no position to complain and was way past being out of time. I put them on over my T-shirt, stuffed my jeans in my bag, and ran to find the infamous Mrs. M.

I'd met Mrs. Mitchum the day before during my second shift on the third floor, the geriatric oncology floor. I didn't think I'd do very well with kids. I still felt like a kid myself sometimes, but older people were awesome and usually so kind and accepting. The thing I loved most about being around them was that I could be myself, and when they did get personal and ask a lot of questions, I found it easy to make stuff up. They usually seemed happy just to have the company. And so was I. They reminded me of my grandma, and I missed her so much sometimes my stomach ached.

Historically, I considered myself to be a "normal" person. Well, at least in regard to bodily functions and normal body mechanics. I ate, slept, and drank like everyone else, walked like everyone else, and contributed to society in my own way. My life was unusual, indisputably so, but I swear, I wasn't usually such a spaz. But today proved to be a freaking humdinger! I couldn't seem to do anything in a normal fashion. It had to be the lack of caffeine.

I found Mrs. Mitchum's room, knocked on her door, and

pushed it open with just a little too much force. Of course, the door slammed against the wall, and, *of course,* it caused all the boxes of latex gloves in the little metal dispenser affixed to the wall to fall down onto the floor. And then, when the actual metal dispenser box fell, hitting the tile floor and making the loudest clanging noise *ever*, all I could do was hang my head and breathe through my nose to try to calm myself.

I counted to ten silently and looked to the bed to make sure I hadn't caused Mrs. M to have a heart attack. Thankfully, she only seemed amused, sitting on the edge of the bed with an indulgent smile on her face, like she might be holding in a little giggle.

And then I took two steps toward her and tripped over the cord to her IV stand, landing on my face in front of her feet, smacking my forehead on the floor. Hard. Oh. My. God. Apparently, asking the universe for a break had only made her angry and she was taking her revenge out on me. I was embarrassed, but I figured making a sick old lady laugh wasn't a bad thing, so I just stood and dusted off my scrubs.

"Oh! Eve, dear, are you okay? I heard your poor head hit the floor."

"I'm fine, Mrs. Mitchum," I lied. "It sounded worse than it felt."

As I turned to move the cord that almost killed me, I stuttered an attempted apology for being late and collided with a very tall, very solid wall of muscle and man. I looked up—way up—to see who I had body checked and gasped.

The man, who held said cord in his hand, was smiling at me. He had the most beautiful smile. Small on his lips and kind of crooked, it lit up his eyes and made the skin crinkle around them. I didn't think I'd ever seen anything so perfect.

But then his smile vanished and he lowered his eyebrows and frowned.

"Miss, you're bleedin'. Please, sit down," he said in a super low, rough voice that felt like velvet inside my head. Grabbing my hand, he pulled me to sit in a hard, plastic chair under the window. All I could do was stare up at him. I couldn't even find my wits enough to be mortified, the way I definitely should've been.

I closed my eyes, feeling a little dizzy, and when I opened them again, he'd disappeared. I closed them again and took a few deep breaths. Had I imagined him? Maybe I hit my head harder than I thought.

The fresh oxygen helped with the dizzy feeling, so I opened my eyes slowly, worried about what I might—or might not—see, but he was there again, kneeling in front of me with a bright white, wet washcloth in his hand, aimed at my forehead. He pressed the wet cloth there and dabbed a few times. It stung a little, but the cool moisture felt good against the throb I could now feel about an inch above my right eyebrow.

I winced, and he sucked in a quick breath of air through his teeth. Holding the cloth to my head, he looked at me. His eyes searched mine, my face, my neck, and my hair, searching for... sanity? Or maybe just further injury.

He was breathtaking. His face looked kind of rough and tanned, like he spent a lot of time in the sun, with short, dark stubble on his clenched jaw and above his upper lip. And that lip was plump and soft, just like the bottom one.

But all of that barely registered because the only thing I could focus on were his eyes. They were a wild hazel color, green and amber with little flecks of bright turquoise blue. I couldn't look away, like he had me in some kind of trance.

"Eve? Eve, honey, can you hear us?" I heard Mrs.

Mitchum, but her voice sounded far away and quiet, and the light in the room seemed to be fading, even though I knew it to still be mid-morning.

And then he spoke again.

"Miss… Eve, can you hear me?" When I didn't respond (I'd been completely unable to form words when he spoke in that low, gravelly voice, or maybe it was the violent knock to my head), he lifted his hands to my face, held it gently between them, and said, "Eve, say somethin'… Does your neck hurt?" He caressed my bottom lip with his thumb so softly, his eyes still searching mine, and I moaned. I couldn't help it.

I said, "My name is Everlea."

Aaand then I passed out.

CHAPTER THREE

JACK

CATCHIN' her from slidin' outta the beat-up plastic chair when she blacked out, I carried her over to the bed and laid her down. She smelled like autumn apples in the afternoon sunshine and vanilla cake.

Mrs. Mitchum jumped right up when Everlea slumped in the chair. She'd been distraught over the state of this beautiful woman. She and some young doctor were in the room with Everlea now, checkin' her over, and I found myself pacin' the same hallway I wore a path in not four days before.

Who was this woman? While we waited for her to arrive this mornin', Mrs. Mitchum chattered away about this Eve— Everlea. She said Everlea was new to Wisper and had started volunteerin' at the hospital in Jackson just a week before. She'd moved here from somewhere in the Midwest about a month back. It sounded like the two women had become quick friends.

Of course, I'd heard about Everlea from people in town, though I hadn't known her name at the time. I'd never been one to involve myself in town gossip, but even I had to make my monthly trips to Bob's Feed and Tack and occasionally to the farmers market for Finn. Last week, I'd heard from Bob himself we had a new resident in Wisper. Unmarried and with no family to speak of, she'd rented Mr. Masterson's daughter's house while the woman studied overseas.

I'd been to school with Carolyn Masterson, though she was a year younger than me. She'd gone away to California for her bachelor's degree and now lived somewhere in the UK while she finished vet school.

Thinkin' about Miss Carolyn livin' overseas led me to thinkin' about my mama. As a boy, she'd taken me on long drives in Pop's truck. Sometimes, we'd drive over to Idaho Falls, to the department store there, where she'd try on long fancy dresses and silly shoes. She'd douse herself in expensive perfumes, then we'd go to the Italian restaurant next door, where we'd eat spaghetti Bolognese and gelato. I remembered her talkin' about travelin' to places like England, France, and Italy. She said she'd never been anywhere excitin', and she used to tell me it was her dream to travel the world.

Even at the tender age of seven or eight, I'd felt her melancholy and knew she'd been unhappy with her lot in life. She'd grown distant from my dad and even from us boys. Then, one day, she was gone. She left a note, and I'd read it after my dad let it fall to the floor in the kitchen. It said, "I'm drowning. I'm sorry. I love you boys." That was it. She'd gone, and I'd known then we'd never see her again.

I remembered worryin' when Kevin was a baby 'cause she spent all her time with him, and she'd become pregnant again not long after he was born. I whined and complained that I had too many brothers, and I remembered her laughin', sayin', "You're such a good big brother. I thought you wanted fifty brothers." My dad wasn't the cuddliest guy on the planet, and I'd missed my mama, missed her attention. She promised she'd always be there for me. I was the "first in her heart," but it didn't stop her walkin' out the door.

And it didn't make her come back.

Dad went out alone to the mountain for three days. When he came back, he smelled like sour whiskey and sweat. He'd taken a shower and come to stand in the kitchen, and I remembered lookin' to him for an explanation or some kinda support, or somethin'. Anything. Not for me, but for my brothers—they'd been so young and confused. But he just patted my head, closed his eyes, blew out a long breath, then pushed open the creaky screen door and headed to the barn to feed the horses.

He never talked about my mama after that. Granny tried to explain it to me once. She said sometimes love ain't enough to hold a person. My dad had all the love in the world for my mama, but maybe Mama'd never really been able to feel his love and thought she might find a better love somewhere else.

I didn't understand it at the time, but I knew then I wouldn't ever bother with it. With love. It seemed to me to be too painful a thing. When a person said they loved you, they made promises they couldn't keep. They caused pain and destruction, and eventually, you'd find out they never really loved you anyway.

What was the point?

I would be a good son and a good big brother, and that would be just fine for me. I'd gotten to work on it right away, helpin' Granny with the house chores at night, helpin' my brothers with their homework, and spendin' time with my dad in the barn, tryin' hard to make him forget about the pain my mama had caused.

I guess I never really stopped doin' all those things. I supposed that was how I ended up right where I was, worryin' about the future and takin' care of everyone around me. And that was enough.

Besides Mrs. Mitchum, all women were nothin' but a pain and a burden, always needin' somethin' I didn't wanna give.

I never dated, never bothered to get to know any women. There'd been a few to chase after me, but I always told 'em no thank you in the most polite way I could. One woman, Cara Thompson, screamed at me in a bar full of people after I'd told her just that. She cried for a few minutes, then shouted at me that I was a cold, unfeelin' bastard and I would be a miserable old man, alone for all my life. I sat there, silent, while she told me off till her girlfriends came over to rescue her, then waited out in the parkin' lot till they left, to make sure she got home safe.

After that, I'd taken to drivin' out to the city when I felt the need. There were a couple bars there big enough to be anonymous, and there'd never been any shortage of pretty ladies lookin' for a "cowboy" for the night. Women that, like me, weren't lookin' for love, just a night of hard sex and release. And I lived far enough away, if they did decide they wanted more, they weren't likely to find me. Usually, though, I just used my own fist. Less hassle.

But this mornin', lookin' into Everlea's beautiful green eyes, I'd wondered what it might be like to be with her. What would she taste like—

The sound of Mrs. Mitchum's shrill, irritated voice callin' my name pulled me right outta my sour mood. "Jack! Pay attention, boy. I've been callin' your name for five whole minutes."

"Yes, ma'am. Sorry." Jesus, the woman always had the ability to turn me right back into a twelve-year-old boy. I turned to see her sittin' in a wheelchair with a male orderly pushin' her to stop in front of me.

"Where's your head at, Jack? You're not usually one to daydream," she said with a little smirk on her old face and her right eyebrow popped up. "Listen here. Poor Everlea needed two stitches and Dr. Patel says she has a concussion. Now, you know I don't like to be a burden, but the doctor thinks she and I are gonna need a little lookin' after. She's not able to care for me today like we'd planned, so I've set my mind to us girls comin' home with you."

Say what?

I dragged my fingers through my hair. "Um wha— Uhh, are you— Ma'am, I don't think—"

"Oh, stop your sputterin'. It'll be fine. Dr. Patel says Everlea needs to rest today. She's feelin' dizzy and nauseated. You'll just have to get over yourself. It'll only be for a day or two."

"But, ma'am, Kevin is still laid up there with his—"

"Oh, Kevin will love the company. You can't tell me that boy won't fully enjoy havin' such a pretty lady holed up at the house to commiserate with."

It had just occurred to me Dean, Finn, and Jay were on their way up to an auction in Billings, Montana, then they'd head on to two more in South Dakota. They wouldn't be back for another week, at least. I couldn't pawn this off on them.

My whole body broke into a sweat, and I felt like I might lose my breakfast. I crushed my hat in my hands. "Mrs. Mitchum, ma'am, I'm not sure I'm the best—"

"Don't be silly, Jack, it won't kill you to look after us a few days. You remember how weak I get from my medication. Honey, I wouldn't ask this of you if I didn't absolutely have to, but Everlea has no family. We can't just send her home alone. I just couldn't live with that," she said, and dammit, I knew she was right. I wouldn't be okay with it either. And I couldn't say no to Mrs. Mitchum. Never could. I'd lost the argument before it had even begun.

"I'll go get your things and pull the truck 'round front."

"Perfect," she chirped as I walked back toward her hospital room, to where Everlea still lay in a hospital bed, injured and beautiful.

Well…

Shit.

CHAPTER FOUR

EVERLEA

THE COMPLETE AND utter humiliation had finally caught up with me. I had no idea how long I'd been out, but when I came to, Mrs. Mitchum and some guy with shiny, black hair pulled back into a man bun stood above me, looking at me with some kind of expectation. Dr. Patel, Mrs. M explained, was the attending doctor in the ER, and he had very kindly come up from downstairs to stitch the cut on my forehead and assess my condition.

Condition?

Oh no. It all came flooding back: my rush this morning, Ms. Cummings, my stellar entrance into Mrs. M's room, and the man. The tall, solid wall of man! *Oh God.* I was so embarrassed, I thought I might throw up. I groaned, which caused Mrs. M to go into hysterics. She patted my arm and my head, trying to be gentle, but it felt like she was slapping me, which made me groan again.

Dr. Patel laughed and explained that a headache was normal with a concussion and I might experience a little nausea. He said I could go home, but I would need someone to keep an eye on me while I rested. How annoying.

Wait... why? Oh, yeah, concussion. Maybe he was right. They both left the room a few minutes later, Mrs. Mitchum now sitting in a wheelchair with her very own chauffeur/orderly, a chubby man with ruddy skin and really hairy arms.

I lay there for a long time, remembering my awful day and thinking about the man I'd crashed into. *Those eyes*. I really hoped he'd gone home because I couldn't face him again. The indignity was acute, and my day from hell was far from over. I just hadn't known it yet.

But then the door opened and that very man walked in.

Could a person die of embarrassment? If he looked at me, I might. As it was, I tried to blend in with the scratchy off-white sheets on the hospital bed.

I hadn't noticed earlier but now could see he had thick, rich brown hair, which had probably been lightened from the sun—I couldn't imagine him sitting in a salon to get highlights—at the tips and throughout some flips that lay just around the back of his neck and ears. I wondered if he normally wore his hair shorter. It looked a bit messy and he didn't strike me that way.

He had to be six-foot-one or two, at least, and he looked strong. Not like a lunkhead bodybuilder, but well-muscled and powerful, like he worked hard every day and his body showed the proof. His legs were long and thick, arms muscled and hard. He wore black steel-toed boots and a green baseball cap.

He radiated cowboy, even though he wasn't dressed like one. His jeans were dark and faded, and he wore them low on his hips in that sexy, every-woman's-fantasy kind of way with a long-sleeved charcoal grey T-shirt that hugged his chest and abdomen like... I didn't know. I couldn't find the right word for it.

He was mesmerizing.

He bent to pick up Mrs. M's suitcase and his shirt rode up a little, showing the skin above his hip. It looked hard and tanned. Just that little bit of skin lit some kind of fire in me, in my lower belly. I moaned. *Oh my God, was that out loud?* But I had a condition. Surely, he'd think it was because of my concussion, right?

I snapped my eyes shut. I didn't hear any movement, so after a few seconds, I opened them just a fraction to see if he'd noticed me. He hadn't turned to look and I was grateful for that, but he stood ramrod straight, not moving, facing the wall and just kind of breathing deeply through his nose.

Finally, he about-faced and walked out of the room, taking the suitcase with him. He didn't look at me or speak to me. Was he angry? Probably. I mean, I had pretty much ruined his day. He was probably mad that I was supposed to be caring for Mrs. M, and now she was kind of caring for me.

She came in soon after he left to inform me that I would be accompanying her to the beautiful, angry man's house, and he would take care of us until my concussion danger period had passed.

And now I *knew* he was angry. He'd be stuck with me and Mrs. M, by no fault of his own. I already knew Mrs. Mitchum could be a feisty lady, and if my cowboy assumption proved correct, he wouldn't tell her no.

The humiliation came back with force.

No, this was not a good idea. I didn't want to be a burden, and I wasn't accustomed to being taken care of. I'd been on my own for a long time, and I didn't want to drag these innocent people into my world.

I would just have to convince her to let me go home. I didn't feel *that* bad. At least, not if I didn't move my head at all.

I attempted to talk Mrs. M out of her cockamamie plan, but she would not be moved. Then I made myself an even bigger burden when I tried to stand to further my argument and passed right back out. Only for a few seconds, but damn it!

So, a few hours later, I found myself sitting next to this man, Jackson, Mrs. M had called him, in an old red pickup truck, acting as some sort of barrier between them as she scolded him about his driving for the last ten miles and he said not a word.

My mortification rode front and center in the truck with us, especially after he'd insisted on lifting me out of the wheelchair (the one the nurse made me use to make my super-graceful exit from the hospital—Mrs. M was allowed to walk!). I tried to stand when we arrived at his ancient pickup truck, but he walked over to me, bent down, swiped his arms behind my back and calves, and scooped me up. Like a child.

So, as we drove through the small town of Wisper, past the street where my little blue rental house was, all I could do was look out the window at the passing homes, quaint main street, and breathtaking mountains in the distance. My thigh rubbed against his, and I had to try really hard not to fan my face with my hand because the heat it caused through my whole body made me sweat.

I'd never lived in a small town before, staying mainly in big cities where I could blend in easily. But big cities were expensive, and my money needed to last a long time. So, about two months ago, I decided to head west to try to lose myself in the anonymity of a tiny town in a big land. Steady jobs were hard to come by when you lied about your name and didn't have a social security card, but I'd been good at saving every penny from odd jobs through the years. Though, if I didn't find work soon, I might be in trouble.

I felt safe in Wisper—as safe as I ever could feel. People knew their neighbors here. They looked out for each other. I'd met the sheriff already, who had been really kind. He offered his assistance in any way I might need and gave me his card with his office number and cell. I hadn't told him the truth about who I really was or why I'd moved to Wisper, and he hadn't seemed suspicious, only asking the basic "Where ya from? What do you do for a living?" kind of questions.

Mr. Masterson, my landlord, had been so nice when I moved in, helping me bring in what little possessions I owned from my car. He didn't mind that I had no rental history to speak of or a good credit score. He was happy with cash.

I found Iggy that day, hanging around the house, and he told me to keep her if I wanted to—he didn't mind! And then he'd gone out and bought her a litter box, litter, and kitten food. It was the nicest thing anyone had done for me in a very long time.

I'd never been able to keep a pet before, and Iggy quickly became the best friend I'd ever had. Though I couldn't quite work out how I'd take her with me when I moved on (I couldn't condemn her to life in my car, and where would I put a litter box?). I hoped Mr. Masterson might take her in. He and his wife Susan offered a standing invitation to weekly Sunday dinners at their house. I hadn't gone yet, even though one of them stopped by every week to offer again. I hadn't told them the truth either. I knew as soon as I showed up for dinner, they'd start asking questions.

So, I didn't trust this man whose house I would be staying in for who knew how long, and I didn't trust Mrs. M either. It wasn't that I thought they would hurt me, but people talked, and if people around Wisper knew the truth about me, it would spread like wildfire. And who knew where, or more importantly whom, that gossip might make its way to. I couldn't risk it.

I wanted to risk it. So many times, I'd wanted to confide in someone. To bare my soul and allow someone to know me. The real me. I'd had a couple friends over the years, people I'd worked with doing under-the-table jobs for cash, and one person I'd been close to, but he was dead now, so I couldn't bring myself to do it.

No matter how much it hurt to be alone in the world, it could always hurt worse.

If he found me again, he would make it hurt...

We drove for another fifteen minutes or so, then turned off the highway onto a gravel drive, passing under a big aged wrought iron sign. It arched over the entrance to a huge, sprawling green property lined with pine, fir, and aspen trees, surrounded by majestic mountains in every direction, and said, "Cade Ranch" with a figure of a mom and baby horse on each side.

We followed the road for maybe half a mile until a big, two-story house with a wraparound porch appeared in front of us. It had been painted white, though not recently, and the sun glinted off its many big windows. Five or six assorted chairs littered the porch with a hanging swing at one end. I imagined sitting in the swing at night, looking up at the stars and breathing in all the fresh country air.

Parking in front of the house, Jackson stepped out of the truck and went to the back to get Mrs. M's bag while she and I carefully scooted out the other side.

There were pretty wooden fences everywhere for the horses, I assumed, but I didn't see any. When I turned my head to look past the truck to the mountains beyond, I caught him watching me, studying my face again. He looked away quickly and came around to help Mrs. M.

"Where are your horses, Jackson?" It was the first time I'd spoken to him since passing out earlier, and he didn't respond. He took Mrs. M's arm and led her to the house.

"Wait there," he grumbled over his shoulder as they walked.

Mrs. M said something to him but I couldn't hear it, so I did as he commanded and waited. He definitely seemed irritated having me around, and I didn't want to make his mood worse. As much as I hated to admit it, I did need him, at least for the next twenty-four to forty-eight hours. My head pounded, and all I wanted to do was wrap myself in a blanket and sleep.

They disappeared inside the house after he'd helped Mrs. M slowly climb the porch stairs. While I waited, I leaned against the truck so I couldn't make a bigger fool of myself by falling down and looked out at the big, blue, cloudless, western sky above the dark, craggy Grand Teton mountains, feeling dazed and small in comparison.

When Jackson reappeared, another, younger man stood next to him in the open doorway. The younger man held himself up with crutches and wore a cast on his right leg, below the knee. He had Jackson's same brown hair, though his was wavier. He talked and laughed at Jackson, and Jackson stomped down the steps toward me, which seemed to make the younger man laugh harder.

I didn't have a suitcase or anything, just the messenger bag I wore across my chest and low on my hip. It went with me everywhere, so when he got back to where I stood against his truck, he picked me up like he had outside the hospital, bag and all.

"You don't have to carry me, Jackson. My legs are fine," I mumbled as embarrassment made another comeback.

"Jack," he growled.

Oh my God, now he was growling at me? Like a bear.

I couldn't help myself. I looked up into his eyes. They were still beautiful, but hard and guarded. They intimidated me—*he* intimidated me—and I felt awful about the mess I'd made and the inconvenience I had become. Shame and embarrassment made me lower my head and look away, but then he spoke and I peeked up again.

Trying not to smile that tiny, crooked smile again, he climbed the stairs to the porch. "Please, Everlea, call me Jack. Most of the horses are in the back paddock or in the barn. And I am not a bear."

Ohhh no, I so said that out loud.

———

Lying on the sofa in the living room of the big white house, I'd been at Cade Ranch for about two hours. Mrs. M sat in a dirt-brown recliner next to me, and the other guy, broken-leg guy (Mrs. M had introduced him to me, but I'd forgotten his name and was a little embarrassed to ask) stretched out on a beanbag chair on the floor with his head resting back by my feet at the end of the couch and his casted leg propped up on the coffee table. The chair dwarfed Mrs. M, but she wouldn't hear of trading places with me.

I felt awkward being in their home. I wasn't part of their family and they all seemed so close, even Mrs. M, although she said she didn't normally live at Cade Ranch. But they were kind and welcoming, and already, I'd been included. For lunch, broken-leg guy wheeled in snacks and bowls of soup for all three of us on an old rickety metal serving cart. Where in the world would a person get one of those things? It looked like something from the 1930s. I declined the soup and potato chips. I still felt so nauseated.

They tried talking to me, asking me questions about where I'd grown up, how I ended up in Wisper, what I did for a living, but I couldn't answer any of their questions, not without putting them in danger, so I lied, redirected, and pretended to sleep.

Mrs. M knitted, and they watched Jeopardy on a humongous, high-tech, flat-screen TV that looked ridiculously out of place with all of the old furniture and decorations in the house. The living room probably hadn't been redecorated since 1987, but it was clean and cozy and that was all that really mattered. Besides, it was a hell of a lot nicer than ninety-nine percent of the motels I'd stayed in on the road, and that was if I could even afford a no-tell motel. Usually, I just slept in my car.

I hadn't seen Jack since he'd deposited me on the couch and stomped back outside. Broken-leg guy and Mrs. M shared some kind of look then. I couldn't be sure what it was about, but I thought it might have had something to do with Jack's mood. He seemed kind of hot and cold, from the little experience I had with him.

He was the most beautiful human being I'd ever seen. I wondered if he knew, if he'd known the effect he had on me in the hospital, the effect he undoubtedly had on every woman he encountered. It only lasted a few minutes, but it had been powerful.

I'd never been so instantly and insanely physically attracted to someone.

It didn't matter though. I needed to get out of his house, and I supposed I would probably have to move on, too, and find a new place to hide. Already, I felt like Mrs. M and Jack had gotten too close. Just me being in their personal space put them in danger.

I fell asleep thinking about where I might go, and of Jack and what it felt like when he'd touched my lip.

———

I slept through the night, which was unusual for me, especially out here in the valleys and mountains. Someone tried to wake me several times. I vaguely remembered swatting and batting at whoever it was, and I think I even cursed at one point.

Places like Wisper could be really quiet, though I couldn't say I'd been in many of them. Normally, the quiet would freak me out, but I guess I'd really needed the rest. My head pounded, and I still couldn't even think about eating anything.

I dreamt all night of running and being chased, and when the monster would get close, I'd try to fly, flapping my arms and expecting them to carry me away, but it wasn't working. I couldn't get lift-off, and I was *seriously* angry about it. So, when someone woke me again, I reached out instinctively to whack them.

A big rough hand grabbed my wrist mid-strike and held it firmly, and I heard a low, sexy chuckle. "Whoa there," Jack rumbled. "You're okay. You were dreamin'."

I opened my eyes to find the lights on in the living room, and it brought the pounding in my head front and center.

"Oh!" I yelped, pulling the blanket someone had tucked in around me over my head. "Turn it off. Please?"

"Sorry, it's off." I heard him flip a switch, so I uncovered my head a centimeter at a time, and when I knew it was safe, looked at him through squinted eyes.

A soft light from the kitchen illuminated the living room a little so I could see him. And wow. He wore faded blue jeans again, a well-fitted black T-shirt, his green baseball cap on backward, and straight-up sex!

"Water?" I croaked. He handed me a fresh bottle of mountain spring water from the coffee table. "You know these end up in our oceans and kill our planet, right?" I scolded, shaking the bottle in front of me, but then pushed myself up onto my elbow and drank the whole thing down, to the last drop.

"Uh huh. That really the first thing to pop into your head after sleepin' like the dead for hours on end?"

"Yes."

Carefully, he sat on the edge of Mrs. M's recliner, like he might be afraid to startle me, as I sat up on the couch. Lying down in front of him seemed too intimate and made me think about other things I could be doing with him if I were lying down. I slammed my thighs together, staring down at the blanket like I could see every fiber of the fabric and found it to be the most interesting thing I'd ever seen in my life.

"You were dreamin' about somethin'. Must've been pretty scary 'cause you were thrashin' 'round on that couch awful hard."

"What time is it?" I asked, and a disgusting, dizzy feeling began to flood my whole body. I laid my head down on the arm of the couch.

"It's four in the mornin'," he said, looking at his watch. "What were you dreamin' about?" His voice was that low, sinful velvet again.

"Nothing. I don't remember," I lied, squeezing my eyes shut. *Oh no*, my stomach did that clenching thing that crawls up your esophagus right before— "Jack?" I clutched my arms around my middle, taking measured breaths through my nose.

"Hm?"

"Do you have a bucket, maybe, or garbage can I could borrow?"

"Oh, shit. Okay, hold on." Quickly lifting me into his arms like a toddler, he rocketed us to the tiny bathroom under the staircase, threw the toilet seat back, and wrapped his body around me while I knelt and barfed my guts out. He held my hair back with one hand and rested the other gently under my sternum to steady me. Even through the yakking, I felt his warm breath on the back of my neck.

When I'd finished and completely humiliated myself again, he carried me back to the couch and laid me down. He jogged out of view for a minute but returned quickly with a wet washcloth, and I lay there, head lolling, while he wiped my face and neck. I watched his eyes as he tended to me. They were nervous but tender.

"I don't feel so well," I remember saying, then... nothing.

When I opened my eyes in the morning, Jack was there again, leaning over me and caressing my cheek with the backs of his fingers.

"Wake up, Everlea. Doc's here to see ya."

"Huh? No, I don't have insurance." Did I really just say that? *Oh my God, my breath!* I clapped my hand over my mouth and jolted up to run to the bathroom but got dizzy before I made it there and listed to the side, knocking into some kind of table with a lamp on it. Jack caught me and lifted me into his arms. Seriously, I was no waif. How strong was this guy?

"Whoa nelly, calm down. You gonna be sick again?"

"Did you just say 'whoa nelly?'" I spoke from behind my

hand, and he looked at me quizzically, walking back to the couch.

"There's a bucket on the floor there, see?" He sat me down next to the bucket and backed away. "This here's Doc Whitley. Mrs. Mitchum thought we oughta call him to make sure you're doin' okay."

A tall, skinny man, probably in his seventies with snow-white puffy hair and crinkly, smile-lined skin, stepped forward with an old-fashioned mercury thermometer in his fingers, aimed right at me.

"Open please," he said, and I opened my mouth to protest, but he jammed the thermometer in. "Under the tongue."

I pulled it out of my mouth. "Dr. Whitley? I'm fine, sir, thank you. Seriously, I really don't have insurance, and I'd rather you check on Mrs. M and broken-leg guy anyway. I'm fine... uh, I already said that. Sorry." I knew I sounded like an idiot, but if the doctor asked questions or wanted to do a physical, I'd be screwed.

"Look here," he said while trying to shine a penlight into my eyes.

"I'm fine, really."

"Maybe so, but Jack says you vomited early this morning. How are you feeling now?"

I opened my mouth again to tell them I felt fine, but Jack stepped forward, glaring at me. "Everlea, if you say 'I'm fine' one more time, so help me—"

"So help you what? I'm feeling *well*, Dr. Whitley. I threw up because I guzzled a bottle of water after not eating or drinking anything for almost two days. My head is sore, my neck and shoulders are a little stiff, but other than that, I feel fine." I glared at Jack as I spoke to the doctor and flashed him a "so there" look. He narrowed his eyes and gritted his teeth, jaw muscles flexing.

Sexy.

"I have been the boys' doctor since birth, miss Everlea," the doctor said, pulling me out of my inappropriate ogling, and I looked back at him. "And Mrs. Mitchum is a long-time friend of mine. There is no charge. I'm simply doing a favor for my friends." He yanked the thermometer out of my hand and aimed it back at my face. "They asked me to check on you, so I intend to. Open please, or there are other orifices I can stick this in to get a temperature." He smiled his own "so there" smile at me, and I opened my mouth in defeat. Out of the corner of my eye, I caught Jack looking smug while I sat there for the allotted minute and a half with the damn thermometer sticking out of my mouth.

The doctor walked around to the back of the couch, and I froze. I couldn't protest his exam without outing my secrets. Luckily, I'd kept my Metallica T-shirt on underneath the scrubs so no one would see my scars.

He felt my head with his fingers, moving it from side to side, and then my neck and the top of my spine, moving my arms around a bit before coming to stand back in front of me. My fingers stayed clutched around the neck of my shirt, ready to yank if the doctor got too nosy. He didn't.

"I think you are correct. You seem to be fine," he said, pulling the thermometer from my lips and checking to see what it said, then shook it, "but, if this excessive lethargy and dizziness continue, Jack will call me and I will be back. Got it?"

"Yes, sir, thank you." Jeez, was everyone around here so pushy?

"You may take acetaminophen for your headache. Now, I'll come back in a week or so to remove your stitches. Won't take but a minute, and it'll save you the trip to the hospital. I'm told you live alone?"

I nodded. Ouch, that hurt. I winced and hoped they hadn't noticed, but of course, I wasn't so lucky. Wait, why did the doctor care that I lived alone?

"Then you will stay here so you can be monitored. No exerting yourself physically for a couple more days, and you need to eat and drink—small amounts. You are probably a little dehydrated, and if you're not careful, you'll end up in the hospital for IV fluids. Have I made myself clear?"

"Yes, sir, very." I felt like a five-year-old being scolded for getting caught with her hand in the cookie jar.

A couple days? A week? This was not a good idea, but I would just have to figure a way out of it. I didn't have my car, but maybe I could persuade Jack to drive me back to the hospital. I looked over to see him shaking his head slowly with one eyebrow raised, like he knew what I was thinking and was already saying no.

"Okeydokey then. I would like to go up and check on Sara and *Kevin*." The doctor looked at me, shaking his head too.

"Yes, sir, thank you," Jack said, grasping the doctor's hand and clapping him on his old, frail shoulder.

The doctor turned and walked to the stairs, carrying one of those old-fashioned, black leather doctor's bags I hadn't noticed before. Where the hell was this place anyway? Mayberry? Old mercury thermometers, house calls, and black doctor's bags... I slumped back on the couch, pondering this and feeling relieved my secrets were still intact.

Jack still stood by the recliner, now with his arms crossed over his hard chest. "Broken-leg guy?"

"I forgot his name. Concussion, remember? It's just the way I thought of him in my head."

He didn't say anything more, just stood there looking at me.

"You wouldn't happen to have a toothbrush I could use, would you?"

"C'mon," he said, holding his hand out for me to grab.

"I'm not a baby. I can do it." Great, now I sounded like a baby. I stood quickly to prove myself capable of doing so on my own and immediately felt dizzy, falling back to the couch on my butt.

"I can carry you again, *baby*, if you prefer."

When I could stand without swooning and falling over like a starved debutant, he grabbed my hand and turned to pull me behind him. He was gentle with me but I could sense his irritation still. The muscles of the wide expanse of his shoulders tensed every time he touched me.

Leading me to the bathroom under the stairs again, he motioned with his hand to the sink where a pink toothbrush sat, still in its packaging, and a tube of toothpaste, the kind with multi-colored stripes. I tried to shut the door for a little privacy, but he lodged himself in the doorway, shaking his head.

"I also need to pee, warden. Do you mind?" I turned for the toothbrush but was hit with another dizzy spell and grabbed the sink for support.

"Whoa, okay, sit down."

"Stop saying that." I sat on the toilet, breathing deeply.

"Stop sayin' what?" He pulled the toothbrush from its package, ran it under the water, spread a little paste on the bristles, and handed it to me.

"Stop saying 'whoa.'"

"Stop fallin' over."

Smartass.

I brushed my teeth, and he passed me a little paper cup of water to rinse with, then turned and said, "I'll be right outside the door if you need help," and closed the door quietly.

I took care of business, then washed my face in the sink, and when I lifted my head after drying off with a hand towel, felt dizzy again. Damn it. Reaching behind me to find the wall, I leaned back and slid down to sit on the floor. How ridiculous. I'd taken care of myself for years. I'd never needed help from anyone, but now I couldn't go two steps without it. I was so frustrated, and it made me nervous, relying on these people. On Jack. I couldn't afford to get comfortable here, to get attached.

They couldn't afford it either.

But I needed food, and it seemed I didn't have the ability to stand up straight long enough to do anything about it, so I would just have to depend on him and accept his help for the time being so I could gain the strength I needed to leave.

"Jack?" I said his name, hoping he could hear me. My voice sounded weak.

"Yeah, I'm here."

"Can you— I need you." I sighed, completely defeated.

He cracked the door an inch but it bumped my leg, and when I tried to scoot over so he could get in, the motion caused a whole new bout of dizziness. I moaned, sliding the rest of the way down to melt onto the floor. *Ohh*, the laminated floor felt blissfully cool against my face and body. It cooled my hot, clammy skin, so I lay there with my eyes closed, trying to breathe through it.

"Dammit." He gently pushed the door open, moving my legs with it, and then I heard, "I gotcha. C'mon, let's go lay back down."

I moaned when he lifted me and carried me to... a bed? My eyes were still closed against the nausea, but when he laid me down, I could tell I was in *his* bed. The sheets and pillows smelled just like him, a woodsy, clean, sexy man scent. It was delicious and so calming.

"I think you need to eat somethin'," he grumbled in his velvet voice. "How 'bout some toast and a scrambled egg? Just a few bites. I'll be back in a couple minutes. Try to relax."

"Mmhm," I murmured. "I'm sorry." I said it but didn't think he heard me.

While he was gone, I snuggled into his pillows and sheets. They were so smooth and cool against my skin and felt divine all around me like a silky, fluffy, cotton cocoon. A breeze floated in through an open window, and I let it take my thoughts with it as it traveled over me and continued on through the bedroom door.

I had no idea how long Jack had been gone, but after a short while, I heard him speaking with Dr. Whitley again. I couldn't make out what they said though, so my thoughts kept drifting… and then Jack was there, and the side of the bed dipped down as he sat.

"Open your eyes for me. Can you sit up just a little?"

I did as he asked and scooted up the headboard a few inches.

"Here, let's try a little toast." He held half a piece of perfectly toasted bread to my lips, and I took a nibbling bite. The creaking sounds of the old house were the only noises surrounding us, and the slow second-hand ticking of an old-fashioned clock. "There ya go, slowly."

He watched my lips as I chewed, and I watched his eyes. So beautiful and kind. He opened a bottle of water that lay next to his leg on the bed. "Take a sip." He held it to my lips as I finished swallowing the toast, but I sat up a little higher, took the bottle from him, and took a drink. I held the water bottle in my hands as he lifted the fork with a small clump of egg on the tines and fed it to me.

I chewed a little and smiled. "Thank you, Jack."

He cleared his throat, sitting up straighter, and his eyes raised to mine. "Um, yep, you can probably do this yourself. I'll be in the kitchen if you need anything else. I need... coffee." Standing abruptly, he walked quickly through the door and disappeared.

CHAPTER FIVE

JACK

STUMBLIN' blindly into the kitchen, I couldn't see where I walked 'cause the image of Everlea's lips and the light in her eyes when she smiled at me blinded me.

Muscle memory led me to the kitchen counter, and I stood there like a statue for what felt like hours but had probably only been five or ten minutes. I went upstairs to take a shower after checkin' to make sure she hadn't thrown up again or passed out.

I peeked at her from around the corner. She ate slowly, chewin' and takin' sips of her water in a careful rhythm.

Good Lord, she was *beautiful*, all big green eyes and pale, soft skin. What I could see of it anyway. She still wore those ugly blue scrubs.

Her hair lay long and wild down her back, a curly and wavy light brown tangle with golden streaks and a little bit of red when the sun from my bedroom window shone down on it. She had freckles everywhere, but mostly on her cheeks and across her nose, which was cute as a goddamn button.

She looked so fuckin' sexy in my bed. I had to force myself, physically, to walk away.

Standin' under the scaldin' hot spray of the shower, lettin' the water work its magic on my shoulders for a while, I thought about the last couple days' events, wonderin' how I'd ended up here, with this woman in my bed.

Then it hit me: Mrs. Mitchum.

She was exactly how I'd ended up here. I remembered her phone call from the other night. She'd set this all up. She was up to her matchmakin' again. She couldn't have planned for Everlea's stunnin' lack of coordination at the hospital, but it had all worked out in her favor anyway 'cause now we were stuck in the same house together, Everlea and me.

Much to my consternation, that led me to thinkin' about Everlea. The last two days all came rushin' back at me, every single time I'd been near her, lookin' in her eyes before she passed out and the feel of her lip still lingerin' on my thumb. Her thigh against mine in my truck, her warm body pressed against me when I carried her in my arms. I could still hear the little moans she made in her sleep this mornin' on my couch and could still see her mouth as I fed her.

I couldn't take it anymore. I was so hard, when I grabbed the base of my dick, it hurt. And not in a good way. I stroked myself slowly, tryin' to ease the ache. I didn't mean to do it, but I imagined Everlea's hands on my body instead of mine.

I pictured her in the shower with me, the water slidin' down her skin, between her legs. She'd look up to see the need in my eyes, and I'd see it in hers too. Wrappin' her arms around my neck, I'd lift her up with my hands grippin' her hips, and she'd wrap her legs around me.

With my arm behind her lower back to protect her from the hard shower tiles, I'd guide her shoulders back against 'em to hold her up. Takin' my time, I'd kiss and lick the water from her lips, her neck... her breasts. *Fuck.*

And then I'd slide my finger into her wet, hot sex, lookin' into those sultry green eyes, to make her ready for me. She'd writhe against me, moanin' like she had this mornin', but louder.

My cock had grown harder in my hand while I stroked faster, every muscle in my body strainin'. I bit my bottom lip hard to hold back my release. And then I imagined removin' my finger and swallowin' her moans of frustration at the loss of me inside her body as I kissed her. Then, I'd take her, enter her in one *hard* thrust and—

I barked out a curse and came so fuckin' hard, I blacked out for a second, tastin' blood.

Everlea was sittin' at my kitchen table when I came downstairs a while later, clean and dressed. I couldn't look at her, or I knew I'd end up right back in the shower like a teenage boy in the throes of puberty. Mrs. Mitchum and Kevin sat across from her with their heads together while she sipped coffee.

Set up on the old ash dinin' table, there were pancakes and bacon on a servin' platter, hash browns in a cast iron skillet, and fresh-cut fruit in a bowl. It looked just like it used to when we were boys and we'd have Sunday breakfast with my dad, Pops, and Mr. and Mrs. Mitchum. I woulda smiled at the big ol' spread and the good memories it brought to me, but I remembered my epiphany from the shower, that Mrs. Mitchum meddled with things she shouldn't.

"You must be feelin' better," I grumbled, sittin' at the head of the table between her and Everlea, tuckin' a napkin into my lap. I kept my eye on Mrs. Mitchum as she smiled and batted her eyelashes at me.

"Good mornin', honey," she said.

"Mornin'."

"I got a phone call this mornin'. I don't remember if I told you before, but I set up a home health nurse to help me once my treatments start again. Remember Ida Johansen?"

"No, ma'am," I said, spoonin' food onto my plate, not lookin' at what it was. I threw a pancake on top, doused it with syrup, and shoveled it into my mouth. I felt Everlea watchin' me but I ignored her. I tried anyway. The whole right side of my body felt electrically charged from her nearness.

"Yes, you do. Ida Johansen?" Mrs. Mitchum hedged, like just sayin' the name again would make me remember. "She helped me last time, drove me to my treatments and stayed with me when I wasn't feelin' well. Remember?"

"Uh, yeah, I guess. Sure."

"Well, she was plannin' to help me again this time, but her daughter's just gone into premature labor. The baby's comin', and she's gonna have to stay with them in Sheridan awhile."

"Okay. Want me to find someone else?"

"Well, I was thinkin' I'd just stay here with you boys. And Everlea's here. She was supposed to help me anyway. Why don't I just hire her?" She looked at Everlea and smiled, and Everlea froze in her seat with her cup of coffee almost to her lips. *God, those lips.* Perfect, freckled, pink, and soft. What would they taste like on my tongue? I licked my lips, took a deep breath, and looked at my plate.

"Oh, um, you know, Mrs. Mitchum, I'm not trained. I mean, I'm not a nurse. I was volunteering as, like, an aide or something. A buddy. I'm not qualified to—"

"Oh, nonsense. I don't need a nurse," Mrs. Mitchum argued. "I need someone to help me bathe when I'm weak, comb my hair, and make sure I take my medicine. You don't need a nursin' degree for that. And you can go with me to my treatments."

"Oh, right, but I-I don't drive. I don't have a car so…"

"Well, that's okay. Jack can drive us, and you can keep me company."

"Um…"

Finally, I looked at her. She didn't seem happy to be offered the job, and it sounded like she was makin' excuses.

"You got some other job to go to?" I asked.

"Uh, well, no. Actually… no."

"Okay then, what's stoppin' ya?"

She clicked her tongue. "Well I… Nothing, I guess. Okay. For a little while. Till your nurse gets back?" She looked at Mrs. Mitchum and smiled but doubt colored her face.

"Wonderful. I'll pay you. Sounds like you need a job anyway. Volunteerin' don't pay."

"Yeah, true. I could actually use a job. I hadn't gotten around to it yet, but yeah, I do… need a job." I could see the gears turnin' in her head. What on earth was there to think about? Yeah, you want the job, or no, you don't. "Oh! I have a cat."

"That's nice, dear."

"No, I mean, I forgot about her. I need to feed her. She's probably freaking out."

"Jack can feed her for you. In fact, why don't you just go pick the cat up, Jack? Bring it here since we don't know how long Everlea'll be here."

"No!" she yelped. "I mean"—she looked around the table —"she's really shy. I should go. That would be better." She chewed the inside of her lip but tried to smile.

"Fine. I'll take you a little later. I got some stuff to get done first."

"O-okay."

Jesus. What could be the big deal? I didn't see any reason for her anxiety. Over a cat? The only problem I could see was that I would have a fuckin' cat in my house. And a woman.

Like I said, nothin' but a burden and a pain.

I grumbled through my chores and then all the way to Bob's Feed. I'd just been to his place a week ago. Why he couldn't have my whole order ready at one time was beyond me. Pain in my ass.

I picked up my eight thousand gallons of all-natural horsefly spray from Bob, ignorin' his attempt to fill me in on all the new town gossip, and headed to the grocery and the farmers market to pick up food for the week, feelin' even more annoyed I had to do it. Finn usually did the shoppin', but I'd sent him, Dean, and Jay up to the auction. So, I was the shopper, cleanin' lady, and all around do-every-goddamn-thing-for-everybody sucker, on top of everything else I had to do every day with the ranch and the horses.

I was so annoyed, I decided to skip the hassle of drivin' all the way back out to the ranch to fetch Everlea so she could come with me to pick up her cat 'cause, apparently, the cat suffered from some kinda wallflower affliction. Whatever. I was already in town.

The little blue house sat at the end of West Street, back-endin' the football field behind the high school. I wasn't sure how I knew where Carolyn Masterson's grandparents' house was, but she and Dean had been all hot and heavy back in high school, so I figured I must've picked him up from there a time or two. It occurred to me as I pulled into the driveway that I didn't have a key, but these old doors were easy to wiggle open, if it had even been locked. Most people in Wisper probably didn't lock their front doors.

It had been locked, though, so I wiggled and wiggled, but the damn thing wouldn't budge. But, turned out, I didn't need a key after all.

"Jack Cade? Is that you?"

I turned to the voice behind me on the short sidewalk leadin' to the porch steps and saw Carolyn Masterson's mama. She'd been a good friend to Mrs. Mitchum, and we'd been invited to her Halloween parties over the years. I never went.

"Yes, ma'am."

"Whatcha doin'?"

"Oh, um, sorry. The girl, the woman who rents this place—"

"Eve? Is everything alright? Is she okay?"

"Yes, ma'am. She's stayin' out at the ranch with us and Mrs. Mitchum. She hired Ever—Eve to help while she's gettin' her treatments."

"Oh. Well, that's nice. I'm so sorry to hear about the cancer, Jack. She's the strongest woman. This is her third bout, isn't it?" she asked, walkin' up the steps. "I'm glad Eve can help though. She's such a nice young lady."

"Yes, ma'am," I said to answer her question and to be polite and agree with her statement. She just kept chatterin'. I didn't really hear her 'cause I was too busy wonderin' why Everlea had lied about her name to the Mastersons too. Or maybe Eve was just a nickname.

"Are you picking her up? Her car's not here so I don't think she's home."

Her car? Thought she didn't drive.

"No, I'm just pickin' up the cat. I was supposed to bring her with me but I was already in town, so I just figured—"

"Oh, that's sweet of you. Here," she said, pullin' a set of keys from her purse. Sweet? No, efficient. But I didn't argue. "Go ahead, get whatever you need. Take the key and lock up behind yourself." She handed me the key. "I'm just on my way to a fundraising meeting at the church, so just give the key to Eve. I'll get it from her later. And please tell Sara we're thinking about her and praying for her. Tell them to call me anytime. You, too, if you need anything."

"I will, ma'am. Thank you."

"Sure thing. Oh, I almost forgot." She pulled some papers from her purse and handed 'em to me. "Give these to Eve too. Glen put in a new fridge before she moved in. Oh, it's state of the art. I think that thing will even order your groceries for you. But he brought the instructions home, and I'm sure she'll need them. The customer service number is on there. She'll probably wanna call to set it up. I don't have any idea how that stuff works. Glen says he knows, but you know, I think he's fibbin'. Are you good at that kinda thing? Maybe you could help her." She looked me up and down, smirkin'.

"Uh, no, ma'am. I ain't good at it either. My brother Finn is though. I could have him come out to take a look when he gets back from auction. I'll, uh, I'll let her know."

"Oh, that's perfect. Okay, well, I better get goin'. Don't forget to lock up."

"I won't forget. Thanks again," I said as she turned and walked back down the steps toward her car on the side of the road. She waved as she pulled away.

Jeez, that woman could talk. She was kind though. Mrs. Mitchum said she spent her Sundays drivin' around town and the surroundin' areas to pick people up for church, folks that didn't drive or their car was broke down or whatever. Then she drove 'em home after and took food to some of the elderly people livin' out in the country who couldn't make it to church 'cause they were sick or ornery.

I watched her drive away and looked at my truck in the driveway. Why would Everlea lie about havin' a car? What could possibly be the reason to lie about somethin' like that?

Shakin' my head, I unlocked the front door to the little blue house, pushed it open, ducked under the doorjamb, and somethin' came flyin' at me. It launched itself straight from the floor to my shoulder, latchin' on with knives. At least, that's what it felt like. The damn cat. It perched up there like a bird, purrin' and trillin' at me and whippin' its tail in my face.

I tried pullin' it down, but it just dug its little daggers in deeper, so the damn cat stayed up there as I found my way to the tiny kitchen. I cleaned out the food and water bowls I'd found on the floor by the sink after the cat jumped down to the counter, then went lookin' for a bag of cat food. I didn't see it in the kitchen, so I looked through the hall closet and went out to the garage.

The side door to the garage creaked and swung open when I got to it. Oftentimes, the wind would knock these old fiberboard doors loose when it came down into the valley from the mountains. The overhead light was on when I walked in, but I figured Everlea had probably forgotten to turn it off and to check that the door had been latched in her haste the other mornin'.

But when I walked in further and found the cat food sittin' atop an old Maytag dryer, I also found an aged and rusted metal cabinet that had come away from the wall and fallen over, all its contents scattered across the empty garage floor. My first thought had been raccoons, or more likely a bear, given the size of the cabinet, but then I remembered the open bag of cat food in my hand—no wild animal would leave that untouched…

Pushin' the cabinet back against the wall, I tidied up a bit, then locked the garage up tight. I walked the bounds of the property, twice. Then I went back through the house with an eye for anything outta place. 'Course, I'd never been inside the Masterson house before, so "out of place" was relative to me, but I could at least look for "out of the ordinary."

I looked in every room, every cupboard, every closet, searched through the old basement and root cellar, and even crawled up into the attic. That damn cat followed me every step, but I didn't find anything causin' me to worry further over someone messin' around inside Everlea's house.

I did find a few things that struck me odd.

The first thing was that Everlea might've been a slob. I wasn't sure if it was just 'cause she'd been outta sorts the other day, or if her house always looked like a clothin' bomb had gone off inside it, but Jesus. There were clothes everywhere, in literally every room, on the floor, hangin' off nearly every piece of furniture, though I noticed the place had been pretty sparsely decorated. That wasn't an oddity, I guess, but it did surprise me. She was just so small and soft. I didn't imagine she could make such a big mess.

The other things I found kinda odd were in a small room off the kitchen. I'd figured it for a broom closet on my first pass through the place.

When I walked into the tiny room, the only thing I could see at first was a huge five-foot by three-foot map of the US. That wasn't strange by itself, but it looked old and ratty and the sides curled in, like it had been rolled and unrolled many times.

Everlea had tacked the map to the wall, about four feet off the floor. It looked to be right at her eye level. There were lots of tiny sewin' pins stuck in it, each pin a different color and stuck in a different city. There were pins in Minneapolis, Indianapolis, St. Louis, Louisville, Nashville, and Dallas, and there were also pins in several moderately sized cities, scattered in between all the big ones.

But there was only one pin stuck in a small town, and that was this very town of Wisper, Wyoming.

But what struck me most about the map were the big red slash marks, most likely made by a wide permanent marker, through a whole host of cities and areas that didn't have any pins in 'em. There was a big, red X through the whole state of Illinois, one through Oklahoma and Northern Texas, and another through New York and New Jersey.

The damn cat jumped up onto a folded pile of blankets sittin' on the floor, pullin' my eye down.

Against the wall, under the map, was a green canvas duffle bag. It had been packed full and left open, and on top I saw a pair of folded blue jeans, a white T-shirt, and a pair of black Chuck Taylor tennis shoes.

And... money? There were several small stacks of bills rubber-banded together. Not enough to make me suspect Everlea of robbin' a bank, but definitely enough to make me worry she might be in some kinda trouble. There were also two sets of keys hooked to the straps of the bag with carabiner clips, and I could see rolls of change in an open zippered pocket. In another pocket on the other side of the duffel, was a thick book of state maps.

There was no other word for it. This was a go-bag.

What. The. Hell?

I found a cat carrier in the livin' room, and when I opened it, the damn cat walked right in and made itself comfortable, so I locked the house back up and brought it with me, throwin' the litter box, litter, and food in the bed of my truck. I left the duffle where I found it.

Everlea was runnin' from somethin'. I didn't know what, but it put a pit in the bottom of my stomach, so I decided to call my friend Carey, the sheriff of Teton County.

He answered on the second ring. "Hey, man, how ya been?"

"Good. Doin' good. You?"

"Yeah, good. Got a new cruiser. Not sure why the state of Wyoming decided to allocate its budget in my direction, but I ain't complainin'. So, what's up? It's a rare delight I get a call from you."

"You know the Mastersons got a new renter?"

"Yeah. Met her when she moved in. Why?"

"Oh, uh, well, she's stayin' at the ranch. Mrs. Mitchum hired her to help while she's goin' through chemo. She's decided she and this woman are gonna stay with us. Lucky me, I guess." I sighed, rollin' my eyes.

"Lucky you is right. She's sexy as shit. Wouldn't mind hand-cuffin' her to my bedpost. She seemed nice enough. What's the problem? You wouldn't call unless there was one."

"I just stopped at her house to pick somethin' up for her. The garage door was open, and somebody or somethin' left a big ol' mess in the garage. Haven't gotten any calls about it, have you, or maybe 'bout a bear in the area?"

"No, haven't heard anything but probably just animals."

"Yeah, probably."

"You think there's a problem?"

"No. I'm sure you're right. Probably animals. I just thought you might wanna check with the George twins, make sure they haven't been helpin' themselves to a free party pad again, thinkin' the place is vacant."

He chuckled. "Good idea."

"Alright then. Talk at ya later."

"Jack? If you think somethin's up, I can run her name. She seemed innocent enough but you never know."

"No. Don't. It ain't necessary. I'm sure it was just a couple 'coons or a bear or somethin'."

"Alright. You good otherwise? How's Ma doin'?"

"She's okay, man. She starts her treatments in a few days. She seems cheered up to have this woman around so…"

"Well, maybe you oughta take a page outta her book and try to be happy 'bout it too. Seriously, I wouldn't complain if she was stuck in my house for a while." He chuckled again.

"Shut up, Carey. Go arrest somebody or somethin'."

"Yeah, yeah. Hey, call me when the guys get back from auction. We'll do lunch. I mean, sit around and guzzle beer. Sound like a plan?"

"Sure does. Later."

I didn't tell him about the other things I'd found. At least, not yet.

Kevin stood in the kitchen, leanin' against the counter drinkin' a cup of coffee when I walked in the door with the cat.

"I thought you were gonna take Everlea to get the cat?"

"Yeah, well, I changed my mind. I was already in town. I ain't got all the time in the world, you know, to drive back and forth all day."

I opened the carrier, and the damn cat shot out of it like its ass had caught fire. It launched itself on top of the icebox and literally flew from up there to the back of the couch in the next room.

"Oh shit. Everlea's asleep on the couch." Kevin hobbled after the cat but stopped in the middle of the livin' room and spun in a circle on one crutch lookin' for the thing. He stood starin' at somethin', then whispered loudly, "Get in here. Look at this."

The cat lay with Everlea like a baby. The damn thing tucked itself into her chest, facin' her with its head under her chin and its paw on her arm like it was givin' her a hug. Kevin hopped a couple of steps closer to the couch, and that damn cat twisted its head around like a tiny demon, glarin' at him with obvious malice in its eyes. I had no doubt if he took one step closer, the thing would launch itself at him and rip his face off with its tiny daggers.

"Looks like you made a new friend," I whispered, walkin' back into the kitchen to feed the evil home invader. Kevin hopped, jumped, and skipped after me. "When did she fall asleep?" I set a bowl of food on the floor next to the sink and filled another with water, settin' it next to the food. I had no idea where to put the litter box. It wasn't goin' in the kitchen. Disgustin'.

"I don't know, man. I just came back downstairs a few minutes before you got back."

"And why ain't you in bed with your damn leg up?" I asked him, eyebrows raised, the big brother in me comin' out. "Have you rested that leg at all?"

"I got a date," he said, grinnin' like a fifteen-year-old horndog.

"A date? You're not a week outta surgery. How you gonna go on a date?"

"She's a nurse. Ha! You remember Jillian from my time in the joint? She wants to 'take care of me.'" He leaned on one crutch, scrunchin' two fingers up and down in quotations.

"You're a dipshit, Kevin. And 'joint' means prison, dumbass."

"Close enough."

I inched closer to the livin' room, tryin' to peer over the back of the couch to set my eyes on Everlea. Although probably unnecessary, I figured I'd better check to make sure the damn cat wasn't maulin' her, but it seemed like the thing thought she was its mama. They were both asleep, and I could hear the cat purrin' from where I stood at the edge of the kitchen.

I didn't know why I felt the need to check on her, but I did and it annoyed me.

"What?" Kevin cocked his head to the side, considerin' me. "You like her."

"Shut up, Kevin."

"You do! Holy shit. Never thought we'd see the day."

"Fuck off. She ain't bad to look at, that's all. Even you can agree with that."

"What the fuck's that mean?"

"Nothin'. I got work to do," I said, reachin' for my dirty work gloves on the counter.

"Whatever. Just be sure not to talk too much, if you wanna get laid."

"I've known her two days, Kevin. Save your words of wisdom for your date."

The sound of a quiet little car approachin' saved me from any more heart to heart.

"There she is. Alright, brother. Wish me luck. I'm hopin' for a sponge bath at her place." He took a deep breath and held it, released it slow, then flashed a grin Lucifer himself would be proud of, pulled the screen door open, and hobbled through it. "Don't wait up."

With Kevin gone and the girls nappin', I had time to get some work done. It had been pilin' up, but the horses were fed and watered and grazed out in the paddocks.

What to make for dinner? Somethin' easy but fulla good stuff for Mrs. Mitchum. Stew. We had some venison left from Dean's last haul and all the fresh vegetables from the market, so I set about gettin' it all ready, and when I'd thrown the last potato in the pot, my phone rang. It occurred to me then Everlea didn't have a phone. Or at least, I hadn't seen her use one. Kinda odd in this day and age.

"Yeah?"

"Hey, brother."

"What's goin' on, Finn? See that stud yet?" I stepped out onto the porch so I wouldn't wake my new houseguests.

"Yep, just had a look. He's a handsome fucker, a handful too. The auction's in the mornin'. We'll get him and head over to Rapid City, see what we can see. What's goin' on there? Dean said Ma's sick again?"

"Yeah. She's here, sleepin' upstairs. I think she wants to stay here till…"

I heard the pain in the crack of Finn's voice. "Um, so, how long then?"

"I dunno, Finn. Doc said there's no way to know. They're gonna try more chemo but—"

"What's goin' on? Finn?" Jay nagged in the background.

"Hold on, Jay, dammit."

"Maybe you oughta head back after Rapid City, just in case. The stud's the only horse we need. The other auction was just a long shot."

"Yeah, I'll let the boys know. Call if there's any change."

"I will, Finn."

"Hey, what's this Kevin says 'bout some woman stayin' at the house?"

"It's nothin'."

"Sure sounds like somethin', way Kevin tells it."

"Uh huh. And how often does listenin' to Kevin ever work out for ya?"

"You got me there, brother, but somethin' tells me, this time, he ain't wrong." He sniggered, and I could tell he was suspicious and laughin' at my expense. *Damn Kevin.*

"I got work to do. See you when you get back."

"That you will. I'll be glad to get away from these ripe assholes. See ya." He hung up, and two minutes later, my phone pinged with a text from Jay:

Tell Ma we love her.

I set a timer on my phone to remind me to put some dough in the oven so we'd have fresh bread with dinner and headed out to tend to my blissfully silent horses. If I had to listen to one more opinion about what I should or shouldn't do, I was gonna strangle somebody.

Sex, sure. I wouldn't have minded gettin' my hands on Everlea for that. In fact, I had a hard time thinkin' about much else with her livin' in my house, but there was no way in hell I'd jump into a relationship with the woman. I already knew she lied. And that bag in her house? She would run at some point.

So, why would I bother?

CHAPTER SIX

EVERLEA

WAKING SLOWLY, awareness coming back into my body an inch at a time, starting in my toes, I felt safe. Instinctively, I knew it was unusual, but I was too comfy and warm to care. I heard people murmuring in low voices and the clanking and sliding of silverware on ceramic plates, but when I opened my eyes, the first thing to register in my mind was the darkness outside. It seemed wrong.

Feeling the first hint of panic when I finally realized I didn't know where I was and couldn't remember falling asleep, I sprang up off the couch, automatically assuming a fighting stance, a heavy quilt falling and pooling around my bare feet. No shoes? Where were my shoes? I never went without them, even in sleep. My lungs heaved in quick heaps of breath, and my heartbeat pounded in my head.

The screen door to my left was thrown open, and suddenly, he stood in front of me.

Jackson.

Jack.

His hands went up in front of his chest, and my eyes went straight to them, looking for weapons. Why would Jack have weapons? I relaxed my stance and straightened. Jack was a good guy. I knew that instinctively too. Maybe not a very friendly guy, but good. I was safe in his house for the moment.

"Everlea, honey, you awake?" Mrs. Mitchum called from the kitchen. I looked around desperately, trying to find somewhere to hide. I needed a minute to collect myself.

Jack must have recognized the panic in my eyes. "Yes, she's up. Give her a minute, please," he called over his shoulder in the direction of Mrs. M's voice, his eyes kind and never leaving mine.

The air became silent and still around me, so I lowered myself back down to the couch and tried to stop shaking.

He walked slowly over and sat next to me, covering my trembling hands with his large, warm, rough ones and waited for me to look up. When I did, it took every ounce of strength and self-preservation in me not to cry and fall into his arms. He wanted to help me, to calm and steady me. I saw it in his eyes. He had no reason to want to do that. Why? Could he really be that good and kind of a person? Did those kinds of people really exist?

I'd given something away just then, in my fight or flight response. Did he understand that?

If he did, he didn't say.

"It's okay," he said softly, so no one else could hear. "Everything's okay. You're safe."

The low rumble of his voice was so soothing, I imagined for a moment I really was safe, and an almost silent sob escaped me before I could stop it. I'd been so not safe for such a long time. I had no idea what safe felt like. If this was it, if he was it, I could lose myself in him.

No. My attraction to him was clouding my mind. I wasn't safe. Anywhere. Not here. I wouldn't let this aberration in time ruin everything I had been planning and preparing for. I'd let Jack get to me before, let my guard down, but I couldn't let it continue.

Dropping my hands from his, I practically jumped off the couch. "No. I'm fine," I lied. "Just a little headache. Do you have any more coffee?"

I noticed out of the corner of my eye that his were closed, and he'd pulled his hands into hard fists, but then he stood, slowly faced me, and opened them again.

I stared straight ahead, trying desperately to hold on to some kind of control, to signal to him that I was fine on my own—I didn't need his help. But I felt a profound pull to look at him. It confused me, and for just a second, I felt defenseless and my eyes snapped to his. There was something on his face, in his expression, his soul, that I felt in mine.

I didn't know what it was, but I struggled not to reach for him.

Shit. I jerked my mental walls back into place, and instead, walked away from him to the kitchen.

I'd been shoveling food into my mouth at an alarming rate, even to me. I might've even moaned a couple times. It was a little embarrassing, but I was *so* hungry and thirsty. I'd only been able to eat a few bites this morning, but the nausea was gone so I assumed it safe to eat and drink again. If it weren't, I'd be sorry later but for now, I was ravenous and there was a feast in front of me.

Finally, I took a break from my animal-like consumption of calories to breathe and to wash the food in my mouth down with some delicious coffee. When I looked up to locate my mug, there were three sets of eyes on me, watching me.

Mrs. M looked a little worried, like she thought I might choke on my food, a possibility for sure since I barely bothered to chew before gulping it down my throat. Kevin laughed under his breath, leaning back in his chair.

And Jack— I didn't know what the look on Jack's face meant. Was it... pleasure? Satisfaction?

He looked pleasantly smug, but when he noticed me looking, his face changed into the hard, guarded mask I'd seen before. I dropped my eyes to the table. He was still annoyed about me being in his house. I felt bad about it and was frustrated with the situation, too, but there wasn't anything I could do about it at the moment, and there was still food on my plate, so I dug back in. I couldn't help it. I was that hungry.

Kevin and Mrs. M chatted lightly while I continued to gorge myself. When I could finally slow down and eat like a normal human, I realized what I'd been eating was absolutely delicious. I hadn't had a homemade meal like it since I was eleven years old. And I definitely hadn't sat around a table with family or friends, chatting and enjoying good food since then either.

"What is this? It's so good," I asked, my mouth full of potatoes, looking up in anticipation of the answer to my question.

My eyes desperately wanted to zoom in on Jack. I still felt drawn to look at him, but thankfully, I spotted a half-eaten loaf of fresh baked bread sitting in a little wooden basket. I smelled it from where I sat at the other end of the table. I eyed it with longing until Kevin barked out a laugh, grabbed the whole breadbasket, and shoved it at me.

"Here, have at it." He chuckled.

"But slowly, dear," Mrs. M warned.

Tearing a piece off, I took a big bite. Okay, so maybe I

hadn't slowed down that much.

"It's venison stew. Isn't it good? Jack made it," Mrs. M said, and I whipped my head up to look at the man in question. No way that big rough-and-tumble guy made this. He was big and strong enough to lift my whole body with one hand, but cook a delicious, tender meal with fresh baked bread? I guess that was kind of sexist of me but come on.

Wait, did she say venison? So, I was eating Bambi? It kind of made me sad, but it was so good. I didn't eat a lot of meat. I wasn't a vegetarian or anything, just didn't usually spend the extra money. I kept a bottle of multivitamins in my car and in my duffel to replace the lack of iron and other nutrients from being on the road a lot.

"You made this?" I asked, disbelief clear in my voice.

He nodded once with an expressionless look on his face. A man of many words, he was not.

Mrs. M looked at him, frowning. "Oh now, don't let him fool you. Jack cooks all the time. He's modest. I taught all the boys to cook. In fact, one of 'em makes a big Sunday dinner every week. Whose turn is it this week?"

"Mine technically," Kevin replied, "but seein' as I'm injured and all, I guess the honor will go to Jack since Finn is MIA."

"So, you two are brothers?" I deduced with my mouth still full of bread. "How many of you are there?"

"Five boys, dear. Well, they're men now." There was obvious pride in Mrs. M's voice. "Kevin here is the rascal of the bunch," she said, motioning to him across the table with a wave of her hand, and he snickered. "By the way, what happened with your date, Kevin? You said you'd be late."

"Oh, uh, yeah, it didn't— It wasn't— Oh, just never you mind."

Mrs. M eyed Kevin for a few seconds, then took a deep

breath. She turned back to me. "The others are up in Montana at an auction. They'll be back in a few days. Never a dull moment 'round here."

"Five?" My eyebrows shot up in surprise, the stitches on my forehead pulling and protesting the little bit of movement.

I couldn't imagine five siblings at all, especially five big guys like Jack and Kevin rambling around in this old house. I was an only child, and even when my parents were alive, besides my grandma, I hadn't known any other family members, if there were any. My parents had been only children too. They probably had cousins or something, but I'd never looked into it. I was better off alone anyway.

Less people to be hurt that way.

"Yes," she said proudly, "and I taught them all to cook and clean so one day, when they marry and have families, they will be able to impress everyone with their fine home-makin' skills. I was kinda hopin' the impressing would happen sooner rather than later. Luckily, I'm a patient woman."

Jack grumbled something under his breath that I couldn't hear, and Kevin laughed out loud at him. Mrs. M smiled but didn't make a peep.

"I got work to do," he said as he stood from his chair, threw his napkin on top of his empty plate, and marched out the kitchen door. He was so moody. He'd been so gentle and kind to me in the living room just a little while before, but he obviously still felt angry having to deal with me at all. I made a mental note to stay out of his way.

"So," I said after the screen door clapped shut behind him, "Mrs. M, how are you feeling? I feel terrible. I didn't mean to fall asleep." I sat back in my chair, pushing my empty plate away from me, but I dipped my finger in the left-over sauce and licked it like a three-year-old.

"Oh, don't worry about me, dear. I'm doin' just fine." She patted my hand on the table. "You must've needed the rest."

"I'm so embarrassed. I don't know what came over me at the hospital. I swear, I'm not usually so ridiculous."

Kevin barked out another laugh. "You should be embarrassed. You were like a tornado on two legs, way I heard it."

My face turned apple-red and I hung my head.

"Nonsense"—Mrs. M stared at Kevin with threat of bodily harm in her eyes—"everyone has a bad day every now and then."

"I'm supposed to be helping you," I said, shaking my head, which of course, hurt and I winced. Kevin laughed again. I'd formed the opinion that he didn't have much of a filter between his brain and mouth, but it made me like him more. He reminded me of myself.

"No matter. You'll help me now." Her smile was so open and kind that I felt like I might cry. "Now, you'll wanna wash up." She stood and began to clear the dishes from the table. "There are fresh towels and toiletries for you in the bathroom. Can't miss it. First door on the right at the top of the stairs. Bring me your clothes when you finish, please, and I'll wash 'em. Kevin laid out some fresh ones for you."

"Oh, you don't need to do that, Mrs. M. I'll take care of it. You've all done so much for me already." I looked down at the awful powder blue scrubs I still wore. "Thank you so much."

"Nonsense, young lady. Bring 'em to me. Now shoo. Go take your shower. Relax."

Just as I opened my mouth to argue, a cat jumped up onto the kitchen table and headbutted me.

"Iggy!" I pulled her to my chest, nuzzling my nose in her silky fur. "Where did you come from, silly girl?"

"Jack went ahead and brought her over," Kevin said,

standing, and he limped over to take the dishes from Mrs. M. "Sit," he told her. Iggy watched him and meowed, and he made a sound between a snort and a hiss. "That cat is somethin' else. She's been followin' me around since she got here, scoldin' me with her judgy yips and yowls. What'd I ever do to you, huh?" he asked her. She stopped cuddling me for a few seconds to glare at him, and she made a little noise that sounded a lot like "hmph."

"You sit," Mrs. M scolded him. "You're gonna ruin that leg of yours. I'm perfectly capable of taking a few plates to the sink." She took the plates from his hands, eyeing him until he sat in her chair. "Good boy."

"But how did he get in? I didn't give him the key." Damn it. He just helped himself? What had Jack seen in my house? My heart dropped into my stomach.

"I think he probably woulda broken in, but Mrs. Masterson showed up. Here, she said you can give it back later." He pushed some folded papers and a single key toward me from the middle of the table. "She gave him those papers for you, too, somethin' 'bout a new fridge."

"Oh, o-okay. Thanks."

"By the way, you know you talk in your sleep?" He laughed again.

What? No. I didn't know that. I'd never been around anyone while I slept, not for a long time anyway.

"Don't worry, you didn't say anything embarrassin', Everlea. You talked a little about a monster and huntin', of all things. Must've been havin' a bad dream."

"Yeah, I guess. Must be all the fresh air out here," I joked, but my voice sounded thin and shaky. I hoped they hadn't noticed.

Jack seemed like a gentleman, so maybe he hadn't snooped when he'd gone to my house, but if he had... I'd need to come up with a reason for what he might have found there.

First things first. I needed a shower, and I didn't want to rush out to find Jack. That would give me away for sure. Plus, the hot water would help ease the pounding in my head. The food helped, especially the coffee I'd had with dinner, but I still felt sore and achy and a shower would address that.

"You stay here, Iggy, and make friends. I'm gonna go take that shower. Top of the stairs?"

The shower had to have been sent from heaven above. The water pressure felt fabulous on my head and neck, and it stayed scalding hot the whole thirty minutes I stood in it.

Now, my hair was clean and shiny. I'd caught a glimpse of myself in the mirror while I'd undressed and had been mortified. Bedhead was an understatement. But now it hung wet down my back, the ends curling into wide ringlets like they always did.

I inherited two things from my mother, one of them my hair. Hers had been fiery red, though, and mine was light brown, but both were naturally curly, the kind of thick, wide, waving curls that millions of women had to pay for. Not me. It was the one thing about my physical appearance I took pride in.

The rest of my attributes were either a casualty of my past or a result of my efforts to outrun it. I didn't really pay much attention to how I looked. I needed to be strong, so I worked out and trained when I could and that kept me fit, but it had become a necessity of survival, so I just did it no matter what it made me look like.

The clothes Kevin left out for me were way too big, but

fresh. I wore a humongous kelly-green T-shirt that looked like it came straight from the eighties and had "Bob's Feed and Tack" printed across the chest in big rainbow-colored bubble letters, and a pair of red and black buffalo-plaid boxer shorts.

The T-shirt was so big, the sleeves came down past my elbows, hiding the scars I didn't want anyone to see. The neck was a little too wide to hide my shoulder, but I would just have to keep it pulled to the left. The socks I'd been given were white tube socks with green stripes around the tops, and they went all the way up to my knees.

I looked like a deranged Christmas elf, but I was clean from head to toe and it felt good. I brushed my teeth with the pink toothbrush I'd used... *yesterday? Today?* I still felt a little disoriented.

But I felt almost reborn. My head hurt a little but the pounding had gone. The stitches on top of the goose egg on my forehead were sore, and my neck and shoulders were still a little stiff, but it wasn't too bad.

After cleaning up the mess I'd made in the surprisingly pink bathroom, I went back downstairs in search of my shoes and bag. I intended to head outside to find Jack. Somehow, I needed to suss out what he'd seen at my house and then figure a way to talk myself out of it.

If he'd seen my secret room, then it would definitely be time for me to leave. I didn't want to go. I'd really grown to like this little town of Wisper and its occupants. But affection for a place, or a person, remained an extravagance I couldn't afford.

I felt terrible about leaving Mrs. M when she needed help. She seemed perfectly capable now, but chemotherapy would quickly change that. And I couldn't imagine Jack trying to help her bathe, and Kevin with his broken leg wouldn't be much help to her. But as awful as it made me feel to think of abandoning them, the urge to protect them was so strong.

I would not allow him to hurt them.

Silence and darkness greeted me downstairs, with only a little light coming into the living room from under the kitchen cabinets. I didn't see or hear Mrs. M, Kevin, or Jack. I found my bag and shoes by the couch, so I slipped my feet into my Chucks and sat there awhile, pondering how to go about figuring out what Jack had, or had not, seen at my house.

Jumping up onto my lap, Iggy took advantage of my distracted state to get me to pet and love on her. She was such a good friend. She always seemed to know when I needed her, and I was proud of her for not freaking out about being in a big unknown house. Leaving her would break my heart. I knew it would be the best thing for her though. Maybe Mrs. M would keep her.

What could I tell Jack about what he'd most likely found? Would he want answers? I'd never tried to explain my life to anyone. I hadn't wanted anyone to know any details, for fear of the knowledge coming back to haunt me. Or them. I'd had one good friend in the last nine years, and he'd paid for my friendship with his life.

Toby had been my one and only real friend after I'd run. He'd been so kind and helpful to me as I learned my way around Louisville, and after a short time, became a sort of big brother figure to me. The urge to confide in him had been strong. But I hadn't, not on purpose anyway.

I'd been scared enough by then, by the danger hunting me, to be careful.

We had worked nights together mopping floors and cleaning at an old run-down strip mall in Louisville, Kentucky for less than minimum wage, but cash. One night, when we'd finished working, we sat down at Lou Vulle's

Pizza to eat throwaways and talk. I told him I'd gone to high school in Peoria; Toby had been telling me about his little sister's first promposal.

We'd cleaned up and gone home without me ever realizing my mistake. I had been so tired. I hadn't been sleeping well because I'd been hearing strange noises at night again and swore I could feel his eyes on me. I planned on leaving the following Friday after I got paid, but never got that far.

I didn't want to leave the only friend I'd ever had, and I thought for one second about telling him my secret, but Toby hadn't had any other family, and he and his sister depended on each other. I couldn't put either one of them in a position to be hurt. But the next evening, when I showed up for my shift, our sleazy manager, Gary, told me Toby had been found with his throat slit outside the door to his apartment. Dead.

I'd known he'd killed Toby. I knew my slip of the tongue had nothing to do with him finding me or killing Toby, but it didn't matter. I'd stayed too long, gotten too comfortable.

Toby's death had been a warning. I hadn't been playing the game and that was unacceptable, but at the time, I hadn't known the rules.

I caught a glimpse of him watching me through the window in the pizza parlor when I learned of Toby's death. He smiled. He was proud of what he'd done to an innocent person.

And he was proud because he'd done it for me.

I left right then out the back door, didn't go home, didn't even take my car. I just ran. I hopped my first train that night.

It had all been for nothing. Toby didn't get to see his sister dressed up and glowing before her prom. She'd never get to see her brother again.

I cried and screamed all night on that fucking train.

When it stopped, I found myself in Chicago.

CHAPTER SEVEN

JACK

"EVERLEA?"

Whippin' her head around to look at me when I threw the screen door open and barreled into the kitchen, her eyes were as big as golf balls. I could see 'em all the way in the other room, in the dark.

"Sorry, didn't mean to startle you."

"It's okay. I just, I was— I'm fine," she stammered, smoothin' her hands down her thighs a few times. I couldn't tell for sure in the dim room, but I thought they might be shakin' again. The cat jumped from her lap to the back of the couch to sit behind her head like a guard, givin' me the evil eye.

She was wearin'— Goddamn Kevin. What a fuckin' a joker. *My* boxer shorts? Nice. I shook my head and tried not to look at her legs.

"C'mon." I grabbed her hand, pullin' her to stand.

"Okay. Um, you went to my house, I know—"

"I got a horse in labor. Stuck foal. I can't get my hand in there to pull it. Your hands are smaller. Will you do it? I called the vet but he's got another emergency. By the time he gets here, it might be too late."

"Oh. Um. Okay," she said in a quiet voice, tuggin' on the neck of my T-shirt she wore. I dragged her through the kitchen, out the door, and down the lawn to the barn. She didn't say a word as I pulled her beside me, just stared at me. I felt her eyes on the side of my face again. Realizin' I still held onto her, I yanked my hand away like she'd burned me.

When she saw the mare lyin' on her side on the floor of the stall, she gasped. "Wow."

"Never seen a horse before?"

"Not up close. She's beautiful."

"She's in pain. Just talk low and don't make sudden movements. Look here." Pullin' her to Biddie's backend, I motioned to the tiny hoof stickin' out with a wave of my hand. "See that hoof?"

"Oh my God."

"That's the problem. We gotta get it back in and then align the foal's legs and head into a divin' position. I can get the hoof back in, but it just keeps poppin' out when she has a contraction."

"Okay. What do I do?" Her eyebrows jumped but then scrunched down into a determined little v, her eyes dark in the shadows of the barn but still green as could be as she stared at me, waitin' for instructions.

"I'm gonna push the hoof in, then you gotta get in there and hold it back while you get your fingers 'round it and the other leg. Around the ankles. Like this." Grabbin' her wrist, I held it and wrapped my fingers and thumb around her fore and middle fingers and tugged. "Get the legs 'tween your fingers like this. You'll feel it when you're in there, and once the legs are aligned, the head should follow, but I want you to try to feel for the head to make sure." I eyed her for a few seconds. "You're not gonna throw up again, are ya?"

"No." She looked apprehensive but resolute, and I released her hands.

"Okay. Ready?"

Takin' a deep breath through her nose, she released it slowly from her mouth. "Yes." She stood tall, then pulled her long tangle of hair away from her face, wrappin' the whole length of it into a knot behind her head.

Dammit. I couldn't afford to be distracted by her beautiful face or lips. Or that hair. I wanted to feel it in my hands, fallin' between my fingers as I—

I cleared my throat, closed my eyes, and refocused by takin' a deep breath of my own, then got down on my knees and eased the foal's hoof back in. But, as this was Biddie's first pregnancy and she was small in stature, my hand was too big to get a good feel of the foal without worryin' about tearin' somethin' or hurtin' Biddie. She had already struggled with the foal tryin' to push out the wrong way.

"Okay, you're up," I said, scootin' against the wall.

"'Kay."

"Make your hand into the shape of a torpedo. Point your fingers and push your thumb up underneath."

"Like this?" she asked, holdin' her hand up in front of her chest.

"Yeah. I know it's gross. We're outta gloves." She knelt next to me, and I grabbed the bottle of lubricant from the floor of the stall to squeeze some onto her hand and fingers. "Now, just push in slowly. You'll know when you're there and I'll guide you. Just tell me what you feel and avoid jabbin' your fingers into anything unless you know for sure it's the foal's legs."

She did it. Didn't hesitate. Didn't scream or squeal. "Feels weird. Is she pushing? She's squeezing the crap out of my arm."

"Yes, but that's good. The hoof will try to pop back out but grab it, and it'll lead you back to the other one. Feel it?"

"Yes! It's hard." Leanin' over, she lay next to me, tryin' to find the right angle, but she didn't seem scared at all. She yanked my T-shirt, exposin' her left shoulder, and I found myself havin' a hard time lookin' away from it, from imaginin' what the rest of her body looked like under my shirt.

"Okay, now push it slowly back and feel 'round with your other fingers carefully for the second hoof."

"I feel it. I think I felt his head too."

"Okay. Grab both hooves like I showed you. Does it feel like the head is lined up to dive?"

"I think so? I can feel his nose against my knuckles. At least, I think it's his nose. It's soft and squishy. Oh, yep. I'm pretty sure I just stuck my pinky up a nostril."

"Okay, now slide your arm out *very* slowly and guide those hooves through the birth canal. Don't pull, just gently guide. Biddie's gonna do the work. You just wanna help her a little. But hold on tight. Don't let go."

"Oh my God. She's pushing my arm out!" Biddie protested the pain and neighed, then rolled a little, but Everlea just moved with the mare. She didn't startle like I thought she would.

"Yep, and since you're holdin' the legs, she's pushin' the foal out too."

I held my breath, watchin' as Biddie expelled Everlea's arm with the two hooves, one slightly behind the other. The foal's nose poked through, and I hoped we were in the final stretch.

"Don't let go."

"I won't."

"That's good," I said when the foal's head made its first appearance, then popped free. Scootin' behind her, I reached around to wrap my fingers above hers. "Now, with the next contraction, we're gonna apply a little traction. We're *not* pullin'. Just givin' Biddie's push a nudge to help her pass the shoulders. A small nudge."

"'Kay. He's so cute."

"He's covered in guk," I complained next to her ear. I felt the warmth from her cheek on my own and involuntarily scooted closer.

"Oh, it's the most natural thing in the world. Who cares? Look at his cute little nose."

"It could be a filly. You keep sayin' he but could be a her." We tugged a little and the foal's shoulders popped free.

"Oh! Look at that. She did it. Good girl, Biddie," she cooed. "What a good mama you are." I watched her face and the smile that overtook the whole thing as the foal blinked the goo away and flared his nostrils, tryin' to suck in his first breath.

We coulda let go, and Biddie woulda delivered the foal the rest of the way on her own, but I didn't wanna ruin the moment for Everlea. She seemed mesmerized by the whole thing. Also, I didn't wanna stop touchin' her. My front was glued to her back, my arms wrapped around her as we guided the foal to be born.

It occurred to me again that I didn't pull away as soon as I could have.

"Okay, one last tug."

"Oh my God. This is amazing, Jack!"

When he was all the way out, I unglued myself and we stood. As Everlea dusted herself off, I bent to clear the foal's nostrils and check his breathin', and I looked between his legs.

"Guess you were right. It's a boy. C'mon. Mama will do the rest. Let's give 'em some privacy."

"I think I might need another shower." She breathed a laugh, lookin' down at my Bob's Feed and Tack shirt, which was now covered in goop and wood chips from the floor along with a little blood from the membranes. Her arm and hands were covered, too, but she didn't seem bothered by it. Grabbin' a rag hangin' from the stall door, I handed it to her, and she used it to wipe up the mess.

"Yeah," I grunted, walkin' outta the stall, closin' the door behind us.

"Does this happen a lot?"

"What? A stuck foal? Not too often. Go ahead if you wanna jump in the shower. I got a few things to do still."

"Do you mind if I stay? Can I watch?"

"I, uh— Sure."

She cocked her head to the side. "What's this music? I've never heard it before."

"Oh, I dunno. It's my brother's thing. 'Scuse me for a sec. I need to call the vet back." I left her standin' outside Biddie's stall to make my call, and when I got back, she was sittin' in front of the door, singin' softly to the new mama and baby.

Her eyes were closed, and she rested her head against the door but occasionally peeked into the stall. I didn't know the song and could barely understand the words, but the melody was sweet and soft and her voice sounded like an angel's. Somehow, it seemed like it came from the music on the speaker in the corner playin' quietly. She moved her fingers on her thighs, like she was playn' a piano while she sang.

Steppin' back into an empty stall, tryin' to be silent so I didn't disturb her, I listened for a minute or two. But I didn't want her to know I'd heard her, and I reminded myself, she'd lied to me. And to Mrs. Mitchum. I stepped back out into the aisle.

"Go on up to the house now. Get your shower."

Gaspin', she looked up. The bite in my voice snapped her outta whatever zone she'd gone into, and she stiffened. "Oh. Right. Okay." Lowerin' her eyes, she stood but peeked back in at the horses.

"They'll be fine. They been doin' this without you for all a' time."

She didn't say anything more, just nodded, pressed her lips together, and walked away. I watched her go, feelin' like a gigantic dick, but my family was too important to me to let some woman manipulate 'em.

As attracted as I was to her, I wouldn't let that interfere with keepin' my eye on her.

I slept like shit. I still felt bad for barkin' at her after she'd helped me, and I felt like a jerk for not offerin' her my room, or Dean's or Jay's, to sleep in. I wouldn't offer Finn's room to my worst enemy, as disgustin' as he'd most likely left it. I wouldn't know since I hadn't stepped foot in it since we were teenagers.

But by the time I'd finished up with Biddie and the new foal, she'd showered and changed back into her scrub pants and her black T-shirt and fell asleep on the couch again. Her shoes were back on her feet, danglin' over the side.

I laid Mrs. Mitchum's quilt over her and went to bed but left my door open so I could hear if she decided to up and leave in the middle of the night. I wanted to know so I could break it to Mrs. Mitchum. She seemed so fond of Everlea, but I couldn't figure out why. I knew they'd had a chance to get to know each other a little while Mrs. Mitchum had been in the hospital, but they'd only met a couple times.

Mrs. Mitchum could be somewhat of a collector of lost kids. She'd been a mom to my brothers and me after Granny died, and to Carey after his dad died and his mama had to work two, sometimes three jobs. But Mrs. Mitchum didn't know what I knew, that Everlea was hidin' something from us, that she was runnin' from somethin', and that she'd lied.

An hour later, I lay in my room, down the hall from where Everlea slept, wide awake and starin' at the ceilin' in the darkness. I couldn't shut my mind off. Why had she lied about her car? And why was she wearin' her shoes? Had she planned on leavin' tonight? If she did, why'd she tell Mrs. Mitchum she'd help her? Would she go back to her house, or would she run and leave Wisper?

What could she be so afraid of?

And she was afraid. I'd seen it in her eyes when she'd woken on the couch earlier. She'd had a terrified look to her, like a startled colt, ready to flee at any sound or movement. I'd wanted to hold her, to make her feel safe, but that was stupid. I barely knew her.

And I had no clue what she was runnin' from. Could I protect her? Why would she even let me try? She didn't know me either, even if there was a pull there, some kinda attraction. I felt sure it was only my upbringin'. My mama, Granny, and then Mrs. Mitchum had ingrained it in us to help people, no matter if we liked 'em or not. If a person needed help, you helped 'em.

And what if she would let me? What if the thing she was so scared of was somethin' I knew nothin' about? Was it money? Yeah, 'cause I was a bona fide genius when it came to that. Besides, I'd seen all the cash at her house in her secret room.

All that led me to thinkin' she was runnin' from a guy. An ex-boyfriend most likely, as beautiful as she was. She probably had no shortage of admirers. But whoever it was had hurt her. Physically. It was why she jumped at loud noises, even in her sleep, why she'd been ready to fight in an instant this evenin', crouched down, legs shoulder-width apart, arms up in front of her, hands balled into fists.

Where was all this comin' from? It wasn't like me to get involved in people's problems. This whole train of thought was so stupid and a waste of my time. I threw the covers to the floor and flipped onto my side, hopin' the thoughts of Everlea would go out the window with the movement.

They didn't. Those same thoughts from earlier crept into my mind. How she'd felt in my arms. How soft and warm she'd been. And tonight, how she'd gotten right in there with Biddie and the foal. She didn't hesitate at all. I imagined most women woulda whined and complained about the mess. Everlea hadn't. Thoughts of that mess and of her undressin' to take a shower led me right back to...

It had been so long since I'd been with a woman, and I couldn't deny I wanted her, even though I knew she wasn't bein' honest. I didn't think her a bad person. She seemed kind, and I could tell by the way she treated the horses she cared about animals. That could tell you a lot about a person. But I still didn't trust her.

It didn't mean I didn't wanna bury myself inside her.

I knew better of it, but I crept down the little hallway leadin' from my room to the livin' room and stood behind the couch like a damn stalker, watchin' her sleep.

She was restless, sawin' her legs together, then she flipped onto her stomach and moaned. She'd kicked the blanket down by her feet, and all I could see was a hint of her ass under those ugly blue scrubs. I imagined what she would look like without the stupid pants, what her thighs would look like as she opened 'em for me.

Damn. I wanted to pick her up and carry her to my bed. I wanted to throw her on it and rip those scrubs from her body, to lose myself so deep inside her she'd feel me there, between her thighs, for days.

Jesus. If she woke, she'd see me standin' behind her like a pervert. I crept back to my room and locked my door, leaned against it, then jacked off for maybe a minute before the thought of her wet, moanin' mouth around my dick made me come.

Finally, I fell asleep, with less than four hours till I had to get up and start my day all over again.

In the mornin', I dragged myself outta bed, past Everlea still asleep on the couch, and out to the barn to feed the horses. I finished my mornin' chores and went back to the house for breakfast, and I found her there in the kitchen with Mrs. Mitchum and Kevin again.

"Oh, good. What took you so long? We been waitin' on ya," Mrs. Mitchum chirped while I scrubbed my hands in the sink.

"For what?" I dried my hands on a towel and sat at the head of the table.

"For breakfast, silly boy, and I wanted to let you know the plan."

"Plan?" I yawned.

"Here," she said, handin' me a plate of scrambled eggs. "Why so tired?"

"Had a foal born last night. Didn't get much sleep. Everlea helped." She passed me a plate of sausage links and, I was so exhausted, I just tipped the platter, lettin' four or five of 'em roll onto my plate.

Mrs. Mitchum looked at Everlea. "You did?"

Everlea smiled. Big. I peeked at her outta the corner of my eye.

"Yes! It was amazing. I stuck my arm in there and helped pull the baby out. He's so cute."

Kevin snorted. "I told you to keep your mouth shut so you make her shove her hand up a horse's ass instead? That is so you, Jack."

"Shut up, Kevin," I said, and Mrs. Mitchum scolded him.

"Watch your language."

"Sorry, Ma."

"I didn't mind. I mean, yeah, it was kind of gross but so cool. It's amazing how the horse knows just what to do, the way she takes care of the baby after he's born and—"

"So, what plan? What's goin' on?" I interrupted her. With my brothers gone and Kevin outta commission, I still had a lotta work to do and didn't much feel like listenin' to all their chitchat.

"Oh, well, since it's my last day before my treatments start up again, Mrs. Whitley's takin' me to one of those fancy spas in Jackson. She's planned the whole day for us. Lunch and we're gettin' manicures. Everlea, I would've invited you but she planned this without me knowin' about it. But I figure you can stay here, get to know the ranch and the house a little. Relax before your first day at your new job." Mrs. Mitchum smiled at Everlea and she smiled back, but her smile slipped a little when she noticed me lookin' at her. She sipped her coffee to hide it.

"Please, don't worry about me, Mrs. M. I'll be fine."

"Okay, good. And then, tomorrow we start. I have an appointment at the hospital at nine with my oncologist, so

Jack, you'll have to take us and drop us off. We'll go down to the chemo clinic after that for my first treatment. I'm not sure how long we'll be there. There's paperwork, and they have to get me all set up."

"Yes, ma'am."

"Everlea, you and I will have plenty of time to talk and get to know each other. I feel like I know nothin' about you." Mrs. Mitchum dipped her head, archin' one eyebrow, and Everlea let out some kinda nervous laugh. "Oh, and I was thinkin', Jack"—she looked at me—"we could bring the bed from my spare room over here for Everlea. Set a little bedroom up for her in the parlor. She won't wanna stay in a stinky boy's room."

"Oh, please, don't go to any trouble. I can sleep on the couch. It's comfy."

"I'll get it today," I said. No need to argue about it. I wouldn't have her sleepin' on the couch indefinitely.

"Really, it's—"

I cut her off. "I'll get it."

"Ooookay," she said, hidin' her face in her coffee mug and takin' a big ol' slurpin' sip.

CHAPTER EIGHT

JACK

MRS. WHITLEY CAME by about ten to fetch Mrs. Mitchum. They left laughin', the doc's wife fillin' her in on all the town gossip. I told Everlea to stay at the ranch while I went to get the bed, but she asked me to take her to her house to pick up some clothes. She seemed nervous when she asked, but I didn't say anything about what I'd found there, and she didn't offer any explanation.

We sat in complete silence in the cab of my truck while I drove to town. When we pulled into her little driveway, she coughed awkwardly.

"So, um, I'll just be a minute. I just want to grab a few things."

"I'll come with," I said, turnin' my head to look at her. I wanted to gauge her reaction to my next words. "I wanna check your garage door. When I was here to get the cat, the door was open. There was a mess in there. I think maybe a bear got in, knocked some stuff over."

Her eyes snapped to mine and her whole body locked in place. "A bear?"

"Probably. You remember if you left the door open?"

"Oh, uh, yeah, I-I probably did. I, um, did laundry the other night. I probably just forgot," she lied. I could tell 'cause she glanced at the seat between us nervously, then turned her head to look out the window, wringin' her hands in her lap. "Okay, sure, come with me."

That had been a little too easy.

"Okay then."

We stepped outta the truck and made our way slowly up the walk to the front door, and her steps were measured. I walked behind her, so I couldn't see the look on her face but her shoulders were stiff. She pulled her keys from her pocket and tried to unlock the door, but her hands shook and she dropped 'em.

"Oh." She forced a giggle.

"I got 'em. Lemme do that." Pickin' up the keys, I stepped around her to unlock the door, and she backed away. Normally, I woulda held the door for her and let her go before me, but she seemed scared to death. If somethin' waited inside the house for her, I wanted to find it first. I opened it and walked in.

"Thanks," she said, steppin' around me. "So, um, just wait here. I'll be quick."

"Sure. Lemme know if you need help."

She flicked a glance in my direction but didn't look at me, then turned to walk down the hall to her bedroom. I thought about just tellin' her what I'd seen in her tiny secret spy room, but she knew I'd been in her house and she didn't bring it up so, obviously, it wasn't somethin' she wanted to divulge. And, stubbornly, I didn't wanna give her the out. I wanted her to tell the truth 'cause she wanted to, not 'cause she got caught.

After a few minutes, she backed outta her bedroom and shut the door. She'd changed into black jeans and another band T-shirt, black again with two F's inside a red circle. She carried a trash bag and came to stand in front of me but looked behind her toward the kitchen, where the spy room was.

"Somethin' else you wanna grab?" Probably her go-bag.

"Uh, no. No, I think I have everything I need for now." She turned to smile at me but glanced back one more time. "I guess I'm ready. Will you lock the door behind you, please? I'd like to check the garage."

"'Course."

Walkin' around the house to the garage, I found the key to fit the lock and we stepped inside. Everything looked just how I'd left it. She walked to the middle of the small, one-car garage and looked all around. I didn't know what she searched for but whatever it was, I didn't think she found it. She released a pent-up breath, shook her head a little, and her shoulders dropped three inches. We left and I locked up.

"So, where is Mrs. M's house?"

"'Bout a mile from here."

She took two steps to walk past me, but I grabbed her wrist, and she turned back as I took the garbage bag from her.

A moment passed as we stood there. Her eyes lookin' up into mine, in the shadow between the house and the garage, caught me and held me in place. I saw so much uncertainty in 'em, and I felt that urge again to hold her close. I got the other urge too.

Finally, her eyes traveled down to her wrist still in my hand, but she didn't pull away. And, surprisingly, I didn't feel the need to push her away either.

I slid my hand over hers slowly, lettin' my fingers trail across her skin and under her fingers to her fingertips. Shiverin', she closed her eyes and I held my breath. I liked touchin' her, feelin' her warm skin, but it quickly turned into somethin' I wasn't in a position to do anything about, and I kept havin' to remind myself she was hidin' somethin'. Turnin' her hand palm up, I dropped her keys into it.

"Ready then?"

She sucked in a breath. "Yes."

I retrieved the mattress and box springs from Mrs. Mitchum's spare bedroom. Everlea tried to help me carry 'em but they were only full-sized, and I was pretty sure her little arms wouldn't have been much help, so I shooed her away. I loaded 'em into the back of my truck, then went back into the house to find her. She stood in front of the couch, lookin' at all the black and white photos on the wall behind it.

"Is this Mr. Mitchum?" She pointed to a picture of Mr. and Mrs. Mitchum on their weddin' day. I'd seen it a million times and heard the story to go with it probably twice as many.

"Yeah."

"They look so happy."

"They were."

"What happened to him?"

"Heart attack. Six years ago, I think. You ready?" I asked, but she didn't move.

"Did you spend a lot of time here as a kid?"

"Some."

"How are you related to Mrs. M? You call her Mrs. Mitchum but Kevin calls her Ma. How come?"

"We ain't related. She was my granny's friend. Granny died and Mrs. Mitchum took over for her. She raised us, I guess. Or helped." I ignored her question about why I didn't call Mrs. Mitchum "Ma" like my brothers. It wasn't the time to delve into my pathetic defense mechanisms.

"Of course she did. She's just about the nicest person I

think I've ever met. She reminds me of my grandma sometimes."

"Yeah?"

"Yeah. She died a long time ago though."

"Were you close with her?"

"She was my best friend," she said, crossin' her arms over her chest, huggin' herself a little, and I got the feelin' she didn't wanna talk any more about her granny.

"Ready then?"

Finally, she looked at me. "'Kay."

―――――――

We arrived back at the ranch, and I sent her inside to open the doors and windows in the den. We didn't ever go in it much, so it probably needed a good dustin' and airin' out.

I unloaded the bed and set to carryin' the box spring in when I heard a sound comin' from the open window on the side of the house. Was that Granny's old piano? The sound floated, just a faint sigh in the air, but I was sure of it. I walked to the window so I could see into the back den where the piano had been sittin' untouched for years.

Everlea sat at the old upright piano, on the wobbly, wooden bench, playin' softly and singin' in a whisper. Her head was down but she didn't look at the keys—her eyes were closed. She was playin' from memory. The melody was sad, and it stirred that stupid need in me to go to her.

I didn't plan to do it, but I turned and headed to the kitchen door at the same time I heard the sound of gravel crunchin' under tires. The music stopped, and I looked back through the window at Everlea. She stood abruptly, knockin' the piano bench over, then jerked her head to look out the window. When she saw me, she froze for two seconds, then spun around and ran from the room.

Followin', I sprinted the distance separatin' me from the door, jumpin' onto the porch when I reached it.

"Everything okay, Jack?" Mr. Williams hollered, climbin' outta his car.

I called over my shoulder, "Yes, sir, gimme a few minutes."

Throwin' the screen door open, I searched frantically for Everlea. The look of panic and fear on her face when she'd heard the car approachin' shot a bolt of dread right through me. I needed to find her. I wanted to tell her everything would be okay. She was safe.

Finally, I did find her, curled into a ball under Dean's bedroom window with her arms wrapped around her knees.

She looked up when she heard the door open and then hung her head so I couldn't see her eyes. "Jack," she whispered.

Crouchin' down in front of her, my heart was beatin' a mile a minute. "It's okay. It's just Mr. Williams and his daughter Cadence. I've known him all my life. He won't hurt you."

Lookin' up at me then, her eyes were as big as green saucers. "I'm so sorry. I panicked. I-I'm sorry. I'm fine, really, I'm…"

But she wasn't fine. Her whole body shook, the look on her face gut wrenchin', like a kid when they'd done somethin' wrong, knew they'd been caught doin' it, but also, there was terror there.

I sat next to her on the floor, but still, she trembled, so I pulled her onto my lap, holdin' her tight to my chest. Her heart raced.

After a minute, her body relaxed a little and she let out a

shudderin' breath. I spoke low and soft to her, tellin' her she was safe and I had her. I wouldn't let anyone hurt her. We sat there a few minutes longer, just breathin' together. The tension began to seep outta her body and she pulled back, away from mine, to look at me.

"Don't you need to go and see what Mr. Williams needs?"

"He'll wait."

"No, oh God, I'm so embarrassed. I'm so sorry. I'm ruining everything. That's a client out there and I'm interrupting your business." She tried untanglin' herself from my hold but I didn't let her. I held her wrists loosely, but firmly, in my hands till she stilled.

"Mr. Williams is a friend not a client, and his daughter adores our horses, so they're out there enjoyin' themselves while they wait. There's no rush, Everlea."

Her legs straddled mine from her attempt to get away from me, and I knew the moment she felt my attraction to her, hard against her body, in the warm vee between her thighs.

She gasped and licked her lips, drawin' my eyes to 'em. I felt her soft puff of breath against my face and closed my eyes to try to control the overwhelmin' urge I felt to lay her down right there on the wood floor and take her.

When I opened 'em, she'd moved her face closer to mine and stared at my lips.

"Everlea," I whispered as a warnin' to myself, thinkin' about all the reasons I shouldn't do what I wanted to, but didn't heed it. Instead, I closed the distance between us and took her lips in mine, kissin' her slowly, lookin' into her eyes for any sign she didn't want me.

That wasn't what I got though.

Closin' her eyes, she leaned into me and moaned. It was a small sound, but it roared loud throughout my whole body, makin' my cock punch out behind the zipper of my blue jeans. I growled, couldn't help it, and fucked her mouth with my tongue. There was no other way to describe that kiss. I let go of her wrists and wrapped my hands around her waist, diggin' my fingers into her skin over her T-shirt.

She kissed me back wildly, bitin' and suckin' and rubbin' herself against me. Her hands wrapped around the sides of my neck, and she shoved her fingers in my hair and pulled. It was so erotic and intimate. There were no other sounds in the world besides her little pants of breath and my loud ones.

If I didn't stop it, I'd come. I was almost there, as a matter of fact. Her hands on me, clutchin' at me and beggin' me to touch her everywhere, urged me into a frenzy. She felt so good in my arms, against my skin—I could barely control my body.

It took all the strength I had to stop that kiss. Slowly, I pulled my head back, placin' chaste little pecks on the outside of her lips, her jaw and chin, before I pulled back completely, whackin' my head on the windowsill to knock some sense into it. She opened her eyes to see why I'd stopped, and the heat and need I saw in her was almost my undoin'.

Suddenly, she launched herself backward two feet, landin' on her backside with a look of surprise on her face.

"I didn't mean to do that!" Scramblin' to get up, she ran out of the bedroom and into the bathroom down the hall, slammin' the door shut behind her.

Well, fuckin' A.

Not how I saw that endin'.

I tried to talk to Everlea through the bathroom door, but she wouldn't come out, said she needed a minute. Kevin stuck his head out his bedroom door, saw me standin' in front of the bathroom like an idiot, rolled his eyes and laughed, then disappeared.

Reluctantly, I went out to talk to Mr. Williams, adjustin' the steel pipe in my jeans as I tripped down the stairs.

"Hey there, Cadence. How ya been, girl?" I hollered to her as I walked across the yard, shakin' out my hands to try to forget the feel of Everlea in 'em.

Cadence stood at the wooden fence by the open doors of the barn, feedin' apple chunks to Sammy. Always such a cute little thing, her light brown cheeks glowed golden in the sun, vibrant against her short, curly black hair. She was a pure soul, and I was always glad to see her.

"Mr. Williams, sorry 'bout that. How ya been, sir?" I held out my hand and he shook it.

"Good, Jack, real good. How 'bout you? We heard Mrs. Mitchum was back in the hospital. Everything okay?"

I breathed out a long sigh. I hadn't thought about all the people stoppin' by to see her or ask after her.

"Well, sir, she's okay for now. She's home, here with us. She's gonna try chemo again." I tried to find a way to sum it all up. "She's at peace about it, though."

"Oh, Jack. Well, I'm real sorry to hear it. You'll let us know if she needs anything?"

"Yes, sir, I will." It wouldn't be easy talkin' about this day in and day out. I cleared my throat. "So, what brings you by? Cadence missin' Sammy again?" Cadence looked over at the sound of her name, and I gave her a wink. "How's Carl doin', Cadence? How'd he like that lettuce I gave you last week?"

Carl the rabbit was the star of all the stories she liked to tell me. They'd stop by once a week so she could pet the horses and help feed 'em. I was still tryin' to convince her to let me take her for a ride. Sometimes she talked to me, sometimes she didn't.

Nine years old and autistic, Cadence was shy and had a hard time dealin' with people. I could relate, so I'd let her have the run of the ranch when she had a hard day. Mr. Williams said it calmed her like nothin' else could. Hearin' that made me feel good, and I had to admit, she was one of my most favorite people in this world. She was never nothin' but honest, never tried to hide what she felt. And oh how she loved my horses. I took a lotta pride in 'em, so that made me feel good too.

"Whatcha feedin' Sammy today? Oh, you bring him the green apples? You know how he likes the sour ones, don'tcha?"

She giggled, flashin' me the biggest smile as she twisted the ends of Sammy's mane in her fingers, his buttery, palomino colorin' settin' off his white mane and tail in the sun.

"Jack, you ever hear about those therapy animals they've got over in Jackson?" Mr. Williams asked as Cadence grabbed my hand to pull me closer to Sammy.

"No, sir, don't think I have." Somehow, she knew I didn't much like touch, so she used to be shy with me, but Cadence was innocent, would never hurt anyone, so I relaxed with her real quick. Now she just grabbed and pulled.

"There's this place over there, works with kids and some adults, I think, who have emotional troubles, or like Cadence, have a hard time around people. They've got a mini-horse, rabbits, dogs, even a llama. It got me to thinkin'. Your Sammy would make a fine therapy horse. He's always so gentle with her."

"Huh, guess I never really thought about it. I just assumed Cadence is special and that's what makes Sammy love her." She rewarded me with a shy grin and I smiled back. "He sure does, sweet girl. He waits for you by this gate every time you drive up." She whispered to him, and he snorted, rubbin' his nose against her hand through the fence. Well, that was all the attention I would get from Cadence. She and Sammy were in their own little world.

They stayed another fifteen minutes or so, just long enough for Cadence to calm and center herself, even if she didn't know that was what she was doin'.

When they'd gone, I was left still thinkin' about the therapy animals he'd talked about. But what did I know about any kinda therapy?

I knew horses, though, and it'd always been true they could calm and guide and bring a person happiness like nothin' else I'd ever seen.

CHAPTER NINE

EVERLEA

EMERGING from the bathroom like a cat burglar, I looked both ways before stepping out. I took a big breath and descended the stairs. I didn't hear or see anyone, so I stood there for a few minutes in the muted sunshine coming in the old, thick, glass windows, just listening. And thinking. Should I talk to Jack? Should I broach the topic of our mutual attraction? Or the fact that I practically accosted him not even an hour ago?

If he hadn't stopped the kiss, I would have ripped his clothes off right there on the floor and mounted him. I wanted to then. I still wanted to.

Touching him like that, the feel of his hard body against mine—it took the whole half an hour I hid in the bathroom for the burn in my body to dissipate. I sat on the uncomfortable linoleum floor, head between my knees, trying to convince myself that I didn't want to attack him and push him down into a pile of hay and rip his clothes off.

But now, as I thought of his tongue in my mouth again, his hands all over me, fingers digging into my skin, the wild desire came back full force. I bent to try to breathe more effectively.

Damn it. How ridiculous. I was a grown woman. I could control myself. I wrenched my body upright, taking another deep breath, blew it out, then went to the kitchen door to peek out, trying to rub my thighs against myself as I walked to relieve some of the pressure in my you know what. Oh my God, I could have humped a doorknob to ease the ache.

The big door had been left open again, only the screen as a barrier to anything lurking outside. I'd noticed they never shut the big door, and I wondered if they left it open year-round. It made me nervous. Not like a door could protect me, but at least it was one more obstacle between me and the monster. Would they notice if I shut it at night?

The only vehicle in the drive was Jack's truck, so Mr. Williams and his daughter had gone. Mrs. Mitchum hadn't come back from her spa day, and Kevin was upstairs in his room, I assumed. I heard a TV up there.

So, the only thing left to do was to go out to talk to Jack. Or, at least, offer to help him with his work in some way. I couldn't just sit on the couch and do nothing all day. Oh, but I could set up the bed in the den. It was what we were supposed to do anyway, before I freaked out.

I walked back there, happy to have something to allow me to avoid him a little longer, but when I got to the den door, my smile vanished. Jack had already set the bed up. He'd even put clean sheets on and a blanket and pillow. His productiveness and all around "get 'er done" attitude was seriously getting on my nerves. No way to avoid him now.

Looking at the bed, all I could see was me naked on my back, writhing underneath him as he thrust into me, over and over and over, his tight ass clenching, low between my bent legs.

Fine.

I crept out the kitchen door and made my way to the barn, my eyes scanning every inch of the property. There were so many places a person could hide on this ranch. It made me nervous. But something about the big blue sky and the yellow trees glowing in the afternoon sun also calmed me. I was at ease here. I'd never felt anything like it before, and it confused me.

Wondering why, I stood there, growing more and more anxious, realizing just how many places he could be, watching me, until Jack stepped out of the barn with a saddle in his hands, his biceps bulging under the sleeves of his T-shirt. My mouth watered.

And my anxiety ebbed a little.

"Goin' somewhere?" he asked, squinting against the sun. I looked into his eyes, licked my bottom lip remembering the taste of his mouth on mine, and had to force a moan back down my throat.

He wore his baseball cap backward but shifted the saddle into one hand so he could turn it forward to shield his eyes.

"No. I just thought maybe I could help you? You already set up the bed, and I know you have a lot of work to do. Can I help?"

His eyes roamed all over me, and I thought he could tell I was anxious. He scanned the ranch and the mountains in the distance too. He didn't say anything about our earlier encounter, and neither did I.

"Sure. Wait here a minute. I'm gonna set this saddle in the sun to dry out. We got a leak in the tack room."

"Okay. What's a tack room?"

Walking over to the fence, he set the saddle on top of it, balancing it there. "The tack room is where we keep all our gear, saddles, blankets, medications, and the like."

"Oh, like a horse barn supply closet?"

"Guess so. Tack is what we use to ride the horses. Saddles, bridles, bits. Rope. That's why it's called a tack room. I assume you never brushed a horse before?"

"Nope."

"Well, there's a first time for everything. Betcha didn't think, before last night, you'd ever deliver a foal."

"Uh, no. Not in my wildest dreams."

"C'mon, you can brush Gertie. She loves it. Plus, it'll help me 'cause she yammers at me all day if I don't do it. Finn babies her."

"Finn. He's one of your brothers?"

"Yep."

I followed him into the barn to the first stall on the right. He opened the door, grabbed a bucket from the floor, and walked in, patting the horse who stood munching hay. She was the prettiest almost pink color, with millions of tiny white speckles and a white face, and she had a strawberry blond mane and tail.

"She's pink."

"It's called strawberry roan. It suits her. She's a princess. Here, use this brush first." He handed me a black oval plastic thing. "Put the handle over the back of your hand. See?" He slid the brush over my fingers. "It's called a curry comb. You're gonna start on her left side and comb in circles with the grain of her hair. Don't brush against it. You wanna brush any debris in her coat loose. But do *not* stand directly behind her, hear me?" he ordered, waiting for me to respond.

"So I don't get kicked, right?"

"Right. Gertie's an angel, but all horses can get annoyed real quick. You wanna use a firm hand, but don't dig the comb into her skin. You'll definitely get kicked if you do."

"Okay. Then what?"

"Don't curry her legs. She only likes the dandy brush on her legs."

"Which one is that?"

"So, curry comb, number one." He touched my hand with the comb on it. "Then, dandy brush, it's stiffer." He held up a heavier wooden brush with stiff bristles. "Careful when you go over bony areas. Be gentle. And knock it against your curry comb every few strokes to get rid of the dirt and hair."

I nodded. "Got it."

"Then, use this wide comb to detangle her mane and tail." He grabbed a wide-tooth comb from the bucket then dropped it back in. "Hold the tail up and to the side. Start at the bottom and work your way up. There's a bottle of spray in the bucket if you need somethin' to help get through the tangles."

"Now this, I know how to do," I joked and smiled, tugged my hair, then flipped it behind me.

He chuckled.

"Did you just laugh?"

"No. You misheard me. I don't laugh," he said with the most serious look on his face but then smiled. He tried not to but it broke free. Oh my God, that smile. Still barely there, still crooked, and still the most beautiful thing I'd ever seen. And his eyes sparkled in the dappled sunlight coming into Gertie's stall. "Alright then. When she's lookin' her Sunday best, use this brush. Brush number four. It's called a finishin' brush. It gets all the dust off and makes her shine. She likes this brush on her legs, too, but call for me when you get there. I'll help and I gotta check her feet."

"Okay."

"I'll be down the aisle. Not far. And don't forget—"

"I know, don't stand behind her."

"Yep. And if she starts stompin' her feet or tryin' to get you with her tail, or if her ears go back, she's getting irritated.

Just ease up on your brushin' and talk quiet to her. Gertie loves to gab."

"Okay." I laughed and he watched my mouth.

"Okay, just lemme know if you're not sure about somethin'."

"I will," I said as he stepped out of the stall, sliding the door closed behind him.

I got to work and Gertie and I became fast friends. She loved her belly to be curry combed. She leaned into my hand and nudged my arm with her nose when she could reach. She seemed indifferent to the dandy brush, and she didn't seem to be a fan of getting her tangles combed out of her tail, but she liked when I combed her mane. Her whole body relaxed and she hung her head a little.

I had a ball. It was like brushing a doll's hair, but a giant one I could talk to. She didn't understand me. At least, I didn't think she could, but she liked when I talked to her. When I'd stop, she'd nudge me again or whinny. I told her about the foal I'd helped deliver the night before while I twisted little braids in her mane every few inches. She did look like a pink princess.

Then, while I brushed her with the finishing brush, I told her about my new job and about how I liked her ranch. How pretty the mountains and the trees were and how the air smelled like Halloween when I was a child—the crisp, cool, clean breeze ruffling my hair but the sun warming me.

I remembered getting ready for trick-or-treating and then playing on the patio behind my house while my father read one of his gazillion books, waiting for my mother to dress up too. She always had to dress up and she went all out. Sometimes, she'd even hired people to do her makeup. She had to be the most beautiful, the most desirable woman in our neighborhood. Didn't matter that it was a holiday for children. And

I remembered her laughing about it later, after we'd returned home with my bucket of candy, telling my father how the other moms had looked at her with envy.

"'Bout ready for me?" Jack asked, appearing in front of Gertie's stall and pulling the door open.

"Oh!" I jumped and Gertie stepped to the side.

"Sorry. Didn't mean to scare ya."

I took a deep breath and blew it out through my mouth.

"You're awful jumpy. Anybody ever tell you that?"

"Yeah. Um, yes, she's ready. We were just getting to know each other," I said, feeling my racing pulse slow a little when Jack entered the stall.

"I heard that. Somethin' about trick-or-treatin'?"

"Yeah." I laughed awkwardly. "I always liked fall."

He smiled. "Me too. Cool but sunny. Winter on a horse farm ain't much fun at all. And spring's all freezin' fingers and mud. Summer's not so bad 'round here though."

Bending next to Gertie, he lifted each hoof, using some tool to pick out dirt and pieces of debris. Then he used the soft finishing brush on her legs, and she rubbed her lips on his shoulders, clearly a fan of having her legs brushed. I wanted to rub my lips on his shoulders, too, preferably without his T-shirt as a barrier. He used a soft towel to wipe around her ears and face, and he sprayed something on her coat.

"It's lunch time. Hungry?"

"Starving."

"C'mon then. I'll find us somethin'."

We made our way to the house, and Jack dug through the fridge, then pulled out the stuff to make grilled cheese sandwiches, which were surprisingly good. He used real cheese, not the processed kind, and added slices of fresh tomato and avocado. We sat at the table, and I moaned when I took my first bite and heard him gasp softly.

Could it be possible he was a gourmet chef? I supposed it more likely I'd just been eating junk for so long, everything homemade tasted fancy to me. He finished his sandwich and stared at my mouth while I ate. It wasn't uncomfortable. It was... Whatever it was, I liked the way it made my body feel.

He took a sandwich up to Kevin, then came back down and stood in front of me with his hands on his hips while I finished my milk and carefully set the empty glass on the table.

"I'm done. Thank you."

"Wanna meet my new filly?" he asked, and I smiled so big, my cheeks hurt. "C'mon," he said, grabbing my hand to pull me back to the barn.

He led me past the red barn into a big rounded building with huge double sliding doors that stood open. Once we were inside, he led me to a line of stalls, but they seemed bigger than the stalls in the barn.

Smiling again, he turned me slowly around by my shoulders, and we stepped forward a couple of feet, and there, in the first stall, stood the most beautiful horse in existence. She was a tiny little thing, at least compared to the monster horse standing next to her.

"That's Lucy, her mama," he said, stepping back away from me a little.

Lucy was *huge*. Taller than Jack, way taller, and almost all white, but she had a very faint freckling of light grey speckles all over her body, as if her skin had been darkened by a wet mist. But her baby, the filly, was strikingly beautiful. Her coat was blinding-bright white with hundreds of black, reddish-brown, and grey spots, dots, and speckles all over her little body, her mane and tail shock-white with black roots. I didn't know horses could be so beautiful.

"What's her name?" I whispered. I didn't want to startle the baby.

"Dunno yet. Got any ideas?"

"Rubato," I blurted out the name that came first to my mind. "You can call her Ruby."

"What's it mean?" he asked, and I could hear and feel him smiling.

"It means robbed or stolen in Italian, but in music, it loosely means freedom of expression." I remembered my mother sitting with me on her piano bench, teaching me about all of her musical terms and then playing a few bars to let me hear what each one meant.

"It's perfect. Look there, as she turns around. See the mark on her left flank, her hip?" He pointed in front of me and through the stall door.

I gasped. "A ruby?" She had a spot there, just above where her back leg met her side, and it looked like a red cut gem. Really, it was a chestnut brown color, but against the white of her skin, and with the sun shining in, it looked deep ruby red. I reached out with my hand through the metal bars on the stall door toward Ruby without thinking, and Jack tensed.

"Careful. Mama horses can be *very* protective." Tugging my arms gently, he pulled me back from the stall, but Lucy stepped forward slowly and rubbed her nose on my palm, then dragged her big horse lips across my fingers. Jack let out a breathy laugh, standing still right up against my body, placing his hands on my hips, ready to pull me away if Lucy decided she didn't like me. Just that little touch sent an electric shock from my hips, up to my breasts and back down, right to my... I squeezed my thighs together.

But there was no need for his anxiety because she turned her head and bumped Ruby's back leg with her nose, encouraging her to walk toward me.

"Well, I'll be damned," he whispered.

Ruby approached my hand slowly, sniffing my fingers, then rubbed the whole left side of her body against them as she paraded in front of the stall door.

"Can I go in there? I want to pet them," I asked in awe, and Jack laughed out loud, pulling me to step backward.

"No, not today. I won't sacrifice your life so easily. Just ask Kevin's broken leg, with the metal pins in it, what it's like when ol' Lucy here decides she's had enough of you. We'll take it slow, but I've never seen her walk right up to a person like that. And I have never seen her let someone so close to her foal like that. It was pretty amazin'." He turned me around by my shoulders, looking confused. "Are you magic?"

Oh, I was magical all right.

I knew how to make myself disappear.

We spent the rest of the afternoon and early evening touring the humongous barn—which was really like three barns stuck together side by side so there were six aisles—walking through the paddocks, petting the different horses, and feeding them apples and carrots. Jack worked here and there as we went, checking on each horse and showing me how to lunge them.

"So, what exactly do you do here? I mean, I know you breed and raise horses, but what for?"

"Quarter horses are used for all kinds a' things. Mostly people buy our horses for ridin', but some for barrel racin', some work horses. Some for showin'."

"Did you ever do that? Show horses or barrel race?"

He laughed. "No. No time for it."

"I meant when you were a kid."

"That's what I'm talkin' about. Our dad was a strict son of a bitch. I been workin' this ranch since I was nine or ten years old."

"Nine?"

"Yep."

"Wow. That's young to be doing such hard work."

He shrugged. "It was fine."

"I bet you guys had a lot of fun though, playing out here, you and your brothers?"

"I'm sure we did."

"You don't remember?"

"Not really. I mean, I guess I remember a few things."

"Like what? Tell me a story."

He looked at me, but then his eyes slid to the side, and I could tell he was seeing a memory. "We used to play cowboys and Indians. I was always the cowboy, and Finn was always the Indian chief. You haven't met him yet, but you'll understand when you do. He even made a headdress outta fallen bird feathers. Our mama was so disgusted by it. She threw it in the wastebin, but Finn fished it out, and we hid it from her over by my granny's house. I haven't thought about that stupid feather hat since I was probably eight years old." He shook his head.

"I don't know what Finn looks like, but I can picture you as a little boy, running around here, getting into trouble. Why aren't there any family pictures in the house? With so many kids in the family, I'd think the walls would be covered in them."

"I don't— I guess my dad wasn't much into that kinda thing."

"What about your mom?"

He took a deep breath as we walked further into the pasture. "Have I introduced you to my main man yet?" he asked, changing the subject and waving his arm out in front of us to where a yellow horse stood, munching grass. "This here's Sammy. I like him better than all my brothers combined. 'Specially Finn." He clicked his tongue and the horse loped over to us. "Hey, buddy. Havin' a good day?" he rumbled in his velvet voice, patting Sammy's chest, and the horse practically hugged him. He pressed his big horse cheek next to Jack's and let loose a slow, deep whinny. "Wanna ride him?" he asked, turning to me.

I sucked air in through my teeth. "Okay?"

"Scared?"

I raised my eyebrows and grimaced.

"Don't be. Sammy's the kindest bein' on the planet. He's gentle and carin'. He'd never hurt you. C'mon. I'll lift you up. Throw your leg over."

"Wai—" I squealed as he grasped my hips and lifted me, and the sound echoed between the mountains. I threw my leg over and he plopped me down on Sammy's back. "But we don't have a saddle."

"Ah, we don't need one. C'mon buddy. Walk us home," he said, and I wobbled as Sammy took his first steps. Jack walked beside us.

"I think I'm gonna fall off."

"No, you won't. Hold onto his mane."

"You want me to pull his hair?"

"I didn't say yank it. I said hold it. He won't mind. But I won't let you fall."

"Okay," I said, but it sounded more like a whiny question. Riding Sammy was fun though. He was gentle. I could feel it in his gait. He went slow, like the horse could feel my nervousness.

"What about you?" he asked. "Got any brothers or sisters?"

"No. Just me."

"Where do your parents live?"

"They don't. They died, I mean. When I was young."

"Oh, I'm sorry. Car accident or somethin'?"

"Something like that." He raised his head to look at me, but I kept my eyes straight ahead. I wasn't about to tell him how my parents died.

"Scoot up."

"Huh?"

"Scoot forward a little." I inched forward, squeezing Sammy with my thighs, and Jack jumped up to sit behind me. Just like that. He barely tried. Sammy jumped to the side a little.

"Ohh, oh no. I'm gonna fall!"

"No, you ain't. I gotcha," he said, scooting up right behind me. He wrapped his arm around my stomach, holding me against him, and grabbed a fist full of Sammy's hair, then clicked his tongue, and we flew.

I clutched his arm with both of my hands like my life depended on it. It probably did.

"Jack!"

"Relax. Feel how my body's movin' with Sammy's? Let your body do that too." He spoke next to my ear, and his lip touched my skin, and I felt that burn travel down my chest to my lower belly. I tried to relax. I closed my eyes and trusted him to keep me from falling. "That's it. Now, open your eyes."

I did and the world raced by us. The feeling was amazing. Like flying. I felt so free. There weren't any thoughts about hiding or running or monsters. Danger. I raised my arms, spreading them out to my sides, and Jack's arms touched mine as he lifted his too.

"*You* have hold onto something!"

"No, I don't. Sammy knows where I wanna go. I'm tellin' him with my legs."

"Oh my God."

"Fun, huh?"

"It's amazing!"

Jack's body behind me, his arms around my waist enveloping me into his warm chest, felt so good. I pressed my hands against his thighs so I could feel him command Sammy, and the flexing and loosening of his thick muscles made me imagine him tightening them as he thrust into my body.

My hands wandered higher, and he hissed a breath in my ear, pressing his body closer to mine. He was hard. I felt the stone length of him against my back, and if I hadn't been certain I'd fall on my head, I would've flipped around, ripped his jeans open, and mounted him right then and there on Sammy's back.

We rode back to the barn, watered Sammy down with a hose, and Jack called all the horses in, leading each one to a stall, so we could feed them and fill their hanging water buckets. We fed Biddie while her new foal nursed, who I also got to name. I named him Trumpet because his whinny sounded a little funny, and it reminded me of a horn. Jack laughed at the name but said it kind of fit. He explained that most of the horses had official names to display their pedigree, but he and his brothers used their barn names. We said goodbye to Trumpet and Ruby, then headed inside to find something for dinner.

"Thank you for showing me your ranch. It's incredible. I love it," I said while we walked slowly across the lawn, like nothing else in the world mattered. Like monsters didn't exist and I was just a normal girl.

We'd climbed the stairs to the front porch when he spun

me around to face him and crowded me against the house next to the screen door, looking down into my eyes, his hands on either side of my head, only touching the wood behind me.

"What're you doin' to me?" He sounded so serious, his voice low and gravelly again, and I almost thought he looked angry, but I saw a hunger in his eyes that sent goosebumps down my body and put that burn right back in my belly.

"What? I'm not—" But I couldn't finish my sentence. I couldn't even remember what I'd been about to say because he kissed me. Different than the last kiss, he was slow and gentle, with his wet, plump lips and teasing, testing tongue.

The smooth slow strokes of his tongue against mine and the gentle nibbles with his teeth on my lips were all so intense, the sensations sending signals to my body I'd never felt before. I slid my arms around his waist tentatively. There was a pressure, a growing buzz in my body that I needed to let loose, but I heard a car driving up the lane and froze. I dropped my arms to my sides and turned my head away.

I knew it would most likely be Mrs. M, but the realization that someone could see us, see what we were doing—that he could be watching—stopped me cold. He wouldn't like it. He would take it out on Jack.

"This isn't a good idea. I'm sorry. I shouldn't have—"

"Nope," he said, stepping back. "No apology necessary. You're right. Not a good idea."

Glancing behind him at Mrs. Whitley's car pulling up in front of the house, he threw the screen door open and stomped inside.

I released my breath and walked down the stairs to help Mrs. M, my eyes searching the descending darkness for any sign of danger.

CHAPTER TEN

JACK

HEATIN' up the rest of the stew for dinner, I left it sittin' on the stove, but didn't eat any. I went straight to bed and lay there, floppin' around like a fish outta water. Everlea slept in the den, the room next to mine, and I imagined her in there on the bed, wrapped up and naked in the sheets.

Two different parts of my mind fought for control all night. The part that didn't trust her poked and prodded me, stranglin' me at times. She gave away nothin' about herself. She wouldn't talk about her parents. All she'd said was they died in "something like an accident." What did that mean? Had it been an accident or not?

It felt all day like we were connectin', gettin' to know each other a little. I'd talked about my family, things I liked, things I didn't. And, at the time, I thought she'd opened up to me too. But when I really thought about it, I couldn't remember one thing she'd said about herself, except that she'd been an only child and liked fall and Halloween, and she hadn't even said it to me. I'd overheard her tellin' it to Gertie. A horse.

Okay, so maybe more like I'd eavesdropped.

But then, the other part of me, the part that wanted her, beat back the suspicious part with a broomstick. I hadn't touched another person as much as I'd touched Everlea in years. Usually, the necessity to touch another person made me uncomfortable. I did it if I had to, but only for exactly as long as need required and then I'd disconnect myself, fast as I could.

Not with Everlea.

I didn't wanna let go of her. I liked the way she felt. On my fingers, my hands, in my arms, against my body. My lips and tongue.

Maybe if I just got it over with, screwed her, I could get this thing outta my system. I'd be able to sleep again. I could focus on all the damn work I needed to do.

Didn't seem like she wanted it though. I thought she might have today while we walked my land, when I showed her my horses, my work. She stood so close to me. She was always lookin' at me. I had to admit, I was way outta practice, but I was sure she'd wanted me too. The way she'd kissed me on the porch and earlier, in Dean's room? Pure need and want. I didn't think I'd ever felt that level of desire before.

But we heard Mrs. Whitley's car comin' up the lane, and it felt like a switch had been flipped. Maybe she'd just been embarrassed or shy and didn't want anyone to see us, but I thought it had been more than that. Somethin' else held her back. Stopped her. I could almost hear the gears turn in her head. I felt 'em cease their movement when she turned away from me and dropped her hands.

My skin burned where she'd touched.

It felt like the back and forth in my mind would give me whiplash. Finally, at four in the mornin', I gave up. Rollin' outta bed, I took a shower, forced some of Kevin's sugar cereal down my throat, and headed to the barn. I fed the horses and let 'em out, then worked on the leak in the tack room, movin' everything in it to the aisle and cleanin' like I'd been paid to do it. Liftin' the saddles helped, allowed me to expend some of the excess energy I'd been fightin' against for days.

By the time the sun peeked over the mountain tops, the tack room sparkled like a diamond on a finger. I'd been so into it, I didn't hear Mrs. Mitchum behind me.

"What've you been doin' out here all mornin'?"

"Jesus!" I whipped around, droppin' a whole bucket of brushes and hoof picks.

She laughed. "Isn't like you to swear."

"You scared the— You scared me."

She looked around, surveyed my work. "Barn looks nice. Your pops and granny would be so proud of you, Jack, the way you've taken care of it."

"Dunno 'bout that."

"They would. I know you're worried about the future, but you'll figure it out. I have faith in you."

"Thank you."

"Jay was tellin' me about this idea he's got to turn this place into a dude ranch. What do you think about that?"

Oh God, not her too.

"Yeah, he's mentioned it a time or two."

My baby brother Jay had been tryin' to convince me to turn our ranch into a tourist destination. Every day for the past year, from mornin' till night, he'd been followin' me around while we did our chores, tryin' to convince me a dude ranch could be our way to financial salvation. He came home from his fancy college when our dad died, spoutin' all this nonsense. Now he'd moved back home for good, drivin' me batshit, sayin', "We need a new plan, a new opportunity. We need to do somethin' different if we don't want this ranch to die its final death," blah, blah, blah. No matter how many times I told him no, slammed a door in his face, or punched him, I just couldn't shut him up.

I knew he was right—in my head, I knew.

But what the hell could he be thinkin'? A dude ranch? Really? Did he imagine I would sit around sippin' hot tea and eatin' fancy finger sandwiches while I discussed global warmin' and politics with all my guests? I was pretty certain eatin' canned dog food would be more pleasant. I couldn't imagine strangers hangin' around on our land all day or sleepin' in our house. Yeah, there'd still be some horse ridin' but—

"Well?"

"Huh?"

"Whatcha think about it?"

I sighed. "I think… maybe Jay's ideas are a little too big for his britches."

I bent to pick up the brushes, and she patted my head like I was four years old. "Well, maybe you boys should sit down, discuss it. You're both smart, Jack. If a dude ranch isn't the answer, maybe you can put your heads together and come up with somethin' else. Hm?"

"Did you need somethin', ma'am?"

She sighed. "It's almost time to leave for my appointment. Just wanted to remind you."

"I didn't forget."

"Listen, I know I'm puttin' a strain on you. You're not used to havin' women around but—"

"No, ma'am, I like havin' you here. You know you're welcome, long as you want. You can stay forever if it pleases you." I smiled. It was probably the closest I'd ever come to tellin' her I loved her. My brothers told her all the time, but for me, it wasn't easy.

"Oh, Jack. That smile of yours could light the world, you know it?"

I laughed. "Shield your eyes."

She tsked her tongue. "So, what's got you in this mood then? You sure been grumblin' a lot."

"Just tired. Haven't been sleepin' well, I guess."

"Oh yeah? That wouldn't have anything to do with a certain houseguest, would it?"

My face heated like somebody'd shoved a red-hot poker under my skin, and I turned back to my crystal clean tack room to look for somethin' else to do.

"I like her a lot," she said. "She's a sweet girl. But… I think, maybe she's hidin' somethin' from us."

I turned right back around.

"Yes, I noticed it too. She doesn't ever talk about herself. Her family. And she just about spit her coffee out the other day when I suggested you could go get the cat. Why do you think that is?"

"I dunno, ma'am."

"Well, did you notice anything while you were there? You know I don't like to gossip but—" She held her hands up in front of her.

"Who you? No." I chuckled.

"Jack Cade, I would never. I did call Susan Masterson though. Just to get her opinion. She's known Everlea longer."

"Ya did, huh? And what did Mrs. Masterson have to say?"

"Nothin'. You know they call her Eve? Must be a nick-name. But all she said was that Everlea seems pretty private. She moved here from Iowa, I think she said. Or maybe it was Oklahoma. She pays her rent in cash and she doesn't own a television. That's odd, isn't it?"

"Not everybody lives like Finn with their head stuck in a TV."

"I suppose you're right. But I was thinkin', maybe she's in trouble, Jack. Have you noticed how she jumps at every little noise? Like a scared little lamb. And she's always lookin' around, like she's expecting somethin' to jump outta the shadows."

"I noticed."

"Maybe you can keep your eye on her? Could be she's just not used to havin' so many people around. Susan did say she doesn't think Everlea has any friends or family. I heard that from Bob too."

Was there some kinda telephone tree for Wisper gossip I wasn't aware of?

I shrugged. It wasn't my place to tell Everlea's secrets. Plus, I didn't actually know any of 'em.

"Well, let's get goin' then. We've got plenty of time ahead of us to get to know her." She turned to leave the barn but stopped and twisted back in my direction. "She sure is pretty though." Dippin' her head, she peered at me with a little sparkle in her eye.

"Hm. I hadn't noticed," I lied, lookin' at the floor.

"Oh? Thought you might have when you had your face stuck to hers last night on the porch," she quipped, and she walked back up to the house.

"You know what? I just remembered, the first appointment is pretty easy. Standard stuff. Just paperwork, insurance and all that. So, Everlea, why don't you go with Jack? Maybe you can show her around town? I don't think I'll be long. That way you don't have to drive all the way home and back again. Hm?"

"You're not getting chemo today?" Everlea asked. She sat

between Mrs. Mitchum and me again in my truck. I'd just pulled up outside the hospital in Jackson to drop 'em off for Mrs. Mitchum's oncology appointment.

"Yes, I will, but the first dose doesn't usually do anything. It'll be another day or two till I notice it."

"Oh."

"You sure, ma'am? I don't mind waitin'."

"I'm positive. It's such a nice day. Go on. Enjoy it. Everlea, you and I'll relax later, watch an old movie. Sound good?" She patted Everlea's leg.

"Um, sure. I guess. Are you sure though?"

"I am," she said, climbin' outta the truck.

I opened my door to run around to help her. "Here, ma'am, lemme—"

"I'm not an invalid yet, Jack. Shoo. G'on now." She pushed the door shut, smiled, and walked into the hospital.

"Um. Shouldn't I go with her?"

"No point." I pulled my door shut. "There ain't a thing in this world you can talk her into or out of once she's set her mind to it."

"Okay. But you don't have to play tour guide. If you want to go back to get some work done, that's okay. I don't want to be in your way." She scooted away from me, huggin' the passenger side door and puttin' three feet of distance between our bodies.

"It's fine. She's right. No sense drivin' home and back again. Waste of gas. C'mon, we'll find somethin' to do." I pulled away from the entrance to the hospital, headin' into town. "I know you volunteered here a bit, but have you had a chance to see Jackson yet? Seen the antler arches?"

"No. The what? No, I haven't done much sightseeing."

"The antler arches. It's a big thing in the town square. I'll show you."

"Okay." Sittin' back against the seat, she attempted to look relaxed, but she kept her hands on her lap, tightened into fists.

We drove in utter silence till I parked next to the Jackson town square.

I turned the engine off and waited for any movement or sound from her. It took a couple minutes.

Finally, she took a deep breath. "I'm sorry... about last n—"

"Don't mention it. It's fine. We just got a little carried away."

She peeked at me but I stared out the windshield.

"Yeah."

"You probably got a man somewhere. He wouldn't like to know you been messin' 'round with me." I opened my door.

"No." She opened her door and hurried around to my side. Shuttin' my own door, I stood against it with my arms crossed over my chest. "No. It's nothing like that. I don't. I don't have a... boyfriend. A man." She laughed at the expression.

"Well. Don't really matter why you changed your mind. You're allowed to. C'mon. Can't see nothin' standin' in the road." Pushin' off the truck, I made my way to the wooden walkway surroundin' the little park in the middle of Jackson, Wyoming.

Four big arches acted as entrances, each one made outta thousands of elk antlers, one on each side of the park. I intended to show her every one. By then, I figured we woulda wasted enough time, and Mrs. Mitchum might be done at the doctor.

She followed me. "It's not that I changed my mind. I didn't. I mean, I did, but not for the reason you think."

"It's okay. No need to explain."

"But I want to."

We'd reached the southwest arch and I rounded on her. "Then explain."

"What *are* these things? They didn't kill a bunch of deer to get them, did they?"

"No. They're elk antlers. They fall off in the spring. People collect 'em, I guess. They look real pretty 'round Christmas all lit up. I thought you might like 'em."

"As long as no one killed Bambi to get them, then yes, they are kind of cool."

"No, I think Bambi's safe. Least till huntin' season." I smirked, walkin' into the square, and she followed on her short little legs, joggin' to catch up to me.

"Wait, Jack, come on. Please stop walking."

I stopped and waited.

Steppin in front of me, she said, "I want to explain, but I... can't."

"Why not?" I wanted to know the answer, surprisingly.

"Because. Because I just can't." Eyes dartin' all around, she looked just like Mrs. Mitchum had said, like a terrified lamb. Well, if she was scared of somethin', I intended to make her feel safe. Maybe then she'd tell me. I grabbed her hand and she didn't pull away.

"Hungry? That's Punky's Pizza over there. Best pizza in Jackson. Um, they probably ain't open yet though. But I'm sure we could find somethin'. There's a coffee shop."

"Coffee?" she squeaked, and a tiny smile brightened her whole face.

"Yeah, coffee, ya little junkie." I laughed. "C'mon."

"I like when you laugh," she said, and her cheeks turned bright pink. She looked down.

"Oh yeah? Then tell me somethin' funny."

"I'm not funny."

I waited for her to look at me, and when she did, I said, "I think you are. That thing you said about Bambi was funny enough."

"You don't want to hear the weird thoughts I have."

"Sure I do. Like what?"

"Like… Like, when I saw that big antler monstrosity, I thought, 'They've killed Bambi for this thing? Who's gonna take care of Thumper? They've disturbed the natural order and I *cannot* condone that.'"

"And who's 'they?'"

"You know, 'the man.'"

I snorted. "See? Funny. Wait, you know Bambi and Thumper ain't really friends, right? I mean, I guess they're not enemies, but neither one probably cares about the other."

"How do you know? Did you ask them?"

I laughed again, shakin' my head. *Cute.* "C'mon. Coffee's this way."

We strolled through the square, and I pointed out the Veteran's monument in the middle. My pop's name was on that thing. She thought it was pretty cool, and I supposed it was. As we crossed Cashe Street and Deloney Avenue, I asked, "What else you got floatin' 'round that noggin'?"

She stayed quiet a minute, but I felt her gaze on my face again. "When I first met you, I thought"—she took a deep breath—"I thought you were the most beautiful man I'd ever seen."

I stopped square in the middle of the road to look at her. My heart raced. Her eyes kept flickin' up to mine, but then they'd wander all around us, searchin' for somethin' again.

Squeezin' her hand, I pulled her to the little boardwalk near the coffee place. It was kinda like an alley, but there were all these little tourist shops linin' the walk. It was still mornin', though, so the shops were all closed. I found a little nook to hide away in and guided her back against the buildin'.

"Now, you can't say somethin' like that and expect me not to respond."

Leanin' down, I spread her legs with my knee between her thighs, touchin' my lips to hers.

She breathed, "Jack."

"What? Gonna tell me it's a bad idea again, that you don't want me?"

"I do. More than I want air to breathe."

"But?" I sucked her bottom lip a little and licked it, lookin' in her green eyes.

She gasped softly. "But nothing. Kiss me."

Oh, I did. I took her mouth in mine and devoured her. I pressed harder against her, pinnin' her to the wall, and she rubbed herself on me and moaned.

Good God, the smoky sound of her breathy moan was like kryptonite to me. All my best laid plans, all my careful considerations, they flew right out the window when I heard her make that noise and felt her hands on my shoulders, then my neck, reachin' up to tug my hair in her fingers.

She moaned again. "Jack."

"Still want coffee?"

"What's coffee?"

I groaned. "C'mon."

Pullin' her back to the square, we sprinted to my truck. A raincloud peeked through the ever-blue sky and tiny drops fell on us as we ran, but by the time I opened her door, it poured. I shut her in the truck with a promise of a look and rushed, quick as I could, to my door.

When I climbed in, there was a beat of silence, but then she attacked me, throwin' her leg over my lap and straddlin' me, hittin' her back on the steerin' wheel.

"Ow."

"You okay?"

"Yes. Kiss me again."

I gripped her hips and shoved my tongue in her mouth, pressin' the hard length of me into the soft, hot, wet core of her. Even through our jeans, I could feel it. She rubbed back and forth against me and I groaned. "Fuck. Stop."

"Oh. I'm sorry." Hangin' her head, she tried to climb off me.

"No, I don't mean stop, stop. I mean, not here. Put your seatbelt on. I know a place."

"Oh, thank God."

CHAPTER ELEVEN

EVERLEA

JACK CHUCKLED, turning the key in the ignition. He backed out of our parking spot slowly, and we made our way through the downpour to some place by a river.

The sexual tension in the truck was palpable. His hands gripped the steering wheel at ten and two, his knuckles white with blood loss from squeezing so hard. I wanted to touch him again, but the rain was relentless and I didn't want to cause an accident.

Fiddling with my shirt, I made sure the neck covered the edges of my scars and pulled my hair up into a bun, but then, realizing how unsexy it probably looked, released it, letting it fall back down my shoulders.

Jack didn't make a sound. I couldn't even hear him breathe. Finally, he pulled onto an empty dirt path. I didn't think it would have mattered if there'd been people everywhere. The rain came down so hard, no one would've been able to see us anyway.

"What is this place?"

"Flat Creek. Used to fish it."

I hadn't really cared where we were. I just made conversation for the sake of it and to distract myself from the over-whelming need I felt to mount him.

Before he'd even stopped the truck, I'd pulled off my shoes and jeans and climbed back over him.

"Wait, wait, wait," he said, shoving the truck into park and turning it off.

He reached between my legs to unbutton his jeans and slid his fingers inside my panties, dragging them through my nearly dripping arousal. My hands clutched his shoulders as I kneeled above him, with my legs on either side of his, and my arms shook with anticipation.

I'd wanted him since the first moment we met. I tried to deny it, to push the desire away. I knew I was being foolish, putting us all in danger, but I'd never wanted anyone more, and I couldn't hold onto the fear in my mind long enough to convince myself to stop what we were doing.

"Okay? Is this too much? We don't have to—"

"Oh my God, shut up."

He laughed.

"Shit. I don't have a condom." He groaned. "Wait, Kevin's a randy son of a bitch. Reach behind you, look in the glove—"

"We don't need it." I slid my fingers inside his jeans, under his boxers, wrapping my hand around his hard cock, and he shuddered and moaned. It felt like satin wrapped around a steel pipe and I wanted it inside me, like, now. "I'm on birth control and I've never..." Thank God for the invention of IUDs and Planned Parenthood—no time for crippling cramps when you're on the run.

"You never...? What? Had sex?"

"No."

"Everlea," he breathed.

It wasn't like I was a virgin, technically. I had owned a

vibrator at one point, but there wasn't a lot of time for masturbation on the run either.

"I'm not completely without experience."

"Really?" He looked doubtful. How could he know I lied?

"Okay, fine. I've never had sex that wasn't battery or finger powered. Happy?"

Arching a brow, he gripped my hips again, and just when I thought he would buck his hips and fuck the bejesus out of me, right through my panties, his phone rang.

He lifted his ass to reach his phone in his back pocket, pushing him harder into my hand, and we both groaned.

"It's Mrs. Mitchum," he grumbled, and I released him.

Answering with a swipe of his thumb, he closed his eyes and lifted the phone to his ear. "Yes, ma'am, you ready?" I heard her chirpy voice on the other end of the line. "No, ma'am, we're still in town. Over by town square."

He opened his eyes, looking at me while he listened to her. They sparkled, the little blue flecks in them almost glowing against the brown and green. "Okay, we'll be there in a few minutes."

His hand gripped the steering wheel behind me, but he lifted it into my hair, then twisted it, wrapping the long locks around his wrist, tilting my head back. "No, ma'am, I won't have you sittin' there waitin'. We'll be right there." He hung up. "She's ready," he said, leaning forward to press his face against my neck, and the scratchy stubble on his cheek gave me goosebumps.

I very reluctantly climbed off of him and dug on the floor of his truck for my shoes and jeans, then pulled them on. I sat back against the seat, blowing out all the dizzying anticipation in a slow breath through my lips.

We drove again in silence back to the hospital. I wanted to talk to him but I was freaking out. The careful, weary part of me screamed at me in my head that I was being stupid. It didn't matter how much I wanted Jack. I knew better, and I didn't want him to be hurt by my reckless actions.

I knew how bad things could get if I became involved with him. For him, for Mrs. M, Kevin.

But damn it. I'd never felt like this, never wanted something so much that I even considered risking the wrath of my "admirer."

There was a pull inside me, like a string connecting my gut to my mouth, and it yanked and twisted and I opened my mouth to speak, to tell Jack my secret. I wanted to. I was desperate to tell him... until Toby's face flashed before my eyes. My only friend in all these years. Dead. And I'd barely told him anything.

I took a deep breath, and the intake of fresh oxygen cleared the confusion out of my mind.

No. I couldn't tell Jack. I couldn't be with him.

I couldn't hurt him. I wouldn't do it.

We pulled up in front of the hospital, and just before he got out of the truck to open the door for Mrs. M, he leaned over, whispering, "Meet me in the barn as soon as she falls asleep."

But I wouldn't.

Mrs. M had been wrong. She felt the effects of the chemo later that afternoon. She didn't get sick, but I watched as the color drained from her face and all the light left her eyes. Stumbling into her bedroom upstairs, she practically fell onto the bed, and I flapped my hands around her, trying to find some way to help.

"Oh, honey, I'm okay. It just hit me hard this time, is all. I wanna lay here awhile. You go on. Relax. I'll be fine."

"I'd like to stay with you, if you don't mind. It'll make me feel better."

She rolled over and lay back, and I adjusted her pillow under her head. She smiled but she looked so defeated.

"Have I told you about my Mr. Mitchum?"

Removing her shoes, I let them fall to the floor. "No, but I'd love to hear about him."

She patted the bed next to her, and I walked around to the other side, kicked off my Chucks, and climbed in. A throw blanket lay at the foot of the bed, so I grabbed it and draped it over her, tucking it under her chin.

Her eyes drifted to some faraway place, and she smiled again, but this time, it was joyous and it changed her whole face, making her look thirty years younger. Pulling her arms out from under the blanket, she folded them on her stomach, and I lay on my side, propped up on my elbow as she spoke.

"We met June 27th, 1967, right here in Wisper. Every once in a while, the town would hold a dance at the, well, it's a discount store now, but it used to be a big town hall kinda place where they'd hold meetin's. Once or twice a year, all the ladies in town would get together and decorate the place till it sparkled and glowed, and then they'd get dressed up in their fanciest dresses, the men in their suits, and they'd drink and dance and laugh all night.

"It was a big to-do 'round here, though we were just a poor farmin' community. But for us, it was like a ball at the biggest castle.

"I was just a young lady. I'd just graduated from high school and hadn't yet turned eighteen. I had the world at my fingertips. My best friend Alba and I'd primp for hours—we loved gettin' all gussied up—then we'd sneak into the dance. It always felt like such an adventure, though the adults knew we were comin', and they never hollered at us. By the night's end, there'd be just as many young people as there were adults."

She took a deep breath, closing her eyes. "That night, I wore a deep blue dress my mama had made for me. I'd worn it to graduation, and Alba poked fun at me for wearin' it again so soon, but it was the nicest thing I owned. Her family ran some big farmin' equipment business, so she always had nice things. But I loved that dress, and I loved how I looked in that dress. It wasn't fancy or anything, but it made me feel so grown up. So confident. And the shoes I wore with it? Oh, you girls today know nothin' 'bout pretty shoes." She laughed.

Iggy jumped onto the bed, curling into a fuzzy ball by Mrs. M's feet.

"So, there I was, all dressed up and feelin' a'fire. Every boy had on his nicest suit, if he owned one, or his best shirt and pants. Now, mind you, Wisper was even smaller back then than it is now, so I knew every single boy who lived here.

"But when Roger Mitchum walked in with a tall boy followin' behind him, I nearly fainted. I knew Roger. He was in my class at school, but I'd never seen the other boy. Oh, I woulda remembered if I had.

"He had the nicest dark brown hair. It was very well groomed, not like a lotta boys back then. You know, it was the sixties. And his suit was so smart. Crisp and clean and it fit him like a glove. It was a dark brown color too. And his smile? Oh, it liked to bowl me over. He had a light in his eyes I didn't think I'd ever seen before. He looked so alive, so... enigmatic. He knew something I didn't. I was sure about that.

"Well, he noticed me too, right off the bat, and I

blushed but I never looked away. He came right at me. Didn't hem and haw about it like boys did back then. He walked right up to me and said, 'My name is Gregory Mitchum, Roger's cousin, and I'd like to dance with you. May I?' And he held out his hand. Well, I took that hand, scared as I was—my heart beat a mile a minute. But I knew then, if I didn't take his hand, I'd regret it for the rest of my life."

She yawned and opened her eyes.

"Would you mind gettin' me a glass of water, dear? All this rememberin's makin' me thirsty."

"Of course, I'll be right back."

She closed her eyes again, and I made my way down to the kitchen, hoping desperately Jack wouldn't be there. He wasn't. I saw him, though, through the window, standing in the paddock with Sammy. The rain had stopped and the sun had come back out, and Jack stood with his face turned up to it while he stroked Sammy's back.

I watched for a minute as he pet the horse and talked to him. They had such tenderness between them. He could be so gruff and grumpy with people, with me, but with his horses? He was a teddy bear. The sound of his voice when he murmured to them was so sweet and gentle, and the velvety texture made me ache for him to talk to me that way.

I took a deep breath and huffed it out. I kept having to remind myself I couldn't have him.

When I opened the door to Mrs. M's room, she rolled onto her side, snoring, so I set the glass of water on the bedside table and tiptoed over to climb back into the bed. I lay there for a long time, just looking at her face and imagining what her life had been like. Every line in her soft skin came from some worry she'd had or some adventure, and I hoped she'd tell me about each one. I'd never met a stronger woman, and I hoped I could learn something from her about survival I didn't already know.

She tossed and turned in her sleep a little, so I hummed and sang softly to her and she relaxed. I'd always loved to sing and play, and I missed having music in my life, but it hurt, made me sad.

I remembered how brilliant my mother had been. I'd always looked up to her, wanted to be like her and play music all over the world like she had.

I remembered her playing her piano for me. She'd play lullabies to help me fall asleep as I lay in my father's arms, and when she was happy or excited about something, she'd play fast and cheery songs in the living room, and I'd jump and dance to celebrate with her. Her music had been beautiful, ethereal. It made me feel loved back then.

The sounds of her playing would haunt me until the day I died. Now, I couldn't stand to listen to it. It hurt so much, I stopped breathing and had to hold back vomit when I heard it.

She'd taught me to play her piano and I'd loved it. I'd been good at it, too, worked hard at it to please her, but I hadn't played since the day my parents died. I loved music. It sustained me when I felt like I couldn't run another step or drive another mile. And it protected me from the silence in my head.

But her music…

It was the knife in my fucking gut forcing me to have to run in the first place.

An hour flew by, and I knew I couldn't avoid Jack forever. Mrs. M still slept peacefully, so I left her room and wandered around, peeking in all the different upstairs bedrooms.

Kevin had gone outside with Jack when we'd returned to

the ranch, so I looked in his room first. I didn't go in, just opened the door for a few seconds. It had been easy to see the differences between each brother just by a quick look in their rooms.

Kevin's room was messy, clothes strewn around, with lots of art on the walls. None of it had been framed, though, just photographs taped or tacked up. His blinds were left down, the curtains pulled shut, casting the room in darkness.

He had a computer and some kind of camera gear sitting on his desk. He'd left his bed unmade, the sheets and blanket still on the bed but pushed down to the foot. It kind of resembled my bedroom at my rental house, though I didn't have a computer.

The room I'd hidden in yesterday when I freaked out, the one Jack had kissed me in, was neat as a pin and bright, the window coverings up and open. I didn't know who it belonged to, but whichever brother lived there was exceptionally clean and made his bed with precision.

There was a desk but nothing on it. No art or decorations of any kind on his walls and only a small flat screen TV atop a wooden dresser. I would've thought no one used the room, but a sweatshirt hung over the desk chair. It said, "U.S. Marine Corp" on the back with some kind of emblem underneath.

The room next to it had also been kept tidy and light, but there were tons of books on the desk and some lining the walls on the floor. A few pictures hung on the walls, and they looked similar to the photos in Kevin's room. There were also a couple of framed certificates on the wall behind the bed, but I didn't go far enough in to see what they said. The third room's bed was made but rumpled.

And the last room, besides the guest room Mrs. M slept in, was a freaking disaster zone. Jeez. There were clothes hanging from every surface, from the open closet doors, the desk, the desk chair, off the bed, dangling from the window blinds—everywhere! A serious-looking computer with three screens sat on a desk in the corner with a T-shirt hanging off of one, and there were food and candy wrappers and completely recyclable empty water bottles all over the floor and desk.

No books in this room, but there were stacks of DVDs on the floor and a huge TV mounted to the wall opposite the bed. An acoustic guitar rested in a stand in one corner, and two more hung from braces mounted on another wall. The bed sheets and comforter lay in a heap on the floor in the middle of the room. And there was a not-so-pleasant odor coming from the fourth room. I shut that door and backed away in horror.

Finally, out of sheer boredom, and I had to admit, a need I felt clenching in the center of my body to see Jack again, I wandered outside and down to the barn. Kevin sat on a bale of hay next to the first big open barn door.

"Hey, girl. How's Ma doin'?"

"She's sleeping."

"Yeah, she'll probably do a lotta that. I stayed with her awhile at her house last time she went through chemo." He frowned, picking at the hay. "She's not in pain though?"

"No, I don't think so. Just tired. How are you? How's your leg?" I pointed to his cast.

"Ain't so bad."

"Yeah," Jack said, appearing in the doorway, leading a horse by a rope, "that's why you fell when you tried to put weight on it." He flashed me a quick smile, and Kevin looked back and forth between us. Jack backed the horse up a few feet and clipped two ropes, one hanging from each side of the aisle, to the horse's halter.

"Who's this? Why's he covered in mud?" I laughed, motioning to the beefy horse with a swing of my arm. His coat resembled the rich, deep, auburn-brown color of whiskey, and he had a black mane and tail, his legs and belly crusted with dried mud.

"Tank, though we oughta call him the Postman. This damn horse just can't help himself. Rain, mud, sleet, snow. If there's any kinda mess, he can't stay out of it. He's gettin' a bath today." Jack laughed, and Kevin whipped his head over, looking at him with squinted eyes.

"Hm. Guess, I'll head on up to the house. Might take one of them lovely pain pills and get me a nap. My leg does hurt a bit after all." He spied Jack again, who pet Tank with an easy smile on his face, then blinked a few times, shook his head infinitesimally, and stood on his good leg.

"Can I help you?"

"Nah, I got it. Thanks. Hey, thanks for helpin' Ma though. I think she kinda likes havin' another girl around."

I shrugged. "Me too."

"Ain't you a girl?" Jack joked.

"Ha ha. I forgot to wear my pigtails today," Kevin quipped, grabbing his crutches from against the barn behind him. "Somebody took his funny pills this mornin'," he mumbled and shook his head again, then hobbled up to the house.

"Wanna help?" Jack asked, bending to grab a curry comb from the bucket at his feet.

"Sure." He handed it to me, and I stood on the other side of Tank, brushing in circles.

"Ma didn't— Mrs. Mitchum didn't get sick, did she?" He cleared his throat.

"No. She said she's just really tired. The medication hit her pretty hard."

"Yeah, that stuff sure does a number on her. It did my dad too."

"Your dad had cancer?" I asked, peeking over Tank's back at Jack's face.

"Yeah. He passed last year. Lung cancer," he said, looking intently at the horse.

"I'm sorry."

"Mm. What about your parents? You said they passed in an accident?"

"Yes."

"Car accident?"

"No."

"How old were you?"

"Eleven."

"Jesus. I'm sorry, Everlea. Well, who raised you then? Your granny?"

"Can we stop talking about this, please?"

"Sure," he said, and he stepped around to Tank's head. "Here, we'll finish this up later. C'mon, I wanna show you somethin'." Reaching to grab the curry comb from my hand, he dropped it into the bucket, then unhooked Tank and led him back to his stall.

"What?" I asked as he walked back toward me and took my hand.

"Just hold your horses, young lady." He smiled and my heart squeezed in my chest.

I knew then I had to leave, but I thought it might kill me to do it.

CHAPTER TWELVE

JACK

"MY GREAT GRANDPOPS built the barn and put in this foalin' room. We hardly ever use it."

I'd led Everlea up the stairs in the last aisle, and we stood in the doorway of the little room. It had been meant to be used as a place to catch some sleep when waitin' for a foal to be born, but I usually just slept leaned up against the mare's stall door. That way, I could hear everything goin' on, in case of problems.

There wasn't much in the room above the barn with its peaked roof and wood panelin'. A few bits and halters had been left on the small, square table next to the only window, and a metal foldin' chair sat in the corner, and an old, full-sized bed stuck out into the middle of the room from the back wall. A stack of folded blankets sat atop the bed. Not much else.

I stood in front of Everlea but turned and reached behind her to shut the door.

"Jack," she whispered when I rested my hands on her hips, urgin' her backward against it. I ducked my head to kiss her, just on the edge of her bottom lip.

"Hmm?"

"We can't," she said, hidin' her face in my chest as I lifted my head.

"No? Why not?"

"I… I just can't."

I pulled away so she'd be forced to look at me, but she lowered her eyes.

"I know you're runnin' from somethin'. You don't have to hide it from me."

"You don't understand," she whispered.

"So, explain it to me. Please." I couldn't keep the annoyance outta my voice.

She shook her head and I stepped back. She wouldn't even try to talk to me even though I'd opened up my home and my family to her, and it was startin' to piss me off.

"What are you so afraid of, Everlea? Tell me. Look at you. You're shakin'."

She looked down at herself like she could see her own fear, like it was a visible, pliable thing shrink wrapped all around her.

"So, what, you're just gonna stand there and lie? Gonna say it's nothin'? Then what? Gonna run?" I could picture it, her stealin' away in the night, and I hated how it made me feel. Angry and… sad. I didn't want her to go.

I wanted her to trust me.

"I saw the bag at your house, the map. You just gonna take off one night, leave Ma? Dammit. Mrs. Mitchum. You said you'd help her and you're just gonna leave? Find somewhere better, more excitin'?" She shook her head furiously, but the look of doubt in her eyes gave her away.

I was right.

She'd run. An image of my mama, before she'd left us, flashed in my mind. "You know what? Just go. Now. Take your fuckin' garbage bag and go. We'll take care of Mrs. Mitchum. I'll make your excuses." I tried to step past her, but she latched onto my arm with her greedy fingers and wouldn't let go.

"Jack, please."

"Please what? Did you just wanna fuck and then you'll go? Is that what this is?" Not that I'd blame her, but at least she could be honest about it.

"What? No!"

"Where's your car? I'll drive you back to it." I turned my head, lookin' down at her, and the accusation in my question stunned her into silence. "Yeah, I know you lied about that too. This is a small town, darlin'. Can't hide much for long." I imagined the disdain in my voice slicin' through her like a knife.

"I'm sorry," she whispered. But was she really? Sorry about what? Lyin'? Or gettin' caught?

"Yeah, well, I'll survive it, but you're gonna break Mrs. Mitchum's heart. She likes you and she needs your help."

"No," she whispered, almost cried.

The pain in her voice sounded so real, and I wanted to believe her. Somethin' inside my chest ached for her. But I pushed it away. I wouldn't fall for it. She'd leave. Wasn't that what all women did? Took what they wanted, maybe gave a little, made you believe they gave a shit, then left.

"C'mon, get your crap." I grabbed the cheap gold door-knob to yank the door open and storm out, but she squeezed my arm, dug her nails into my skin.

"Jack, stop. Please."

I sighed, shakin' my head. I'd known this was a bad idea. I'd known it and I ignored my better judgement. I didn't have time for her games. Yeah, I want you, no, I don't. Yeah. No. What-the-fuck-ever.

"What, Everlea? Is there a problem here, or are you just some wanderin' flake, goin' from sucker to sucker? Is that what Mrs. Mitchum is to you?" It was what I was to her. I already knew it. I let go of the door and shook her off, and she backed away till she bumped into the wall, slidin' down to the floor.

"There's a man."

Right. Another man. I'd called it. She'd lied again.

"What man?" I turned and leaned back against the door with my arms crossed over my chest. Everything inside me screamed at me to leave the room. To walk away from her. I didn't know her. I never would. I shouldn't have wanted to.

So why couldn't I open the fuckin' door?

"A bad man."

"What, he didn't buy you the diamond you wanted?"

She tucked her knees to her chest, wrappin' her arms around her legs. She shivered.

"This man your husband? Boyfriend?"

Pressin' her lips together, hard, squeezin' her eyes shut, she shook her head in tiny jerks. "No. He's— There's something wrong with him. He won't leave me alone."

"What does that mean, Everlea? What is it you ain't sayin'?"

"He wants me. For himself. It's a game to him. If he finds me here with you, he'll hurt you." When she looked up from the floor and into my eyes, she cried, tears on her thick lashes she wouldn't let fall. "Please, I don't want to hurt you. Mrs. M, Kevin. You've all been so nice to me, and I can't bring you into this. I can't put you in more danger. Please understand."

The tears did fall, down her face, drippin' onto her shirt. I crouched down then and sat in front of her. It felt like I couldn't move. Like she'd hexed me. She'd snared me and I knew I was stupid, but the look on her face tore at me. The fear, and so much sadness.

"You don't need to worry about me. Kevin and I can take care of ourselves, and we'll take care of Mrs. Mitchum. Everlea, look at me," I demanded, and she looked up. "Start talkin'. What kinda danger? You think this man's here? In Wisper?"

"I don't know. When you said my garage was ransacked, I thought it might have been him. I mean, how often do bears break into people's garages?"

"'Round here? All the time. Bears, racoons, mountain lions, drunk teenagers."

She smiled but it didn't reach her eyes. "I don't think it was him, though. There wasn't a note. He always leaves a note."

"Has this man hurt you?" I already knew the answer and I felt rage. I shouldn't have. She wasn't mine.

Her face crumpled and she nodded.

Inhalin' a long breath, I had to force myself to keep my mouth shut. The words threatenin' to pour out would hurt her, and if she could hear the anger in my voice, it would scare her too. I wanted to yell at her. Why had she stayed with this man? Why had she allowed herself to be treated in such a way? I would never do that to a woman, raise a hand against her. Never.

I tried to steer the conversation in a different direction. "You been in Wisper, what, a month?"

"Four weeks and five days."

"And have you seen this man here? Talked to him?"

"No."

"When's the last time you did see him?"

"Two months ago, maybe a little more. In Texas."

"So then, why you so afraid he'll come here? Texas is hundreds of miles away."

"It doesn't matter. He'll find me. He always finds me."

"God, you're shakin' like a leaf." I grabbed a blanket from the bed and wrapped it around her shoulders, and she clutched at it. "You're safe here. I wouldn't let anybody hurt you."

"He'll hurt you."

He could try, but when I shoved my shotgun up his ass, bet he'd cry like a baby.

"This guy bigger'n me? He some kinda trained assassin? Ex-military?"

She shook her head. "I don't think so."

"Well then, I don't think we got a problem. I got a gun. I got lots a' guns, actually. Who is he? You sleep with this man? Date him?"

"No. H-he knew my mother."

"Your mama? So he's older than you?"

"Yes."

"Wait a minute. You said your parents died years ago."

"They did. I didn't lie about that. He had a relationship with her. A long time ago."

"Why don't we call Carey? Sheriff Michaels. He's a friend of mine." I pulled my phone from my back pocket. Maybe this was a little too big for me. I knew I could protect myself and my family, and I would protect her, but if this guy was fixated on her, then he probably wasn't dealin' with a full deck. I wanted Carey to look for the guy, put his creepy ass in jail. And honestly, I wanted him to look into it, to tell me she wasn't lyin' again.

"No!"

"Why not? He can keep an eye out 'round town for this guy."

"Please don't call him. I-I don't want to get anyone else involved. Please? Promise you won't call him." I studied her face, lookin' for answers I knew she didn't wanna give for some reason. "Please? Not yet."

"I think he can help."

"Please? If you call him, I'll have to leave. I don't want to. I don't want to leave this place. Mrs. M." She looked in my eyes. "I don't want to leave, Jack. I can't tell you everything. If you can't accept that, then I have to go. But I don't want to. Not yet. Please don't make me." She got up onto her knees, grabbin' my hands. "Please?" Movin' between my legs, she wrapped my arms around her back. The blanket fell down around her as she begged and leaned into me. "Please?"

"Everlea."

"Please? I want you." She pushed against me, and I lay back on the floor in defeat. I knew then I'd give into her. "I want you so much."

I groaned. "This ain't exactly fair."

"I know." She pushed my shirt up, flattenin' her hands on my stomach, and the heat from her skin traveled down to my dick, and it thickened to near pain. She unbuttoned my jeans. "I'm sorry," she whispered, and I sat up, pullin' off my shirt.

I knew she wasn't tellin' me everything and I knew she'd leave, but in the moment, I didn't care. I'd wanted her from the very first second I saw her, and no matter her intentions, that hadn't changed. I grabbed the bottom of her shirt, but she stopped me with her hands on mine.

"No. You can touch me everywhere, anywhere you want, but not under this shirt."

"Everlea. What—"

"No, Jack. That's the deal. Take it or leave it but I promise, if you agree, you can have as much of the rest of me as you want." She stared me down, darin' me to tell her no. It wasn't like my body didn't give me away. She knew I wanted her, and she offered as much as she thought she could. If only for a day or two.

I wouldn't deny her. I thought I'd already passed the point where I could. It pissed me off and turned me on at the same time.

She bent, kissin' my shoulder, then licked from my chest to my neck, and I growled and grabbed her hips. "Take off those jeans," I said. "Now." She stood and kicked off her shoes, and as she unzipped her jeans, I gripped 'em and yanked 'em down her legs. "Get on the bed."

I got up onto my knees and knocked the pile of blankets to the floor as she sat in front of me. I fisted my hands at my sides to stop 'em tremblin' as she opened her legs, and the look in her eyes was sheer verdant fire, which just made it worse.

"Lie back," I growled through clenched teeth to stop the tremble in my voice too.

I was desperate to touch her. I'd waited days to be with her like this. To be inside her. I'd never wanted anyone more. Shakin' out my hands, I placed 'em on her stomach, over the damn shirt, and waited for my heart to slow a little. I didn't want her to feel me tremble.

The overwhelmin' need I felt to touch every inch of her, inside and out, confused me. I closed my eyes and concentrated on my breathin', but the heat from her body seduced me like Eve in the fuckin' garden, and I couldn't wait. I didn't have time to figure out her secrets.

I had to have her.

Slidin' my fingers under the little stretch of fabric coverin' her hips, I yanked her panties to her knees, and she gasped.

As I stood to push my jeans down, she lifted up onto her

elbows to watch me, and her eyes consumed my whole body. She was hungry for me, too, and so fuckin' beautiful. Even with the stupid shirt. It covered her whole torso, but it fit her like a second skin, and I could see every curve, every peak and valley. My imagination did the rest.

She moaned and fell back, rubbin' her legs together. "Please, Jack," she begged, "put your hands on me, like you did before. Touch me."

I grasped her thighs, pushin' 'em open, and shoved my face into her, spearin' her with my tongue, and she shuddered, pumpin' her hips into my face.

Her sweet taste in my mouth made me wild, and I sucked and swallowed her arousal, then licked up to her clit and pressed my tongue flat against it. I sucked it in between my teeth, flicked it, and her whole body arched up off the bed. She gasped and moaned and clutched the bedsheets, and the sounds spurred me on, made me frantic.

I couldn't wait anymore. I'd wanted to make her come on my tongue, but I had to get inside her. I pulled away and lifted her to reposition her on the bed, then crawled back over her.

Hoverin' there, I waited for her to open her eyes—it was the longest three seconds of my life—and when she did, when I saw 'em dance and sparkle for me, I pushed into her as far as I could go.

She gasped and the sound that came outta me was guttural. Animal.

Fuck. She felt so goddamn good, soft, like silk, so warm and wet. And tight.

"Oh!" she cried out and whimpered.

"Don't move." I held my torso above hers, brushin' my chest against her breasts, soft, even through her shirt. I rested my forehead against hers. "Give it a minute. I don't wanna hurt you." Squeezin' my eyes shut, sweat dripped down my face, and I bit the inside of my lip hard to keep from movin'.

She gripped the hair on the back of my head and pulled, and when I opened my eyes, she whispered, "Jack Cade, if you don't start moving inside me, *I'm* gonna hurt *you*."

Well.

Fuck me.

Growlin' approval of her erotic demand, I thrust my hips. Her body squeezed me so hard I could barely move. I tried to go slow and be gentle, but it was the most difficult thing I'd ever had to do.

The sounds she'd made while I licked and sucked her were so sexy. They lured me in, but now, with my body buried inside hers, she moaned and writhed.

Her voice was husky and needy, and the sound of it all around me intoxicated me. I dug my fingers into her outer thigh so I could lift her knee to fuck her deeper, and she growled low and long. I almost came just from knowin' I'd caused her to feel good enough to make such a sound.

Her hands were everywhere, learnin' my body. Everything inside me had been so frantic and rushed till then. I hadn't been able to control the urge to touch her, to kiss her, to be inside her, but I slowed my hips. I knew I wouldn't last long. Whatever this thing was between us felt too good.

The urge to fuck hard and come was nearly impossible to ignore, but I was desperate to make her feel good, to make her understand how much I craved her, and I wanted to feel her on my body for as long as I could. I knew she'd leave. I knew this would probably be my only chance with her.

Maybe I was desperate to give her a reason to stay.

Her neck was long and sexy with her head thrown back against the pillow, the skin freckled and dewy. Those freckles trailed off underneath her shirt, and I wanted to rip it off so I could see every part of her, but for now, feelin' her in my hands through the shirt would have to do. Something kept her from showin' her whole self to me, and I didn't like it, but I knew I had to respect it. For now.

I leaned down, suckin' her breast into my mouth through the shirt, and she groaned. The shirt had ridden up a little though, and I looked down between our bodies to the soft pink-peach flesh of her belly. Watchin' her thrust her wide soft hips to match my own thrusts and the sight of myself movin' in and out of her body was so erotic. I moaned, scrapin' her nipple with my teeth, and she shoved her hands into my hair, graspin' and pullin'. It hurt but it felt good, too, and I loved that she had some physical control over me.

She yanked at it to lift my head, and her fingers caressed my face. She drew 'em over my cheeks, my ears, my eyebrows. She searched me, desperately trying to find somethin'. I watched her eyes the whole time and saw a look in 'em I couldn't name—rapture and remorse, all at the same time.

"Everlea…" I pleaded with her, beggin' for somethin', but I didn't know what.

At the sound of her name, she dragged her fingers down to my chin, rubbin' her palms along my jaw, my lips, and I grazed her thumb with my teeth, pullin' it into my mouth. Her eyes followed, watchin' me suck it in and out.

Spreadin' our legs a little wider, I used the space to thrust my hips at a deeper angle, swivelin' every time I pushed in deep. I fucked her faster and faster and then my hips just pistoned my cock in and out. It became automatic so I could concentrate on her, on her face, as she came closer and closer to comin' undone. I wanted to see her come apart. Let go.

She couldn't lie to me then.

Her breathin' became erratic, and she made these tiny

little gaspin' noises. Rippin' her hands from my face to claw my back, my ribs, my ass, she threw her head back, moanin' and archin' her body into mine.

She was ready to come, her inner muscles grippin' my cock tight, and thank fuck 'cause I couldn't last one more minute. Seein' her like that, ready to explode all over me was —the pleasure was searin'.

It was almost unbearable.

Her eyes were closed, her mouth open as she held her breath, so I took it, fuckin' her mouth with mine while I fucked her body with my whole soul. I knew I'd regret it but I gave her everything, even though I didn't understand the impossible need inside me to do it.

She moaned and begged, "please," and I swallowed the sounds of her pleasure just like I'd dreamed of doin'.

"Open your eyes, Everlea. Come," I commanded into her mouth. I needed it, the connection. I needed to see inside her so maybe the power she held over me would make sense.

She opened her eyes and that was it for me. I felt her contractin' and squeezin' me, and she breathed my name, her voice raspin' and broken. I took her lips in mine again, almost brutally, and she bit me when she came.

My eyes rolled back in my head and I came, too, roarin' my release, breakin' into a million pieces inside her.

CHAPTER THIRTEEN

EVERLEA

"THAT WAS... DO IT AGAIN," I breathed.

"I'm gonna need at least a few minutes to recover." He twisted, falling down onto his back beside me on the bed, and we both exhaled loudly. I turned on my side to face him.

"You surprised me."

"Whatcha mean?" he asked, breathing hard. We both did, like we'd just run ten miles.

"I don't know. I guess, I thought you'd be, mmm, reserved."

"Reserved."

"Yeah, 'cause you're usually so quiet. You don't say a lot." I thought for a moment, remembering how he'd ordered me to the bed, to open my eyes. To come. My cheeks flooded with heat and I looked down. "You're kind of bossy."

He laughed. "I am the boss 'round here. Get used to it." Rolling onto his side, too, he kissed my nose. As soon as he said it, I flinched internally. I wouldn't get used to it. I wouldn't be around in a day or two.

If I could find the courage to leave.

I changed the subject. "Now, I'm hungry."

"Whatcha wanna eat?"

"You." I pushed him back, climbing on top of him, and he wrapped his fingers around my wrists like manacles, holding me in place.

"Evvie, take this damn shirt off. Lemme see you."

I stiffened. "No, Jack."

"Why not?"

He released my wrists, and I pulled my shirt down by the hem to make sure it covered my scars. I would never let him see. "Did you just call me Evvie?"

"Yeah, guess I did. Don't like it?"

"I love it. I've never had a nickname."

"No? Your mama never called you Evvie or Lea? Evie?"

"Nope."

"Your dad?"

"No, my father was… He was a weird guy. He loved to read, always had his nose in a book. He barely ever looked out of them, didn't notice anything going on around him. Every memory I have of him, he was reading."

"What kinda books?"

I shrugged. "I don't know. I was too young to notice. There were piles of them everywhere, all different colors and sizes. My mother hated them. He was very intellectual. Probably *War and Peace* or Nietzsche and Kafka or something. So different than my mother."

"What about your mama?"

"My mother was a musician," I stated it, so matter of fact.

"Oh yeah? What'd she play?"

"Piano."

"Do you play? I heard you a little the other day."

"Not anymore."

"Why not?"

"What about *your* mom?" It was cruel. I already knew his

mother wasn't his favorite subject. He'd dismissed my question about her in the paddock yesterday. But I couldn't talk
about my mother either, and any time I thought about her, I'd
just get angry and sad. I didn't want to be like that with Jack.

"She's gone," he said.

"Did she die?"

"Nope."

"You see how you don't want to talk about your mother?
That's how I feel about mine."

Thankfully, a loud noise distracted us. It sounded like a
really big truck, and it creaked and bounced on the driveway.

"What is that?"

"That's probably my brothers. They're back earlier than I
expected. C'mon. Let's get you dressed."

I hesitated. More people who could be hurt because of
me. But I didn't have a choice unless I left the ranch now.

I didn't want to. Mrs. M still needed me. Or maybe I
needed her.

Maybe I needed Jack.

I took a deep breath. "'Kay."

When we were properly clothed, Jack took my hand and
we made our way outside. A big black truck with a trailer
hitched to the back sat parked on the gravel lane in front of
the barn. Behind it, three men struggled to contend with the
biggest, blackest, most gargantuan horse I'd ever seen. And
he was not a happy camper. He stood on his hind legs, trying
to pummel the men with his front hooves, snorting and
making an awful screeching sound.

"Some fine horsemen you fuckers are!" One of the men
turned when he heard Jack's voice, staring open-mouthed at
Jack and me while the horse tried to knock his head from his
shoulders.

"Pay attention, Finn! Jesus," Jack yelled, dropping my

hand, running over to help. He jumped right in with them, grabbing the rope attached to the halter on the horse's face.

So, these were the infamous brothers: Dean, Finn, and Jay.

Finn had sandy blond hair pulled back into a little pony-tail. He stood a few inches taller than Jack, but thinner, not as densely muscled. He looked like a rugged surfer.

The man standing next to Jack was about his same height, but big, very densely muscled and he looked tense. His sandy blond hair had been cut short, unlike Finn's. He faced away from me so I couldn't really see his face clearly, but he seemed hard. Intense. He held his body in a rigid stance.

And the guy next to Finn was shorter than all of them, though only by a few inches, with the same brown hair as Jack, but kind of curly and a little longer.

Suddenly, I was nervous.

Jack took control, pulling the horse back down onto all four of his feet, guiding him to walk along the wooden fence, then ran by the horse's side, letting him exert his excess energy. He looked so confident, so in control, handling the horse. So sexy. I imagined what he would look like without his shirt…

I'd been too distracted, still in my first ever post-properly-screwed haze, admiring Jack to notice all three of his brothers converging on me, until Finn stood in front of me and pulled me into a bone-crushing hug.

"Hey, baby girl. You must be Everlea."

"Can't breathe!" I choked out. Finn chuckled, lowering me onto my feet, and he shoved his big hand out to me, grasping mine and shaking me like a rag doll.

"Sorry, I'm Finn. Nice to meet ya." He flashed a smile I was sure had the ability to make many women swoon and drop their panties. What a smile. And his eyes, they were the deepest light blue, like looking into a tranquil tropical ocean. I shook his hand and he dragged me beside him, hooking his arm around my shoulder. I must've looked like a doll standing next to him. I didn't think the top of my head even cleared his rib cage.

"This here's baby Jay, and crabby pants over there is Dean." He motioned to the big guy with a nod, and crabby pants scowled in our direction. I looked up at him and saw a flash of kindness, maybe even tenderness in his big, gray eyes, but then it disappeared, a hard look replacing anything I thought I'd seen. He grunted and turned to walk back toward Jack, who now stood still, holding the horse by his halter, talking to him and smoothing the horse's wide, silky, black cheek gently with his hand.

Looking up, Jack saw Dean approaching and peered around him to me with a worried expression, then back to his brother. He said something to Dean that I couldn't hear, and Dean shrugged, took the rope from Jack, and led the horse to the arena.

Jack jogged back down the small hill to where I still stood under Finn's big, sweaty arm.

"These are my brothers." He cleared his throat. "This is Everlea. She's, uh—"

"Yeah, we've already been introduced," Finn said, looking between Jack and me, then over to Jay who smiled.

"I'm Jay," he said, extending his hand to me.

"Hi. I've heard a lot about you guys. How was your drive?"

Jay laughed. "Good, the drive was good. Although, listenin' to Finn whine the whole damn way about Dean's choice in music was exhaustin'." He rolled his eyes at Finn.

"Yeah, well, you'd complain, too, if you had any fu—any taste. 'Scuse me, Everlea."

"C'mon, let's go check on Mrs. Mitchum," Jack said, nodding toward the house. Finn and Jay followed behind, and I could hear them whispering to each other but not what they said, though I was pretty sure it had something to do with me.

Walking into the big white house, we found Mrs. M and Kevin in the living room, Mrs. M rocking and knitting in the brown recliner, and Kevin lounged on the couch, asleep, with his head rolled back and kinked in a really uncomfortable position. He was snoring, his mouth hanging open and his broken leg resting on the coffee table. Finn walked past me, slapping him on the back of his head, hard.

"Honey, I'm home!" he sang.

Kevin jumped up out of his sleep ready to rumble. "You asshole!" He tried to punch Finn but Finn danced backwards, like a boxer, laughing.

"Language, young man," Finn mock-scolded Kevin.

"Kevin, watch it or I'll—" Mrs. M tried to actually scold Kevin, but then I heard a chorus of male voices recite, "—wash your mouth out with soap!"

"Yes, ma'am, sorry," Kevin apologized and sat back down.

"Yeah, sorry, Ma. Couldn't help m'self. How ya feelin'?" Finn walked over to her, bent down, kissed her cheek, and crouched by her legs, looking up at her and waiting for her to answer.

"I'm fine, Finnie. How's the new horse?" She patted his head like a puppy and he stood, pivoted, and fell onto the couch next to Kevin.

"And I'll smack your behind, Finnigan Cade. Did it occur to you to ask the lady if she would like to sit down?" Ma chided him, and Kevin smacked the back of his head, exacting his revenge and dislodging Finn's ponytail.

"Yeah, *Finnie*."

Finn jumped up, stepping on Kevin's uncasted foot intentionally. "Sorry, miss Everlea, would you like to sit down?"

Dean came in from the kitchen, walked through the living room to Mrs. M, bent to kiss her cheek, and continued on. "You'd think you morons were born in a barn," he grumbled in a deep voice, ascending the stairs, two at a time.

"Um, technically," Jay said, "I *was* born in the barn, but I'm not the one without manners. I apologize for my brothers, Everlea. It's been a long time since we've had a young lady in our house."

"Oh, it's okay. I'm not a lady anyway," I said, feeling small and awkward. These guys could finish each other's sentences. They were that close. I'd never known anyone that well, and the realization had me feeling alone until I looked down and saw Jack's hand holding mine behind the couch. He squeezed, and I looked up to see him smiling so warmly at me. How did he know? Could he really read me so well, so quickly?

Looking back out to the other people in the room, I froze. Every set of eyes was on me. Everyone seemed to be surprised by something.

"Did I say something wrong?" I whispered to Jack.

"No, dear, you haven't said anything wrong. It's just that we're not used to seein' Jack smile." Mrs. M winked at me, and Jack dropped my hand.

"Get up, Kevin. Let Everlea sit with Ma—Mrs. Mitchum," Jack said. I caught his slip, but no one else seemed to notice. He flicked Kevin's ear (jeez, poor Kevin), leading me around to sit as Kevin stood, grumbling something that sounded like "kick *all* your asses."

He stumbled and hopped to the stairs. "I'm goin' to bed."

"It ain't even four o'clock yet," Jay pointed out.

"Yeah, well, some of us have been here takin' care of

things while the rest of you were on a road trip or"—he looked between Jack and me—"otherwise engaged. Good night."

Mrs. M shook her head, chuckling, as he stumbled up the stairs. She looked down at her knitting project, which appeared to be a pink baby blanket. "Poor Kevin."

"I'll be right back," Jack whispered, leaning over the back of the couch a little. "I'm gonna go check on the horse." He patted the couch twice, then turned and walked away.

Finn plopped down next to me. "Did he just whisper sweet nothin's in your ear? You know, you can sue him for that kinda thing nowadays."

"Everlea, what's your story? Where you from?" Jay asked, pulling a dining chair into the living room, sitting on it backward. My stomach dropped to my feet. All eyes were on me again.

But then Iggy jumped up onto Finn's lap, staring straight into his eyes and saving me. The startled—and kind of terrified—look on his face made me laugh. He held his arms away from his body, up in the air, like if he touched her, he'd be electrocuted.

"What the f— What is this?" He looked at me, eyebrows raised to the ceiling.

"It's a cat, Finnie," Jay said. "You remember, C-A-T, cat? Say it with me."

"What's it doin' in the house?" Finn speared Jay with a look.

"That's Everlea's little friend, Iggy," Mrs. M said. "Looks like she's taken a likin' to you, though she's not very fond of Kevin." She laughed, and Iggy stood, jumping from Finn's lap to mine, then curled up on my legs and rolled her head back, upside down, staring at Finn and ogling him with half-closed bedroom eyes.

"I can't believe Jack let that thing inside. She is kinda cute, though, and she has good taste," he said, reaching over to scratch her little black and white head. "What kinda name is Iggy?"

I shrugged, scratching Iggy's belly, and the sound of her purring filled the room while Finn eyed my Sonic Youth T-shirt, then Iggy, then me.

"Welp"—he popped his lips—"I better go help Jack with the trailer. I'm gonna run to the store." He stood, giving one last look to Iggy. "Any requests for dinner, ladies?" He looked at me and I shook my head.

"Whatever you wanna make will be fine, Finnie, but Mr. Jameson has a prescription for me at the pharmacy. Would you mind pickin' it up?"

"Sure thing, Ma."

"Get beer!" Jay called to Finn as he opened the kitchen door.

"Duh."

"Mrs. M, how are you feeling? Did you sleep well?"

"Everlea, you know you don't have to call me that. You can call me Ma, like the boys, or Sara, which is my name." She smiled. "I had a nice nap and I feel fine. A little tired still, but that's gonna be par for the course from now on. I'd like to take a shower and snuggle up in my jammies, and you and I can fall asleep watchin' that movie." She winked at me. "Then tomorrow, I think I'll need to go get some more clothes and things from the house. When I packed for the hospital, I didn't plan on movin' in here with all of you."

"Are you hungry, Ma? Everlea? I could make us a snack or somethin'. Finn'll make dinner but it'll probably be late."

"No, I'm fine for now, sweetheart. Thank you."

"Everlea, hungry?"

"No, thank you, Jay," I said, my voice sounding small.

Actually, I was starving, but I felt awkward now with all the brothers and activity in the house. I didn't want to be a burden, and I didn't know what to do, where to be.

I didn't know where I belonged.

"C'mon, Everlea," Mrs. M said, looking at me. She leaned forward, setting her knitting on the coffee table. "Help me upstairs. You can start the shower and I'll get my things ready."

CHAPTER FOURTEEN

JACK

"WHO IS THIS WOMAN, JACK?" Finn asked, climbin' into Dean's truck so we could move the trailer.

"Just a woman," I said, startin' it up.

"Where'd she come from? Never seen her in town."

"She just moved here."

"From?"

"Dunno."

"Ain't you just as talkative as ever," he said when we pulled up to the south side of the barn. We got out and walked behind the truck to unhitch the old, rusted trailer.

"She's just a woman. She moved here 'bout a month ago and started volunteerin' at the hospital in the city. She was assigned to Mrs. Mitchum as an aide or somethin' and was supposed to help her get settled in at home after she left the hospital, but she got hurt and Mrs. Mitchum said she'd feel better if they came here to stay."

"Look at that. You do know words."

I grunted.

"Well, whatcha know 'bout her? Where's she work?"

"Here. Mrs. Mitchum hired her to help while she goes through chemo."

"Oh. So, you mean she's gonna stay here? Like, live here? On the ranch?"

"Yeah, I guess. For a little while."

"And that's okay with you?"

"Yeah. Why wouldn't it be?"

"I dunno, 'cause you're a cranky curmudgeon." He chuckled. "You're just not usually so... acceptin' of new people. Women in particular." I didn't say anything. He wasn't wrong. "So, what *do* you know about her?" I didn't answer again. I didn't know much, and what I did know, I couldn't tell him.

"Jack?"

"I dunno, Finn. Not much."

"You know *somethin'* about her. You were holdin' her hand earlier." He eyed me. "You sleepin' with her?"

I didn't say a word, which told him everything.

"Thought so."

I walked away but turned back. "Just keep your mouth shut about it. This is a small town. She don't need to be the focus of everybody's gossip."

He snorted. "Too late for that. She became gossip soon as she met Ma."

"*Finn.*"

"Okay, okay." Raisin' his hands in front of his chest, he surrendered. "I'm gonna run to the store and the pharmacy for Ma. I'll make somethin' for dinner when I get back."

I threw him Dean's keys and went back up to the house, but Ma and Everlea had gone upstairs. I didn't exactly know what I woulda said to Everlea if I'd seen her anyway, and I had work to do, as always, so I went back to the barn till dinner was ready.

Dean and Jay came down to help with evenin' chores, and Jay tried talkin' to me about Everlea, askin' the same questions Finn had, but I blew him off. Dean didn't bother. He probably talked less than me, as a rule. He finished groomin' Tank while Jay and I fed and watered and cleaned up.

The whole day flashed over and over in my mind, and I found myself lookin' around every few minutes for anyone not supposed to be on our land. We had a few motion sensor cameras set up around the barn to look for bears and wolves and such, and I wondered if I could figure out how to access 'em on the old computer in the arena office. But I proved pretty hopeless with that kinda stuff. I'd need Finn's help with it. He was the one who usually dealt with 'em.

Everlea didn't want me tellin' Carey about the man stalkin' her, so I assumed she wouldn't like it if I told my brothers, but I wanted to. If she really was in danger, I knew they'd fight hard to protect her. 'Specially if I asked 'em to.

Other than yellin' at 'em to get to work, I didn't ask my brothers for much. I handled the ranch business pretty much on my own. I paid the bills, spoke with the clients, placed the orders, and I went to the bank to take out loans when we couldn't afford any of it. I knew Jay'd been itchin' to get his hands on our books, and he probably had a million ideas he wanted to implement to further our business, but all of it would take money. Money we didn't have.

I thought again about sellin' some land. My pops woulda rolled over in his grave if he'd known the things runnin' through my mind, but times had been easier for him. The ranch had a lotta success back then, but after our mama left and Granny and Uncle Jon died, my dad ran this place into the ground. They both drank too much, Pops probably literally to death, and my dad just checked out. He became mean. Angry and sad, he drank, smoked, and worked till he got cancer. And he lost all the relationships my pops worked so hard as a young rancher to build, with customers and the community. I'd worked my ass off tryin' to rebuild 'em, and I knew I'd succeeded somewhat, but I also knew customer relations would never be my strong suit.

I couldn't fathom givin' up though. And truthfully, even though I knew sellin' some of our land would fix all our immediate problems, I couldn't imagine what it would be like to do it, to have another business or family on the land we'd been brought up on. We'd spent our whole lives here. There wasn't another place on earth I felt at home. There never would be.

Maybe it had come time for me to stop actin' like my dad and ask my brothers for help. Part of me felt like a failure to have to do it, but the other part of me knew Ma was right. We were all smart, resourceful men. And my brothers loved this land just as much as me. It wouldn't be fair to let the ranch fail without at least askin' their opinion.

But what would I be willin' to do to keep the place afloat? What would I be willin' to give or compromise? I decided I oughta give it some more thought.

After muckin' a few more stalls and sweepin' a few aisles, I figured it had probably been enough time, and Finn would be gettin' ready to ring the dinner bell, but before I headed up to the house, I booted the computer up, just to see if I could figure my way through the videos.

The computer took forever to load, and I finally gave up, but while I sat there waitin', I wondered what the hell I was doin' with Everlea. She could be lyin' about the whole thing. She'd already lied about her name and her car, and she'd admitted flat out she wasn't tellin' me the whole story. She hid her body.

She hid a lot.

I knew in my gut she wasn't lyin' though. I'd seen the look of fear and panic on her face when Mr. Williams stopped by, at her house when I'd told her the garage had been broken into, and today, when she dropped to the floor in despair. All the details could be lies, sure, but the fear inside her was real. Very real. Inside her, all around her, it radiated outta her.

It controlled her.

I wanted to take it away. I wanted to wrap her up in my arms and make her feel safe. I felt an urge to do it, but I just couldn't trust her. Yeah, I still wanted her. I'd thought maybe havin' her would cure me of the need I felt for her, but it just made it worse. I wanted her more now than I did before we'd had sex.

I didn't know what to do about it, but I refused to think about it further.

And I refused to fall in love with her.

Finn made pasta for dinner, with some kinda sauce and shrimp. He grumbled the whole time we ate about not havin' access to fresh seafood, but he also praised himself for makin' it, callin' it a small masterpiece. That was Finn though. He never did have a hard time findin' a bright side to a thing. And of course, he could always find a way to embarrass the shit outta me.

We all sat around the livin' room, even Ma and Kevin, at nine that night after eatin' Finn's late masterpiece, and my brothers told stories about us boys as kids to entertain Everlea. Ma got into it too.

"One time, Finn was chasin' a little girl, Karen Perez, remember, Finnie? She was always such a cute little thing. We'd all gone to the county fair, and Karen was there with her family. Well, he had a crush on her, so he chased her 'round the promenade, and I mean *really* chased her. She was tryin' to run away from him—"

"Uh, no, she was just playin' hard to get. She loved me."

"Anyway," Ma chuckled, "finally, her daddy stepped out in front of Finn intendin' to stop him from annoyin' his little girl. Now, mind you, Manny Perez was about six-foot-six and built like a brick wall. He still is. But Finn saw him and put his little fists up and said—"

"You want her, you fight me for her!" I said, imitatin' an itty-bitty Finn. Fine, I got a little into it too.

"I did not. I said, 'Hello, sir. I'd like to ask your six-year-old daughter on a date. May I please have your permission?'"

"Nope, I was there. Mr. Perez picked you up by your skinny little arm and dangled you in front of his face like a Christmas ornament. You peed your pants," Dean chimed in, even blessin' us with a rare laugh.

"I did not. Everlea, they're liars, the whole lot of 'em. Ma, you're killin' me here. I thought you loved me."

"Oh, I do, Finnie, I do. You were a precocious little thing. S'pose you still are, though you ain't little anymore." Ma giggled and Finn stood, flexing his biceps like a moron.

"Well, it's clear I have always been a ladies' man. And I shall be forevermore!" he roared and fell back to the couch, laughin'.

Everlea laughed and she seemed surprised by it. I sat next to her on the bean bag chair on the floor, watchin' her when she didn't know I looked. She'd taken a shower and her wet hair fell down her back, curlin' into thick spirals and wettin' her long-sleeved T-shirt, and the shampoo she'd brought over from her house smelled like autumn apples. My mouth watered.

"Oh, you schmucks think you're so funny. I got a story

for you, Everlea, oh, ho ho. Entitled, ahem, Dean and the Pepto Bismol Kid."

"Who's the Pepto Bismol Kid?" she asked, smilin', and everybody looked at me.

Everlea looked, too, and she laughed, but she seemed confused that I would be the star of a silly story.

"Well, Pops was in the middle of buildin' Granny's house —Jack, have you showed her?" Finn asked, and I shook my head. Why would I show her an old rundown house? "So, he enlisted Jack and Dean's help to paint." I groaned at the inevitable embarrassment, and Evvie sat forward toward Finn.

"Granny picked out this awful Pepto Bismol-pink color for the livin' room. I think you can still see it on the walls there. Anyway, they were no more than five and six themselves, but they were very excited to be chosen for this extremely important job. They were out there for hours, paintin' away, but, eventually, they finished and Pops sent 'em home.

"Well, Jack knew how much Granny loved this ugly color, so he brought the still half-full bucket of paint back to the barn with him—pulled it the whole way in his little red wagon—and he decided, if Granny liked it so much, then she'd be so happy with him if he painted her favorite horse's stall that color, too, and if she'd love that, then she'd definitely love it if he painted her favorite horse too. So he did!"

"All lies," I whispered in her ear, and she whipped her head around to look at me. We were face to face, an inch between us for about thirty seconds, until I pulled away, watchin' her green eyes glitter when she smiled at me.

Finn, Jay, and Kevin laughed, and Ma shook her head.

"Jack pranced that horse all the way to the front porch and called out, 'Oh Granny, come see, come see what I did for ya!'" Dean said. He laughed, too, and slapped his leg. He actually snorted, which made the three buffoons fall over onto each other in a fit of stupidity. I tried hard not to let the smile I held in crack my face. But it did. Finn could be a regular clown, but we hadn't laughed so much in a long time.

"Diane was fit to be tied." Ma giggled. "She knew how proud you were of the job you'd done, but she had to punish you. That poor horse. I remember the look on your granny's face, Jack. It was utter horror, and then she burst out laughin' so hard she fell down and landed on her backside!"

"Yeah, I remember and it broke my heart. She didn't appreciate all the hard work I put into that paint job."

"Oh, and Dad was *pissed*," Finn said. "Jack got his butt whupped that night."

"How do you know? You were barely three years old," I snapped at Finn but chuckled, smilin' at Everlea when she looked at me again.

"Oh, Jack, you're a legend. I've heard that story many a time. I remember Granny tellin' it at the dinner table. Tickled her pink!" And they all fell into bellowing guffaws until Kevin punched Finn and Jay, who were literally lyin' on top of him on the couch.

"But what about the horse?" Everlea asked with the most adorable look of worry on her face.

"Oh, he was fine. We just had to scrub him down with some of that lava soap Ma's so fond of," Dean said, flashin' Ma a smirk.

"Oh, you mean the kind she used to shove in our mouths when we cursed in front of her? Blech. That shit's disgustin'," Kev said, and Ma got up outta her chair as Kevin's eyes popped wide open and his mouth formed a perfect O. "I'm sorry, Ma! Oh, no, no, no. I'm sorry!"

She strolled over to the sink, grabbin' the bottle of liquid dish soap, then marched back over to Kevin.

"Open up, you naughty little devil." And she tipped the soap over his head in the air. The cap was on but she looked dead serious. Kevin twisted over the side of the couch, wrappin' his arms around her middle, huggin' her, and she threw her head back and laughed. She looked forty instead of seventy. She was beautiful.

Everlea laughed so hard, she had tears in her eyes, and she watched the whole thing with rapt attention.

Finally, after a few more stories about frozen horse manure snowball fights and Kevin bein' tied to the fence for half a day after eatin' a bag of Finn's gourmet potato chips, everybody wandered off to their rooms. Ma fell asleep durin' the potato chip incident, so Dean helped her up to bed.

Which left Everlea and me standin' in the livin' room.

Alone.

CHAPTER FIFTEEN

EVERLEA

JACK DIDN'T SAY anything and neither did I. I wanted him again, more than before, if it were even possible. He walked toward me with a look so intense, it almost scared me. He lifted me straight up and I wrapped my legs around him, locking my feet together as he carried me into the kitchen, stopping at the screen door.

He kissed me thoroughly, and his hands were all over my body, all at once, so he was too distracted to open the door. I reached behind us, trying to catch it with my fingernails.

When we got out to the porch, he unhooked my feet, bringing my legs back around, and I slid down his body. Oh God, he was so hard and I wanted him so much. I swayed on my feet.

Grabbing my waist, he grasped and pulled at my shirt, bunching it up around my stomach, and when his skin touched mine, I gasped and moaned so loud. I thought the whole house probably heard it. I almost forgot about my scars, but I yanked my shirt back into place just in time.

"Evvie…" There was so much desperation in his voice. I understood. I felt it, too, but I still wouldn't let him see me.

Turning, I jumped down the porch stairs and ran for the barn. I knew he would follow. It was the only place I could think of where we could be alone.

The sky stretched above us, so dark with the night and clouds, the air so still and thick. I could hear him behind me, chasing me, and it sent shockwaves to my nervous system, the building electricity in the air seeming to seep into my skin. It didn't even occur to me to look around, to be suspicious of the world around me.

Halfway to the barn, he grabbed my hand, whipping me around to face him, but he dropped it, severing the brief contact quickly, like I'd burned him.

He stood there just staring at me while little raindrops fell on my face. As the seconds ticked by, they grew bigger and bigger and fell faster, but still, we stood motionless, except for our breathing. He looked at me, into my eyes, like he could see straight into my soul.

What did he see there?

I couldn't guess and it didn't matter.

The sky lit up with long flashes of lightning, and a big roll of thunder sounded all around us. Rain dumped down from above, soaking us instantly, but still, we didn't move. It felt like the electricity grew from inside me. It reached out, trying to pull him to me, the energy between our bodies expanding all around us, but I couldn't move my arms and legs.

I wanted my hands on him, my lips, tongue, but I knew, when I finally touched him, I would lose all control. The tightening feeling in the core of my body had become almost painful in its intensity as it spread throughout me, even to the tips of my fingers.

Raw, unimaginable need. I'd never felt anything like it.

Our lungs pumped faster and faster, breath heaving, and a

look of pain broke across his beautiful face. He reached for me. Something inside me broke free, and I jumped at the same time he lifted me up. Our bodies smacked together, and I cried out when his erection rubbed against my swollen, expectant clit through our clothes.

Wrapping my legs around his waist, I buried my face in his neck, biting, sucking, and licking his muscles and the taut tendons that were hard and raised as he struggled to hold my wet, writhing body up.

"Fuck, Evvie." He growled into my ear as I tried to rip through his shirt and crawl into his skin. The rain continued to pound down on us, and it made everything so much more frantic. Grabbing the back of his T-shirt, I rolled my wrist to create a hold for myself, shoving my other hand into the hair at the nape of his neck and pulling.

Assaulting his mouth with my tongue, I sucked his lips and stubbled jaw as he marched with me in his arms toward the stairs in the farthest barn aisle from the house.

The motion, as he carried me, caused our bodies to rub together in the most primal way, and he lowered me a little, holding me up with just his forearms so every step he took ground his jean-clad cock between my legs, driving my need for him deeper and deeper.

When we finally arrived inside the shelter of the barn, he pushed my back up against a wall, pulling his shirt up and off his body, and my hands and fingers immediately clawed and scratched his chest.

The pressure from his pelvis against mine made me whimper, and it felt good, but it wasn't what I needed. I needed us both naked, and I wanted him inside me.

He tried to walk forward, but we weren't making much progress. I wanted skin to skin contact, and in the frenzied rush of the moment, I reached for the hem of my

T-shirt, but he stopped me. "No. I wanna see you—desperately—but I want you to be sure, not 'cause you were caught up."

Well, that just made me want him more.

My hair, dripping and wild, stuck to both of us, and when I pressed my chest against his, my nipples hard and attempting to poke through the thin, wet fabric, he swayed to the side, and we ended up against the outside of a stall. He tried to untie my sweatpants with the fingers of one hand, but he couldn't do it without setting me down, so I unbuttoned his jeans instead. He lowered his head, biting and sucking my breast through my shirt.

"Jack, hurry." I whispered it above his head while he attacked my breasts with his mouth. He growled into my neck —God, I loved that sound—and climbed the stairs.

His face was drawn, and he looked like he was in pain, so I ground myself down onto him through our clothes, hoping it relieved some of the pressure. He hit the wall, and I thought we might fall back down the stairs, but he corrected our momentum with a fierce look of determination. It was raw and so sexy.

When we'd made it to the top, he kicked open the door behind me, and we entered the small room. It was dark, but I could see a little by the soft overhead barn lighting spilling in from the doorway. Bumping his legs into something, he dropped me, and I landed on my butt on the bed and heard the box springs squeak.

I dragged my eyes up and down his straining body. His hair was a dripping mess, but it just made him sexier in the dark, and his chest heaved up and down with his breath, still wet, glistening, and hard as granite. Pulling and kicking his boots off, he bent to push his jeans down, and I untied my frumpy, sopping sweatpants and jumped up to pull them off, too, but he stopped me with his hands on my arms, stepping behind me.

He stood there, naked, shaking and breathing heavily and waiting for… something. I felt his erection against my back, and I wanted it in my grasp so I twisted toward him, but he dropped down to his knees, grabbing my hips.

"I want you so bad," he whispered against my low back. I felt his breath tickle the little bit of skin there between my shirt and pants.

Gripping the sweatpants at my hips, he pushed them and my panties, so slowly, down my legs, kissing the skin on the backs of my thighs as he traveled lower. When he got to my ankles, he pulled my shoes off, and I stepped out of my sweats and he tossed them somewhere.

I heard him breathing, but there was no other sound in the world.

Rising inch by inch, he dragged his hands up my hips, then my ribs, and my arms, careful not to lift my shirt. He moved agonizingly slowly, torturing me, but then stepped one foot in between both of mine so I had to open my legs, and when I did, he dropped back down to his knees.

With one hand on my back, he guided me to lean forward over the bed. He kneeled there, just barely touching the tops of my thighs, his fingers tracing light patterns over them. I'd never felt anything more erotic than him behind me, looking at me like that.

He kissed down the sides of my cheeks, up in the little hollows above them, and back down to the bottom, to the crease where my thighs began. He placed his hot palms there, sliding his thumbs into my wet, throbbing folds, spreading me open, and speared his tongue into me, then licked up to my clit and back inside me.

Groaning, I pushed back onto his tongue, loving the hot,

intimate touch of his mouth between my thighs, and he wrapped his arm around my leg, his fingers stroking through the wetness, rubbing circles around my clit, which was practically buzzing and so sensitive.

It felt like it took all of ten seconds and I was coming—screaming, whimpering, and moaning, or some combination of all three.

After he licked me clean—which was so arousing in a new way, listening to him groan and swallow my orgasm—he stood abruptly, clutching my hips, and rammed into me, holding me still by placing his palm in between my shoulder blades.

Oh my God, the sensations and the sounds were so hot, so obscene, but so good. I could hear our bodies slapping together, and the wet suction of my body gripping and squeezing his cock as he grabbed a fist full of my wet hair, wrapped his hand in it, and pulled gently, lifting my face and turning it to the side.

His growling and grunting were driving me mad, making the delicious pressure build back up inside me as he thrusted into me, over and over and over again.

He fucked me so hard and deep.

I moaned and growled. I didn't recognize the sounds coming out of me, but he felt so good.

Grasping the thick blanket on the bed, I tried to hold on to something to find leverage to push back against him, but he leaned over me, placing one hand under me, in between my breasts, covering my body with his. He let go of my hair and grabbed both of my wrists, raising them up above my head with one strong hand.

That was it. Him controlling my movement, our bodies both reaching, feeling the sweat and rainwater dripping from him onto me, and with his rough breath in my ear while he pounded into me over and over, I came. My core muscles contracted so violently that it hurt, but it was the best pain I'd ever felt.

Squeaking out his name because my voice was gone, I clenched my thighs together, wrenching my torso up off of the bed, squeezing his cock so hard, and he shouted and cursed and came. I felt it, his hot cock and cum inside me, jerking and throbbing, while he held me up.

When I came down from the atmosphere, I opened my eyes as he continued to gently pump into me. Pulling me tight against his body with his arm against my chest still, he pivoted his feet and sat us down on the bed, his body still inside mine.

I moved to climb off him but he held me there, trapped in his arms, hugging me.

"Just wait," he whispered, rubbing his chin on my shoulder. "Will you wait?"

He meant would I wait to leave the ranch. He didn't have to say it. I heard it in the crack of his voice.

I did wait.

Every time I worked up the courage to leave, I'd let something, or someone, draw me back in. I clung to any excuse to stay. Jack and I were together every chance we got, sneaking into each other's rooms every night or into the room above the barn, fucking every which way from Sunday. Jack was a fierce lover, greedy but generous, and insatiable, and I'd never felt so alive.

The rest of the time I spent with Mrs. M.

Her chemo treatments were in full swing, and I went with her to the appointments and tended to her after, through vomit and nausea, headaches, bad moods. I sat next to the tub while she soaked and we talked for hours. She told me more stories about her Mr. Mitchum and about the boys and all the trouble they'd gotten into as kids. Disgustingly, frozen horse poo snowballs were a common theme. Sometimes, we didn't talk at all. I think it made her feel better just to have someone there. To not be alone.

I brushed her hair and helped her dress, and we finally watched her old movies. *Gone with the Wind* was her favorite, but I really liked Gene Kelly movies the best. He was pretty funny, and boy could that guy dance. Her illness notwithstanding, I didn't think I'd ever been so happy, not since before my parents had been killed.

I loved waking up in the mornings to breakfast with the guys. Finn bought special gourmet coffee just for me and at least four different creamers to try. I loved coconut the best. And he even tried to help me learn to cook. I think they'd all noticed I wasn't any good at it when I burned the eggs and toast I'd made for Mrs. M one day. The most complicated thing I'd ever cooked was macaroni and cheese, and usually the little microwavable bowls of it. But Finn seemed over-joyed at having houseguests to cook for. He probably went to the farmers market four times in one week, looking for new fresh ingredients for his concoctions. Everything he made tasted good to me. And he was constantly looking for things to make for Mrs. M to eat that wouldn't upset her stomach.

Kevin and I played board games while Ma slept, and the guys worked. He pretended to be annoyed, but I could tell he secretly loved it. He especially enjoyed it when he beat me. Once, after crushing me in a particularly grueling Monopoly match, he jumped up out of his chair at the kitchen table in triumph and quickly fell to the floor after putting too much weight on his broken leg. Oh, he screeched and cussed, and the others all came running.

Dr. Whitley had to be called. The vet had already been there to check on a horse, so Dr. Whitley used his portable horse x-ray machine to make sure Kevin hadn't rebroken his leg. He hadn't. But boy, did Dr. Whitley yell at him. I giggled behind my hand because I remembered when I'd been scolded by the doctor. He removed my stitches then, and it hadn't hurt a bit. I'd forgotten they were there.

After that, Kevin had been stuck on the couch or in his bed with his leg propped up on a stack of pillows. Jay even rigged a rope from the couch to a hook in the ceiling to hold Kevin's leg in the air like in the hospital, but Kevin refused to lie still, so the whole contraption came crashing down around him when he attempted to sneak off his makeshift hospital bed to steal some of the hard candies sitting in a box on the coffee table that Finn had bought for Mrs. M. She said candy sometimes soothed her stomach.

Jack began teaching me how to ride and Dean even helped. I rode Sammy at first, but I always had the overwhelming feeling I would fall, even though they both tried to convince me I wouldn't. But finally, Dean suggested I ride his horse, Tank, because he was much wider across his back, and Dean thought that might help me feel more secure eight feet up in the air on a moving thirteen-hundred-pound animal.

Jack said Biddie would be a perfect horse for me since she wasn't insanely tall, but she was still tending to her baby, Trumpet, and couldn't be ridden just yet. But I became more comfortable each time I rode. Jack even said he thought I might be a natural.

The days passed like that. Sometimes I'd get nervous and couldn't keep my eyes from roaming everywhere to look for the monster, but Jack could always calm me down. He'd distract me by leading me into a stall or the tack room to kiss me in secret, or he'd tell a joke. The guys all groaned whenever he did. They didn't seem to like his jokes. Finn called them "dad jokes," or maybe they were just surprised he told jokes at all. He seemed to get more and more relaxed around me as the days wore on.

I never said out loud what I looked for, but he knew and he looked too. I tried to hide it, especially from the other guys and Mrs. M, but of course, they noticed. They noticed the thing growing between Jack and me too.

"Evvie?" Kevin asked, using Jack's nickname for me. They all used it. Even Mrs. M. "You okay?" He and I watched a movie one night after Mrs. M had gone to bed when we heard something knocking against the house, and I gasped and jumped a mile high.

"Yeah. Sorry. Guess I'm still not used to the noises out here. So different from in town."

"It's probably just a tree branch. I'll text Finn to take a look. If it's hittin' the house, we'll need to trim it back anyway. We used to keep all that in perfect shape. Our pops could be militant about it."

"What was he like?"

"Pops? Aww, when we were kids, he was the whole world. Larger than life. He always had a project goin', buildin' something' or fixin' somethin'. He built that whole house for Granny by himself. We worshipped him. Most of the stuff I learned how to do on this ranch, I learned from him.

"But then Granny died. And his other son, my Uncle Jon, died too. We called him UJ. They died on the same day. Car accident. It broke him. Broke my dad too. He'd been hangin' on by a thread after our mama left, and when the sheriff came to tell us they'd died, my dad just disappeared. He was here physically, but otherwise, he was gone. He never really came back."

Sitting up on the couch, he faced me. "That's also the day Jack became the Jack *you* know. Somethin' changed in him too. Before all that, he was just a normal kid. Still bossy, always bossy, but he became an adult that day. Guess he had to. There wasn't another one around. He couldn't have been more'n ten years old. I was five or six."

"I'm so sorry, Kevin."

He took a deep breath. "It was a long time ago. We survived it... But that's why Jack can be so grumpy and serious. He feels like he's got the weight of the world on his shoulders. I s'pose he does since he won't let us help him." He speared me with his eyes, smiling mischievously. "You seem to have a calmin' effect on him."

Yeah, I'd noticed that too.

I changed the subject. "Why did your mom leave?"

He sat back and sighed. "Dunno. Guess you'd have to ask her that." His face changed from open and friendly to closed and angry.

"I'm sorry. I shouldn't have asked."

"No. I'm sorry. Sore subject is all."

"But you have Mrs. M. She's amazing. She's been telling me about Mr. Mitchum. I love her stories."

He chuckled. "Oh yeah? She tell you the one 'bout the time they went skinny dippin'?"

I gasped. "No! You're lying. I cannot picture her skinny dipping, ever, for any reason."

"Well, I s'pose a person will do a lotta things when they're in love."

I laughed, trying to picture Mr. and Mrs. M naked, running hand in hand into a lake. "Well, what about you? You have a girlfriend? You went on that date."

"Oh, uh, no." He shook his head. "I— No. Guess I just haven't met the right person yet. I might never." He looked at the TV.

"You will. It might have to be someone who doesn't speak English, though," I joked, trying to lighten the mood, "so they don't know when you're being so sarcastic." I wondered who would win his heart. It would have to be someone really special, someone sure of who they were, someone who could handle whatever he hid behind his smile.

CHAPTER SIXTEEN

JACK

THINGS HAD BEEN GOIN' well, and more than three weeks passed. Evvie stuck around, and I could tell she was more comfortable around us every day. She got to know my brothers, even Dean, but only a little. He could be even more closed off than me sometimes, always in the background, always watchin'.

She still didn't offer much about herself, other than that her parents had passed, and she'd been really close with her granny. They'd spent a lot of time together 'cause her mama had gone out on tour a lot and her dad had been some kinda busy professor. Her granny died, though, even before her parents, and she'd felt alone ever since.

But she gave of herself in other ways. She went with Ma to every single chemo treatment and spent hours with her afterwards, tryin' to get Ma to eat and bathe. She lay in bed with her while Ma told Evvie all about Mr. Mitchum and their life together.

I sat outside the bedroom for a while, listenin' when I'd gone up to check on Ma one afternoon. She'd been havin' a hard time keepin' food down, even with the nausea medication Doc Whitley had prescribed. But, it seemed, Evvie was able to distract her.

"You never finished telling me about you and Mr. Mitchum. You said you were happy, but I have it on good authority there's more to the story."

"Oh, well yes, there's quite a bit more."

"Will you tell me?"

"Well, we courted. He met my parents, but they weren't convinced he'd be a suitable match for me. Gregory was a bit of a free thinker. He had a lot of big ideas as a young man. And he was a musician. Betcha didn't know that."

"A musician? What did he play?"

"He played the piano."

"He did?"

"Yes. It was his first love. I always told him he should pursue it somehow, professionally—he was so good and he adored it—but he said he didn't ever want his love of music to feel like work. He wanted to keep it for just him and me. Oh, the songs he used to play for me."

"Did he have a favorite?"

"His favorite classical pianist was Beethoven, of course, but he loved jazz. Herbie Hancock, Bill Evans. So many others. We went to San Francisco many times to see jazz shows. We even went to New Orleans a time or two. Oh, how we'd dance." She laughed. "He even got up on stage once. One of his friends played the trombone in a quartet and convinced him to play a little. He loved it."

"So your parents thought he was a hippie?" Evvie giggled.

"No, not a hippie, but they weren't sure he could support me and a family. We never had one of our own. I wasn't able to have children, but, at the time, every woman was expected to have a family and every man to support one."

"Wow."

"So, he left."

"What? What do you mean he left? Like, left? He left you?" Evvie's voice climbed higher and higher, and I stifled a laugh 'cause I'd heard the story and knew the happily-ever-after would come.

"Yes. Stole away in the night. He left me a note, said he'd be back and asked me to wait. I didn't see him again for a year and a half."

"Wait just a minute. You said this was a love story." Now she was gettin' just a tad indignant. If she'd been standin', she woulda stomped her foot.

Ma chuckled. "Well, it is. You just gotta have a little patience. Now, as I'm sure you can imagine, I was devastated. Alba, my parents, even his cousin Roger, they all said, 'I told ya so.'

My parents were happy and considered him leavin' to be good luck. They tried time and time again to set me up with other young men, but I wouldn't have it. I just knew he'd come back, and I intended to wait. Liked to drive my mama crazy. She used to cry and tell me I was givin' her 'the nerves.'

"I bided my time with friends, church, and volunteerin'. That's how I became friends with Mrs. Whitley, you know. She's a native Wisperite, too, and so is Dr. Whitley. We were all friends. And then the bank opened up in town, and they put out a call for a cleanin' girl. I got it into my head that I wanted that job. Thought I could save some money for when Gregory came for me.

"Well, that done put my mama right over the edge. In her mind, no respectable young woman should be workin'. She should learn to cook and clean and prepare to be a wife. She was convinced if I worked at the bank, I'd never get married.

She went to the bank manager and forbade him to hire me, but my daddy disagreed. He was proud of me for wantin' to work hard and be responsible, so he took me down to the bank himself and told that manager to go ahead and give me the job. And he did.

"I worked there for, oh, six or seven months, Monday through Friday. Until one day. It was a Wednesday. November 27th, 1968. It was the day before Thanksgiving. I was cleanin' the lobby and the door opened. Well, by then, everybody in town used the bank, so people were always comin' and goin', so I didn't bother to turn to see who it was. But I didn't need to see him. I felt him. Gregory had come back for me. I turned, and he was down on one knee with flowers in one hand and a ring in the other.

"He'd gone home to Missoula, Montana to make somethin' of himself. And when he felt he'd done a good enough job, he returned. I never looked back. He'd found himself a job in a bank, too, if you can believe it, and made a good wage. It was the only time in my life I ever lived outside Wisper.

"We married two months later and then left for Missoula. We lived there for five years until the manager at the bank here died. Gregory applied for the position and got it. We moved home, and he ran that bank till he passed six years ago. He never wanted me to be away from my parents, and I had a sister, Joanna. She was five years younger than me. She died the year before Gregory. She lived here, too, with her husband and children."

"Were you sad you couldn't have children of your own?"

"I was, yes. But I had Gregory, and I didn't think I could ever love anyone more. And I was close to my sister, and I spent time with her children until they grew up and moved away. And I had my kids at school—I taught the fifth grade for years. And I have my boys. They've been just like my own children, but I was lucky and got to skip the dirty diaper parts." She laughed.

"Mrs. M?"

"Honey, will you just call me Ma?" Ma chided, and Evvie laughed softly.

"Okay. Ma? Can I show you something?"

"What?"

"How do you feel? Do you think you could come downstairs for a few minutes?"

I stood, makin' a little noise in the hallway, actin' like I hadn't been eavesdroppin', and knocked on Ma's open door, pokin' my head in. I thought I knew what Evvie wanted to show her, but I wanted to help Ma down the stairs.

"How you ladies doin'? Feelin' any better?"

"Well, I think I am. Evvie's wantin' to show me somethin' downstairs. Think you can help me? Now, I can walk, Jack, but just in case."

"Yes, ma'am," I said, smilin' at Evvie. She ducked her head, like maybe she felt a little shy about what she wanted to do.

We made our way downstairs, and Ma hooked her arm through mine as Evvie led us to the den. I helped Ma to sit on Evvie's bed and propped her up with pillows, and Evvie covered her with a quilt. Ma griped at us to quit fussin', so I pulled a chair next to her, and Evvie sat at the piano.

She put her fingers on the keys and the whole world faded away. I closed my eyes and let the music reach deep down inside. I'd never heard anything like it. After a few minutes, there was a noise, so I opened my eyes and saw Evvie and Ma both cryin'.

Evvie's eyes were closed as she played, and tears streamed down her face. I'd never been much of a music connoisseur, not like Finn, but I knew whatever she played was a classical song. And Ma watched Evvie. She took in every note and movement Evvie made, and the most joyful smile spread across her face. Then she closed her eyes and just listened and felt the music.

Evvie played for a long time. She'd peek every so often to make sure Ma still enjoyed it, then she'd start in on a new song. She looked like a different person when she played. Her skin lit up and she just seemed so… alive.

She loved playin' music. I couldn't imagine why she'd ever stopped. I figured it might've had somethin' to do with her mama since she'd played piano, too, but Evvie wouldn't say.

The last song she played sounded different than the rest. It wasn't like all those old classical songs. It sounded rich and thick and sad. And Evvie cried the hardest then. I'd wanted to stop her so she wouldn't hurt anymore, but I didn't think she wanted to be interrupted. She was in it. The house coulda fallen down around her, and I didn't think she'd notice.

Ma looked at me, closed her eyes, and shook her head a little because she knew, like I did, the pain Evvie tried to hide had come from that music.

My brothers had gathered outside the den door while Evvie played, Finn with his jaw on the floor, but by the time she finished the last song, they'd disappeared. I think they could see and feel that Evvie had become so emotional and so had Ma. They wanted to give the women some privacy.

I did, too, but I couldn't move, like I was glued to my seat. Evvie'd barely said a word about her life, and it was clear she'd been through a lot. She'd snapped at me when I asked about her mama, but now, she offered this thing to Ma, this thing that stripped her bare and hurt her heart just to put a smile on Ma's face. To give a little bit of love back to Ma, like she was always givin' us.

I didn't think I'd ever seen anyone be so completely selfless.

After dinner, Evvie helped Ma change into her bedclothes, and they talked some more, and Evvie fell asleep next to Ma on her bed. I didn't wake her. I knew whatever she'd given of herself had been hard on her, and she needed the rest. I sat there, in the chair in Ma's room, watchin' 'em sleep.

And all I could think was that I might be in some real trouble.

The next day, I took the afternoon off. I told my brothers to cover for Evvie and me. Well, actually, I asked 'em. They were fine with it. Said they could handle it and I knew they could. I wondered why I'd never thought to do it before.

Ma didn't have any doctor appointments, and she said she felt "relatively good, but tired." Kevin was watchin' some action movie on the TV in the livin' room, and Ma scowled but snuggled into her blanket for the duration.

Evvie had shown me somethin' of herself when she played the piano for Ma, so I got it in my head to show her somethin' too.

"Where are we going?" she asked as I drove us up Route 20 to Highway 10, into the mountains.

"There's a place up on our mountain no one in the world knows about, except Dean and me. Our dad used to take us there and his dad took him. My younger brothers don't even know about it. He took us there when we were little, maybe five or six years old, but we stopped goin' when I was nine.

Until Dean and I were teenagers, no one had been up there. I don't think my dad ever knew we'd gone back."

"Ooo, a secret hideout?"

I smiled. "Yeah, guess it is. It's a little cabin close to this bluff. It's the most beautiful place on earth. I swear it to ya."

"Your ranch is the most beautiful place on this earth," she said, gazin' out her window.

I was surprised at the immense pride I felt at hearin' her words, even though I'd had nothin' to do with makin' it so. I found myself surprised about a lotta things lately.

"I'm glad you think so. I kinda agree."

She didn't say anything more while I drove the rest of the way to the trail that led to the cabin. Barely wide enough to be considered a trail, much less a road, the path to the cabin stayed well hidden behind brush and trees, but I knew the exact bend in the lonely highway to look for. When we parked at the trailhead, I led her by the hand to the skinny path to take us the rest of the way.

We walked for awhile in the bits and pieces of sunlight that had stolen their way through the treetops, in and outta the branches. It warmed us but there was a chill in the air, and I could tell winter would be creepin' down from the tallest peaks, beggin' for attention soon enough.

The crisp pine smell and the sound of our feet crunchin' dead needles on the forest floor brought back so many memories of the cabin and of my pops and dad. Good and bad. I remembered followin' Pops up and down this very trail, feelin' so special to have been trusted with such an important secret. He'd said the cabin was the Cade men's sanctuary, a place where we could come to make important life decisions, to commune with nature, and to be together. I remembered thinkin' Finn, Kevin, and Jay would never understand the significance and import of bein' entrusted with such a thing.

The magic hadn't lasted long anyway. My dad stopped bringin' Dean and me up here when my mama left, and after Granny and UJ died, no one came up here at all. The place stood vacant till Dean and I came lookin' for a place to drink one night back in high school. We'd kinda made a silent pact that we'd never tell our brothers about it. It had been nice to have somewhere to go if we felt stressed or angry or just needed time alone. Dean used it more than me. He'd had a hard time in the military, and when he came back from his tour, spent quite a lotta time at the cabin.

"This place is so pretty. Smells so good," Evvie said, bendin' to pick a wildflower, and I thought the place had never been more beautiful. "Why'd you bring me here?"

"I, um… Well, what you did last night, for Ma? I guess I just wanted to thank you. I know it wasn't easy for you."

"Oh. No. I— No, it wasn't."

"Why'd you do it?"

"Ma had a hard day." She shrugged. "I wanted to cheer her up."

"Here, gimme your hand." I helped her step onto a thick fallen branch, and she hopped off. I stepped over it. "Yeah, but you coulda just told her a joke or somethin'. You didn't have to…"

"What?"

"You were cryin'. It looked to be painful for you."

She peeked up at me but ducked her head, shruggin' again.

We'd arrived at the end of the trail. The cabin stood a hundred yards in front of us.

"Don't do that." I held her hand in mine still and squeezed. "Don't brush it off. You were amazin'. Whatcha did? It was amazin'. It meant somethin' to Ma."

"It wasn't amazing. The piano is out of tune and I made a

ton of mistakes. My mother would have smacked my hands fifty times for all the mistakes I made."

"I couldn't tell and I don't think Ma could either. She loved your playin'. I don't think perfection was the point."

Suckin' in a deep breath, she sighed. "Yeah, I guess."

She took a couple steps toward the cabin, but I stayed put and kept hold of her hand, pullin' her back to me. "Thank you."

She gave a little half-smile. "You're welcome." She seemed to be havin' a hard time makin' eye contact. "So, this is your cabin?"

"Yep. It ain't much, but it's my second favorite place in the world. C'mon." I pulled her to the cabin nestled in the shade of the ancient forest, to the door, unlockin' it while her eyes darted all around. "You don't have to worry. No one knows about this place." She smiled but it was sad, and I opened the door.

It looked like Dean had been up to the cabin recently. There were some canned goods in the tiny kitchen area and a bottle of whiskey on the table, half-empty. Evvie looked around while I opened the windows and checked the food situation. I hadn't thought to bring anything, but now it occurred to me I shoulda packed a picnic.

The cabin consisted of just one large room and, really, not that large with only a small nook for the kitchen, a small pantry, and a tiny root cellar built into the earth crowdin' the north wall. The main part of the cabin was divided into different areas by sparse furniture and a couple wood beams through the middle.

Tucked into a corner, a small bed make up a bedroom, and an ancient loveseat and a wooden straight-back chair surrounded the fire on one side for the livin' room. An old cast iron bathtub sat on the other side, and a small round table with two chairs made up a tiny dinin' room. We didn't even have a bathroom, just a small outhouse about twenty yards away from the door. Each wall had a window and that was about it. But it was shelter and warm in the winter.

"So, this is it. Like I said, not much."

"I like it."

"Hungry? I'm sorry. I didn't think to bring anything, but we got rice and beans and some canned fruit."

"Sure. Sounds rustic." She giggled softly and I loved the sound.

I got to work. I pulled her back outside, and we found wood and kindlin', and then I prepared the rustic rice and beans and set it to cook in an old dutch oven over the fire. She asked me questions about my pops and about the things we used to do at the cabin. I talked a little. And then there was nothin' left to do but wait, and a potent silence hung in the air between us.

Neither one of us moved. We stared at each other. There were so many thoughts runnin' through my mind I wanted to tell her, but I didn't know how. I didn't know what any of 'em meant, and I still had this overwhelmin' feelin' she'd disappear. I didn't want her to, but I didn't know how to ask for it, and I didn't think it was somethin' she knew how to give.

After a few minutes, she rose from her chair at the table and walked to me standin' against the little half-wall separatin' the kitchen from the rest of the cabin. She wrapped her arms around my back, layin' her head against my chest. My heart raced as I listened to her breathe, and she reached up on her toes to kiss my neck. She rubbed her lips against my jaw and her cheek against mine and kissed her way to my mouth.

Her kiss was slow and lazy and scorchin', all heavy breath and bodies pressin' together, but no sound. It lasted a day or so it felt, and I wrapped my arms around her, liftin' her straight up, her feet danglin' above the floor as I carried her to the bed.

I laid her down and pulled my fingers through her hair, spreadin' it over her shoulders and all around her, then slowly removed her shoes and socks and jeans. I removed my own, and my shirt, and sat next to her.

The quiet in the cabin had infected us both, and somethin' about it made me nervous. But she crawled behind me, kissin' my neck and shoulders, pushin' at me till I lay back on the bed.

She kissed me everywhere. Up and down my arms and chest, lickin' and suckin' my nipples into her warm mouth, and down my stomach, my ribs and hips. Still, we made no sound, except for breath.

I didn't touch her then, only watched. I was mesmerized by her, by her confidence, by the fire in her eyes.

She moved down further and took my cock in her hand, spreadin' the cum leakin' out with her thumb, then pumped slowly.

I moaned. Nothin' coulda stopped the sound. It felt so fuckin' good. Takin' her sweet time, she felt me, rubbed her fingers up and down, took my balls in her hand. I felt so bared to her. Even though we'd already had plenty of sex, this felt different. Somehow, more… private.

Watchin' her while she explored my body, I felt like she might be tryin' to memorize it as she stroked my skin, over and over. She pressed her fingertip into the thick vein and followed the length of it up to the head of my cock, tracin' her finger around it, then leaned down and took me into her mouth. My breath hitched and I gasped, and she smiled. She liked the power she held over my body. I liked it too.

But then she released me.

My dick had hardened to the point of pain, and I swore I

coulda cried, but she crawled up my body and mounted me, and I'd never felt anything so perfect in my whole life. Rollin' her hips, she moaned softly, lookin' in my eyes. Holdin' me there, I was caught in her gaze, as she rode me slow and so, so good.

Over and over, she took me further inside her, and I bucked and rolled my hips in time with hers. Reachin' up, I held her face in my hands, caressin' her cheeks and lips with my thumbs, rememberin' the first time I'd done it in the hospital when we'd first met.

The intimacy between us stole my breath away. I'd never before been so vulnerable and open to another person, never touched another person like this. But I didn't feel scared. Not with Evvie.

Somethin' cracked and broke inside me, like I had a two-hundred-pound weight on my chest. I couldn't breathe. It hurt all of a sudden; all this intense connection became too much. She was destroyin' me from the inside out, and the devastation made me want her more.

She made me wanna never let her go.

I wanted to tell her but I didn't know how. I opened my mouth to tell her, but I didn't have the words.

"Evvie…"

Somethin' changed in her expression when I said her name, and she pushed her hands against my shoulders for leverage to fuck harder. She ground herself against me, pullin' me further and further out and back into her body with each wave of her hips. I leaned up on my elbows to kiss her, and the change in the angle caused my body to rub her just right, and she whimpered.

The sound of her voice and the wet, slow glide of her soft, pink skin against my cock made me frantic. I dug my fingers into her hips, buckin' up into her so hard.

She became frantic, too, ridin' me faster and faster, and she shoved her hands into my hair. I captured her mouth with mine and felt her body grippin' my cock inside, suckin' me in deeper and deeper. It felt like there wasn't any part of us not connected.

She huffed her breath into my mouth and gasped, throwin' her head back, and I leaned up as she pulled me by my hair to her chest, strainin' and contractin'. Her whole body enveloped me, inside and out, and we came, silently, as the old bed creaked beneath us and evenin' surrounded us.

CHAPTER SEVENTEEN

EVERLEA

WE SPENT the night in the cabin, tangled up together in front of the fire.

I'd made love to him in that cabin. It hadn't been just sex for me.

I didn't tell him. I couldn't.

It had been three months since the last time I'd seen Paul. Far too long for his liking. He would come for me soon, and every day I stayed at the ranch, I put Jack and his family more and more in danger.

And every day, it grew harder and harder to leave.

But I'd fallen in love with Jack. And I knew then, it meant I *had* to leave. There couldn't be any more excuses. If I didn't go, he'd die, and I loved him enough that I could go because a world where he didn't exist would be a world I wouldn't want to live in.

Even if I couldn't be with him, I needed him to exist. His family needed him, Ma, the world needed Jack. He was so kind and giving. And good. He cared for everyone, even if he didn't say it.

He loved hard.

It would hurt. No. It would destroy me. I didn't know how I'd survive it. My parents were gone. No matter how much I missed them, I'd never see them again. But with Jack, I'd have to *make* myself stay away. And I couldn't even think about Ma. It would be the worst thing I'd ever done to another person, but to keep her safe, to keep Jack safe, I had to go.

I decided. The next day, I would somehow convince Jack to take me back to my car, and I would leave.

But before I ran, I would give all of myself to him. Even if it could only be for one night. I knew I'd never see him again, and I never wanted to forget what it felt like to be in love with him. To make love to him. I realized he'd reached something inside me I hadn't ever known I possessed: the ability to *be* loved by another person.

I did my best to push away the sadness and despair I felt and just concentrated on Jack. On his smile and his laugh and the love radiating out of him. He didn't say the words but I felt it. Or I convinced myself I felt it so I could always have it. It was in the way he touched me, the gentle caress of his strong fingers on my skin. The soft way his lips pressed against mine. The way he looked at me, with his beautiful eyes always searching and trying to capture mine.

We played. I screeched and giggled as he chased me around the cabin, tickling me, and I tickled him too. It never would have occurred to me such a hardened cowboy could be so ticklish, but he was and he laughed and giggled, too, like a little boy as I attacked his ribs and the backs of his knees with my fingers. I would remember the sound for the rest of my life.

We sat naked, wrapped in blankets in front of the fire as he fed me rice and beans from an oversized wooden spoon.

Well, mostly naked, I still hadn't shown him my scars, and I wouldn't. I'd leave and he'd never have to know.

"Will you tell me about this man? What's his name?"

"His name is Paul. I don't know his last name. He's just some guy who met my mother years ago at a concert in New York City and fell in love with her just like every other man she ever met. The glorious Clare." I mocked my mother's name. She never used her last name, like she thought she was Madonna.

"So, she dated him?"

"She had an affair with him or a one-night stand, at least."

"What's he look like?"

"I don't want to talk about him now."

"Evvie."

I sighed. "He's tall. Well, taller than me, but not as tall as you. He has white-blond hair and beady, black eyes. He's just some creep."

"Evvie, if he was just some creep, you woulda gone to the cops a long time ago. Tell me what he did to you. How did he hurt you?"

"Please? I really don't want to talk about him right now."

"I know, but if you'd just speak to Carey. I know he could help us. Maybe put the guy in jail. You wouldn't have to worry anymore. Wouldn't be scared all the time."

"Maybe."

"You gotta trust someone at some point. Carey is really good at his job. Lemme call him."

"No, Jack. Not yet."

"You gotta give me somethin'. How can I protect you if I don't know what I'm up against?" Pushing my hair out of my face, he tucked it behind my ear. "I *will* protect you from this man, Evvie. I won't let him hurt you. I promise."

I knew he wouldn't give up. I didn't want to tell him the

severity of my past. That fucking monster had taken every-thing from me. If Jack knew, I wouldn't be able to stop him from calling the police, and they would lead Paul right to Jack.

I distracted him with my fingers and hands and my mouth.

"Can we talk about this later?" I asked, grabbing an open can of sliced peaches from the hearth in front of the fire. Dipping my fingers in, I pulled one out, then kneeled in front of him and fed it to him. He moaned and chewed and lifted my hand to his mouth to suck the juice from my fingers as I licked it from his chin. I fed him more, licked more, and kissed him with his mouth full of peaches. The juice ran down his neck to his chest, and I feasted on him. He wrapped his arms around me as I crawled over him, taking him inside my body.

We made love twice more through the night, and I committed every single movement and sound he made to memory.

When we woke in the morning, wrapped in each other, pressing our bodies together, seeking heat to ward off the early mountain cold, we made love again, then walked to the bluff. He'd been right. It was beautiful, majestic, and breath-taking as the sun came up in the vast Wyoming sky.

We sat perched on a small cliff with our legs dangling over the edge, watching as the lavender night receded and all the lights in the stars went out and the glowing pinks and oranges and blues rose in the distance, setting our world on fire.

I was jealous of that sky because it would always look down on him. It would always know where he was and would have the privilege of being with him, surrounding him, touching him.

But I only looked out for a moment. The rest of the time, I looked at Jack. His strong shoulders with all the world on top. His capable arms and steady hands, sturdy back. His long, solid legs that held him up and always carried him in the right direction.

And his face.

I studied the lines around his eyes when he smiled at me. His full lips with the little sideways tug. I watched how the breeze ruffled his dark chestnut hair and how he'd push his fingers through it 'cause it annoyed him, then he'd stuff it all in his baseball cap, backward, and how the ends would curl up under the edge of the hat.

And his eyes when he looked at me. They shined and took my breath away. I knew the feeling would be something I'd have to get used to, not having enough air to breathe. He would keep my breath with him when I left. He deserved to keep it because he owned it. My breath, my heart, my skin and bones, my blood.

My soul.

"What's that look for?"

"What look?"

"That silly look you got, right here," he joked, spreading his fingers over my face like an octopus. "Why you lookin' at me like that?"

I swatted his hand away so he'd stop blocking my view. "I just like looking at you. Is that such a bad thing?"

"Well, yeah, when you got the most beautiful view in the whole world in front of you. You're missin' it," he said, gesturing out in front of us with a wave of his arm.

"I'm not missing anything. I *am* looking at the most beautiful view in the world."

He scoffed. "I think you need to get your eyes checked." But he peeked back at me. "Sometimes, the things you say—

Nobody's ever said anything like that to me before. I kinda like it."

"Oh yeah? You like me telling you how pretty you are?" I joked, crawling into his lap.

"Pretty? Oh no. Handsome. *Rugged.* Good lookin'." Wrapping his arms around me, he hugged me and I snuggled back, reveling in how the strength and heat from his body made me feel so safe. "You ready? I'm gonna get the book thrown at me when we get home. The first time I take time off and I don't come back all night? You know what? It's your fault. You're a bad influence." He laughed, kissing my cheek.

"I'll take the heat. You can always blame me."

I deserved it.

He didn't get the book thrown at him. His brothers joked and prodded him, but no one yelled at him, though Dean didn't seem very happy. He always seemed mistrustful of me, and he had every right to feel that way. I hoped when I was gone, Dean would say, "I told you so" and Jack would agree and get over me. I hoped his brothers would help him and Ma, and it would be like I'd never been there. Like I'd never existed.

We stood next to his truck, between the house and barn. "I'm gonna head into the office, make some phone calls. You oughta go up and get a nap. We didn't do much sleepin' last night," he said, leaning down to kiss the edge of my bottom lip.

"No, I think I'll hang out with Ma. I was thinking, though, will you take me to pick up my car later? It's silly for it to just sit there. I can drive her to her appointments so you don't have to stop working every time."

"Sure."

"And maybe we could stop by my house? I'd like to pick up a few more things."

"Oh yeah? What, you think you're just gonna move in?" he joked, lifting my chin with his finger when I looked down at the ground. "I'm just kiddin'. You okay?"

"Yeah, I'm fine. Just tired. Maybe a nap is a good idea. Go on, go to work. I'll be fine," I lied, plastering the closest thing to a smile I could manage on my face.

"Okay. See ya later then." He kissed my nose, and I ambled up to the house.

"Well good mornin', honey. Have a good time last night?" Ma asked when I crawled into bed with her. I'd meant to spend my last time with her talking and listening to her tell me more about Mr. Mitchum, but as soon as I saw her face, my tears broke free. I tried so hard, but I just couldn't hold them in. "Oh, sweetheart. What is it? What's wrong?"

"I'm sorry. I-I'm… I miss my parents." It was the truth, but it had nothing to do with why I cried.

"Oh, there, there," she cooed, wrapping me in her arms, and I cried harder. "It's hard to miss a person, isn't it? There's so much you wanna say to 'em, but you can't. I know, sweet girl."

"Does it get better? Does it always hurt so much?"

"It does get better in some ways. Yes. But it's always there. I can't lie to you. You're just havin' a bad day, hm? You're tired."

Looking at her, I sniffled. "Yes. I am tired." Tired of running, of being scared, being alone.

"I have a feelin' you didn't get much sleep last night," she said, smirking. "You're fallin' in love with him, aren't you?"

"Yes." I cried. I held my breath to stop the sobs I knew were coming, but they broke free too. "I love him so much."

"Oh, oh," she chuckled, "I know it can be overwhelmin'. But the lucky part is, I'm pretty sure he's in love with you too. What are these tears for, girl? It's a good thing."

I couldn't tell her the truth. I couldn't tell her I'd fallen in love and lost it all in one night. "Will you tell me more about Mr. Mitchum?"

"Sure I will. He's my favorite person to talk about. Hmm. Well, he was a charmer," she said, smoothing my hair away from my wet, snotty face. "He always said this thing. Anytime he left the house I'd ask him where he was goin'. He'd say, 'crazy, baby,' and I'd scold him and say, 'now, Gregory,' and he'd waltz back over to me, kiss me, and say, 'you drive me crazy, baby.' Oh, it always made me blush and swoon."

I wiped the tears from my cheeks with the back of my hand. Just the sound of her steady voice helped me calm down.

"I can still hear his voice sayin', 'You drive me crazy, baby.' Did I tell you 'bout the time he brought home four Christmas trees?"

"Four?" I laughed through my tears.

"Four. 'Cause I had the flu, and I couldn't go with him to pick one out. He couldn't decide which one was the prettiest, so he bought 'em all and brought 'em home so I could pick. But then he decided he liked all of 'em, so we decorated two in the house, brought one here for the boys, and the other one we donated to the children's ward at the hospital. I was cleanin' pine needles outta the house for years. I bet there's still some there under the rug in the livin' room."

I listened to her for a while as she told me so many stories. I wrapped them up in my memory, too, so I could take them with me. The way she described Mr. Mitchum made me feel like I knew him. I would take him with me too.

I fell asleep snuggled up to her while she stroked my hair and remembered love, and I prepared to lose it.

CHAPTER EIGHTEEN

JACK

"SON OF A BITCH." I slammed the farrier's bill down on the desk in the office.

"What?" Dean stuck his head in the door as he walked past.

"I forgot to pay the damn farrier."

"Isn't like you to forget."

"No shit."

Steppin' into the room with me, he shut the door. "You been a little distracted lately."

I glared at him. I didn't need him to point it out. I was tired and irritable. Evvie and I'd had the most amazin' night together, but this mornin', there was somethin' in her eyes.

"It's just…"

"Just what? Spit it out. I ain't got all day."

"Just, what do you really know about this woman, Jack? She's nice and all and I know Ma's fond of her, but I mean, we don't really know anything about her. She never talks about herself."

I busied myself with paperwork, avoidin' his eyes.

"I get that you like screwin' her but—"

"Jesus, Dean!"

He raised his hands in front of his chest. "I know. Sorry, but I dunno. It's just a little suspicious. And…" he hesitated.

"And what?"

"And Doc P mentioned we might be a little behind on the vet bills the other day when he came out to check the mares."

"Oh, he did? Did he also mention he raised his prices again? I can't give him money we don't have, Dean."

"Right. I just thought, maybe your head's not in the game? I mean, you were out all night. That's not like you either."

"Don't worry 'bout it. I'll figure it out."

"Maybe it's time we talk about Jay's idea. Just talk about it. It can't hurt."

"No? You ever looked up one of them dude ranches? I have. They're pretty fuckin' fancy. You think rich people are gonna wanna stay in our ramshackle ol' house? Share a bathroom with us? This idea of Jay's would take a lot of money. The same money I don't have to even pay the damn vet."

"Jack—"

"I said I'll figure it out!"

"Brother, I'm just tryin' to help."

I sighed. "I know that."

"Look, I got some money left from my last security job. I'll pay the farrier and the vet if you'll promise to hear Jay out. He's got some good ideas. About money too."

"I don't want your money, Dean. Thanks, but this is up to me."

"Dammit, Jack. No, it's not just up to you. It's up to us all. We all live here. It's my home too. I expect to be here rest of my life, just like you. Lemme help."

Collapsin' back into my chair, I pinched the bridge of my

nose between my fingers. I felt a headache comin' on. "Fine. I'll think about it."

"Good. Gimme that bill. Where's the vet bill?"

Swipin' the stack of unpaid bills from the desktop, I held 'em out for him. Might as well get the shock over with all at once.

To his credit, he didn't react. He took 'em from my hand, looked 'em over and said, "Okay then," and walked outta the office but stopped and turned at the door.

"Oh, almost forgot. You notice somebody hangin' around by the front gate?"

"No. Why?"

"I found a pile of cigarette butts by the road there. Probably somebody just dumped 'em. There were some tread marks in the mud, too, after the storm the other night. Pretty rude to stop right at someone's front door to dump trash. I cleaned it up. Just thought I'd check with ya." He knocked on the door frame twice and left.

Tread marks in mud out in the country weren't anything to get excited over, but they weren't the first. I hadn't said anything to Evvie, but I'd noticed some, too, by my truck at the trailhead this mornin'. Still, not a huge deal, but the turnoff for the cabin was pretty well hidden. Unless someone pulled off there by sheer coincidence, they would've had to follow us to find it.

It had come time to call Carey. Whether Evvie liked it or not.

She slept for hours with Ma, but when she woke, she asked me again to take her to her car. So, we drove out to Jackson in silence. She wouldn't talk to me. Every attempt I made resulted in an "mmhm," a "yes," or a "no." And it made me nervous.

After last night, I'd thought—

"Do you just want to head home? I'll meet you after I stop at my house?" she asked in a quiet voice, almost a whisper, when we pulled up to the employee parking lot across the street from the hospital.

"Alright then."

She smiled at me but it seemed hollow, then she climbed outta the truck, and I watched her walk to an old, rusted brown two-door sedan. While she fumbled with the keys and dropped 'em, I wrote the license plate number down on a slip of paper and tucked it into my pocket. I didn't know why I did it, but I just had this feelin' I should. The plates looked old, and the sticker in the corner had expired two years ago.

I followed her back to her rental house in Wisper, up the sidewalk, and into her kitchen. She didn't say one word till we got inside.

"I thought you were gonna meet me at the ranch."

"Just wanted to make sure you got here safe." I knew she was gonna run. I wanted her to tell me to my face.

"Oh. Right. Thanks."

"Why we here, Evvie?"

"Oh, I just, you know, just wanted to pick up a few more things. Check the mail."

"Oh, yeah? Got a lotta mail comin' to you here? Is it addressed to Eve or Everlea?"

She turned to look at me leanin' up against her fancy new fridge. "I don't know. I guess I probably don't have much mail."

"So, then, why are we here?"

Lookin' down at the floor, she peeked up at me. "I wanted to check, to make sure he hadn't been here."

"Why didn't you just say that?"

"I don't know."

"Bullshit. You asked to get your car and to come here so

you could grab that duffel bag." Noddin' to her secret spy room behind me, I said, "You were gonna run."

Her eyes snapped to mine. "No, I just, I just want to be prepared. That's all."

"Prepared for what?"

She didn't answer. She just stared at the floor.

"To run," I said and laughed, but it was bitter and it hurt. "Here we go again."

She raised her eyes to mine. "What does that mean?"

"It means you're lyin' again."

"I'm sorry." She sighed. "It's been a while now. I guess, I-I'm just getting nervous."

"Why? Don't you trust me to keep you safe?"

"You don't understand."

"No. You're right. I don't. 'Cause you haven't told me shit."

"Jack."

"You know, I got my family to think about. My business. And Ma. She's been through a lot. I don't mean to let you put her through more." It was all true, but it wasn't what made my heart drop into my boots and my breath catch in my throat. The headache I'd been feelin' comin on all day pounded in my head.

She was fixin' to run, and there probably wasn't a damn thing I could do about it.

And goddammit, I'd been right. I never shoulda trusted her. I gave and she took, and she would leave.

"Jack. I, I'm—" Tears collected in her eyelashes, and then she stopped cold. Mid-sentence. She blinked once. Holdin' her breath, she walked over to the slidin' door in the small dinin' room behind me. When she got to it, she looked outside. Even from the kitchen, I could see her eyes scannin' the back yard and football field beyond. She took one step back and pulled a piece of paper from the door frame. It had been folded into a tiny square, but it was neon pink so it stood out. I'd been so pissed at her for wantin' to leave me that I hadn't thought to check the house.

She tried to hide the note, tried to pretend she hadn't just pulled it out right in front of me. "You're right." She swiped her finger under her eyes. "You have your family. Your business. I'll just mess things up. You should probably go," she said, but her hands shook and her voice was so quiet and thin. She was terrified. The color drained from her face, and her eyes wouldn't stay in one place for more than a second or two.

"Evvie, give it to me."

"What? No, it's just time for me to move on. But, um, could you just tell Ma goodbye for me?" She turned so I couldn't see her face.

"Everlea, gimme the goddamn note." I walked up behind her and reached around to pull it from her hand.

"No!" She whipped around and pushed me, and I staggered back 'cause I didn't expect it. "Get away from me. Don't you get it? I *don't* trust you. I don't trust anyone. This was never gonna work anyway. You don't trust anyone either. Not even your own brothers. You're such a fucking martyr. 'Oh poor me. Everybody looks up to me. Everybody expects me to do everything.' Your brothers have been trying to help you, but you won't even let them speak. So don't fucking talk to me about trust!"

"Evvie—"

"No!" she shouted, tears streamin' down her face. "You don't know me. You don't want to know me. There's no point." Stormin' past me to her bedroom, she slammed the door, and I heard the lock turn. I stood on the other side, listenin' to her panic. It sounded like she was grabbin' things outta drawers.

"Everlea, please, let me in."

No response.

"I can't help if you don't tell me what's goin' on."

Still, she didn't respond, and I hung my head. And that's when I saw the pink note crumpled into a ball on the floor. I picked it up. In a messy, all-caps scrawl, it read, "LEAVE HIM OR HE DIES" with a smiley face and heart.

She yanked the door open with another garbage bag thrown over her shoulder. Her mouth was open so she could yell at me some more and pretend to push me further away, but when she saw me holdin' the note, she stopped dead in her tracks.

"Everlea, please, let me—"

She backed up till she couldn't go any further. "No," she whispered. "He means it. He'll do it. He's done it before."

"He's not gonna hurt me," I said, rollin' my eyes.

"No? You think he can't?" Shakin' her head, her face was covered in utter despair. "Well, I. Beg. To. Differ!" she whispered, her voice thick and strangled. Droppin' the garbage bag, she ripped her shirt over her head.

Her hair tumbled down all over her shoulders, and the honey brown color set off the red and pink burns all over her. All the breath rushed outta me and I staggered back, hittin' the edge of the bedroom door, slammin' it closed, and she jumped.

When she'd hid her body from me, I assumed she had some weird scar, an odd birthmark or somethin', but the entire right side of her torso had been burned. Deep, dark, thick burns. Her right rib cage was covered in 'em, under her breast and around to her back. They spread up her right arm, over her right shoulder.

"So, now you know. You see what he's capable of? If I don't leave, he will kill you."

I couldn't speak. My heart thudded in my chest.

Steppin' toward her, I reached for her.

"Are you *stupid*? You still don't get it! He killed my parents. Burned them alive in their bed. I heard them scr— I saw them—"

Her legs gave out and she dropped to the floor, and I rushed to her. I scooped her up in my arms, but she fought me. "Don't touch me! Let me go!" She twisted and kicked, and I held on tighter while she screamed and cried till she lost all her fight.

It took a while, and even then, she still cried. I rocked her and shushed her and wrapped her in the blanket from her bed.

"He's killed everyone I've ever loved," she whispered. "He'll kill you. Your brothers, Ma. He'll kill anyone who gets in his way. Don't you understand? I can't have you. I'm so stupid. This was a mistake. A bad one. The worst I've ever made." In the smallest voice, like a little girl, she said, "He's going to kill you."

"Shh, shh. He won't." I pushed her hair from her tear-soaked cheeks.

"Why do you keep saying that? Do you think this is a joke? He will."

"No, I don't think it's a joke. I'm callin' Carey." I pulled my phone from my pocket.

"What? No. Jack, you promised!"

"Evvie, it's too late for that. Carey can help. Dean can too. He was a sniper in the Marines. He can watch the house. We can protect you."

"What? No. No." Pushin' back against me, she used her elbows to knock my arms away in some kinda self-defense move. She sniffled and crawled away from me, searchin' frantically through all the clothes on her bedroom floor to find a shirt. Pullin' one on, she stood and swiped the garbage bag from the floor.

Her legs shook, so she stumbled but made her way to the bedroom door, then threw it open so hard it hit the wall, some of the plaster fallin' to the floor where the doorknob knocked it loose.

Runnin' to the little room for her duffel, she hoisted it over her back and ran past me standin' dumbfounded in her bedroom doorway. She stopped when she got to the front door, facin' away from me.

"I'm sorry, Jack. I can't let you do that. I have to go." Pullin' the heavy wood door open, she pushed out the screen and ran.

It took thirty seconds for my brain to register what was really happenin', but finally, I went after her, yellin' her name, but she jumped in her car and locked the door.

"Evvie! Stop! Dammit, open the door!"

She shook her head, cryin'. She cried so hard, I didn't think she could even see to drive, but she tore outta the driveway and left me standin' there wonderin' why in the fuck I hadn't thought to park behind her.

I stood there for about a minute, tryin' to breathe, then ran to my truck, threw it in gear, and raced to find her. But when I got off West Street, I realized there were a million different directions she coulda gone in, and my old truck was about as fast as a slug on sand. I turned and headed back to the ranch, callin' Carey on the way.

"What's goin' on, man? Ready for that beer?"

"I need your help. Come to the ranch, now."

He heard the fear in my voice. "I'll be right there."

He'd only been three minutes behind me, but while I waited for Carey, I filled my brothers in. Ma came downstairs, too, and she cried and worried for Evvie.

"She just left? Just like that?" Finn asked.

"That's why she's been so secretive. She's probably so scared, Jack," Ma said, snifflin'.

Dean put two and two together, finally understandin' what had been goin' on. "Those tire tracks and cigarette butts…"

"Yeah, and there were other tracks by my truck this mornin'. Goddammit, I shoulda called Carey weeks ago."

"But who is this guy?" Jay asked. "How does she know he's after her?"

"He left a note." I pulled the pink square from my pocket and dropped it on the table. Dean picked it up, read it, and set it back down, lookin' at me.

"What's it say?" Finn picked it up. "Oh, shit." He passed it to Jay.

Carey walked in then, lookin' around at all of us standin' there. It took me a minute to collect my thoughts, but I started talkin'. I told him everything I could remember Evvie sayin' about the guy, which wasn't much. He called one of his deputies and sent him and two uniformed officers to look for her car.

I handed him the slip of paper with her license plate number. "I doubt it's legal. The sticker's two years old."

"Okay. I'll call it in. It ain't much to go on, but I got somebody I can ask for help on this. Gimme a minute."

Carey stepped onto the porch to make his calls, and I ran back to the den to look through Evvie's stuff. I ripped the place apart, lookin' for anything. Anything that might tell me where she'd go, where'd she been. Somethin' about her parents. I didn't know.

"Jack, lemme help. What are we lookin' for?"

"Anything, Finn. Anything! I gotta find her." I pushed the mattress to the floor, lookin' underneath it and the box spring.

"Somethin' like this?"

I spun around to see him holdin' a book. "What? What is it?"

"It's a book of songs. I'm no piano player but this ain't classical music. It ain't one of Granny's old books. It's a book of songs by someone named Clare Donovan."

"Her mama's name was Clare. Gimme that." I swiped it from Finn's hand and flipped through the pages, but there was nothin' in it except a buncha lines and dots. "There's nothin' here."

"Jack, there is somethin'. Now we know her last name. Everlea Donovan. It probably ain't Smith like she said."

"Okay, I got somebody workin' on this," Carey said, clickin' his cell phone off when he entered the den. "What is that? Find somethin'?"

I shoved the book at him. "It's nothin' but it says her mama's name. Maybe that'll help?"

"Yeah, it might. Jack, why'd you wait so long to call me about this?"

"Evvie didn't want—" The familiar sound of gravel crunchin' under tires stopped me cold, and I bolted from the den. Throwin' the livin' room door open, I watched as Evvie's car came to a stop next to my truck. She climbed out and just stood there lookin' at me.

I couldn't move. I'd never been so angry at anyone in my life, but the relief I felt seein' her safe and in one piece was staggerin'.

My breath shook its way outta my lungs while she walked slowly to the porch and stood at the bottom of the steps, lookin' up at me.

"I couldn't do it. It hurts too much. I can't leave you. I'm sure you'd rather not— I-I've dragged you into this. I wouldn't blame you if you didn't want me. If you want me to leave. I've put you in danger, all of you. I'm so selfish but I want you so much. There's never been anyone or anything I've wanted the way I want you. I'm so sorry. I'm so fucking sorry." She sobbed, huggin' herself.

I didn't say a word. I stomped down the stairs and picked her up, holdin' her so tight. All the air rushed outta her in a desperate exhalation, and she sucked breath back in and sobbed some more. I carried her back up the stairs and sat on the porch swing, rockin' her till she stopped.

Ma walked out onto the porch and cocked a shotgun. "Who's in danger? Not me," she said, plantin' her legs, ready to rumble.

"Jesus Christ, Ma," Kevin whispered, hobblin' through the door behind her to take the gun from her hands.

"Kevin Christian Cade, watch your language."

CHAPTER NINETEEN

EVERLEA

"HIS NAME IS PAUL. That's all I really know about him. He's been hunting me for nine years. It's a game to him. He's deranged. Sick."

I looked around Jack's living room at all the faces looking back at me. Jack sat next to me on the couch, staring at his hands folded together in a tight knot between his knees. The sheriff sat on my other side, holding his phone toward me, recording me. He said it would be important so he didn't forget anything. It could help someone named Billie locate Paul.

"Why? Why is he hunting you?" he asked.

"He thinks I'm my mother. I know that sounds crazy. He was obsessed with her. I... I don't really know how else to explain. My mother was a world-renowned pianist. She was kind of famous. Not like a pop star, but she played all around the world with a lot of really cool musicians. She was beautiful. She had fiery red hair."

I inhaled as much air as I could fit in my lungs. This was the first time I'd ever told anyone my story, and I didn't know *how* to tell it, but I knew I had to.

"When I was eight or nine, she performed at a concert in New York City, in Central Park. A summer concert with the New York Philharmonic Orchestra. I wasn't there—she never let me go with her—but I saw a video of it after. She was magnificent.

"But I wasn't the only one who thought so. She always had fans. Lots of them and some were weird, I guess. Sent her letters and odd gifts, pictures of themselves, clothing they'd worn. She'd show them to me and it creeped me out, but she loved it. She loved the attention.

"But, apparently, she gained a *new* fan that night. They met after the show. She didn't tell me this. He did. Years later. He said they had an affair. I don't know if that's something she did a lot, but it wouldn't surprise me. She was shallow and insecure, and she needed other people's attention like she needed air. My father didn't fawn all over her, so I guess she looked elsewhere.

"When I was eleven, he killed them." It sounded blunt and cold, but I didn't know how else to say it.

Ma gasped.

"How?" Sheriff Carey asked.

"He set our house on fire."

"You were there?" he asked again, his voice the only sound in the room. It didn't sound like anyone breathed.

"Yes. I woke in the middle of the night to a sound, a whooshing noise. Creaking and crackling. I looked out my window, and there was a man standing in our yard holding something in his hand. I knew he was a bad man. I knew he shouldn't have been there. And I knew something was *very* wrong.

"I ran to their bedroom and tried to open their door, but it wouldn't budge and the doorknob was so hot—I heard my skin sizzle." I clenched my fingers into a fist, remembering the pain. "I found something in the hall, I don't know, a curtain or towel or something, and used it to try to open the door, but something blocked it or held it closed."

Squeezing my eyes shut, I tried to push the images away, but they just kept coming. They made my head swim. "I couldn't get it open. And then I heard the sound of glass breaking, and the door swung open so fast, it sucked me into the room."

I held my breath, blinking the quick-forming tears away, but they overflowed my eyes as I saw the fire, like it was raging right in front of me. Like I was back there again. My heart raced and I shook so hard.

Occasionally, I peeked at the walls around us to make sure they weren't on fire too. I knew they weren't but it felt so real. The brutal heat surrounded me, and the light in the room faded as I heard the whooshing and cracking of wood.

"It was only a few seconds, I think, but I remember every inch of that room. The broken window, the dresser, my mother's beautiful antique armoire. All her clothes in flames. I used to hide in it when my grandma and I would play hide and seek. The flames were roaring, engulfing… eating everything. The bed. They were— I-I h-heard them scr—"

Jack grabbed and squeezed my hand, and I looked at him. Whatever he saw on my face scared him. His eyebrows fell and he closed his eyes, then reached for me, pulling me into his lap. I couldn't stop shaking and my teeth chattered. Sobs broke free, and the heaviness of despair settled in my chest, crushing my heart and lungs.

The pain had surfaced and it scared me to death. I'd buried it away so long ago. I hadn't allowed myself to feel it, not once since that night. I hadn't ever thought I could recover from facing those memories.

I wondered for a second if pain could cause a seizure.

Trembling in his arms, I listened to Jack breathing, trying to match my breaths to his.

No one said a word.

"Apparently, our next-door neighbor was a retired Chicago firefighter, and suddenly, I was pulled back out into the hallway. I was burning. I smelled it. Or maybe th-that was from— I couldn't feel it, the burning, and I don't remember much of the rest of that night. I know he got me out of there, and they took him in an ambulance too. I guess I kind of checked out. Does that make sense?" I turned my head, looking at Jack, and he nodded, wiping the tears from under my eyes with his thumbs.

I gulped in breaths. I'd survived the hardest part.

Afraid my confession had scared them or made them angry, I looked around again. Tears streamed down Ma's face, her hand covering her mouth, and Jay crouched next to her, holding her other hand. Dean stood looking out one of the living room windows. Kevin had moved to the stairs at some point, and he peeked at me through the wood slats of the railing. He closed his eyes when I glanced his way. I didn't see Finn, but I heard him behind me in the kitchen, pacing. And the sheriff hadn't moved an inch.

"Were you questioned?" he asked.

"I don't remember. And I didn't remember the man in our yard until years later. After the... fire, when I was released from the hospital, I lived in a state home, an orphanage, I guess, until I turned eighteen. They pretty much just kick you out at that point. I'd already graduated so I could work. I lived in a halfway house until I found a job and could get my own apartment. I did, though. Find a job. At a globe factory." I shook my head, remembering the oddity of my old job. "My job was to pull a lever. That's all I did. I pulled the lever to make a machine press a sheet of acrylic into a half circle shape.

"It was a good job. I even had health insurance, well, for a month or two. I loved working. I loved the people. I was getting to know them, and they were getting to know me. I'd even been invited to one of their children's birthday parties.

"But, one day, when I went in for my shift, we were all sent home. Later, there was a meeting and the managers told us the factory was closing. Going out of business. We were all out of a job. I felt so bad for my new friends. Lots of them had kids, families, and they cried and got angry. I was terrified because I didn't know how I would feed myself.

"I looked for a new job. I had a tiny studio apartment and bills to pay. I needed food. My parents left me some money, but I didn't have access to it until I turned twenty-one, and by then, I was too afraid to try to get to it.

"I only got one interview from all my applications. At a record store. A really cool place that sold vinyl and vintage concert tees.

"Anyway, when I turned in my application, the owner set up my interview, but she said her son would be interviewing me. I remember thinking it was funny, a guy named DJ running a record store. The job didn't pay very well, but it was a job and I thought, if I got it, it could at least tide me over while I looked for something better."

"What was the name of the store?" the sheriff asked.

"Uh, Rage Rock Records. I don't remember the owner's name. She's dead." His amber-brown eyes searched mine for a moment, trying to decide if he believed me, maybe.

"When I arrived for my interview, a man met me at the door, and he felt familiar somehow. He was very polite, but something just seemed off about him. But I needed that job, so I dismissed the feeling in my gut. We stayed out in the main part of the store, but there was no one else there.

"He asked me questions about my life, what my hobbies were, what the state home had been like, if I missed my parents, things I wasn't sure potential employers usually asked interviewees, but this was only my second interview, so what did I know? I was young and stupid.

"Finally, he told me he'd get back to me, and I quickly went to leave. I was really uncomfortable. He didn't hit on me or anything, but it all felt too personal, too intimate, the things he wanted to know. And the smile on his face freaked me out.

"When I got to the door and pushed it open, he said, 'I saw your mother play once in New York. You look a lot like her.' It sent racking shivers down my spine, and I ran all the way home and cried myself to sleep. I didn't know why what he said affected me so powerfully, if it was just the overall interview or his words as I left the shop.

"The police were beating down my door the next morning. They told me the owner of the record store and her son had been murdered—found dead in the office in the back of the store the night before—and I was on the books as their last interview.

"I told the cops about the man, who they said was not DJ, and that I thought he was familiar somehow. That's when I remembered, when I figured it out. He was the man from my yard, and the thing he'd been holding back then was a red gas can.

"After I calmed down and stopped crying, I told them about the fire and who I thought the man was. They seemed to believe me, said a detective would follow up. A week later, an old guy showed up, said he was the detective.

He was... bored with my story. It's the only way I can

describe how he acted. He told me he'd look into it and get back to me. He didn't give me any information, not even a card so I could call him if I needed to. I got the impression he didn't want me to call him, that I was just a distraction he didn't need. I never heard from him again."

"What was his name?" the sheriff asked.

"I don't remember. I'm sorry."

"It's okay. Go on."

"I hadn't even thought about the possibility that the man could have my address, but about a month later, I went to the corner store two blocks from my apartment. I could only afford a few things so I wasn't gone long, and when I got home and went to put the milk in the fridge, there was a note on the freezer door, right in front of my face. It said, 'I'm watching' and 'We'll be together soon.'

"I knew it was from him, the man from the record store, the murderer. The monster who killed my parents. He'd been in my apartment. I packed a bag, went to the bank, took all the money I had, closed the account. And then I ran."

Jack squeezed his arms around me, pressing his lips against my shoulder. "Where'd you go?"

"Um, well first, Louisville. I took a bus and just got off at the first big city."

The sheriff wrote in a little notebook, and I relaxed back against Jack. His embrace in the moment evoked feelings in me I'd never experienced before. I felt protected, cared for. I felt like I was part of something, part of a family. Like I wasn't alone anymore.

I guess I hadn't expected such acceptance. I'd been so afraid to tell anyone what happened to me. I assumed they'd be angry because I'd lied and put them in danger, or they wouldn't believe me, but I felt warmth all around me, safety, and love.

Suddenly, I needed to get up, to walk around or get some fresh air. Just thinking about being safe made me feel the need to move.

I was never safe.

And now I had someone besides myself to think of. More than one someone. The fear slammed back into me like a freight train. "Can we take a break? I-I need to move or something. I need air."

The sheriff looked up and then at Jack. "Yeah. I'm gonna get someone on this information. Go ahead, get some rest tonight. Dean, a word?"

Dean opened the living room door and walked onto the porch. Finn and Sheriff Carey followed, and Kevin hopped on one foot after them, the screen door clacking shut behind him.

"Ma? I'm sorry I lied to you." Fresh tears coated my face. The shame I felt for lying to her burned, and I hung my head.

"Oh, honey. It's okay. I understand. Everlea, will you look at me please?"

I lifted my eyes, but not my head.

"You're forgiven," she said and I wept. I cried so hard, I couldn't breathe, until Jack lifted me up and took me out to the barn. He carried me the whole way, and I buried my head in his chest and cried and snotted all over his T-shirt.

"Hey," he said, setting my feet on the floor. "C'mon. Sammy needs a good brushin'. I think he's got a little crush on you."

"Jack, I don't feel like—"

"C'mon now. Trust me."

And I did.

Taking my hand, he led me to Sammy's stall, grabbing a bucket of brushes on the way. Sammy nickered and blew raspberries at us when Jack opened his door. "Grab a curry comb and get to work. Just concentrate on your circles."

When I didn't do what he said, he took my hand, pushing the comb over my fingers, lifting it to Sammy's back and moving it in big round strokes. Sammy leaned into my touch, and I felt the warmth from his body travel into my fingers, up my arm, and into my chest, and finally, I did what Jack told me.

Jack stood back while I concentrated on combing Sammy. I placed my other hand on his back so the peace Sammy always exuded would work its way through me. Combing in circles over and over, soon, I didn't have to think about it. My body just did it. I dropped the comb and hugged Sammy, pulling my fingers through his mane, and he reached his head back to touch my side with his nose.

Jack pulled me backward and down into the soft stall bedding. He held me in his arms like a baby, and my fear and sadness dripped and seeped and bled into him. He soaked it all up, carried it for me so I could just be.

CHAPTER TWENTY

JACK

I CARRIED Evvie to my bed, and she fell asleep within seconds of her head hittin' the pillow. I stood there, just lookin' at her for a long time. I knew she'd gone through somethin' bad but…

I felt *rage*. I'd never wanted to kill another human bein'. I did now. I needed to.

If he'd left the note at her house recently, then this monster had already found her. Us. If he didn't know she was at the ranch, it wouldn't take him long to figure it out. Already he had some clue since he'd been pokin' around.

"Jay." I called his name as he came down the stairs, and we walked into the kitchen. He'd taken Ma up to bed and came down to see what the guys were doin'. He knew we needed to do somethin'.

"Stay with Evvie. She's asleep but I don't want her to be alone."

"Okay, brother."

"I'll let you know what's goin' on as soon as we have a plan." Walkin' to the back-hall coat closet, I pulled out a shotgun and a box of shells, set 'em on the kitchen table, and looked at Jay. He inhaled deep and loaded the gun as I left the house.

The guys and Carey had all congregated in the barn.

"She okay?" Finn asked.

Closin' my eyes, I tried to find some semblance of calm inside myself. There wasn't much. "She's asleep. Have you found anything?" I asked Carey, openin' my eyes and willin' him to give me some kinda information. Anything.

"Jack. I know this woman might mean somethin'—"

"I saw the burns, Carey," I said through gritted teeth. "I saw the sheer fuckin' terror in her eyes when she saw the note at her house. I know you're tryin' to be the impartial sheriff right now, but just tell me what we can do."

He sighed. "Okay. The woman I called, Billie, she's a… hacker, of sorts. I've worked with her before. She's freelance now but she works similar cases. Mostly missin' persons cases, but she can find just about anybody. She's a friend. She's on it and I've asked her to come here. She'll find him, Jack."

He cupped his hand on my shoulder, but I shook it off. I knew he was tryin' to be comfortin', but the fury I felt inside my body simmered so close to the surface. He understood and he dropped his hand.

"Listen, I dunno how this guy finds Everlea—I'm sure there's more to her story—but I think we need to assume he's good with computers. I don't want anybody usin' their cells. No Wi-Fi. Don't even turn on the fuckin' TV. In fact, unplug it. Unplug anything that can connect to Wi-Fi. Gimme your phones."

He held out his hands and we all dropped our phones into 'em. "Don't go lookin' online for anything. We're gonna let Billie do that 'cause she can cover her tracks. I'm gonna run, get some pre-paid phones. Don't use Everlea's name in any calls or texts. I'm gonna assume he knows she's here, but in case he don't, let's not make it easy for him."

"Why don't Jack and Evvie just take off? They could go somewhere—"

"No, Kevin," Dean argued, "we don't know enough about him yet. And besides, if she runs, he'll just follow. He seems to be able to find her no matter where she goes. We need to stop him so she doesn't *have* to run anymore." He looked at me. "We got the motion sensor cameras around the barn for predators, but I wanna get more for the house."

"Yeah," Carey said, "that's a good idea, but don't connect 'em to Wi-Fi, Dean. Billie will be here in the mornin'. I want her to set it all up. She can make sure your computer is secure."

"Fine. Finn and I'll set traps around the house for tonight."

"And Jack, don't leave the ranch. Stay here 'cause it'll be easier to keep her close. If you go to town, there's a million places he could be lurkin'. There are here, too, but at least here, you know every inch. And here, you can protect your-selves if you have to. Your land. I'll have Lee and Sims patrol 'round town, and they can do hourly drive-bys."

I nodded, hopin' it would be enough. My mind raced, tryin' to come up with ways to protect Evvie.

"While Billie's lookin' for this guy, I'm gonna have an old buddy of mine get as much info on the fire as he can, and the record store owners. He works for the government, based outta St. Louis, so I'm gonna see if he can drive up there, to Peoria, get his hands on the actual paper files. I think, if this guy really has killed four people, there's bound to be more. I'll be back tonight with those phones." Carey looked at Finn, Dean, Kevin, and me, one at a time. "Everybody, get armed. And don't let Everlea outta your sight."

We made it through the night, though I didn't think any of us got more than a few minutes sleep here and there. Even Ma. She got up three or four times to check on Evvie. She called me out to the kitchen before, finally, Kevin convinced her to take the sleepin' medication Doc Whitley had prescribed for her. Chemo could cause insomnia, and she'd had a hell of a time gettin' any rest durin' her last bout of cancer.

We sat in the kitchen, and she wrapped her hands around one of mine on the tabletop. "Are you okay, honey?"

"I'm fine."

"Jack," she sighed, "it's okay to say how you feel."

"I'm just tired."

She looked at me then, studyin' my face. "You want her, Jack. I see it in your eyes and on your face every time you look at her."

I felt the skin on my neck heat up at the embarrassment of hearin' her talk about Evvie and me, and of wantin'. But more than that, I was angry at her words. She was tryin' to force this on me, tryin' to force me to admit to what I swore I never would. It was one thing to say it to myself in my head, but I knew what was comin', and it pissed me off and terrified me at the same time.

"You deserve love. I know how hard you tried to avoid it since your mama left, but it's time now."

Time? Time for what? For me to fall in love with someone who would probably leave? Or be taken away from me?

No.

"She needs help. I wanna help her. That's all that's goin' on here," I lied. "G'on up to bed now. You need your rest."

"Don't you condescend to me, Jack. You don't need to

tell me what's goin' on here. I can see it plain as day. Now, if you're gonna choose to deny it, well then, I reckon that's your choice, but I never figured you for a coward."

Evvie slept like the dead all night, and I lay next to her, wrapped around her, with a pistol under my pillow, a shotgun next to the bed, and a knife next to the pistol.

Watchin' her chest rise and fall with breath, I thought about her out in the world, alone, about how she'd survived—the strength it must've taken. To be on the run, to pick up and leave her home every time she heard a strange noise. Although, from the sound of it, she hadn't had a home. Just a place to sleep in each new city she'd been to, and sometimes she hadn't even had that. She told me she'd spent plenty of nights in her car, cold 'cause she'd turned the engine off to save gas.

I thought about her mama. I coulda strangled the woman if she hadn't already been dead. The pain she'd caused her daughter made me so fuckin' angry. I had to get outta the bed 'cause I couldn't lie still.

I paced the little hallway outside my bedroom till Finn interrupted me. "Brother, go on. Go back to bed. I ain't sleepin' anytime soon. We got the house covered. You can rest. We'll take care of the horses in the mornin'."

"I can't sleep, Finn. I can't stop thinkin' about—" I stopped my pacin' and rested my head against the wall. "I almost want him to come here so I can fuckin' *kill* him."

Finn stood next to me, fidgetin' with the stupid ponytail holder he wore around his wrist. I felt the apprehensive energy comin' off his body and knew he wanted to say somethin'.

"What, Finn? Just say whatever it is."

"You love her, Jack?"

I looked at my brother. I wanted to deny it. I didn't want him to know how vulnerable I felt. How raw and ripped open. I opened my mouth to tell him no, to lie to him the way I'd tried to lie to Ma, but I couldn't say the word.

"Yes. I love her. I want her," I said, slidin' down the wall to the floor. I held my head in my hands and he sat next to me.

"Alright then. No deranged jumped-up psychopathic motherfucker is gonna hurt my sister *ever* again."

I must've fallen asleep at some point 'cause in the mornin', I jerked awake to the sound of the kitchen door clappin' shut. I heard my brothers and Carey talkin' though, so I knew it had only been one of them and not an intruder.

Evvie opened her eyes, blinkin' the sleep away, her eyelashes flutterin' on her cheeks like little wings.

"Hi," I said, lookin' in her eyes.

"Hi." Her voice was thick with sleep and raspy.

I'd closed my bedroom door and drew the blinds and curtain so we were in relative darkness, but I could still see the green of her eyes, like emeralds. As she looked at me, she must've remembered everything that had happened the night before. She gasped, sittin' straight up.

"Hey, it's okay. You're okay."

"I-I don't… know what to do."

"'Bout what?"

"I've never told anyone before. It feels strange for someone else to know." She lay back slowly and rolled to face me. "What time is it? Ma has an appointment today. Probably soon, if we haven't missed it."

"It's"—I looked at my watch—"eight fifteen. Finn and Jay will take her today."

"Oh, okay, good. Is she okay?"

"She's fine. Evvie, what's wrong?"

Tremblin' next to me, she sucked in a breath, like she'd just remembered she needed air. "I can't take it back. I crossed a line last night and I can't go back."

"Why would you wanna take it back? You mean tellin' us?"

"Because now you're in it. You're all in the middle of this thing, and I can't fix it. I can't save you. I can't—" She gasped in breaths, clutchin' at her chest.

"Evvie, calm down. Look at me, please?" She looked in my eyes, and I smoothed her hair away from her face with the palms of my hands. "Take a deep breath."

She did and blew it out.

"Now, kiss me."

"Jack."

"Kiss me. And then I wanna show you somethin'."

A few minutes later, we stood on the lawn, squintin' into the blue October sky, lookin' up at the roof of the house. I whistled and Dean popped up over the back of the peak. He lifted his rifle in the air so Evvie could see. He wore his camo pants and vest. More pockets for ammo, binoculars, phone, and anything else he might need stuck up there all day.

"Oh."

"And we already have motion sensor cameras 'round the barn and far paddocks to look out for wolves and bears, but we got more on the way. Finn will pick 'em up while Jay takes Ma for her chemo. Carey brought us disposable phones.

Here's yours." I reached in my pocket, pullin' out the cheap flip phone, and handed it to her.

"Mine? I've never had a phone."

"You got one now. I already sent you a text."

"I don't know how to text," she said, lookin' at the phone, turnin' it over in her hand.

"I'll teach you." I kissed her cheek. "Carey's got someone comin' out to set it all up. She's some kinda hacker or somethin'. She's good at all this stuff."

"Billie?"

"Yeah."

Carey walked out onto the porch then, sippin' a cup of coffee. "Mornin'."

"Good morning," Evvie said.

"Come up here a minute. I wanna talk to you."

When he, Evvie, and I were all seated in the old mish mosh of chairs on the porch, he brought her up to speed about his buddy in St. Louis. "And Billie's on her way. She should be here in a couple hours."

"Okay." She twisted her hands in her lap.

"Jack told me about your map. I took a look. Can you tell me 'bout it? Why'd you X out so many places?"

"Oh. Well, New York and New Jersey because that's where they met. I didn't mean to put the X through Jersey, but it's so close to New York. I thought I should stay away from that whole area. I thought he might be from there. Illinois because that's where we lived. I wanted to stay away from anywhere I knew he'd been. Texas and Oklahoma because that's where I saw him last. In Odessa."

"Where in Odessa? You remember?"

"Yes. At the Texas Star motel. He started a fire there too."

"You said that was about three months ago?" Carey looked from Evvie to me.

"Yes. Before that, I was in San Antonio, but only for two days. I thought I'd seen him there so I left. I was headed toward El Paso but decided to go east. He chased me on the freeway. It had been three days, almost, since I'd slept and I was so tired. I had to stop. I had to. I couldn't keep my eyes open. I thought it'd be safer to get a room than to sleep in my car because there'd be other people around.

"I got a room in the disgusting motel for thirty-five dollars. I barricaded the door, but he must've come through the tiny window in the bathroom. I woke up to him on top of me trying to tie my arms behind my back. The motel was on fire. I think he was trying to scare me, but the place was a dump and the fire got out of control. He seemed confused by it, and, in the chaos, I got away."

"Jesus." This guy was out of his fuckin' mind.

"After that, I went to Dallas, but it just felt too close. I ended up in Oklahoma, and that's when I decided to come west."

"Had he ever caught you before? Before Odessa?"

"Yes. One other time. In Chicago. I got away that time too."

Carey frowned, pursin' his lips. "I guess, I don't understand. I mean, obviously he's fixated on you, but if he killed your mama, then he knows you're not her. Why wouldn't he — Sorry, but why wouldn't he just kill you if that's what he wants?"

"Does there have to be a reason? He's out of his mind. Sometimes he seems lucid, sometimes he doesn't. I've only been close to him a few times, but it's clear he's not well. But he's capable and strong."

She thought for a moment then shook her head. "And he doesn't want to kill me. At least, that's what he said. He wants to be *with* me. But he likes the game. He likes me to suffer so he can rescue me. He likes when I get desperate. When I run out of money or whatever. He leaves food for me, gifts, or even cash. If I take what he leaves, he sees it as an invitation. I only made that mistake once. I didn't know the food was from him. It was drugged."

He fuckin' drugged her? I clenched my hands into fists. They ached to wrap around his neck.

"How'd you get away?" Carey asked.

"I just fought. He had a piano there, in the house he'd taken me to. In Peoria. A block away from my home. Well, where it used to be. He untied my hands so I could play for him. He played my mother's music over and over on some old CD player. But someone heard it, I think—it was loud— and when they knocked on the door, he panicked. I screamed and bit and kicked and ran."

"Okay." Carey's eyes darted up to mine, then back to Evvie's. "Is there anything else you think we should know?"

"He had a gun. In Odessa. He had a gun."

"Okay. That's good to know." Carey looked at me again, and I tried to distract Evvie from the worry on his face.

"C'mon. Let's get some breakfast and then we got some more horses to brush. If you're lucky, you can help me muck stalls," I said, smilin' and pullin' her to stand.

"Sheriff?" She turned back to Carey but squeezed my hand.

"Yes?"

"He killed my friend, Toby. In Louisville. Toby Armstrong. He doesn't like me to have a friend. And he *really* doesn't like it if the friend is a man."

CHAPTER TWENTY-ONE

EVERLEA

THE SHERIFF RETURNED to the ranch soon after Jay and Finn had come back with Ma after her chemo treatment. She went upstairs to take a nap, and we heard his SUV pulling up to the house, so everybody went out to the porch. He climbed out of his truck and walked up the stairs, then, behind him, a woman carrying a heavy black backpack stepped out.

The woman was gorgeous. A little shorter than me, maybe, and strong, she looked like she could kick some serious ass. Not necessarily physically, but like she knew herself, was a confident woman.

Thick fringe bangs and black sunglasses hid her eyes, and dark brown, stick-straight hair fell past her shoulders. She had many curves—mostly in the chest area—which she covered with a short black skirt, a black tank top, and a soft, black leather jacket and shiny black, shit-kicking boots.

This woman would never be hunted; she was the huntress. And probably Kevin and Jay's wet dreams. They stared at her with bugged eyes, and I waited for drool to drip from their mouths. Finn smacked Kevin on the back of his head again. Poor Kevin.

"Ow! Finn, you fucker."

"What's goin' on here?" the sheriff asked. "You guys havin' some kinda porch party and didn't invite me? Well, screw you too." He was trying to be funny, but I could see the tension in his shoulders.

Dean cleared his throat to remind the sheriff there were ladies present, and the woman snorted. "You weren't trying to protect *my* delicate sensibilities, were ya, big guy? 'Cause, like, fuck that shit. You Everlea?" I nodded, following her like an annoying little sister as she barged her way into the kitchen.

"Carey, what's goin' on?" Jack demanded.

"Found him," the sheriff said, and my pulse pounded in my ears.

"The fuck you say?" The woman glared at him.

"Sorry. Everybody, this is Billie, and *we* found this Paul guy."

"I found him, you asshole. You gave me a first name and the location of a concert. I'd like to see anybody else locate a motherfucker with more." She kicked her foot out, crossing her leg at the ankle as she leaned back against the wall next to the kitchen door. "We. Pfft."

"Well, where is he?" Finn asked, and everyone took a seat at the kitchen table. Billie stayed by the door.

"I meant we found *who* he is. We still don't know his location." Carey pulled a thick folder from his leather satchel, set it in front of him, and looked at me. "I have a couple pictures of the man we found. Think you can look at 'em to identify him?"

"Yes." I closed my eyes and held my breath. I hated the feeling in my body anytime I saw him, like my stomach had a heartbeat and it twisted and wrung itself, trying to make me throw up.

He pulled a few stiff pieces of paper from the folder. "Ready?"

Taking a deep breath, I opened my eyes. "Ready."

He placed three photographs, one at a time, in front of me. I looked at Jack. It felt so wrong to be with Jack but look at Paul. The two worlds should never have met. I didn't want Jack to ever have to see him. If Jack was close enough to see him, Paul would be close enough to hurt Jack.

Jack smiled his sideways smile at me, grabbing my hand under the table. I took another deep breath and looked at the photographs.

"That's him," I said, exhaling slowly, trying to quell my stomach. "He looks a little different. Younger, but that's definitely him." The man—the monster—was skinny and scrawny in the photos, with really light blond hair, almost white. He had dark shadows under his eyes, his eyes themselves black, soulless beads. He really did look like a monster in the pictures. Like something supernatural.

I had to stop looking. I turned my head back to Jack to see him staring at the pictures, like he could set them on fire with just his eyes, and I shuddered.

I pushed the pictures toward the sheriff across the table, and he passed one to Dean, who passed it down the line, so everybody would know who to look out for. Jack scooted his chair closer to mine and squeezed my leg. Grabbing his hand with both of mine, I held it like it was a buoy in the middle of the ocean and I'd been shipwrecked.

"How did you find him so fast?" I asked.

"Easy peasy," Billie said, rolling her eyes. She waved her hand, like it had been the simplest thing in the world to do. Nine years of running, hiding, and panic, and she dismissed it all with a flick of her wrist.

"His name is Paul Mancinno. He's registered as a resident

of New Jersey. Newark, right across the bay from Manhattan. He's married and has two children with a woman named Angela Mancinno. Their children are teenagers, fifteen and sixteen."

"What?" I gasped. "He has *children*?"

"Yep," Billie said, "but he hasn't been there in years from what I can find. His kids seem normal. Both boys work after school at a fish market. They're pretty active on social media, but there isn't one mention of their father. The mother struggles financially. She works two jobs but they mostly pay their bills.

"I also found old work records for this creep. He used to work for the New York City Parks Department. I think that's why he was in Central Park the night of your mother's concert. I found a video from that night of them talking. Wanna see? There's no audio."

"Yes."

Billie pulled a square, boxy laptop from her backpack and walked around to stand next to me. Setting the computer in front of me, she opened it, angled it so I'd be able to see, and hit a key. On the screen, I saw a grainy, black and white video. It showed a woman—*oh!* My mother.

My heart raced, and my hand flew up to clutch my chest to try stop it.

I'd forgotten just how beautiful she'd been. Even through the poor-quality video, I saw it. She had this… air about her. She had been so magnificent and magnetic.

And Paul Mancinno had *definitely* been drawn to her. In the clip, he leaned forward toward her as she talked and played with her hair. As she flirted with him. He'd been so fixed on her, with his beady eyes and his body bowing toward hers. Disgusting. How could she ever have found him attractive?

I could see my hair and the shape of my face in my mother. I remembered looking at myself in a mirror before she'd died, wondering if I had that thing. The thing everyone seemed to love about her. The thing that addicted everyone to her.

All this time. It was surreal to be able to see the exact moment when our lives had changed. The exact moment I'd lost my family. He didn't kill them until three years later, but the exchange on the screen in front of me had decided my fate. It was confirmation to me that my mother had been selfish, shallow, and stupid. I watched as she seduced him while my father and I were home, trusting her, loving her, and waiting for her to come back to us. But our love had never been enough for her.

"Evvie?"

Jack's voice brought me back to the present, and my eyes snapped up to his. He wiped the tears I hadn't known I'd cried from my cheeks while he looked in my eyes. The sadness I saw reflected back at me made me ache. He pulled on my hand and I leaned into him, the warmth from his body luring me right in until I couldn't stop myself. I stood and sat in his lap, and he wrapped his arms around me, holding me and protecting me. He nestled his nose into my hair, and I felt his chest expand as he inhaled.

"Billie also found videos from the concert itself," Sheriff Carey said. "There's audio if you'd like to listen—"

"*No.*" I hadn't meant to yell at the sheriff, but I couldn't listen to my mother's music.

Billie reached around me to close the laptop and picked it up. Shoving it into her bag, she finally sat down. "I've been trying to figure out how he finds you," she said. "Short of this sick fuck injecting you with some sorta magical, black-ops, alien substance to track you using his space scanner, I can't figure it out.

"So, that leads me to believe he's just been using old-school tracking skills. It's possible he used a simple tracking device, in your car maybe, or even a cell phone if he could figure out a constant power source. Carey's already searched your car, but I plan to rip it to shreds today. Maybe we'll find something. He already knows where you live, so I guess it's not that important but—"

"Oh no. The Mastersons, they're in danger! He knows where I live. He can easily find who owns the house—"

"They're not in danger, Everlea," Carey said in a low and soothing voice, trying to stop my anxiety. "When I spoke to 'em, they were at the airport in London, on their way to visit their daughter, Carolyn. She was in a car accident, and they went over to stay with her while she's on the mend."

"On the mend?" Billie said, sniggering. "Is this a hoedown?" Carey stomped on her foot under the table. "Owwwuh!"

"What kinda accident?" Dean asked, fidgeting in his chair, which was unlike him. If it weren't for his hulking presence, he usually sat so still and silent, I'd forget he was there.

"Uh, just a minor thing but she hurt her wrist. You know how her mama is. A stubbed toe is an international incident." Carey looked at me. "Everlea, I'm gonna have my deputies and a couple trusted officers lookin' out for this man, but I've made it known they are not to approach him or pull him over. They will only be authorized to take note of his location and then contact me directly. I wanted you to know I was doin' this. Are you okay with it?"

"I guess. But why won't they arrest him? Isn't that what we want?"

"Unfortunately, no, it's not so easy, Evvie," Dean answered for the sheriff in a careful voice.

I looked at him. "Why not?"

"Because, as of now, we don't have any proof of what he's been doin' to you. He would spend a night in jail and then walk. That is *not* what we want."

"Okay. So then, what are we going to do?"

"Well, right now," the sheriff said, "we're gonna get set up and then we're gonna wait. Billie's lookin' into it. Let's get the new surveillance gear in place. She'll make sure everything is secure and can't be hacked. I'm still waitin' to hear back from my guy in St. Louis."

"Okay," I said, like it was just that easy.

But I knew it wouldn't be.

"All right, who's got the fastest computer? Lead me to it," Billie said. "Unplug the rest."

"We already did," Kevin snapped. "We may talk slow here at the hoedown, but we ain't stupid."

"C'mon," Finn said to Billie, rolling his eyes at Kevin. He stood and led Billie upstairs, and I heard Finn's bedroom door creak open.

"No fucking way!" Billie shrieked. "I'm not going in there. Something *died* in there."

"Bite my ass!" Finn yelled at Billie.

Jack groaned behind me. "Dammit, they just woke Ma."

We heard Ma's bedroom door creak open. "Finnigan Francis Cade! You did not just curse at a young lady."

Billie giggled. "Furr-ANCIS?"

And then Finn whined, "But she said the F word," like he was twelve, trying to get Billie in trouble too. Iggy meowed and yowled at them, scolding them for waking Ma. She'd taken to sleeping with Ma after her treatments. I could picture her weaving in and out of their legs, looking up at them with her adorably-judgmental kitty eyes.

"*She* doesn't belong to me. Now, you may be twenty-seven, and I may be old and weak, but my hand still works and your backside is still sensitive. Watch your language."

"Yes, ma'am."

"Don't worry, ma'am, I'll smack it for you," Billie said, laughing.

"Oh my God." I snorted, and the whole thing wiped away the tension and sadness I still felt after seeing my mother. "I *like* her."

"Billie can be a little," Carey hedged, trying not to laugh, "um, you know, she might be a little much to handle."

"Doesn't sound to me like she needs anyone to 'handle' her, Sheriff."

"Oh, no, I didn't mean—"

Kevin snickered and I laughed.

"I'll be on the roof," Dean mumbled and he left the kitchen, and Kevin and Jay made their way upstairs to watch the Billie, Finn, and Iggy show.

"Everlea, you know you can just call me Carey." He smiled at me. "Just try to relax today, if you can, while we get things movin'. I gotta run to the station for a while, but I'll be back. And I'll let you know if I hear anything from Peoria."

"Thank you."

We spent the day tending to the horses, watching Billie work on the cameras and computers, and listening to her argue with Kevin and Finn. Finn had been mostly playful with Billie, but Kevin didn't seem to like her very much, and I thought it might have had something to do with Billie "outsarcasming" him. Even Ma had a hard time not laughing, even when Billie used "foul language for such a pretty young lady."

Jay had been oddly silent and incognito most of the time. Maybe he didn't like Billie's brand of humor, but I did. I loved having her around. I'd never really had a girlfriend my own age. She was strong and independent, and she reminded me that maybe I could be that way too. Maybe this would work. Maybe we'd find and stop the monster, and I could have a normal life.

Jack had been distant all day. He rarely left my side and I couldn't go anywhere, not three steps, without a shadow, him or Kevin or Finn, but he barely spoke to anyone.

I worried.

Maybe he thought all the burden and inconvenience had become too much. Maybe he'd rather I left. His family would be safer if I did. He would be.

I sat on the porch with Kevin, watching him take my car apart with Billie. He didn't say much to her either, and when they finished, after she'd ripped out seats and pulled up floor-boards without finding anything, I'd made up my mind to ask him why, but he pulled me aside first.

"Let's go somewhere."

"Carey said not to leave the ranch."

"We ain't leavin'. We're goin' for a ride. And Dean's got us covered." He nodded to the roof and Dean waved.

"'Kay."

We rode Sammy, using a bareback pad instead of a saddle, through the paddocks and over the beautiful fields. The afternoon sun blinded me until Jack took his green base-ball cap off and put it on my head, pulling the brim down low. He carried a pack on his back with water and apples for us, and a shotgun strapped to the side.

All the guys carried some kind of weapon, though you

couldn't tell just by looking at them. He said nothing bad would happen, and it had only been for protection from bears, mountain lions, and other animals, but I saw his eyes roaming everywhere, looking for danger. For Paul.

We came to a blue and gray stream with millions of multi-colored stones of all different sizes glittering in the sunshine, on the banks and leading into the water, and Sammy waded through it. Just on the other side sat a ramshackle, little two-story house right next to the edge of the woods, at the bottom of Jack's mountain.

It had been made of wood and stones, just like the ones in the stream, and a white porch wrapped around it like the ranch house. Technically two stories, the roof had caved in over a large part of the second story. It looked like maybe a tree had fallen on it and caused a whole lot of damage. A huge piece of black plastic sheeting covered the open cavity.

I turned to look behind us and saw the big house in the distance, close enough to see, but too far to walk to.

"There's a dirt path between the houses. We have a couple ATVs we use to get around the property if we're not ridin' the horses. Pops built this for Granny years ago. They lived here a while, but Granny died and Pops abandoned the place. I think… he lost his heart when she died."

Jumping down, he held his arms up for me, and I slid into them, letting him lower me to my feet. He turned me to face the little house, standing behind me with his chin on my shoulder and his arms wrapped around my waist. Pulling his baseball cap down on the back of my head, he raised the brim up a little, allowing me a much larger view of our surroundings.

"It's so pretty, with the mountain behind it, the stream, and the sun shining down. I can picture them here, your grandparents. I bet they were happy."

Jack cleared his throat and I felt nervousness coming from him, which was unusual. "Wanna go see?"

I turned my head to look at him, and the skin crinkled around his eyes, and his lips curved up into my favorite smile. He grabbed my hand, and we ran to the falling down porch.

Jack pulled a key from his pocket, an old-fashioned, long, brass key, and unlocked the door. I pushed it open, and it made a creaking sound when we stepped over the threshold, and a forbidden future flashed before my eyes.

I saw us there, cooking dinner, eating at the big wooden table sitting empty in the middle of the first floor, and snuggling up on a couch by the fire. I saw us making love on that couch, on the floor, on a dining chair. I saw babies, and then little kids running around—a boy who looked so much like Jack with his dark brown hair flipping up around his ears, and a little girl with red ringlets falling down her back.

I imagined a black piano in the living room, rays of sunshine coming in through the window, making it glow as I played while Jack sat listening, holding our children on his lap, talking softly to them. I saw us getting older, graying, and the kids became bigger, teenagers.

Tears ran down my face. I wanted that future. I'd never dared to dream of something so good. When I saw it, imagined it, it hurt because I wanted it with so much desperation.

I clutched my arms around my middle.

"Evvie? What's wrong?"

I opened my eyes and Jack stood in front of me, reaching his arms out toward me.

"Nothing. Sorry, I just— It's nothing. I'm emotional, I guess. Everything that's happened the last few days— I'm fine." I dropped my arms and stood straight.

"You don't like the house?"

"No, Jack, I love it. You should fix it up."

"I was thinkin' about that," he said, looking around.

I walked a few feet further in and peeked out a window, walked over by the stone hearth fireplace, trailing my fingers over the dust coated mantle. "I can picture a fire in here on some cold fall night." I pictured it with him—us—wrapped up in each other on the floor in front of the fire.

"Whatcha thinkin' about?" He studied me, watched me intently.

"Just picturing your grandparents here. Ma showed me their picture from when you were little," I lied. I was too afraid to tell him the truth. Too afraid to tell him how much I wanted a life with him.

Too afraid he'd give it to me and it would be ripped away.

He didn't say anything for a few minutes while I wandered around, touching the pink walls, the broken-down furniture, kicking at the dead leaves and sticks littering the floor.

"It made you sad today to see your mama. I'm sorry."

"It's okay." I shrugged. "I hadn't seen her in so long. I don't have any pictures. I forgot how pretty she was."

"C'mere."

I walked to him and he lifted me, turned, and set me on an island jutting out from the kitchen wall.

"She ain't got nothin' on you," he whispered, kissing my nose. "Why didn't you wanna hear her play?"

I shook my head. "Her music hurts. I hear it in my head sometimes. When it's quiet, no cars, no TV. When I'm alone, I hear her music. It's like a... a soundtrack to the terror I feel all the time. It used to make me sad. Now, all I feel is anger. This is all her fault. She did this to me. She's the reason I have no home, no family. The reason I'm scared all the time. The reason my body is ruined. Why I can't have—" I almost said, "this. I can't have this." A home. With him. A life. "I *hate* her."

"Can't have what?" he asked, cocking his head, looking in my eyes.

"Nothing. Let's go back outside. I feel cooped up. It's dark in here."

"Evvie. Can't have what?"

"Nothing. Just, you know, a normal life."

CHAPTER TWENTY-TWO

JACK

I WANTED to give her that life.

I saw the way she looked around Granny's house. She longed for it. She yearned for normal and everyday. Safety and a family. A home.

And I wanted what Ma said I deserved. Happiness. Love. I wanted it with Evvie. I wanted her to know me inside and out, and I wanted to be a better man for her.

My own parents had been no example, but I remembered Mr. and Mrs. Mitchum's love for one another. No two people ever loved each other more. They touched every time they'd been near enough. He'd kiss her deep when he'd come home from workin' all day over at the bank, and he'd whisper in her ear and nuzzle in her neck, and they'd laugh and laugh. They'd gaze into each other's eyes sometimes, sayin' somethin' to each other I couldn't ever hear, couldn't understand.

And the smiles she'd given him? The sun had risen and set in his eyes for her. I remembered thinkin' the world must've felt warm all around her when she smiled like that.

I hadn't ever wanted to understand it. I'd wanted to reject it 'cause, if I did, no one could ever steal it away from me.

But when I thought of Evvie in my arms, in my bed—in my life—growin' old with her, I wanted all the things Ma said I could have. I wanted 'em bad.

Includin' a woman into my life on the ranch had never really occurred to me. I hadn't ever thought a woman would want to be a part of this kinda life. My life. My mama hadn't. So hard and dirty, ranch life didn't agree with most women, and they liked fine things, fancy things. I wouldn't have the first clue about any of that.

But Evvie didn't seem to care much about womanly things like hair or clothes and shoes. She didn't wear makeup. But then, she didn't need to. I'd never known another woman to compare to her. Her beauty and kindness. Sometimes, I ached to look at her. She had a wildness to her, and it appealed to me in a way I didn't understand. I saw it in her eyes, her hair, her hands, heard it in her voice, and in the way she moved.

Could she live on the ranch? With me? She said she loved it here. She loved the horses, my brothers. Ma. Could she love me?

'Cause I loved her. And I wanted her. I wanted a life with her.

I couldn't remember ever wantin' to trust someone like that.

"C'mon. I wanna show you somethin' else." I plopped her down on the floor and took her hand. We made our way back to Sammy and rode out behind Granny's house, to the meadow beyond.

"This place is so beautiful, Jack. You're so lucky you got to grow up here," she said, lookin' all around. I wrapped my arms around her and rested my chin on top of her head while Sammy plodded along.

"I guess you're right. We did have a lotta fun when we

were kids. There was always some adventure or somethin' to explore."

"I can picture you guys as boys running around out here, little cowboys." She laughed.

"Yeah, or soldiers. Pirates lookin' for buried treasure."

"Jack, look at the deer!" She pointed out to the northwest and there, hidden in the high grass, stood a herd of elk.

"Those are elk." We startled 'em and they took off runnin', and she gasped, watchin' 'em leap and race away.

"Beautiful."

A few minutes later, we arrived at the meadow I wanted Evvie to see. It had been one of my favorite places as a boy, and I remembered hikin' out there with Granny for picnics. I really missed her. I tried hard to suppress those memories usually but lately found myself lettin' 'em through. She had been a hard woman, but she'd loved us and showed us all the time.

"Granny used to bring us out here when we were little. I loved this place." I hopped off Sammy and pulled her down, and we stood there a minute, lookin' around.

The meadow had to have been created by some kinda god. The blue-black mountains with their white snow caps surrounded us, but down in the valley, the grass grew so green. The trees glowed yellow and orange with their white bark trunks, and little purple and blue flowers popped up everywhere.

But none of it compared to Evvie.

The sun set high in the cool, late October sky, and I was too warm in my sweatshirt, so I pulled it over my head, and when I opened my eyes, Evvie stood in front of me like an angel. She'd taken off her sweatshirt, too, my UC Berkeley hoodie that hung down to her knees, revealin' a deep blue tank top.

Her hair flowed long and thick, cascadin' in wide rings and waves down her back, shinin' in the sun. I couldn't see her face. She stood with her back to me, but I could see her bare arms and I was overwhelmed with pride. Her burns showed, and she didn't try to hide 'em like she usually did. Her soul, her wild beauty, it radiated all around us.

"Evvie," I whispered her name, but the wind carried it away from me.

She turned to me then, and I grabbed my chest. I swore, I'd never seen anything so perfect. The blue from her shirt made her eyes so green and brought out all her Irish freckles. Her cheeks were rosy from the crisp air, and the flush traveled down her neck and onto her chest.

But her eyes darted all around, her face grew wary, and she bit the inside of her lip.

"We're safe here. Promise."

"Jack. We're not safe anywhere."

"Evvie, look." I pointed toward the house and waved my arms high in the air. The sun glinted off somethin' in the distance, probably Dean's rifle, and my phone rang. I hit speaker.

"I see you," he said. "Followed you from Granny's house."

"Fire a shot."

Dean put his phone in his pocket. We heard the fabric rustlin' the speaker, then, ten seconds later, a bullet whizzed nearby and hit a dead tree that had fallen into the meadow. It lay less than twenty feet away from us.

Evvie jumped.

I hung up. "We're safe."

She closed her eyes, took a slow, deep breath, released it, then spun in a circle.

I reached out to grab her waist to pull her to me, but she turned and ran away.

"Catch me if you can!" She ran across the field, hair whippin' in the wind, and disappeared through the trees.

"Oh, you are in so much trouble, woman. When I get my hands on you, I'm gonna put you over my knee!"

"Promise?"

Oh, really? A whole barrage of indecent images flooded my mind, but I blinked 'em away. Listenin' to where the sound of her voice came from, I took off in the same direction.

When I reached the edge of the trees, I stopped to listen again. Damn, I couldn't hear anything. I closed my eyes and *really* listened. I had a hard time concentratin' 'cause my heart pounded through my ears in anticipation of gettin' my hands on her, but I could hear the sound of the brook, the water flowin' and bubblin' over the stones in it. I heard a couple birds singin', and then... there, the snap of a twig.

"You ain't as stealthy as you think." With my left arm, I snagged her around her waist, but she ducked and twisted and ran back into my meadow, laughin' all the way. I growled and spun, catchin' up with her in six big strides, reachin' out with my hands to grab her, but I tripped on somethin' and fell face first into the grass, arms up above my head.

"Shit." I rolled onto my back, groanin' and spittin' flowers outta my mouth.

"Oh!" She laughed and came to stand above me. "Poor baby, are you okay?"

"No, I'm injured."

"What's wrong, what hurts?"

"My pride, it's achin' real bad." I flashed her my saddest poutin' face.

"Oh no, not your pride. What will we do without it? Look

at that face." She laughed and shook her head, little waves of her hair dancin' around her, twistin' and floatin' in the lazy breeze and shimmerin' like strings of gold in the light. "Can I make it better?"

"Yes. Kiss me."

Kneelin' beside me in the blue and purple flowers, she touched my arm with just the tips of her fingers, pushin' the cuff of my T-shirt up to my shoulder, splayin' her hand open on my bicep. She leaned over to kiss my lips softly, then sat back up, crossin' her legs like a little girl.

"Look at my hand on your arm. It looks like a child's."

I looked down at her hand and back into her eyes. She drew a line with her finger from my arm, up along my carotid artery, over my jaw, to my lips. She pushed my too-long hair away from my eyes and lay down next to me, snugglin' in close.

My skin soaked up her touch, every stroke of her finger makin' me greedy for more, and I rolled onto my side, moldin' my body to hers so there could be no crook or corner of us left bereft.

"Why didn't you like to be touched?" she asked.

"What?"

"I noticed. When we met, you were really careful with me when you touched me, and sometimes, when I touched you, you'd get tense. Why?"

Of course she'd noticed. I sighed. I didn't wanna talk about my mama, didn't wanna ruin the afternoon, but I wanted her to know.

"Until I met you, I never wanted to be touched or to touch anyone. In fact, it was the opposite. Made me uncomfortable. So, when I found myself wantin' to touch you, wantin' you to touch me, I wasn't sure how to. If I should, if you'd want me to. I wanted my hands on you so damn bad, but I didn't wanna hurt you, be too rough. It felt like all the years of not touchin' anyone or lettin' anyone touch me, had built up inside me—filled me up—and with just one look, you unleashed it. It was... intense."

"You like me touching you?" She dragged her fingers over my ribs and back, under my shirt.

"Like it? No. I *crave* it, Evvie. Sometimes, it feels like I can't stop touchin' you. If my body ain't connected to yours in some way, it hurts."

"But *why* didn't you want to be touched, Jack? Will you tell me?"

"It ain't a big deal. My mama left when I was nine. She wasn't happy with my dad or livin' on the ranch, or maybe both. I dunno. One day, we woke up and she was gone. Never saw her again. I decided then I wasn't gonna bother with lovin' someone. Just didn't want it. Guess that translated to touchin'."

"You don't think that's a big deal? You were nine years old, and the person who's supposed to love you the most in the world leaves, just walks away and never looks back? That's a big deal."

"Well. Maybe so."

"Do you ever wonder where she is?"

"No. I hadn't even thought about it till..."

"Until what?"

"Till you." Till I fell in love with her, and she made me question every thought I'd ever had. I pulled away to look in her eyes. "Evvie. I won't let him hurt you."

She sighed. "I know you think that, but you don't know him. It's not me I'm worried about."

"Evvie—"

"So, tell me about Granny," she said, tryin' to change the subject. "What was she like? When she'd bring you here, what did you guys do out here?" She'd had enough sadness and fear to last a lifetime, so I let it go.

"Oh, I dunno." I propped myself up onto my arm. She lay flat on her back, and I pushed her hair away from her face. "We'd bring lunch. Peanut butter and banana sandwiches and a thermos of cherry Kool-Aid—oh, and celery sticks. Ugh, there's probably still a pile of 'em over there by the creek. We all hated 'em—and we'd eat and goof off.

"Finn usually got hurt somehow. Broke his arm over there"—I nodded to the south—"tryin' to climb a tree like a damn orangutan. And Kevin would wander off, followin' an animal, or lookin' for rocks or somethin'."

I laughed. "We were carefree back then. Granny had stories for days, usually 'bout her own brothers, or her mama, and we'd sit and listen to 'em. She loved to make us laugh. She was real good at trickin' us. She'd tell a story, and throughout the whole thing, we'd be scared or sad, thinkin' somethin' bad was gonna happen at the end, but then she'd stop—all dramatic-like—and the next thing outta her mouth had us rollin' on the ground." Evvie giggled. "Actually, you remind me of her sometimes."

"I do?"

"Yeah, 'cause you're funny. You can be so serious, hoppin' mad about somethin', the look on your face so severe, and next thing I know, I'm laughin'. I've never laughed so much, not in years, not since I was little, out here with Granny and my brothers."

She smiled a genuine, whole-body smile. It blinded me, eclipsin' the sun into shade. "I'm glad I make you laugh, although, I think that might have more to do with you guys laughing *at* me, not because I'm actually trying to make a joke."

"I think you might be right, but the other day, when you

threatened to shove Finn's empty plastic water bottles up his ass if he didn't start recyclin' 'em, oh my God," I chuckled, "the sound of your voice, so serious, and the look on his face. I liked to die, I laughed so hard."

"Yeah, well, he deserved it. He leaves those things everywhere. Have you seen his bedroom? They litter the floor like glitter. Ugh. Why can't he just fill a glass from the tap and drink that?"

She sighed and grew quiet, twistin' a lock of hair around her finger.

"What?"

"Nothing. It's just, it's so hard for me not to think about— Usually, it's all I do. I don't go anywhere without looking around to find the exits, places to hide."

"Don't think about it. Carey and Billie are gonna find this guy. You don't know him very well, but Carey's damn good at his job. I guarantee he's not thinkin' about anything else."

"Yeah but—"

"No buts."

I leaned down to kiss her nose and then her cheeks and lips. Once I started, I couldn't stop. I kissed her chin and moved down so I could reach her neck.

"Why are you always trying to distract me?"

"It ain't purposeful. It's just that you got magnets under your skin, and they pull me to ya. It's biological. I just can't help m'self." I hugged and tickled her a little, but it became somethin' entirely different so fast. I pulled her harder against my body—so hard I wondered if she could breathe. "He won't hurt us."

"Promise?"

"I swear it," I vowed and released her, climbin' up on my knees.

The look she gave me, the shy smile with her beautiful eyes, stoked a fire in me.

"Evvie—"

"Dean's watching."

I'd forgotten. I pulled my phone from my pocket and sent him a text: *Mind your business.*

He texted back: *10-4*

I knew he wouldn't watch, and the grass stood tall enough, there wouldn't be much to see.

"He'll give us privacy," I said, pullin' my T-shirt over my head, then sat back. I'd waited so long to see her body. The burns.

She peeked up at me, then lifted her shirt by the hem slowly, and I watched as she revealed her secrets to me. I glanced at the burns, but I couldn't take my eyes away from hers. She stared at me. Into me. I saw so much fear and doubt. Hesitation. I thought, in the moment, she was deciding whether she could really trust me or not. Whether she could trust me to love her despite the thing she'd thought would push me away.

And I knew.

I needed to tell her. I wanted to give her my trust so she'd give me hers. I wanted to earn it.

Reachin' out with my finger and thumb to release the clasp on her bra between her breasts, the white fabric fell away. I leaned in to kiss her and down to kiss the burns, but I stopped, lookin' back up. "May I?"

She breathed, "Yes."

"Wait." I whistled for Sammy and he came lopin' over. Takin' a blanket from my pack, I spread it on the ground, then lifted her and laid her on it, pushin' my sweatshirt under her head.

I removed my boots, jeans, and boxers, then the rest of

her clothes, too, and lay beside her. I reached out with my finger toward her arm, to feel the burns for the first time, and she shivered at the first touch of my fingertip. I pulled it away.

"No." She grabbed my hand, guidin' it back to her arm, and I watched her throat dip as she swallowed hard. "I want you to touch me everywhere. I'm just not used to it."

I hadn't been able to really see her scars yet, not fully—there'd been so much goin' on—but now I could, and they were... soberin'.

They extended from the middle of her right side, all the way up her body, her waist, movin' back and forth as they traveled up her rib cage and over her elbow on the back of her upper arm. Her right breast and underarm had been spared, but the scars continued from her arm to surround her entire shoulder, front and back.

They were a red or pink color in some areas, and her natural, pale-peach skin tone in others, though the texture felt thicker than the rest of her skin. The red spots had raised spiderweb patterns on 'em, and the peachy skin-colored areas looked similar but were not as pronounced. She had patches of freckles all over her body, wherever the sun had touched it and she had 'em on her left shoulder, but not on the right.

I kissed her shoulder, placin' my hand on her hip to hold her still while I moved, so slowly, down her arm, then reached for her hand, raisin' it above her head so I could kiss the back. She lay motionless, with her eyes closed, but when I moved to her ribs, she drew in a ragged breath and opened her eyes.

She watched me then as I touched and kissed every inch of her, down to her toes and back up. I guided her to roll onto her stomach, tracin' the edge of the burns with my tongue, up her side, to her neck and back down.

Spreadin' her legs apart with mine, I held myself above her, nestlin' my face in her hair and inhalin' her into me as I rubbed my erection between her ass cheeks, and she raised her hips to push back against me and moaned.

But I needed to see her face, to look in her eyes. "Turn to me."

She did and she cried. I leaned down to lick and kiss the tears away, coatin' my lips with 'em, tastin' her sadness and relief on my tongue. She opened her legs and I knelt between 'em, kissin' her cheeks, her closed eyelids, her nose, to her mouth. I kissed and licked her lips and chin and neck, and she pushed her fingers into my hair as I entered her body.

"I love you." I said it. My heart raced and I shook, but I said it.

"Jack," she whispered into my mouth, gazin' into my eyes. "I love you so much. I want you so much. *Please*."

"Please what, baby?"

"Please, don't let this end."

"Never," I promised, and I made love to her like our lives depended on our naked bodies touchin'.

CHAPTER TWENTY-THREE

EVERLEA

BILLIE HAD BEEN WORKING NON-STOP, looking for Paul Mancinno. She'd gone back to Oregon, where she lived, but she monitored the camera feeds remotely and kept up her searches.

Carey's friend from St. Louis overnighted everything he found from the fire and the record store murders, but there hadn't been any real substantive evidence. The police found fingerprints at the record store, but none of them had been matched in any national databases, including mine.

I'd been mentioned in the report as a possible witness but had been ruled out as a suspect by the timeline and by my age, sex, and history. The fire that destroyed my childhood home burned away all evidence, though the fire marshal concluded that it had been started by an accelerant—plain old gasoline. They'd never figured out who set the fire.

Everything appeared normal at the ranch. The guys worked in the barn, preparing it and the horses for a big storm headed our way, but the air felt charged and tense. Everyone looked over their shoulders every few minutes, and the anxiety it caused in me worried Jack.

Ma noticed my discomfort, too, and she called me inside to play the piano for her. She said it would help her relax, but I knew she hoped it would help me. I didn't want to be a distraction to Jack and his brothers though—they had so much work to do before the storm hit—so I wandered inside to play a little.

Finn had called a friend to come tune the piano for me, so when I placed my fingers on the keys and pressed, a rich, warm sound filled the room, and somehow, it filled me with hope and happiness.

I didn't know how long Ma and I'd been in the den, and I'd gotten used to cars pulling up the long drive to the ranch house, so I didn't notice when someone arrived, but out of nowhere, a little girl sat beside me on the piano bench.

She didn't say anything, and when I stopped playing, she gently lifted my hand back to the keys.

"Everlea, this is Cadence Williams. Cadence, this is our friend, Everlea. We call her Evvie," Ma introduced us.

Cadence smiled and poked the back of my hand, so I played. I banged out "Mary Had a Little Lamb," "Chopsticks," and "Three Blind Mice." When I finished, I looked at her. She had the most beautiful warm, dark brown eyes, and light brown chubby cheeks, and I felt the need to wrap her in my arms. I didn't. Jack told me all about her, how shy she could be and how careful with people.

"Do the faster song again," she whispered.

I smiled back at her and played Beethoven's "Fur Elise." Cadence watched my hands the whole time. I made so many mistakes—it had been years since I'd memorized and practiced it—but she didn't seem to care. I finished and placed my hands in my lap.

"Do it again."

During my fourth pass through the song, better than the

second and third as the notes came back to me, she mimicked my fingers on the lip of the wood.

When I finished, she looked right in my eyes and said, "Please?" hovering her fingers over the keys.

I spent the next half hour teaching her to play the piano. We didn't use sheet music or books, though I'd seen a few in the nook under the bench, but she picked it up. She'd somehow been able to hear the change in note and octave, even chord changes, and then reproduce it. She made mistakes, of course, but seemed to know when she did and tried to correct them. I was completely amazed by Cadence, and the look on Ma's face had been utter joy. She sat silent, watching, until Jack's deep voice interrupted us.

"Hey, ladies. Sorry to interrupt, but Evvie, I need to talk to you. Mr. Williams, this is Evvie, Everlea. She's stayin' with us."

I stood, and Mr. Williams walked over to shake my hand. "Nice to meet you. Looks like you've gained a fan. You ever taught piano?"

"Oh, no," I said, laughing awkwardly. "I just started playing again. I haven't played in years."

"Well, if you ever decide you want to, give me a call. I think Cadence might like to learn," he said, smiling at his daughter who still sat at the piano, poking keys and testing sounds.

"Ma, would you mind hangin' out with Cadence for a minute? Mr. Williams and I'd like to talk to Evvie 'bout somethin'."

"Oh sure. Cadence, you can show me what you learned."

Cadence seemed at ease and eager, so I followed the men to the front porch.

"Evvie, Mr. Williams is a mechanic. He saw your car sittin' up on the wood blocks and asked about it. He found this." Jack held out a square, black piece of plastic with two huge round magnets attached to it.

"What is it?"

"Well, I texted a picture of it to Carey, and he and Billie seem to think it's some kinda trackin' device."

I gasped and froze.

"It's dead. Billie said there'd be a green light flashin' if it worked. It looks old or like it's been there a while."

"Yes," Mr. Williams said, "I've actually seen one before. A woman came into my garage for an oil change, and I found one under her car. Turned out her husband didn't trust her very much. I looked over the rest of your car. I didn't find anything else."

"Thank you." I exhaled, and Jack grabbed my hand to stop it from shaking.

"I don't know what's goin' on, but I mean it, Jack, you call me if you need help. With anything. Ya hear?"

"Yes, sir. Thank you."

Finn hopped up onto the porch as Mr. Williams and Cadence said goodbye a few minutes later.

"I'm serious about them piano lessons, Evvie," Mr. Williams said. "I bet there's a lotta kids around here who'd be interested."

"I was thinkin' the same thing," Finn said. "We haven't had a music teacher for a long time."

"Not since your Granny, I don't think."

"Yeah." Finn nodded, winking at me.

Me? A piano teacher? I didn't know what kind of teacher I'd be, and didn't you have to go to school for that? I only had a high school diploma. But I loved the idea. If it meant I'd be able to see Cadence and play music with her, I'd do it.

If I ever got free from the monster. The one who'd been

tracking me this whole time, using my car to do it, and I'd had no idea.

The storm hit around eight that night. Finn lit a fire in the den, while Dean set one in the living room. We lost power about eight thirty, so Jay went through the whole house with a flashlight, lighting candles everywhere.

Usually, I loved storms—they filled the silence—but this storm was so big, the thunder and lightning so intense, it shook the house.

The guys worried about the horses and I did too. It would be Ruby and Trumpet's first big thunderstorm. I wanted to go out to try to keep them calm, but Jack said it would be too dangerous; the horses could get so spooked by the sounds of the storm and the change in the air, they'd kick and jump to get away.

We stayed inside, playing Uno and Go Fish, trying to keep each other entertained. Finn persuaded me to play the piano while he played his guitar, but the noise from the storm had me on edge, too, and I couldn't really concentrate.

Ma couldn't sleep through the sheeting rain hitting the windows and the thunder rattling the roof either, so we sat with her around the kitchen table, while Finn cooked to give his hands something to do.

I sat in Jack's lap. Since he told me he loved me, he rarely stopped touching me. The guys all made fun, joked about it, gave him hell, but it didn't bother him. It didn't bother me either. I loved when he touched me. I'd seen couples before, with their hands all over each other in public, and like everyone else, rolled my eyes and thought, "I would never do that." But the way I felt, knowing Jack loved me so much that he couldn't stand to be separated from me, made me so happy. And I felt safer in his arms.

And him touching me all the time often led to other things. I pretty much stayed horny twenty-four seven. We'd just made love not an hour before, on the side of the porch in the rain, up against the house. I smiled remembering his hands between my legs and his mouth on my breasts, and a little moan threatened to escape me. I coughed to try to cover it up, and Jack squeezed my hips.

"What are you making, Finn?" I asked when he yanked the old refrigerator door open for the fourth time, looking inside for divine inspiration.

"Well, I was gonna cook up this ground beef, make burgers, but that just don't sound good right now. I feel like we need some comfort food. Somethin' warm and gooey. So, I'm makin' Irish slop. It ain't fancy but it's damn good."

"What is Irish slop?"

"Ever heard of goulash? It's kinda like that, except without the noodles."

"Umm, goulash is a food? Like, you eat it?" I made a disgusted face. "It sounds like something you get on your muck boots in a cow pasture after a storm."

"Yes," he laughed, "goulash is food. I'll make it for you and you'll love it. Irish slop is just ground beef cooked up with some onions and garlic. You basically throw a buncha stuff in a pot with it, then we eat it over homemade mashed taters with sourdough dinner rolls. It's Ma's old recipe. It's fu —it's delicious."

"It is very good," Ma said, smiling at Finn, proud of him for cooking her food and for stopping the casual curse ready to leak out of his mouth.

"What's your favorite food, Evs?" he asked.

"Mine? Um, I don't know. I really liked fish when I had

it, but that was years ago, and I don't remember what kind I had. Oh, and I ate at this Mediterranean place once. I don't know what it's called, but it was grilled chicken on a pita with this tangy white stuff—some kind of sauce—and veggies and chickpeas. It was so good."

"That does sound good. I bet it was chicken shawarma."

"Shawarma?"

"Did you just say chickpeas tasted good?" Kevin asked, incredulous, sticking out his tongue. "Ugch. What's a' matter with ya?"

Finn snorted. "You wouldn't know good food if it slapped you upside your ugly mug."

"I was thinkin' about that," Jay said, setting his book down on the table, bending the spine. "The other day, when Carey mentioned Carolyn Masterson. Imagine the amazin' food she gets to eat everyday overseas."

"What, like haggis? That's *way* worse than chickpeas." Kevin groaned.

"Dean, you've been overseas. What'd you eat?" Jay asked.

Grumpy pants grunted, "Hot dogs."

"Hm. Fine dinin' then," Finn said with a serious face.

"Listen. I been thinkin'. Speakin' of fine dinin' and shit we can't afford. It's time we start talkin' 'bout the ranch," Jack said, interrupting abruptly, and the whole room grew silent. We heard the rain running down the roof in rivulets, pooling on the porch.

"Really? 'Cause I got a lotta ideas, Ja—" Jay practically jumped in his chair, but Jack held up his hand.

"We *ain't* doin' a dude ranch. It's not us, Jay."

"Yeah, but Jack, they make a lotta money."

"Actually, I drove over to one, over past all them resorts north of Jackson the other day. They're—"

A deafening cracking sound cut Dean off. It shook the house. I could feel the electricity in the air all around us, and a piercing ringing sound invaded my ears. There was one second of complete and utter still, then we all jumped up, the four guys running to the porch, while Kevin hopped behind. The thunder boomed and I felt the rumble in my body, and my heart kicked into a sprint.

"Shit! Jay, call the fire department!" Dean shouted. There was a lot of cursing, and Jack, Dean, and Finn all threw on their boots and ran outside. I followed after them to the front porch, but Jack yelled back to me.

"Evvie, look after Ma. Stay inside!"

"Oh no." The barn was on fire! Had it been hit by lightning? It looked like the fire burned only in the first aisle, but the rain poured down, making it hard to see so far away. I felt panic at the sight of the huge flames; I'd seen that kind of fire before. The big kind. I squeezed my eyes shut.

"Evvie, come back in. C'mon now, they got it," Kevin said, pulling me back through the screen door by the hood of my sweatshirt. His words were meant to be reassuring, but the tone of his voice was not. I stood there, inside the door, watching as utter chaos reigned in front of me. I couldn't do anything to help.

I prayed like hell the rain would keep the fire from spreading. All those horses! My Ruby. Trumpet. There were horses running everywhere. Somehow, they'd gotten out of their stalls. *Oh God. Jack. Be careful.*

"Dammit!" Jay slammed the phone back into its cradle on the wall. "I can't get through to nine-one-one. The landline's out and there's no cell service. Fuck, fuck, fuck. Shit, um... okay, I'm gonna take Dean's truck and go sound the alarm. Kevin, stay here. The last thing we need is you screwin' your leg up worse. Look after Ma and Evvie."

"Dammit, Jay, I can help."

"No, you can't. You'll just get your crutches stuck in the mud." Jay looked at me and through the kitchen to Ma. She stood in the living room, looking out the window there, worrying about her boys. "Stay inside. Someone needs to stay with Evvie and Ma."

"I'll keep tryin' my cell. Maybe I can get a text out," Kevin said, worrying the inside of his lip with his teeth, deciding he might still be useful from inside the house.

Jay pulled a jacket out of the closet in the little hallway behind the kitchen. He yanked it on, flipping the hood over his head. "I'll be back as soon as I can." He ran out the kitchen door, slamming it behind him and jumping from the porch.

"Okay, Evvie, let's go sit down. Ma's worried. Help me distract her."

"Oh… okay." I walked backward, looking out the screen door until I couldn't see anything anymore, then turned and set my sights on Ma.

"C'mon, Ma, sit down here," Kevin said, lowering himself to the couch, laying his crutches across the coffee table. "There's nothin' we can do to help 'em out there, but let's try to stay calm. Evvie, put another log on the fire. You know what to do?"

"Um, I think so. Don't I just lay it on top?"

"Yeah, but use the poker to stoke the embers a little so they settle a bit, then lay your log on top."

"Okay, got it."

Ma sat on the edge of the recliner, clearly not relaxed. "Oh, boys, be careful," she whispered, closing her eyes.

"Ma, get your hind-end over here. The wind's suckin' the heat up the chimney. I can feel the temp droppin'. We're gonna get cold real quick." Ma shuffled over to snuggle into Kevin on the couch, and he covered her with a blanket.

"Should I put more wood on the fire in the back?"

"No, just leave it. It won't do us much good, not till this wind dies down some. We'll just huddle up here with the blankets. Grab a couple more. There's some in the trunk there under the window." Adjusting the blanket over Ma, he scooted closer to her and pulled his shotgun, standing on its butt next to his leg at the end of the couch, closer to him too.

I retrieved the blankets and snuck a quick peek out the window. One of the guys raced through the rain on the back of a horse, chasing after one of the rogue horses, but the rain still fell in thick sheets—I couldn't tell who it was. It was pitch black outside, the only light coming from the fire and the occasional flash of lightning. How could they see anything?

The barn still burned but on the side farthest away from the house, so I couldn't really tell if it was better or worse than it had been a few minutes before. I hoped Jay would make it to town quickly to get help.

"Any luck, Kevin?" I asked.

He held up his phone, shaking his head. "Not yet."

I sat next to him and Ma on the couch, careful not to bump the gun, and covered us all with two heavy blankets.

A rush of wind whipped through the house, rustling papers on the counters and slamming the heavy kitchen door closed. I heard something clatter in Jack's room and remembered Iggy was in there.

"Oh no, Iggy's probably freaking out." I jumped up off the couch. "Be right back, I'm gonna make sure the window is shut and try to pull her out from under the bed." I let out a nervous laugh, jogging to the bedroom, calling for Iggy as I stepped through the door.

"Iggy, kitty, kitty?" The window was open, and I felt the wind whipping the rain in. It misted over my whole body, making me shiver. Great. The bed would be soaked. Wait, hadn't Jay shut all the windows when he lit the candles?

I felt a warning in my body. All the little hairs on my arms and the back of my neck stood on end, and I couldn't even see a foot in front of my face. The candle on Jack's dresser had gone out, but the fear came from more than just the darkness.

"The candle's out," I called out to Ma and Kevin. "I can't see anything."

"Look on the desk," Kevin called back. "There's usually a flashlight there."

I waved my hand over the top of Jack's desk, feeling for the flashlight. "No, I can't find—"

"Looking for this?" Barely a whisper but I heard it. A searing light shined in my eyes, blinding me, but I didn't need to see to know who stood next to me. His voice gave him away.

The monster.

He'd found me.

I screamed, and the sound of my voice seemed far away, inhuman somehow, as terror flooded my body and something smashed into my face, then the back of my head and then...

Nothing.

CHAPTER TWENTY-FOUR

JACK

THE RAIN DOUSED THE FIRE, but the lightnin' must have hit the ground and left a huge hole in the dirt at the mouth of the damn barn. If any of the horses tried to run back through, they'd be injured, and we'd be fucked. We'd be lookin' at broken legs and dead horses shortly thereafter.

And I didn't even wanna think about the barn. From what I'd been able to see, most of the first aisle and some of the second had been burned to a crisp, and where it wasn't burned, the horses kicked it, breakin' down stall doors to get away from the smoke and flames. I didn't think the fire made it to the tack room, so all our gear would be safe, but we wouldn't know for sure till we got in there. It would take a lotta work and not a little money to repair.

So far, though, none of the horses appeared to be injured, besides being scared outta their minds. Hopefully only a few scrapes. We'd need the vet to check their breathin' and legs though. Jay would call him. I'd noticed him tearin' down the lane, so he must not have been able to reach the fire department by phone.

Damn.

Sammy and I had rounded up three horses and had been leadin' a fourth back up to the arena when I noticed Finn ridin' toward me on Gertie, fast as whip, wavin' his arms in the air and shoutin' somethin'. Blackness surrounded us, the power still out, and with the fire thankfully also out, it was hard to see him, but I could, just barely, and the look on his face—

Dean reached him before I did, and they exchanged only a couple words. Dean pulled his gun from his shoulder and cocked it, racin' to the…

No.

I reached my brother, heart poundin'. "Finn?"

He shook his head. "Jack, Evvie's—"

I whispered it. There wasn't enough air in my body left to speak. "No."

Evvie. The fire. No.

I couldn't remember ridin' to the house, couldn't remember rippin' the screen door off its hinges.

Dean walked toward me from the little hallway leadin' to my bedroom with the most awful look of despair on his face and his shotgun hangin' from his fingers, and I rushed past him, throwin' the door outta my way so hard, it hit the wall and the doorknob popped out, landin' next to my foot. He stood behind me shinin' a flashlight at my window.

It had been busted out, no glass left in the frame, the screen a mangled mess on the bed, which had been pushed away from the window. Rainwater soaked everything.

I snatched the flashlight from Dean's hand, steppin' closer.

Blood. I saw dark blood on the windowsill.

Evvie.

"Jack," Dean hedged, like I was some caged animal. "Kevin is—"

"Where the fuck was he? How could he let this—"

"He's been shot."

My legs went weak, and Dean reached his arms out but I swatted 'em away.

"He's in the den."

He stepped back and I ran. "Kevin!"

"I'm okay. Jack, I'm so sorry. I'm so *fuckin'* sorry. I tried," he gritted out through clenched teeth. "I tried. I was too slow."

Evvie.

I kept hearin' her name in my mind, like a heartbeat.

Kevin lay on her bed, blood leakin' everywhere, soakin' the covers. Ma held his hand and tears ran down her face.

"Mama." I fell to my knees, wrappin' my arms around her. "You okay?"

"Oh, honey. I'm fine." She cried and then hung her head over Kevin and sobbed.

At some point or another the paramedics showed up, along with the fire trucks and Carey.

I stood there, struck fuckin' stupid. "Is he…?" I looked at my brother's face while they bandaged his wound, and he winced and tried hard not to pass out.

"I'm sorry, Jack," he said again, like he was beggin' my forgiveness.

I shook my head.

Evvie.

"I don't think the bullet hit anything too important, but I ain't a doctor, Jack. I think this might need a surgeon, though. He's still losin' blood." Dan Stephens, a guy from my high school class, and another volunteer fireman whose name I couldn't remember, lifted Kevin on a stretcher and carried him to their rig.

They checked Ma over and she'd been spared. Her blood

pressure was through the roof though. How much more could one woman take?

Evvie.

"Carey!" I screamed for him when the ambulance drove away with two of my brothers inside and my ma.

"C'mon, Jack. 'Round back," Dean said.

Carey and Finn paced the mud near my window, wearin' a ditch into it with their boots, and water seeped in, creatin' a river. Carey held a radio up in front of him, and I heard Billie's voice.

"I tried Carey. Their phones are all out. I called the fire department and you as soon as I could get through. Every-one's cells are down. Dispatch got through on the radio."

Carey saw me, and the look of regret and shame on his face made me stop in my tracks. "I've got Billie on the radio. She's lookin' for a rental car. Ma thinks it might've been red or maroon. It looks like he used somethin' to slide her from the window but I dunno what. There's some kind of red residue on the windowsill and frame. Somethin' scraped against it. Officer Geer's down by the road—this guy drove right through your front fuckin' fence a mile down the highway."

I looked at my watch. It had been an hour and forty-seven minutes since Carey arrived at the house. Time sped by, and I felt nothin' but panic at the thought of Evvie gettin' miles and miles away from me.

"Ma got a shot off," Finn said, pointin' a flashlight at my bedroom window, "hit that motherfucker too. He bled all over the windowsill. She was sure she hit her mark. She said he screamed like a little girl when he pulled Evvie through the window."

Evvie.

"It ain't Evvie's blood?" *Oh God, please let it be true.*

"Jack, I don't know," Carey said, squintin' through the onslaught of rain hittin' his face. "Ma said she shot him, but she don't know what happened before they got to your bedroom door. Between the time they heard Evvie scream and—"

Oh God. I bent at the waist, hands on my thighs, tryin' to breathe. Rain dripped off my body like a shower head. *Fuck. Fuck. Fuck.* She had to be so terrified.

"Okay," Billie's voice rang out from the speaker of Carey's radio, "I've found three maroon sedans, two red, rented in Teton County in the last month. I'm hacking GPS as we speak. How did he get past us, Carey? I've done nothing else but look for this sick fuck."

"I'd like to know that too," Finn said. "Until the storm hit, we had someone on the video feeds twenty-four-seven. We hooked 'em up to an app on Billie's phone. She had constant access, and it alerts her if there's anything movin'."

"I don't know, Finn. I don't know. I think he must've been watchin' Evvie long before we started lookin' out for him. The storm was a personal fuckin' invitation. Ain't no way he coulda predicted how bad it would get, so it only makes sense if he were close by, watchin'." Carey still paced in the mud but stopped on a dime when he heard Billie's voice through his radio again.

"Okay, I've got one red and one maroon in Wisper, actually. They both look parked near the main street in town, one on Franklin, the other on Ophelia Avenue. Then, the other red rental is in Idaho, near Boise, but that's too far. He couldn't have gotten that far yet. There's another maroon— Oh shit, Carey, this could be him. It's not far from you guys, off Highway 10. I can't see through the trees on SAT, but could there be something up there? A house or something? There's trails or off-roads. I don't know. Sending a screenshot of the coordinates now."

"Did she say Highway 10?" Dean asked, lookin' at me.

Highway 10. The cabin?

"Yeah," Carey said, "there's a rental car up there somewhere. Why? That mean somethin' to you?"

"Depends. Lemme see the screenshot." Dean crowded closer to Carey as he pulled his phone from his pocket, and Finn held his jacket over 'em both. I stood there, my body buzzin' with adrenaline. It already knew what my mind hadn't yet realized.

"Dammit, I still barely have a signal." Carey tried for a minute, hittin' the screen over and over. "Okay, I think it's loadin'. There's a tree down on Route 20, blockin' access to Highway 10. I'll send somebody up there to cut it up as soon as—"

Dean watched, and as soon as the picture came up, he sucked in a breath and I ran.

The cabin.

The tire treads.

"Jack! He's at the cabin!" Dean bellowed behind me, but I already knew. "Pop's cabin! Finn, c'mon! You ride with Jack, take the horses, and I'll take Carey. Jack's the only one who knows the location. Go!"

I ran toward the fence and hopped it, jumpin' on Sammy in the paddock, and we flew.

I heard Finn chasin' me. "What fuckin' cabin?"

The rain whipped my face and it stung, the wind pushin' me, tryin' to take me down, but I just rode harder.

Evvie.

Evvie, I'm comin'.

What had I done?

I promised her.

There wasn't a person more innocent or pure, and terror had been pretty much the only thing she'd ever experienced in her life. She didn't have any good memories. She didn't have her family and she'd been alone.

I'd promised her and now…

She'd become my family. My home.

I loved her and he would take her away.

Finn finally caught up to me. We'd wound our way through the trees near the base of the mountain at breakneck speed. It would be hard on Sammy's legs, pushin' up the mountain through brush and mud and rocks, but I couldn't worry about it. "Sammy, I'm sorry, please, buddy, *please*. Keep goin'."

"Jack, where is it?"

I couldn't speak. All I could think about was what that fuckin' monster was doin' to my Evvie.

We'd probably ridden ten miles, but now we were in the thick of the mountain, the brush gettin' deeper by the minute and our speed gettin' slower. I knew we were close, but in the dark, I couldn't be sure. I slowed every so often to check the compass on the watch Pops had given me years and years ago.

Finally, I jumped from Sammy and took off west, to the side of the bluff, at least, I hoped it was the bluff, from the little I could see in the black of the night and rain.

I heard Finn yellin' at Gertie, sendin' her and Sammy back toward home with a smack to their hind-ends. They wouldn't make it much further up the mountain anyway, not in the dark and slidin' mud. We only had light from the flashlight he'd had in his hand when he jumped on Gertie to follow me, and the moonlight.

But I knew I was almost there. I could feel it.

And that was when I smelled the gasoline.

CHAPTER TWENTY-FIVE

EVERLEA

OPENING MY EYES SLOWLY, I realized the panic had gone.

It seemed weird. I should've been freaking out, but all I could feel was a numb fear. I sensed the panic. It was near but I couldn't reach it. I figured it was a good thing. Maybe it was some kind of defense mechanism.

When I'd woken up once before, I was in the trunk of a car; I smelled the gas fumes and heard the road beneath me. The fear had been a physical thing then, like bugs crawling all over my skin—faster and faster and faster.

I was soaking wet from the rain, and the cold had woken me, but even that couldn't distract me from the terror gripping me, every cell in my body. Needless to say, that time I did freak out, and I think I may have hyperventilated myself back into unconsciousness.

This time, I'd been bound and tied to something in the middle of... Jack's cabin? When did I get here? And how did I get from the trunk of a car to the cabin? It was a mile, at least, of hiking uphill from the end of the dirt road and the trailhead. I remembered because I'd complained about having to walk so far on our way back to Jack's truck when we'd stayed the night at the cabin. Jack had laughed and hauled me up, swinging me onto his back, and I wrapped my arms and legs around him and rode piggyback the rest of the way, kissing his neck and shoulders.

I smiled at the memory and winced. My face was so sore and throbbing, the right side, my cheek, ear, jaw, and temple.

Jack.

Jack would come for me.

I needed to stay alive until he did. I took a deep breath, trying to focus, taking stock of my injuries and surroundings. I'd been bound to something hard—a wooden beam in the middle of the room. The only light came from a flashlight that had been aimed at my body from the mantle of the fireplace and a few flickering candles. I couldn't see them, but I could see the dancing shadows their light produced on the walls and floor of the cabin.

My ankles, waist, wrists, and chest were tied to the beam with scratchy rope. Every movement I made felt like agony, like tiny glass shards dragged back and forth across the raw skin of my wrists and ankles. My feet didn't touch the floor because I'd been suspended a foot in the air, and I was freezing. I knew that for sure.

My whole body shook. I couldn't control it. My clothes were still soaked through from the rain, and my arms and legs were sore, muscles burning, fingers and toes numb. I couldn't feel them or move them at all. My breath turned to white steam as soon as it huffed out of my mouth.

But all I could really focus on was the pounding in my head. I heard noises in the cabin with me, but I had a hard time concentrating on them because the throbbing had become so intense, and every sound was amplified.

"I've been watching you," the monster purred. "I knew

you needed time. Our little game of hide and seek can be so hard on you, Clare."

The sound of his voice physically revolted me, nasal, reedy, and shrill as it echoed in my head. I had to try really hard not to react when I heard it.

Suddenly, he stood next to me, dragging his bony hand down my face, my arm, and my stomach. His face and neck sallow and pockmarked everywhere, it looked like he picked at his skin, causing scabs to form.

My head throbbed, and I was dizzy and shaking violently, but when he touched me, my entire body became completely still, like another warning signal had been tripped. I was nauseous and I tried to hold back vomit, swallowing convulsively, tears streaming down my face from the constant effort.

"I know, I know, my love," he whispered. "I feel it too. It's been so long. To touch you again, it makes me whole. How I've missed you, my darling." He pulled back, looking me up and down. "But then you go and fuck that *filthy* horse boy. How dare you!" he shrieked, spitting in my face, in my hair. His breath smelled like cigarettes and rot.

"I watched him fuck you, Clare, right here in this cabin. You-you let him put his hands on you, in you, in *my* body, his filthy hands touched your hair. My hair! You belong to me!" He shook with fury as he turned into me, digging his erection into my leg. Seeing me beat up, shaking, and terrified turned him on.

He put his disgusting mouth on my jaw, grabbed a fist full of my hair, and whispered, "You're mine. If you thought desecrating your body with that man would stop me, you. Were. WRONG!" He screamed it so loudly, slamming my ear to his mouth. My eardrum popped, and a loud ringing sound exploded in my head, making it pound harder.

I'd been afraid before when he'd caught me, but this time

felt different. There was an edge to his words. He was unhinged—not in control. Before, I felt like a mouse in the clutches of my own sadistic cobra whose goal in life was to haunt and terrify me, but now, I just felt like a witness to madness.

I wasn't afraid of the man himself, only of what he could do to me that would take me away from Jack.

He stepped back, lifting something from the table behind my left shoulder. I caught a glimpse of a piece of metal reflecting the light from a burning candle right before he grabbed my hair in one hand, pulled it out from behind me, and yanked my head back. It knocked into the beam, and he dragged it over to him.

It hurt so much, and a black fog washed over my eyes, a numbness that filled them and leaked out, consuming everything. My mind tried to shut down, but I fought it with every ounce of strength I had inside me. If I had any chance of ever seeing Jack again, I needed to pay attention to everything the monster did and said.

I gritted my teeth against the pain and heard a *shck-shck-shck* sound, and my head fell forward because it no longer connected to my long hair. He'd cut it off. My hair.

I tried so hard not to cry. That was my mother's hair, the only thing, besides the piano, I'd shared with her. But I wouldn't let myself feel it. I wouldn't give the monster the satisfaction.

I told Jack I hated her but I didn't. I was so angry at her. I felt rejected by her, and I was sad I had to live my life without her, but I didn't hate her.

The monster lurked behind me, and I felt pure terror at not being able to see him—what he would do to me next. I tried to concentrate on what I *could* see and hear, what I could control, but I'd been so tightly bound.

The only things I had any command of were my thoughts and my breathing, so I slowed my breath, making it deep and even. He made no sound behind me. I couldn't even hear his footsteps on the wooden cabin floor.

When he finally appeared on my right side, he held my shorn hair, plastering it across his face, smelling it, breathing deeply through his nose. The sound of him sniffing and moaning was so disgusting. The repulsive sound in the back of his throat made me sick, and my stomach heaved.

Standing in front of me again, he clutched my hair in one hand and grabbed his penis through his pants with the other, squeezing himself hard. His knuckles turned white, and he whispered, "Look what you do to me."

He wouldn't look at me, not in my eyes, thank God, but I thought he knew I wasn't my mother, and if he saw my green eyes staring back at him, instead of her blue, he'd lose the connection he thought he had to her.

Maybe if I forced him to acknowledge it, I could distract him, or maybe he'd just kill me sooner, but I had to try something. I'd already lost feeling in my feet and hands, the numbness spreading quickly up my legs and arms. I knew he could do anything to me, and I'd be powerless to stop him. He'd removed my shoes and socks so I couldn't run, not on frozen feet, even if I were somehow miraculously able to get free.

He unbuttoned his pants, and I knew I only had seconds to save myself from watching him masturbate, or worse. I couldn't think about worse. I had to try to talk my way out of this hell somehow.

"Paul?"

Whipping his head up, forgetting to keep his eyes from mine, he looked at me and I began to shake again. My voice sounded scratchy and thin, my throat completely dry, but I tried to clear it so he could hear me. I'd never actually spoken to him before, with the exception of the "interview" at the record store. Well, and begging, I'd begged him to leave me alone, to let me go, but I'd never uttered his name out loud. So when I did, even as quiet and weak as my voice was, he heard it loud and clear.

"You know I'm not her. I'm not my mother. I can't give you what she did. You know it. Please see *me.*"

Clamping his eyes shut, he turned away from me, facing the fireplace. He stood completely motionless and it terrified me.

"Oh, I see you. I've watched you for so long. You've changed your hair, your clothes, you even smell different, and you don't play my songs anymore, but you are her. You. Are. My. Clare."

"No, I'm not! Look at me!" My head pounded harder, and the racking shivering made it so much worse. Each breath in became thinner and shallower. I'd never been so cold.

"Please..." I lost the battle not to cry. I sobbed and begged. "Please, *please*, let me go back to my family. Please!"

"You do not have a *family*. I'm the only one you need." He paced back and forth in front of me, stopping every few seconds to look over at my legs, at my body, with nervous and beady, covetous eyes.

But I did have a family. Jack was my family, Ma, Kevin, all of them. Jack had become my home.

"Please, Paul. If you stop this now, you can go back to your family, too, to your sons. Don't they miss you?" I sobbed. Not catching my slip, that I knew about his sons, he shook his head, laughing—he didn't care about them at all. The deranged sound of his cackling and giggling sent new chills up and down my spine. Finally, he stopped pacing and came to stand in front of me, a foot from my body, but not looking at my face again.

"Didn't you miss me at all?" he whispered. "It's been so long since we've been together. I gave you space. I knew you needed it. You like to... have your own life." He shrugged. "I've been so understanding. I'm sure you agree, my love. But after everything I've done for us to be together— I've given up *everything* for you. No one can love you like I can, Clare. You know that. Why? Why do you insist on denying me? Defying me!"

The cold air was so painful on my skin, like millions of needles stabbing me, and I worried about hypothermia. I didn't know how long I'd been in the cabin. Jack's cabin. Maybe he'd think to look here. Maybe there would be a trail.

So lost in my thoughts and losing my battle with consciousness, I couldn't pay attention like I knew I should. I was so cold and so tired. My eyelids became heavier and heavier, and my head dropped forward.

"Pay attention to me! I've waited too long for you to ignore me."

"What?" I wheezed a laugh. Something had occurred to me. I amazed myself with the ability to still string the thoughts together. "You're just like her." I laughed more. I felt crazed, laughing at a time like this, and it hurt but I couldn't stop myself. "J-just like her." I could barely get the words out, my teeth chattered uncontrollably.

"All this time, I thought I was running from a m-monster, but you're not. Monsters are strong and s-scary. You're just pathetic and weak. Just like your p-precious Clare. That's all she ever wanted. Attention. That's why she slept with you, why this is all happening now. She was so fucking insecure that she needed everyone to tell her how amazing she was. And now, listen to you. 'Pay attention to me'?"

I laughed and laughed. My head spun and throbbed so I couldn't hear where he was in the room, but it didn't matter. He would kill me. Maybe he already had. I didn't know if a person could die from a concussion, but I knew hypothermia was a definite possibility.

And I knew, if he hadn't been mad before, he was now.

I hadn't thought I could handle knowing I would die, especially since Jack. But now, Jack's face was all I could see. If he was safe, then I could face anything, even death. I didn't want to. I wanted to be with him forever. How stupid of me to think I could have left him. Now I would be taken from him, and I was so angry at myself for wasting even those few minutes. My laughter turned to wretched, anguished sobs.

But I could still see the vision, the one I'd seen the day Jack showed me his granny's house, and my sobs ebbed away. I pretended the vision had been made up of real memories, that I was Ma's age and all those wonderful things I'd seen had actually happened.

I was fading quickly, my breath wheezing its way faster and faster in and out of my mouth, but I couldn't get enough air into my lungs. I couldn't feel anything anymore, my entire body numb from the cold, but I smiled, seeing Jack and our children, our family, the ranch. We were happy. I could still see it so clearly, and I remembered the smells, the pink color of the walls, the way my body felt reaching and grasping for that forbidden future. I focused on it. If I had to die, at least I could be happy when I did. And I could be with Jack.

"I killed your lover, *Jack*," the monster spat. "That's who you're thinking about, isn't it? You think he loves you. As if I'd ever let you have that. Do you think I'm weak now? Hmm?"

His words ripped me from my fantasy, and my eyes popped open as an electrical rage traveled down my body.

"You're *lying*. You'd be dead if you'd t-tried t-to kill Jack. He would rip your head off your neck in a second. Any of them would. You could never compare and you know it! Jack is *not* d-dead."

He couldn't be. I refused to believe it.

"No? Well, when that old lady tried to shoot me, I shot back. I hit him, your Jack. Do you still think he's coming for you?" He looked down at his left side, wincing and twisting, trying to see it better, and I noticed for the first time that he'd been wounded, blood seeping slowly through his shirt.

Ma shot him? Oh, how I loved that feisty old lady!

It was why we were here at the cabin, still so close to the ranch. He'd been shot and probably couldn't go any further. He was definitely *not* in control.

Neither was I, but maybe this was the mistake Carey or Billie needed. He thought he'd already killed Jack. The storm stopped him from being more thorough, and he'd been shot so he'd had to run, but he didn't get far.

I knew it hadn't been Jack he shot; Jack hadn't been inside the house when the monster came for me. But Kevin had been. He'd confused Kevin for Jack. *Oh God. Kevin. Ma.* They had to be okay. They had to. If Kevin was shot, Ma would get help. They would make it.

I couldn't consider any other outcome.

"I know he is, and when he gets here, y-you better run. You are a *pathetic* excuse for a man. You made a mistake. I just realized it. It took loving Jack f-for me to see, but now I do."

"I didn't make a mistake. I never do. Haven't you wondered how I've been able to find you all these years? I've tracked you, traced you, followed you. You were never out of my sight. I let you believe it, let you believe you'd gotten away. We had more fun that way, don't you think? Allowing you to get comfortable, relax. Make *friends*." He laughed. "Do you think I'm stupid? I will always find you!" More spitting.

"You did make a mistake. Actually, you made two. But the most important one is that you chose me. I didn't know before because I was too… t-too scared, too caught up in it, in my parents' death." I struggled to catch enough breath to speak, but I couldn't give up. I had to keep going.

Hope had snuck back in.

"I was t-too caught up in the past, but I'm letting that go. For the f-first time in my life, I have a f-future. I have a home. Hope. You can't s-scare me anymore. I will *never* give in to you. You got the wrong girl, asshole!"

I tried so hard. To breathe, to stay awake, to stall the monster. I knew in my very soul Jack would come for me. He loved me. He wouldn't give up. None of them would. And the monster was completely unaware of the resources we had behind us. He never would have guessed I could best him in any way, believing himself to be superior, smarter, and in control at all times. Maybe Carey had already identified the vehicle he'd used to take me away from the ranch. I just had to make it until Jack found me.

He *would* find me.

He had to because, if he didn't, none of this would matter anyway.

I could barely see anymore. I wasn't sure if it was the cold or just plain old pain blinding me, pain so intense it bent me from the inside out, but my vision was a lake of black. I couldn't think about it. I pushed it away. If I allowed myself to feel the pain, the fear, I would lose myself, my hold on reality.

I collected it all in my mind: the physical pain, the cold, my fear for Jack, Kevin, Ma, and the others. The pain of my parents being burned alive in front of me. The pain of leaving Jack. That was the hardest to push away. I held on to the thought, trying as hard as I could to push it back so I could focus, but it was just too painful, too big, too intense.

He whispered in my ear, "Does *this* scare you?"

Something pressed against my abdomen. Just a dull feeling for a few seconds, but then I felt a slow, sharp, ripping pain in my gut. The burning and tearing feeling was so intense and enormous, I couldn't even scream.

It took every ounce of energy I had left to survive that pain. And then it was gone, in an instant, and I felt something hot and wet gushing down my frozen legs, soaking my leggings. The heat from the blood actually felt good.

He'd stabbed me.

He held the scissors in his hands. The metal, glinting silver and blood red in the candlelight, broke through the haze in my eyes.

Jack, where are you?

I knew I should be freaking out, but exhaustion was taking over, and I couldn't hold my head up anymore. It hung forward, the jagged pieces of my butchered hair tickling the back of my neck.

"Still think I'm weak? Looks like you're the weakling now. You should see yourself!" He cackled at me. "You're disgusting. You're unclean. You have his filth all over you, inside you." Leaning in close, hands wrapped around my hips possessively, fingers digging painfully into my skin, he whispered, "How could you fall in love with him? You were supposed to love me."

His breath washed over my face like a hot, putrid fog. "You think you're better than me? Well, look who's laughing now, bitch. Look who's laughing now! You think we're done?"

He yanked my head by my hair again, and I screamed so hard and so long. I screamed for Jack, but no sound came out because I'd run out of air.

Jack. Please, please find me.

As I drifted in and out of the darkness, trying desperately to hold on to Jack—he was right there; I could almost feel him—the monster paced and muttered, his words tumbling out in a frantic jumble.

"I'm going to cleanse you again. We'll start over. We need to leave this place. I just have to get him off of you first, out of you. You're not better than me. You're mine. I will have you. You love our game. We'll start over. You'll see. It will be better this time, Clare."

I tried to respond but I couldn't. The words wouldn't come. The pain and cold and darkness began to spill over the dam in my head, swirling around and down my neck. It overwhelmed my mind, and the panic had returned and locked on, entering my body like a dragon surfing the pain. It roared in my ears and in my heart, making it stutter and hurt.

I heard liquid splashing, a lot of liquid, and then a distinct odor invaded my nose. I tasted it, a thick, bitter, chemical film on my tongue, in the back of my throat. I choked and my head swam. I knew the word for the scent, but my mind wouldn't grasp it, and then I heard a tiny *scchhhhk*.

A match.

I tried to follow all the sounds in the cabin. If I could just hold on to one thing… I heard some kind of faint disturbance by the cabin door, and then cold air surrounded me, and colder air still.

A new sound filled my ears, a rustling and scuffling. It felt familiar, but I just couldn't put my finger on it. It didn't matter. I was dying. The pain, the cold, it had all become too much, and I didn't have enough air.

Would Jack forgive me?

"Jack, I love you. Please forgive me," I begged, but my words tripped and fell, slowly slurring their way out of me. I heard Jack's voice in my head. It sounded far away, like an echo, and he was in so much pain.

No, Jack, don't hurt. It's okay.

I love you.

CHAPTER TWENTY-SIX

JACK

I RAN FOR MY FUCKIN' life.

Evvie's life.

'Cause if he lit the cabin on fire, it wouldn't take but a minute to burn, old as it was.

Reachin' the top of the hill, I sprinted toward the cabin, but the rain still pounded, and every step through the mud was a fight, the wet muck suckin' my feet in deeper and deeper, tryin' to pull me down, hold me back, stop me. My legs were so tired from ridin' and climbin', but I pushed 'em, forcin' 'em to carry me forward.

My mama's face flashed in my mind. She laughed at me, mocked me for runnin' toward love. But I stomped her down. She wouldn't stop me anymore. She couldn't.

I wouldn't let her.

I made it to the door and stopped fast. Finn nearly smacked right into my back, and I held up my hand to stop him. I was so fuckin' scared. What would I find on the other side of the door? Would we startle this man and make him panic? Would he set the place on fire, shoot Evvie, Finn?

I didn't know, and every single one of the million possibilities terrified me.

I listened for Evvie's voice, for any sign she still lived, but the relentless downpour made it impossible to hear anything but the thuddin' of freezin' raindrops on wood.

A red plastic children's sled stood against the outside wall of the cabin. It had a rope tied to it, creatin' a makeshift handle. Mud and dead leaves covered it, and somehow it felt like a reminder of all I'd lost in my life. The good times we'd had as kids. The life we'd had.

The sled must've been what he'd used to pull Evvie from my bedroom window—the red residue—and up the mountain from the trailhead. Was it an omen of what more I'd lose? The future I'd barely dared to dream, would I lose that too?

I opened the door slowly, millimeter by millimeter. *Oh God.* Evvie was... *no.* She'd been tied to a support beam in the middle of the cabin, suspended a foot off the ground. Her head hung forward, blood drippin' everywhere.

Rage overtook my whole body. I saw the man not fifteen feet from me. He paced back and forth, mutterin', but I couldn't hear what he said. I didn't think he'd even noticed us come in. A murderous heat spread through my body, my head, my arms and hands, and I needed to break his neck. I coulda broken every bone in his body, one by one, slowly, without battin' an eye.

But I heard Evvie's voice and fear won out. I had to get her outta there. He'd already started a fire. It licked up the floor and back wall. We didn't have much time. I knew Finn would subdue the man, and I couldn't leave Evvie trussed up for one more second.

I ran to her, slippin' in the puddle of blood beneath her feet, but grabbed the support beam behind her to steady myself.

"Evvie. Oh God. I'm here, Evvie. Please, *please* be okay. I'm here. Can you hear me?" I smelled the fire eatin' the gasoline behind me, and I heard Finn wrestlin' with the man, but it was just a vague annoyance in my nose and ears. All I saw was Evvie.

"Jack... Lovuu. Pease f'give me," she whispered. Her words slurred, and she barely had enough breath to push 'em out. She tried to lift her head, moved it a fraction of an inch, but it fell again.

Pullin' my huntin' knife from my boot, I sliced through the ropes, one by one, till she collapsed into my arms. A dead weight.

I carried her, her head hangin' loose, her arms and legs danglin' like heavy stuffed doll limbs over my arms, to the door. She breathed, but not enough and she was *so* cold. I held her to me, tryin' to infuse the heat from my body into hers.

Lookin' up as I neared the door, I saw Finn fightin' with the man. He watched me carryin' Evvie, and a wild desperation flashed in his eyes. He believed his delusions, that Evvie was her mama. He tried to say somethin', spittin' his venom. It sounded like "unclean" and "filthy hands off."

Arms outstretched for Evvie, he took one step toward me, but Finn kicked him with a boot to the gut toward the door, and he hit the wall. His head made a loud thud against the wood before he fell to the floor, unconscious. Finn kneeled over him, checkin' his pulse, then looked up.

"Alive."

"Leave him. Let the fire take him." That man's life lay in my brother's hands, literally, and for just a second, jealousy gripped me, caught me between the door and Evvie's freedom. My hands throbbed to wring the life from his body. To rip his neck open and watch the blood flow out.

Maybe I shoulda cared somehow, if he died, about the loss of life.

I didn't.

Evvie's body shut down. I heard it, just a soft sigh, but the sound made my ears ring.

There was so much blood. It soaked my clothes, flowin' between us, slickin' my skin. I couldn't hear or see anything but her lifeless body. Her chest didn't rise with breath anymore and panic set in.

I wanted to get her to safety, away from the fire, but my legs wouldn't carry me any further than a few feet out the door. I dropped down to my knees in the mud. "Evvie please, *please* don't leave me. I love you," I whispered in her ear, rockin' us back and forth. But she didn't open her eyes.

She couldn't.

"*Please*. Evvie, please, I love you. I'm so sorry. I'm sorry. *Please*, just wake up. Evvie!" I rocked harder, squeezin' her to my chest. If she could feel me breathin', maybe she—

"Jack." Dean dropped to his knees in front of me. The pity and sorrow in his voice made me angry. How could he give up so fast? Didn't he know how much I loved her?

"Brother, put her down." He said it so gently, tryin' to look into my eyes, but I couldn't look away from Evvie.

"I can't. I *love* her. Don'tcha know that? She's so cold, Dean. Help me wake her up," I begged.

"Jack, put her down so I can do CPR. She's not breathin'. Please, brother, put her down." Dean begged too. Why did he want me to give her up? I didn't understand.

"Please don't take her away from me."

"Jack, fucking put her down!" he bellowed, and he ripped Evvie outta my arms.

He laid her in the mud, and I felt my connection to her break, all her shimmerin' strings and threads that had wound their way through me, from her to me, from the first moment I'd laid my eyes on her. My hands shook and I reached out, frantic, tryin' to pick her back up, tryin' to reconnect 'em. To make 'em grow back.

I pushed my brother's hands away from her. "Dean. *Please*."

I tried again, but my arms and legs wouldn't move, and I fought to get free till I realized Finn had wrapped his body around mine to stop me.

Everything came back into focus then. Everything made sense again.

Dean started CPR and I watched, paralyzed, as he pushed so hard. I worried he'd break Evvie's bones, but if he didn't get her heart started, broken ribs wouldn't... matter.

Sound and silence bounced its way in and out of my ears. I heard a rhythmic whirrin', like some kinda machine. I heard my brothers talkin' and shoutin' but not what they said, and the whole time, I held my breath, waitin' for Evvie to breathe.

Paramedics and police crashed through the trees, threw down their gear, pushin' Dean outta the way. Flashin' lights came at me from every direction, focusin' their yellow glow on Evvie's body. Someone cut her shirt a little, then ripped it open and attached pads to her chest, and sounds returned to me all at once, swarmin' me like bees.

So much blood.

"Dear God." Carey.

"Oh fuck." Finn.

"Somebody put pressure on this wound. Now!" Medic.

"That motherfucker gutted her." Dean. "Where is he, Carey? Is he dead?"

"He's dead," Carey said, and I watched as he looked behind me at somethin'. He nodded at me, but I couldn't be bothered. I couldn't look away from Evvie.

They shocked her four times, and still, I held my breath.

"I got a pulse!" the medic yelled, and she puffed oxygen into Evvie with a plastic bag she held over her mouth. A different paramedic intubated her and puffed the bag, and Evvie's chest rose. I sucked in some kinda breath, but I still couldn't feel any air in my lungs. I thought I'd pass out but I didn't.

I wouldn't leave her.

The medic packed Evvie's wounds with gauze and applied pressure with her hands. They were covered in blood and mud.

"Sylvia, back off, let 'em take over. Go!" Carey yelled at the paramedic, and then a tangle of legs blocked Evvie from my view, and vaguely it registered that whoever the legs belonged to wore combat boots and camo pants. I kicked and pushed against Finn to get free.

"What're you doin'? Don't touch her!"

They didn't listen. Slidin' a board underneath her, they strapped her down, then lifted her and took her away from me. I twisted in Finn's hold to watch 'em put her in some kinda bucket. It dangled from a helicopter hoverin' above us, swingin' in the wind—the whirrin' noise.

I retched and heaved as they took her from me, as the last hooks of her strings ripped free from my gut.

Somewhere in my mind I knew this must've been a good thing. Carey wouldn't take her away from me if there wasn't a good reason, but the fear I felt watchin' her bein' lifted into the air blinded me, and I couldn't see through it.

I watched her disappear and realized the rain had stopped. The cabin was engulfed in flames, and I could feel the heat from it behind Finn and me.

"My truck's at the trailhead," Carey yelled over the sound of the helicopter rotors. The leaves and trees rustled and creaked in their wind. They screeched at me that I'd failed. I'd promised Evvie we were safe, that I wouldn't let anything happen to her, and I'd failed her.

Carey looked at me while he talked to Finn, like I wasn't there. Like I didn't exist. Why did he do that? Did he know what I'd done? "Give the guys a chance to get a few more feet in the air and then let go of him, Finn."

"Jack, calm down," Finn whispered in my ear. "I know you're scared, but please, you can't help Evvie if you don't calm down."

"I love her. She's my home. Please, let me go. I have to get to her. I have to— I need to—" All the fight left me. "Finn. Will she ever forgive me?"

"Brother. You haven't done anything wrong. There's nothin' to forgive. She's gonna be okay," he said while the helicopter climbed higher and away from us.

Finn released me and I took off. I didn't tell my legs to lift me. I told 'em to make me fly and they did. I flew the mile to Carey's cruiser, pushin' past brush and trees. They ripped and sliced my hands, but it didn't matter.

Reachin' the truck, I threw the door open, but Carey pulled me out by my arm. He pushed me in the direction of the passenger door, but I didn't spare him a glance. No time.

Tears flowed down my face. I felt 'em and tasted the salt in my mouth. I saw Evvie in front of me, laughin' and runnin' in the meadow. I saw her playin' the piano and the beautiful smile she wore every time. I saw her sittin' next to me on the bluff, in the pink and purple sunrise. Her beautiful green eyes as I made love to her. I saw her in my granny's old house, dreamin' of a life neither one of us ever dared to hope for.

She'd woken me up. She made me alive and I couldn't exist without her. I needed her like the blood in my veins. She made me want and hope and dream.

She made me love her.

And now, she would take it all with her and I'd never get it back.

"They just touched down at the hospital, Jack. She's alive, brother, but it's—she's... critical." Carey placed his cell on the dash and pressed the gas pedal down as far as it would go.

———

It had been two days since they moved Evvie to the ICU and still, she lay unconscious. They'd removed the breathin' tube and the heart monitor after they brought her to the open, gray, cold cavern of a hospital room. Her temperature and vitals were all normal, but she wouldn't wake up. They took her for more tests, another CAT scan, and somethin' called an EEG to measure her brain waves, to make absolutely sure her head hadn't suffered any damage, but everything came back fine.

Why wasn't she wakin' up?

I sat next to her the whole time, caressin' and kissin' her arms, and I even laid on the edge of the bed when no one could see. I begged and cried for her to wake up. I told her I loved her so many times, I lost my voice. I washed her body with warm washcloths and covered her with the blankets the nurses kept heated in a little oven.

Still, she didn't wake up.

I thought I might lose my mind and then a psychologist, of all goddamn things, came into Evvie's room, askin' to talk to me. She wanted to pull me out into the hall, said she'd rather talk in private, didn't want Evvie to overhear. I wouldn't go. I wouldn't leave Evvie's side till she woke up. I told the doctor just to say whatever the fuck she needed to. Evvie could handle it.

"Mr. Cade, I want to discuss the possibility that Ms.

Donovan may be unconscious for an unknown amount of time. She's suffered significant trauma, on top of years of psychological stress and fear. This may"—she backed up a couple feet when I turned my head to glare at her—"take a while."

"All due respect, Doc, but you don't know her. She just ain't ready yet."

Somethin' changed in her expression when she heard my words, and she relaxed, sat down in the chair next to me, and sighed. "You're right. I don't know her. I'm not trying to discourage you, Mr. Cade. I just want to inform you of the possibilities.

"I'll be honest, I've never seen anything like this. She must be extremely strong to have endured what she did these past nine years, alone. I've spoken with Sheriff Michaels, and he says Ms. Donovan has really opened up with you. I encourage you to keep talking to her and touching her. And if there's any help I can provide, please, just call me." She stood and walked toward the door.

"Doc?"

"Yes, Mr. Cade?"

"She's the strongest person I've ever known. But... I think she's gonna need to... to talk to someone when she's better."

"Yes, that will be important. Please, take my card. You can call me anytime. I would be happy to talk with her or help her find someone else if she prefers. You can call, too, if you need to, anytime." She walked back toward me, set her card on the rollin' table between us, and left.

Finn stayed posted outside Evvie's room most of the time. He talked and flirted with the nurses, but I could hear the fear in his voice. He couldn't look at her, and he wouldn't come into her room more than a few feet. He was afraid for Evvie. And for me. Afraid she wouldn't wake up, afraid because he'd seen how badly she'd been hurt. He saw the same thing I did: Evvie lifeless, bloody. And he fought with that man. Finn would blame himself if Evvie didn't...

I understood. I blamed myself. I never shoulda left her side. I asked her to trust us—to trust me. Could she ever forgive me?

I would never forgive myself.

It was three in the mornin' and I jerked myself awake again. I didn't wanna miss it when Evvie woke up. I'd sent Jay and Dean home to take care of Ma and the horses.

Kevin was doin' fine. That fuckin' psychopath shot my brother in the gut, thinkin' he was me, but the bullet missed any major organs or arteries, thankfully. So, Kevin, once again, was soakin' up the attention of every nurse in the damn hospital. The doctor said he could go home the next day. I couldn't even think about what I woulda done if—

It had been hell on earth when they'd both been in surgery at the same time.

Standin' from the awful chair I'd been livin' in for the past two days, I stretched. The incessant checkin' of Evvie's vitals by the nurses made it damn near impossible to get any rest. I couldn't be mad at 'em though. I found myself just as focused on those numbers as they were, now that I knew what they meant. I'd definitely had an education in hospital terminology over the last few days: BP, RBC, O2 sats.

I bent down to kiss Evvie's now-pink lips and turned to walk to the john to take a leak when I heard the most ear piercin', terror-filled scream. It raised the hair on the back of my neck and sent my stomach into my boots. Jumpin' back to Evvie, I scooped her up in my arms as she struggled and flailed against me. She shook. Her whole body convulsed.

"Evvie, Evvie, it's me. It's Jack. You're safe. Shh, shh, you're okay."

Finn threw the door to our room open, and a whole mass of nurses and orderlies came rushin' in.

"Give her a minute," I warned.

Lauren, the head nurse, nodded to the hallway and everyone left the room, but she stayed right outside the door, watchin' us and listenin'.

"Calm down, breathe, you're safe. He's gone. He'll never hurt you again." I whispered it into her ear.

"Jack?" Her voice was so quiet and raspy, but I heard it as she stilled in my arms.

"I'm here, Evvie. I'm here." She turned her head, burrowin' into my chest. "You're okay, you're okay." I kissed her anywhere I could reach, sittin' down on the bed, kissin' her some more. She looked up, searchin' my face with her beautiful green eyes, and I thought I might die from the relief I felt seein' 'em again. But the guilt and shame and fear I still felt wouldn't let go.

"He said you were dead, you weren't coming, but I knew you would. I tried so hard not to give up, but I— It was so cold. I tried, I tried so hard. I'm so sorry." She sobbed, her whole body racked with it, but she was so warm and just feelin' her move in my arms made me dizzy.

But why was she apologizin' to me?

"Try to calm down. You have a lotta stitches in your belly. I don't want you to hurt yourself."

"He stabbed me!" She jerked her hands to her stomach, feelin' around there, locatin' her bandage under her hospital johnny. "It hurt so much. I was so scared, Jack. I thought I'd never see you again!"

She cried and sobbed for hours, then slept for longer in my arms. Lauren checked her over while she cried, and the doctor came in early, examinin' her while she cried. Then suddenly, she stopped and fell asleep. I lay next to her on the hospital bed, wrapped around her, waitin' for her to wake up again. I couldn't get the image of her, lifeless and bloody, outta my mind. I knew she'd be okay; she lay warm and breathin' in my arms, but I couldn't stop the images.

I couldn't stop thinkin' about what woulda happened if I'd been two minutes later. Or one.

Everybody had been in to see her, and Evvie slept through it all. I was startin' to worry about her not havin' any food in her stomach when she finally woke. I held her so tight—it was a wonder she could breathe at all.

"Tighter, Jack," she murmured.

I hadn't even felt her wake up. I jumped up.

"Jack, what's wrong? Are you okay?"

"I'm fine. I just— I don't wanna hurt you," I lied to her.

"I'm okay but I need you."

"Why?" Panic rose up in my chest. I knew it was comin'. Any minute now, she'd realize I'd failed her, broken my promise. I just kept seein' her dyin'.

"Come here."

"Okay, but let's get the nurse. I'm sure they wanna check you out first." She reached out toward me. "No. Evvie, careful, you'll rip your stitches."

"Ow. Then get down here, damn it."

"I can't. I-I gotta get the nurse." The image of her strapped to the beam in the cabin, bloody, dyin', popped into my head again. I couldn't see anything else.

"Jack, please. I need you. What's wrong?"

"No. I'm the last thing you need. I'll get the nurse," I said, and I left the room.

Finn stood outside the door. "Jack? She okay?"

"Yeah. Get the nurse for her. They probably wanna check her out. I-I gotta— I need to get outta here."

"Jack? Jack!" he called after me as I stepped into the elevator, pressin' the button to take me away from Evvie.

———

An eternity passed as I paced the hospital entrance. The old lady behind the reception desk must've thought I was nuts. I couldn't go back up there, but I couldn't seem to make myself leave. How could I face Evvie after what I'd done to her? I'd let her down. I promised her and she died. In my arms!

I heard Finn callin' my name down the hallway, and I nearly busted through the automatic door when it wouldn't open fast enough to let me out. Kevin had been right. This hospital was a prison.

"Jack. Jack! Goddammit. Stop!" Finn hollered at me as I walked away. I didn't know where I'd go. I just knew I couldn't go back in there.

I stopped in the middle of the drive when I realized I didn't have my truck.

"What in the ever-lovin' fuck are you doin'?"

"Leavin'."

"Why on earth would you leave? Evvie's awake. She wants you."

"Yeah, well, can't always get whatcha want." I winced as I said the words.

"Really? You're really gonna go back to bein' a dick? Now?"

I rounded on him. "I can't go back in there, Finn! How can I look her in the eye? I don't deserve her. It's my fault he got to her. I shoulda killed him. I wanna kill him so bad sometimes I can't breathe." I gasped in air. "She died!"

"You know what? I don't have any idea what that thick mass of cells you got in your head is tellin' you, but it ain't your fault. The guy was *insane*. He watched and waited. How could we have known he'd been there the whole time? The storm was the perfect opportunity.

"You're scared. You realized how much you love her and how much it would hurt to lose her. Guess what? You're no different than any other sucker finds himself in love. Yours mighta been a little more traumatic than most, but everybody's story's the same.

"Now, you better march your stupid ass right back in that hospital. She thinks you're mad at her, Jack. She thinks it's her fault you're actin' a fool." He planted his hands on his hips. "If you don't get back in there, you're hurtin' her worse than he ever did. You're rippin' her heart out. You're takin' her hope *and* her home away."

CHAPTER TWENTY-SEVEN

EVERLEA

I SAT up and nearly passed out from the pain when Jack stomped out of my hospital room. My heart dropped into my stomach. Did he hate me for what I'd put him through? What I did to his family? His life?

I wouldn't blame him, but I couldn't live without him.

Would he come back?

A nurse walked in a minute later and Finn followed, and I lost it. I saw his face, the likeness he shared with Jack in the shape of his smile and couldn't hold back the tears.

"What have I done?" I sobbed and the tears fell so fast and thick. I couldn't see through them, couldn't stop them. "I'm so sorry." My stomach burned and my whole body heaved. I pressed into my wound with the heels of my hands, trying to make it stop.

"Give us girls a minute?" the nurse hinted to Finn.

He didn't say anything, just left my room quietly, and she sat on the edge of my bed.

"It's good to see you awake finally." She patted my leg. "Hon, you're gonna be fine. You're already doin' so much better than you were."

"He left. He-he— He left and he's not coming back. It's my fault."

"Oh, girl, he's just scared. He's so in love with you, he wouldn't leave your side. Not once. That boy stuck to you like glue."

"Then why did he leave? You didn't see his face."

"Shh, shh now. He just needs time. Y'all went through a pretty big ordeal. He thought he'd lost you. Give him some time and he'll be back. I promise."

I looked up. "You really think so?"

"I really do. Boy, it sure is nice to see your eyes. You got some pretty ones. Hi. I'm Lauren." She smiled, holding her hand out for me to shake.

"I'm sorry." I cried more, for my rudeness. I knew I sounded irrational, but the tears just kept leaking out.

She chuckled. "It's okay. How do you feel? How's your pain?"

"It hurts so much." I wasn't talking about my body.

"It's gonna. You have about a gazillion stitches. I've got some medicine for you, but everything's okay. You're healin' and you're safe."

"Thank you." I sniffled and the tears slowed. I was safe. Jack said Paul was dead. Carey said it too. I couldn't remember a lot of what happened from the night of the storm, but I knew that much.

"C'mon. Let's getcha up. I'm sure by now you need to tinkle. Wanna brush your teeth?"

"Yes. And I'm starv—"

My stomach rumbled and growled, and she laughed. "Okeydoke. You're on a liquid diet, just for today, just to make sure your tummy can handle it."

"My tummy? Tinkle?" I wiped the tears away from my eyes with the backs of my hands. Lauren stood and I scooted, inch by excruciating inch, to the edge of the bed, dropping my legs over the side.

"Sorry, I work in the PICU, too, so sometimes I forget where I'm at."

The door opened and Finn stuck his head in. "Everything okay in here?"

"Yep. We're gettin' up," Lauren said with way too much pep.

"Is he okay?" I asked, looking at Finn, and Lauren wrapped my arm around her shoulder.

"Now, lean on me, but I'm not gonna pull you up. You need to use your own muscles. Get 'em workin' again."

"Okay." I pushed up on my feet and my thighs burned. My stomach felt like it was being torn open again, and I cried out.

Finn rushed over, arms out, hands flapping. "Here, lemme — I can take you."

"No." Lauren shooed him away. "She has to do it."

"Nonsense. Lemme just—"

"Back off, cowboy. Don't make me hurt ya."

"Okay, okay. Sorry." Finn grimaced, and I laughed because it reminded me of Ma scolding him for cussing, but then groaned because laughing hurt. He stepped back out of Lauren's way. "I dunno what he's thinkin', Evvie. I'm sorry. It's been a rough couple days. I think," he sighed, "I think he's just freaked out."

"See? What I tell ya?" Lauren said, holding her arm behind me, not touching, in case I fell over.

"Are you okay? What about Ma? Kevin? Oh, God, is he—"

"Evs," he said, spreading his arms out to his sides, "Everybody's fine. Kev's okay. He's down the hall. He's goin' home in the mornin'. We're all okay."

The relief was overwhelming.

"The horses?"

"They're all fine too. Didn't lose anybody. Doc stitched a few legs, treated a few for smoke inhalation. But everybody's doin' fine. Iggy's fine. She didn't come out for a good day. Found her under Ma's bed but she's okay too."

"Ruby? Trumpet?"

"Both fine. Mamas too. They were safe in the arena stalls. Nervous as all get out, still, but fine."

"The barn? Oh, God, Finn, the barn." I winced from the pain, taking my first step, and at the thought of all the damage the fire had no doubt caused.

"It's gonna need some work." He flashed his fingers in front of his chest. "Lucky we got ten hands."

"There's *five* of you? Good grief," Lauren said incredulously but then shifted her body so Finn couldn't see her face and mouthed, "Oh my God," wiggling her eyebrows. "Okay, enough chit chat. This girl needs to get washed up." She turned back to Finn, this time so I couldn't see her face. "Why don'tcha go see where your brother mighta got off to? Maybe he'd like to know miss Everlea's up and movin'? I'm sure he just needed a minute to collect himself," she said, but it sounded more like an order.

"Right. I'll just, I'll go see." Finn offered a wary smile and left the room.

"Well, aren't you just the luckiest?"

"How's that?"

"Do they all look like Finn and Jack? I saw one other brother, I think. Dark hair like Jack's, but kinda curly. Dreamy blue eyes." She pulled my IV stand around me, so I didn't step on the cords.

"That's Jay."

"Damn girl, that boy is *fine*. He single?"

"Yes."

"Might hafta get me somma that," she said, and I snorted. "Oww."

We made our way, one agonizing step at a time, to the bathroom.

"You know, I put myself through nursin' school cuttin' hair. I'm good at it. I still do my sister's hair and my mama's. Would you like me to trim yours, even it up? Got my shears in my car," she offered, tugging a little on my butchered curls.

My hand flew to my short, chopped tangle. "Does it look awful?" I asked, holding back more childish tears.

"Miss Everlea, you're a stunnin' woman. Look." She motioned to the mirror with her hand as we shuffled into the little bathroom. "A bad haircut and a little bit of bruisin' can't change that. 'Sides, Jack don't seem to mind." She winked at me.

I couldn't look. And maybe he did mind. Maybe I wasn't beautiful to him anymore.

I ached for him. I needed him.

"But my hair, it was… important to me. It's stupid, I guess, but it reminded me of my mother."

"It ain't stupid at all. A woman's hair is part of her identity. But it'll grow back. Here," she said, leading me to sit on the toilet, "take care of business. I'll be right back. I'm gonna go get your medicine and then we'll get you changed, change your sheets. The whole shebang. You'll feel so much better."

"Okay. Wait"—I grabbed her wrist—"I would like a haircut. Thank you."

"Great. We'll do it after you eat and get a shower. You'll feel good as new," she quipped and left.

"Right. Good as new," I said to no one as I lifted my ugly,

dirty, white hospital gown, dotted with— Were they bows? No, flowers, but they looked like tiny blue vaginas. *Ugh.*

My stomach had been bandaged, and my whole torso looked like a matte oil slick. Purple, black, blue, red, and green. How could I be beautiful to him now? The bandage covered my whole abdomen. I dropped the gown. I couldn't look at it anymore. I couldn't even think about what it might look like under the bandage. Burned and ripped apart.

I finished my business and slowly made my way back to the mirror. I brushed my teeth with the toothbrush and paste sitting on the edge of the sink and washed my face, but I couldn't bend to rinse, so I just wiped with warm water and a washcloth. I still had dirt and dried blood behind my ears. Someone must've washed my hair at some point. It felt wiry and tangled. No conditioner.

Combing through it with my fingers, I peeked at myself in the mirror over the old institutional-looking sink. My hair was an uneven, chin-length bob. My cheek and eye were both still swollen and bruised, and there was a cut above my eyebrow with a couple of tiny stitches in it, almost an identical twin of the soft pink scar I had now from when I'd fallen the first day I met Jack.

I stood there, eyes unfocused, and thought about everything that had happened. The monster was gone. Dead. I was free. I could go anywhere, do anything I wanted.

But all I wanted was Jack.

If he didn't want me anymore, if he was angry with me— his eyes had been so hard and controlled, just like that first day—what would I do? Where would I go? The only place I could picture myself was with him. He was my home. They all were, Ma and the guys.

But I'd made such a mess of things. He already had so much on his shoulders, and all I'd done was add to it. He'd have to rebuild the barn, and it would take money he didn't have.

And Ma and Kevin. Kevin could've been killed. They both could have. I was disgusted with myself. I should have left. It would've killed me but I should have.

"None of this would've happened," I told my reflection. "You are so selfish. This is all your fault. You should have left, you *weak*, stupid girl. You're just like your mother, wanting what you shouldn't." The tears came again, and I tried to wipe them away but just cried more. "You should've left. You ruined everything."

"You didn't." Jack stood behind me. He wrapped his arms around me gingerly and buried his face in my neck.

"Jack. You're not mad at me? I thought—"

"Mad at you? No, Evvie, please don't leave me. I'm so sorry. I-I'm just... I'm terrified."

"Jack." I tried to turn but he wouldn't let me. He held me there in the bathroom, and I felt his tears flow down my neck, wetting the back of my gown.

"Can you ever forgive me? I promised you. I promised nothin' bad would happen and look. Look at yourself. And I'm scared. I've never been so scared. You died, Evvie. And they took you away and— Can you forgive me? Can you ever trust me again?" He lifted his head, looking at me in the mirror. His eyes, now so haunted and sad and guilty, focused on my bruises.

"I *do* trust you. It's not your fault. I'm the one. If I'd never come here, none of this would've happened. Kevin wouldn't have been shot—"

"Evvie. If you'd never come here, I'd still be dead. You brought me back to life. You made me open up and live again. Please don't go. I can't live without you. I don't want to. Please, forgive me." He whispered the last words.

I pushed his hands off my hips, and he stood straight and backed up a step. He thought I was pushing him away. But I turned to face him and reached for his hands, looking into his beautiful eyes.

"There's nothing to forgive, Jack."

"I let you down."

"No, you didn't. You saved me. You changed my life." I stepped into him, reveling in the heat from his skin, his scent, and the way his body, big and strong, enveloped mine. I sighed. "I love you."

He wrapped his arms around me, hugging me. "I ain't sure ya should." Chuckling through his tears, he said, "I love you. Do you know how much? I have missed your beautiful smile, your emerald eyes, the sound of your voice. Evvie, I love you, I love you, I love you," he whispered, and I leaned back as far as I could without ripping stitches. I looked up at his face and touched his cheeks with just my fingertips, caressing his tears away.

He knew what I wanted. He saw it in my eyes. He leaned down and I kissed his lips so softly, and we both groaned.

"C'mon, let's getcha back to bed. I can kiss you better if you're lyin' down." He bent to lift me, but I swatted his hands away.

"Lauren says I have to do it. I won't get stronger if everybody does it for me. And I want to be *strong*, Jack."

"You are. You're the strongest person I've ever met."

He walked ahead of me, turning to wait for me while I hobbled out of the bathroom. I tripped over the cord to my IV stand, of course, like I had the very first time we met, but Jack caught me, his arms warm and home.

And I knew he always would.

EPILOGUE
EVERLEA

A MONTH HAD PASSED since the storm. Thanksgiving was two days away, my first with my new family. Finn had already started cooking and the scents were to die for. Pumpkin pie, pecan pie, and fresh breads. The rest he said he'd cook the morning of and I would get to help.

Jack and I had also been invited to the Mastersons' for dinner, and I couldn't wait. Susan had already spoiled me with her food after I came home from the hospital, and it was delicious. I asked her to help me learn to cook. I wanted to be able to help feed Ma and the guys without giving them food poisoning.

Finn played old-time Christmas songs on his guitar at the table as Jay and Kevin fussed around, trying to clean up after Finn's cooking experiments, and Jack and I danced in the middle of the kitchen like we were the only two people in the world.

He held me up against his body, my feet dangling in the air as we swayed and turned. The room had been full of everyone talking and laughing and Kev and Jay arguing, pots and pans clinking and pinging as they were being washed in the sink, but it grew quiet and still while we danced.

We'd gone to the little room above the barn after and made love for hours.

We began our first annual Christmas movie marathon that evening since they played on nearly every channel. A Christmas movie every night until New Year's Eve. Finn's rule. The guys all groaned and complained but I couldn't wait.

Kevin and I had been stuck on bedrest for a while (Doc Whitley stopped by often to make sure he complied), so we watched a *lot* of movies. Finn and Kevin both insisted on showing me their favorites. Kevin loved *Deadpool*, both the first and second, but Finn was more of a classic movie buff. He liked pretty much any movie, but he made me watch all of *The Godfather* trilogy and said they ranked in his top ten. I liked them all, but secretly my favorite was *Deadpool 2*. Ma scolded us every chance she got for the extremely offensive language and disturbing violence, but I caught her giggling at Deadpool's roommate, the old blind lady.

Life found its way to a new normal. A familiar rhythm. The guys worked on the barn, tearing out most of the first and second aisles and rebuilding while the weather turned colder every day. With all of them working on it, though, it hadn't taken long at all. Carey helped when he could, and so did a couple of Finn's friends, Jeromey and Spade.

Jeromey and Finn played guitar in the arena after they'd finish working in the evenings, and Spade drummed on the crate he sat on or his thighs. Finn told them I played piano, and they inducted me into their band on the spot. They said we'd call it ED, for Everlea Donovan. I thought it was a dumb name for a band, but they acted like it was the best idea since sliced bread.

I'd received a very large check from some lawyers in Chicago after my story made national news. The money my parents had left me. They said they'd tried to find me, but of course, I hadn't wanted to be found. I used a little of the money to pay for the wood for the barn repairs. Jack hadn't wanted to take my money at first, but slowly, he'd been coming around to the idea of letting me and his brothers help him.

We got our first big snow two days before Thanksgiving, and the next day, Dean and Finn surprised me with my first big excursion off the ranch.

"Finn, look at this. Do you think Kevin would like it? Ooo, what about this one? It's perfect. It says 'Adult-ish.'"

Looking through racks of T-shirts and sweatshirts, we shopped for Christmas gifts in downtown Wisper. The small town held a Country Christmas Market in the town square every Friday, Saturday, and Sunday from the day before Thanksgiving until Christmas Eve. Dozens of cheery little booths had been set up along the sidewalk, every brick-and-mortar store decorated to the nines. Lit Christmas trees, wreaths, and reindeer statues littered the town square, and I loved it!

Fluffy white snow covered every building, tree, and road sign, and all the marketgoers were decked out in heavy winter coats, boots, festive hats, gloves, and scarves. It felt like we were in the North Pole. The only thing missing was... Oh, nope, there was Santa, sitting in a vintage sleigh at the north end of Main Street, right in front of the courthouse with a line of children waiting to sit in his lap and tell him what they wanted for Christmas.

I'd been so freaking excited about the whole thing. The guys had been poking fun at me all afternoon while we shopped, but I could tell they enjoyed it too.

"Evs, you have, like, eight gifts for Kevin already. I guarantee he don't deserve 'em all," Finn said, laughing.

"You're just jealous but don't worry, Finnie, I already have all your gifts wrapped and hidden. Now, come on, let's get some coffee. I'm cold." Little did he know, I'd just ordered T-shirts for him and all the guys that would say, "f#ck" or "sh!t" or "a$$" on the front and "Sorry, Ma" on the back. There was a young local artist at the market with a booth selling his own screen-printed artwork. He was excited to get the job and I told him, if we liked the shirts, I'd order a ton more for the ranch, and he could let his artistic juices flow with the design. It was easy to see from the stuff he already had on display, he had talent. And it felt so cool to be able to do something for the guys and pay for it on my own.

"You can have your coffee, you hopeless addict. I'm gettin' hot chocolate... ohh, with a side of beautiful woman. Who is *that*?"

I followed his line of sight to two women walking away from us three stores down the street. "Finn, don't be a jerk," I scolded, swatting his arm as one of the women stopped walking to look at a holiday display in the window of the little bookstore, Your Local Bookie. He was right, though. She was gorgeous, her shiny, chocolate, brown waves striking against the Christmas-red peacoat and white scarf she wore.

"Oh shit, never mind. That's Carolyn." Finn grimaced. He ducked his head, grabbed my gloved hand, and turned around, pulling me in the opposite direction of the woman and her friend. "Don't see Dean 'round here anywhere, do ya?" he asked, scanning the crowd.

"Carolyn Masterson?" I pulled on Finn's hand to stop him walking away. I wanted to meet her to thank her for letting me stay in her house while she was overseas. Her parents talked about her all the time, and I felt like I already knew her.

"Yeah, c'mon, um, let's go over here. I think I saw somethin' Jack might like."

"Let's say hello. Finn? Where are you going?"

"Finnigan Cade, is that you?" Carolyn must've seen him. I wasn't like it was hard since he towered over every other face in the crowd. She walked toward us with a big, bright smile on her face.

"Oh boy." Finn sighed, then plastered his usual goofy smile on his face and waved at Carolyn. "Oly! How are ya? When did you get back?"

"Finn! I knew that was you. I'm good. I just got back yesterday." She walked right up to him, pushing up on her tiptoes to give him a big hug. "How are ya?"

"I'm good. You know me. Life's a beach." He hugged her back, looking over her head, searching for something. He seemed a little worried. "Hey Jules," he said to Carolyn's friend. She was also very pretty, with blond hair flipping up from under her green and white striped beanie, and deep brown eyes. They were both about my height, though Carolyn a couple inches taller.

"Hi, Finn," Jules said with a seductive smile on her face, clearly meant to woo him.

"Oh, hi." Carolyn laughed. "I'm so sorry. Didn't see you there. I just saw Finn's big ol' head above the rest," she said, looking from Finn's tall height all the way down to little ol' me.

"It's so nice to meet you. I'm Everlea Donovan. I lived in your house for a little while."

"Carolyn, Jules, this is Evvie. Evs," Finn said, waving his arm out like a game show hostess toward the women, "Oly and Jules."

"So, you're the famous Evvie. My dad talks about you all the time. He said you and Jack are comin' for dinner tomorrow?"

"Yes, but he didn't say you'd be home. I'm so happy to meet you. I wanted to thank you for letting me rent your house. So, thank you." I laughed. "Your parents have been so wonderful to me. Oh, um, Finn and I were just going to get coffee. Do you want to come with us?"

"Um, sure. Jules?" She looked to her friend, and they exchanged a knowing smile. I wasn't sure, but I thought it might have been about Finn. Jules clearly had a thing for him.

"Great!" Jules smiled, standing a little straighter. She was obviously excited until Finn opened his big oblivious mouth.

"Sorry, Evs, coffee'll have to wait. Just got a text. We've been requested at the homestead," he said, clicking his phone a few times. "Seems there's somethin' there waitin' for you. I'm gonna call Dean. I don't see him anywhere. 'Scuse me, ladies." He searched above the crowd again and stepped back a few feet to make his call.

"For me? Oh, okay. Sorry," I said to Carolyn and Jules. "Another time?"

"Uh, sure. Dean's here?" Carolyn looked over her shoulder. "We-we gotta go anyway. I forgot. I need to pick something up for my mom at the store. C'mon, Jules." She tugged on the arm of Jules' blue puffy coat.

"Yeah, okay. Nice to meet you, Evvie. Happy Thanksgiving."

"See you tomorrow, Evvie."

"Happy Thanksgiving," I called to them while Carolyn practically dragged Jules away. I turned to Finn as he hung up his phone and shoved it into his back pocket. "What was *that* about?"

"Oly and Dean, they used to date. I don't think it ended so well. C'mon, don't tell Dean we saw her."

"Really? What happened?"

"I dunno all the details. It was a few years ago. C'mon. Your chariot awaits," he said, and Dean pulled up next to us in his big black truck. Finn opened the back door for me. "Hop in, lil' lady." Dean seemed clueless to Carolyn's presence.

"What's at the ranch?"

"Wouldn't *you* like to know?" Finn chuckled as I climbed into the way-too-big truck, and Dean actually smiled, eyeing me in the rearview mirror.

We arrived back home, and Jack waited for me in front of the house. The guys slinked off to the barn as I walked toward Jack standing with Sammy. He'd been brushed, and he wore his bridle but no saddle, just a bareback pad, and his reins had been wrapped in red and green Christmas ribbons and battery powered twinkle lights. He nickered and nodded his big head when I patted his side and scruffed his mane.

The smile on Jack's face was my favorite, the sideways one that made his eyes crinkle.

"Hi," I said, grinning like a love-sick fool. Which I was. A sense of relief flooded my body every time I saw him, especially after being away from him for a while, even just an hour.

"Hey there," he rumbled in his velvet voice, his breath coming out in white puffs against the dark, cold, dry winter air.

I cocked my head in suspicion. "What are you up to?"

"Trust me?" he asked, arching an eyebrow. He lifted me straight up with his hands on my hips and kissed me like he never had before. I threw my arms around his neck as my cheeks heated, hoping Ma wasn't watching out a window.

I moaned and declared, "I do."

He pulled back, plopping me down onto my feet.

"Hey. I wasn't done kissing you."

"C'mon, hop up." Turning me by my shoulders, he lifted me up onto Sammy so carefully, like I was made of spun sugar, then climbed up behind me. "Close your eyes."

When I did, I felt the cool, starchy fabric of some kind of blindfold. He placed it over my eyes then tied it behind my head. "What're you doing?"

"Just for a few minutes. Till we get to where we're goin'. Ready?"

"I hope so?"

He chuckled and clicked his tongue twice, and Sammy loped forward. Jack turned him in a circle so I couldn't tell the direction we headed.

"Jack Cade, you're being sneaky. What's going on?"

Rubbing his lips against the skin behind my ear, he whispered, "Just hold your horses, young lady. I got somethin' to show ya." He squeezed my hips and wrapped his arms around me. "I gotta say, I like your hair like this. I like havin' easy access to your neck," he said, kissing my neck and scraping his teeth over my earlobe. I shivered and goosebumps broke out over my whole body, and he rumbled a soft moan in my ear. "Have fun at the Christmas market?"

"Yeah. Got you a present." I smiled.

"You did? What'd you get me?"

"I'm not telling. Hold *your* horses. You have to wait for Christmas."

"Touché, baby. Fair 'nuff." He chuckled.

"Oh, I met Carolyn Masterson. Finn said she and Dean dated. What's the story?"

"Yeah. High school sweethearts. But then she went to school in California and Dean joined the Marines. I think they tried to get back together a few years ago, but it didn't seem to work out. You know Dean. He don't talk about it. And then Carolyn went off to the UK. She must've just come back."

"Yeah, she said she got home yesterday. She'll be there tomorrow when we go to the Masterson's for dinner."

"Yeah? Bet you'll love to hear all her stories 'bout travelin', huh?"

"Sure. I've never been to another country."

"Me neither."

"But I'm happy here. I don't need to go anywhere. There's no place on earth that could lure me away from the ranch. From you." I leaned back, nestling in against his body.

"Boy, I'm glad to hear you say that. Hold on tight. I'm fixin' to go a little faster."

"'Kay." I held onto his arms and squeezed my legs around Sammy, careful not to kick or nudge him in the wrong direction, though I doubted he'd listen to me anyway. He seemed to be able to read Jack's mind and wouldn't dream of going anywhere Jack didn't want him to.

We rode a few minutes more, not talking. We didn't need to, and I'd been surprised to discover how much I liked the silence sometimes. I'd never experienced anything like it, when we'd lay in bed not talking or went for a walk out in the meadow. We could just be together without any words at all, and I'd never felt so connected to another human being.

I'd gotten better at riding but hadn't done much since the night of the storm. I was healing well, but my muscles were still weak, and it took all my concentration to stay upright. I knew Jack had me, but I still got that "whoa, oh crap, I'm gonna fall!" feeling sometimes.

I heard the swishing and splashing of Sammy's hooves in shallow water, and after that, we stopped.

Jack dismounted then held onto my leg. "I gotcha," he said as I pulled my other leg over and slid down into his arms. He set me on my feet and kissed my nose. "Okay, now walk forward. That's it. Right here." We stopped and he stood in front of me. I felt his warm puff of breath misting in the cold next to my face.

"So. I, um…" He exhaled and his breath was shaky. He was nervous.

"Jack? What's wrong? Are you okay?" I laughed awkwardly. If Jack was nervous about something, I was nervous too.

"Never been better," he said in his sexy voice, and I could hear the smile in it. He untied the blindfold, pulled it off slowly, then fixed my unruly curls, swiping them away from my eyes with his fingertip.

Looking over his shoulder, I saw… a forest. A dark mountain. There was nothing out of the ordinary in my view. I saw the creek. It reflected an unusual glow, the gray water glittering with a myriad of colors, bubbling and rolling over the stones coating the bank.

"So, I had an idea. I thought you and me could use a place of our own. I also thought we could make you and me… official."

"Huh?"

He laughed and sighed. "I ain't good at this at all. Okay. Stay right there. Don't peek." He walked around me and I waited with bated breath. "Turn to me."

I turned slowly and gasped.

Behind Jack, Granny's cottage had been covered, dirt to chimney, in bright, twinkling lights. Every window and door had been outlined with them, multi-colored and so beautiful against the dark dusk of the late evening sky. The shadow of the mountain beside it seemed to bow toward it in protection, and the trees stood, watching out for the little cottage like sentries. The roof had been crisscrossed with lights.

"You fixed the roof?" I asked, and Jack dropped down onto his knee.

"I did fix the roof 'cause I thought, well, I *hoped*, you'd marry me, and we could live here. Just you and me." He held up a tiny, square, red velvet box while my heart raced away, and I held my breath. "Everlea Donovan, I love you more'n life itself. I wanna spend the rest of my days makin' you happy. Makin' you laugh and holdin' you when you cry. I want this to be our home, and I wanna watch you take this world by storm. I wanna help you do it, if you'll have me." He cleared his throat, and tears leaked from my eyes. I tried to blink them away so I wouldn't miss one second of the overwhelming love I saw on his face. "Everlea Donovan, will you marry me?" He sucked in a big breath and held it.

"Yes!" I attacked him, throwing my arms around him and pushing him down into the snow. I couldn't have cared less about the pinch of pain from my stomach. "Yes, I will marry you, Jackson Cade. Yes, yes, yes!" I kissed him. I closed my eyes, feeling the color from the lights warm us and surround us like a faerie cocoon.

He released his breath, chuckling. "It needs a lotta work and it'll take a while. Winter's nearly here. And it's small. Only two bedrooms."

"I don't care! I don't care if we live in a shed. If it's just you and me, it's perfect."

"Yeah?"

"Yes." I straddled him, pushed my fingers into his hair, and slid my tongue into his mouth, drowning in his taste, in his breath.

He groaned and sat up with me still attached. "Hold that thought." Lifting us up, he dusted the snow off my knees, then held my face in his hands, looking in my eyes, caressing my bottom lip with his thumb.

He stepped back and held the red box between us, then popped it open. In it sat a delicate, gold ring with one big, round diamond in a square setting. It looked old. And it was stunning.

"Ma gave this to me to give to you. Mr. Mitchum gave it to her the day he asked her to marry him. I think it'll bring us good luck." Pulling the ring from the box, he slipped it onto my finger. "Like it?"

"I've never seen anything more beautiful."

"I have," he said, pulling me against him, kissing the daylights out of me. "C'mon." He nodded behind him toward the house. "Let's go see." Taking my hand in his, we hurried up the crumbled stone walkway to our little house.

When we got to the porch stairs, he stopped me, gently pulling on my hand, and lifted me, carrying me up the stairs to the front door. It stood ajar and he pushed it open with his boot.

"Welcome home, Evvie," he rumbled in my ear as he carried me over the threshold, and the room erupted into cheers as my whole family welcomed us home.

The End
For Now

If you liked the book (or loved it, I hope), please leave a review—even just a few words would help—wherever you buy your books, Amazon, Goodreads, or Bookbub. Self-published indie authors rely heavily upon reviews to get our stories out to the masses. And thank you. I know it takes time to do this. I appreciate the time out of your day and the effort.

BROKEN

Prologue

You don't need her. You have me.

I crouched below the open window of a fallin' down buildin' somewhere in Baghdad. Or Mosul. Or one of the thousand gateways to hell we'd been. The old mud-brick house fell in pebbles and stones. Fell from above, shot up from below, flew sideways at my face, stingin' my skin like the rain whippin' in the Wyoming wind. Bombs. Gunfire. It pounded all around me and nothin' but her voice would break through.

She was seven and I was eight. My world crumbled then too. I held onto her hand that day, in my meadow, the little-boy-adventures meadow where my brothers and I played every day of our lives. I held onto the softest hand, lookin' in the prettiest eyes. Even at eight years old, I knew Oly Masterson was special. A little girl with the fight of some obstinate woman from a black-and-white movie, one without sound, and she scrunches her face and stomps her foot, poundin' her fist in the air. She gets her way. You don't mess with that woman.

That girl.

You don't need her. You have me.

She held my hand that day, but really, she held my heart. I never got it back. I figured it was why I could hear her now. Miles and lightyears and countries and smiles away. Long lingerin' caresses from her ankle to the soft curve of her neck —lazy—a summer's breeze of a touch away. But still, I heard her when my heart beat so fast 'cause I thought I might die. Alone. Separated by worlds from my family.

From her.

You don't need her. You have me.

I wished I did, but I pushed her voice outta my head. Improvise, adapt, and overcome. There was no room in a Marine's head for a girl. A woman. For regrets. There was only the mission. Only honor, courage, commitment. Country.

She wasn't part of my mission. She wasn't part of my life anymore. Hadn't been for a long time.

But still, even through the fallin' down rubble and the earsplittin' sound of the helicopters and gunfire, the punch of bullets into old sun-dried mud stone, I heard her voice.

I wondered, wherever she was with my heart still in her hand, did she feel it throbbin' and racin', tryin' to figure a way out of the mess, tryin' to find its way back home?

Get the next story in the Cade Ranch Series,
Dean's book…

BROKEN: A Cade Ranch Novel

WANT MORE?

Become a Wisperite!
Join my newsletter for exclusive stories, Wisper news, and
The Cade Ranch Sexcapades—naughty little interludes for
my subscribers ONLY!
Jack and Evvie's wedding scenes are there!
Sign up for your first FREE short story, Wild Heart: Welcome
to Wisper.
https://dl.bookfunnel.com/mg0smwmcsl

You can find me on the usual social sites, but I mostly hang
out on Instagram, Facebook, and Goodreads.

Join my Team!
Receive an advanced review copy of my next book. Join my
Street Team, a wonderul group of people who help get the
word out when I release a new book!
Sign up on my website
gretarosewest.com

ABOUT THE AUTHOR

Greta Rose West was a floundering artsy flake until Jack showed up, knocking on the door of her brain, and then pounding on it, and then he just plain kicked it down. She lives in NW Indiana with her husband, her son, and her two precocious kitties, Geoff Trouble and Sally Mae Midnight. When she's not writing, she's reading and devouring music. She enjoys indie films no one else likes, and her favorite food is Aver's Veggie Revival pizza.

CPSIA information can be obtained
at www.ICGtesting.com
Printed in the USA
FSHW010903011021
85160FS

9 781955 633031